The Vanishing Point

A Novel by:

Michael Backus

THE VANISHING POINT

Copyright © 2021 by Michael Backus

Published by:

Cactus Moon Publications, LLC;
info@cactusmoonpublishing.com
www.cactusmoonpublishing.com

Cover art by Dio Cramer

ISBN 978-1-7347865-3-8

To Christine Mahan Backus, whose lifelong love of reading has informed everything I've ever written.

Acknowledgments

First and foremost I'd like to thank Megan Backus and Vija Balakrishnan, who have consistently been the best readers any writer could ask for.

This book was written in part at the MacDowell Colony, The Ucross Foundation and the Millay Colony, the uninterrupted writing time these places afforded me was invaluable.

I've also had a couple of excellent writer's groups over the years and members have provided consistently excellent advice. I'd like to thank Sejal Shah, Magda Maczynska, Cecilia Feilla, Nora Maynard, Melissa Sandor, Patrick McKearn, Julie Huntington, Millie Falcaro and Michael Colvin for their insights about my work. I'd also like to thank Radhika Balakrishnan, David Gillcrist, Parvathy Menon and Darshan Bhagat for their support and help over the years.

And finally, I'd like to thank my parents, Walter Backus and Christine Mahan Backus, they didn't always understand why writing was such a large part of my life, but they were always supportive.

Henry

I wasn't always like this.

For our honeymoon, Jane Renee Philips and I drove 500 miles south and west to a farming town of three hundred people where three days earlier, Annie Steel had killed her four children (Gina, Jenny, Nathan, Fern) and herself. When the paper reported the killings, both of us cut it out and rushed home in anticipation of telling the other and we decided on the spot to get married.

I drove the interstate half of the trip. By the time we switched to Philips driving for the two-lane highways, we were charged, cutting a dangerous swath through the landscape. When she pushed down on the accelerator, the clouds above parted, the front end of the car lifted, wind noise screamed in our ears, children covered their faces as we passed, a rabbit froze in the road, then darted—too slow!, birds panicked and beat the wind with their wings, pickup trucks skidded sideways to avoid us. I unbuttoned her jeans and lay my cheek on the line where pubic hair meets stomach, she bent down and blew her breath on my face, a smell as familiar as my own, drying the sweat. Her lips brushed my eyelids. It felt like flying.

We blew into that town, which was nothing more than a circular collection of houses—like wagons drawn together for protection—surrounded by corn and soybean fields. We believed we were doing something important, getting at basic truths about why people act the way they do, that we had the courage and the insight to look into the darkest places and come out with knowledge. And that we had answers, that's the funny part. When I think back on it now, I'm not sure any of it was real. It's difficult for me to believe a lot of what I remember. It gets harder all the time to be sure about anything.

Leaving

Then I lose my job, which I didn't see coming. Though I suspect it might be for the best, I still make a half-hearted attempt to argue.

"Are you kidding me?" I say to Larry, the owner of the cab company.

"There've been complaints lately. A lot of complaints."

"Country of whiners."

"I have documentation."

"Yeah?" I say, against my better judgment. "Tell me one."

"Mrs. Koppel says you threw dog-shit at her."

"Her dog did it in my cab. What would you do?"

"Clean it up?" He suggests so politely it infuriates me.

"Well fuck me for being human."

"A lady out on West Avenue says her teenage daughter came home stoned out of her mind and she claimed the cab driver got her stoned. According to the logs, that driver was you."

"It was her joint," I say helplessly. "I was just being friendly."

"A Mr. Cordova called to tell us you chased him into his house and forced him to give you his wallet."

"He only had three bucks for a four-dollar fare. That's procedure."

"Mugging clients is not procedure."

"Semantic bullshit. I was retrieving a fare, putting money in your pocket, doing what you want me to do, no matter what the book says."

"He said you went in his fridge, ate his pickles, drank right from the milk carton and stole a bag of home-made tamales."

"First off, the tamales were greasy and I tossed them. The pickles were good," I say, then remember why we're talking. "I was just, well, you know...I thought of it as a tip." But by now, I know it's hopeless and frankly, I'm shocked by the accumulation of details and by the time I leave, I'm actually grateful he hasn't brought up several other incidents that, no doubt, were also reported.

I can't say I'll miss it. Two years of sitting in the same cab, parked more or less in the same spot in a deserted area of downtown near the train station, waiting for some depressed, drunken college student to call the dispatcher is no one's idea of fun. It's just that the other work occasionally available in town—coffee shop counter man, bookstore clerk, day (never night) bartender—pays less and is far more potentially humiliating than driving a cab. I'd moved to this medium-sized New Hampshire college town out of some instinct, a way of thinking that made sense at the time. I no longer remember how it made sense, just that it did. Maybe I came thinking I might be able to get adjunct work teaching the occasional film production or history class, but I've never felt further away from teaching than I do now. Besides, if I'd done even the most cursory bit of internet research two years ago, I would've discovered this college has no film production classes at all and only a single "overview" history class in its most perfunctory form (Edison to Lumiere to Melies to Porter to Griffith to the Germans to the Soviets to sound to Citizen Kane, ad nauseum), a class I swore I'd never lower myself to teach again. Cab driving was far preferable to spewing easy-to-teach bullshit, a moral stand that was never tested because the college's Humanities chair didn't respond to my CV and cover letter which, in retrospect, might've been more combative than was necessary.

At home, I sit at my kitchen table and roll and smoke a joint and start in on shots of tequila. I have a pad of paper and a pen, ready to make a list. This is something I used to do. "Write it down" was once my mantra, the first of many steps towards figuring it out, but it'd been years since I could see the point of implementing a process. What have I ever solved this way? Still, I write *My Options* at the top, then underline it twice and follow it with 1), 2), and 3), three seeming a non-intimidating number, but even this is too much.

A couple of years after Philips disappeared, a year after I fled Santa Fe vowing to go somewhere, anywhere, I took a job teaching film at a commuter college in downtown Chicago. Going back to the city where Philips and I had spent most of our life together wasn't perfect, but I had no better ideas. In the beginning, I liked the relationship with the students, everything was so on the surface. I was one piece of a much larger machine and occasionally an eager student might move by on the conveyor belt, and I'd impart my bit of knowledge, make my adjustment, and send them on. I liked the way students zoomed through my classes, mine was just one point on the map equal to every other point, not much was really at stake.

And after Philips' disappearance and the resulting investigation, with a child who was an infant when her mother left, a toddler when I last saw her, I carried myself in Chicago like I had a secret, an impossibly complex back story too painful to bring to light. I liked playing the sensitive shell of a man routine. It kept people away while hinting at a deeper, darker, possibly dangerous self. No one bothered me and I was calm and in control in a way I never was the last few years with Philips. I felt like a murderer paroled out of prison after years, someone who had been shaped by violence and ugliness. A survivor. Triumphant.

But somewhere it all disappeared without me realizing it and I became the kind of person I least wanted to be, someone who teaches, someone who can't do—someone who won't—and it seemed to me every single human I met every day understood this. After years of brooding, holding myself separate, I found every relationship in my life was the same. I carried on meaningful ten-second friendships with a variety of people around town – the woman with purple hair at the donut shop where I'd get coffee, the newspaper vendor, the gas mini-mart clerk, the health food store cashier, the blond woman in the Saab next to me at a traffic light. Finally I quit teaching and left, heading east, vowing to keep as much of the continent as I could between me and Santa Fe, settling in New Hampshire for no better reason than I'd visited the college when I was 18 thinking I might want to attend. And I took up cab driving again, the perfect job for five-minute relationships.

I no longer own the ability to connect with people on a deeper, more satisfactory level, like it's an organ gone vestigial after 10 million years of disuse. When I see two people together now—and I know how this sounds—I don't believe it, not really. I think they're kidding themselves and they'll come to understand the way I do, they'll come to their senses. All love is a delusion and those most in love are in fact most delusional. And as each year passes, I become less a human being than a collection of strange tics, bizarre reactions, unusual ideas, uncommon fears, as if I am developing into a subspecies with a population of one.

I can't imagine the path I might take to getting close to another person, it is as mysterious as cancer. All life is subtext, I used to tell my students, everything important anyway, but somewhere along the line, I lost the text, and I don't have a clue how to get it back.

Finally I give up on the list altogether and turn on the television. One of my favorite movies is on, the central film in a couple of classes I taught, and I recognize this as a cosmic sign though I'm not at all sure what it might mean. It's the scene where Martin Sheen walks out into a seemingly endless prairie at dusk, the rifle on his shoulders makes him look haunted like a scarecrow, watching lightning illuminate an immense, distant bank of storm clouds; a signal there is another world, another life, but one that's magically, impossibly far away, like a city in the clouds, like a comet passing the earth.

I snort a bit of the opium-speed mix I get from a former cabbie I know living in a survivalist compound north towards Canada. He grows opium poppies out there, dries them, grinds the -seedpods to dust—there's a boiling-water steeping step I'm unclear about— and mixes it with methamphetamine. It's a tiny habit I've picked up. I can take it or leave it and when I say that I'm not kidding myself. I'm old enough to know a real problem when I see it. Old enough to know, but that never helps with the doing. Knowledge is overrated. Introspection is simply a mocking voice repeating the same words over and over but always withholding that single most crucial bit of information; what to do with all the knowledge. For the millionth time, I promise myself my life starts changing in the morning and even as I say it, I don't believe it, knowing as I do, but it still has just enough power, along with the opium, to push me to fall asleep in front of the television.

I dream I'm stoned and falling asleep in front of the television, then I fall asleep and dream within my dream, this time of sitting in front of a different, newer, much larger television in the same room. It has fantastic sound which I say in the dream the way a proud new owner might say it. "This has fantastic sound!" I can hear helicopters behind me and the roar of tornadoes in front, birds chirping above and crickets buzzing all around and I'm insulated and pleasantly spinning, completely content.

When I first wake to that druggy blue glow, I'm disappointed to see my same old 13-inch color TV in its usual spot. Then the content of the dream sinks in. Is this what it has come to; has my subconscious simply given up? Couldn't it try a little harder; would one half-nude teenaged girl lying on the floor begging me to come to her be so out of the question? Or even a nice flying dream, no hard-on required? You get the dreams you deserve, I guess.

"This life cannot continue," I say out loud, having already forgotten my vow of the night before, then I laugh at the seriousness of my pronouncement. Yet one more useless declaration. Think of a word to describe an emotional state—despair, cynicism, exhilaration, antipathy, expectation, whatever—and now tell me each of these has its own distinct feeling and flavor and I'll call you a poor, mawkish fool who's deluded himself into believing in the "wonder" of his own life. Is this what people mean when they argue all life is illusion? The triumph of the subjective, life being whatever a person wants to say it is? I say no thanks to that. I trust in my brain-as-food-processor approach, blending all emotions to a fine, easy-to-digest paste.

Maybe it's not much of a way of living (though I suspect quality-of-life arguments are beside the point), but I figure at least dying will be about the same; just one more thing not to get too excited about. Or it could be the opposite; it'll be scary as shit, and you absolutely fail to control your fear and thus spend the last moments on earth out of your mind and in torment. But if that's the truth, then there's really a very good reason not to dwell on it, no point in going through that more than once, so in a way the opposing arguments come to the same place; the world made up of nothing but gray area. Which would make a fine gravestone epitaph, *His World was all Gray Area.* Much more fitting now than Philips' suggestion years ago of "What the fuck are you looking at?" made during a time when she still believed my death would be bad.

Saying this life has to stop now is exactly the same as deciding I don't care if it stops. I look for another job or I don't. Either way. So I eeny-meeny-minie-moe it and pick *stop now,* then decide I'll try and think of a way out of this but can only come up with the idea that I have to make a plan, the actual plan will follow later. Getting cable comes to mind.

*****

I'm willing to give in to the belief that forces both outside and in combine to create moments of opportunity in a person's life, but I also think I've spent a lot of time waiting and it could be I'm just missing them or maybe that's the way of it. Maybe it's like waiting for an earthquake, a force of nature, the big one might come in the next ten years or ten thousand; either way it's not something a person should count on. But it's easy to simply forget about the possibility of change for years on end, there's always some reason not to think about it.

So I decide to leave town, then go. It is too easy. I'm embarrassed at how small an imprint I've made on the town in two plus years. No job to quit, no friends to see one last time, not even a drug dealer to visit before I go. No matter how hard I rack my brain, I can't think of anyone in town who would do anything other than wonder why I'm telling them this.

I shave my beard, deciding physical change brings spiritual change. I keep going, taking too much off, then trying to balance the other side until I've buzzed it all and my hair is no more than a shadow on a bald head.

It's an unfortunate look. Back in the prime of my marriage to Philips, we used to buzz cut each other's hair right to the scalp then make love, running the tips of our fingers all over the over-sensitive, newly shorn skin; it was like diving into cool, fresh water, like believing that the world was endless and available, like we could blow through or burn down anything in our way.

But in the years since, I've gained weight and the top of my head, shorn of all its hair, is now the smallest point of my body and bald, I look hulking, slightly demented, a little stupid in a back-wards way, someone other people might step away from in a crowd, the kind of person who has an agenda; a biker, a bouncer, a skinhead; desperate and sad, showing his weakness by announcing to all the world how he wants people to see him. I feel dense, befuddled, like I don't have control over myself, like I have no understanding, even after forty years, of my physical place in the world.

Stepping outside and feeling the wind on my freshly buzzed scalp, it's almost worth it.

There's not really a plan. There's only one place to go—back to the town where I grew up—but there's no reason to be excited about it. Last night, I had a half hour of pure panic and unloaded all my possessions, stacking books and saucepans and table lamps on the kitchen counter. I could stay. No one knew I was leaving I was jumping my lease. It's not much, but it's still my apartment. It's not homeless. What was I going to do? Settle back in the town where I grew up? So I decided to stay and fell into a deep and dreamless sleep.

But this morning, I knew it was all insane. I quickly re-packed my truck and wrote a note to my landlord telling her she could sell my couch and kitchen table set to make up for the lost rent, and I left. There's still no plan and no real confidence true change is actually possible, but it's not standing still. I've spent two years in a taxicab, driving in and around this small, snowy town, a couple of hundred miles every day, and at the very least, I won't be driving in circles anymore. I'll be going in a straight line.

*****

When your entire world feels like one endless void, you tend to see the profound in the mundane. In three wandering days of travel, I've cried in my motel room during commercials for fried chicken and diet Cola; I've stood high on the banks of the Ohio and stared at the wake of a garbage barge so loaded down, I lost all perspective and got the sense I was in fact staring at a piece of crumpled paper floating in a creek no more than a few feet wide. I've watched the lights of a tractor at night in an immense field so long, I became certain what I was seeing was more spectral than physical. I've listened to the rhythm of crickets sweep back and forth through the trees like the wind buffeting a huge flag, I've seen thousands of lady bugs gathered in the corner roof of a run-down motel porch in what seemed at the time an ominous portent, I've watched a house burn in the distance, a tiny lick of flame no larger than a lit match held at arms-length, and all of them, if I stare and listen long enough, contain meaning, truth, ideas, knowledge, importance, symbolism just out of my perceptual reach, like a word on the tip of the tongue, the touch of an unseen presence. Today feels like that, the sky a fine crystal blue, a New Mexico sky, a sky out of my past. Not this past—this isn't the kind of sky I ever remember growing up—but a displaced past, 1,400 miles west of here. But what does it mean? Thinking of New Mexico, I only see Philips; pain and bullshit—pain and bullshit.

Or maybe not. Any actual residual pain is buried under accumulated layers so deep, I'm not sure it still exists. The romanticism of angst has its allure. I've been known to drag out Philips stories as evidence; here's my life, here's my pain, I've been through hell, I've felt fear turning to dread turning to horror; you know, back story as proof of present story. It's all kind of comforting in a life-at-arms-length way.

Approaching my hometown from the north there are golf courses and gentle curves in the highway, houses my family almost bought and houses they did. There are lakes and railroad tracks and a cemetery where my family is buried going back a century. There's the murder diner or was that somewhere else? Was that the house where a son killed his father? Maybe that was in Philips' hometown. Places fold into other places. I know it happens but didn't think it would happen to me here. Makes me wonder if this isn't some version of a mistake. Maybe not a full-blown one, but something you realize years later, when you've regained enough spirit to take an honest look at the past.

I've put off calling my Aunt Irene each night so now I'm stuck with the problem of dropping in out of the blue and hoping she and Uncle Eddie won't mind if I stay for a while, hoping they won't be too shocked or angry at my sudden appearance after ignoring them for so many years. I slowly work my way through the three miles of back roads to my cousins' place, acquiring along the way an entourage of impatient and possibly intoxicated teenagers bristling to get past me. When I finally turn off, one of them thrusts out a single finger and I wave back as cheerfully as I can. Teenagers are scary; I'm increasingly drawn to the "too stupid to live, too healthy to die" argument, but it hardly matters. I've reached the age where I'm completely invisible to teenagers, which is (mostly) a relief.

My cousins' road is exactly as it was. Still dirt, it forms an O-shaped tunnel through dense overhanging trees curving along the edge of a lily pad-choked lake. Up a long incline, the road clears the trees and opens up with their fields on my left and the house and barn down a short hill on the right.

I'm happy to see the silo's still here, as covered with ivy as ever but missing the old cone-shaped red roof. Did I used to climb to the top and hang off? I seem to remember that, but it doesn't sound like something I'd do. The yard has been cleared of all the hog shacks and chicken coops, replaced by a single aluminum garage that looks like it was pre-fabricated somewhere else and trucked here.

I pull my truck as far from the house as I can and get out and stand behind it, hoping against hope that someone comes out so they can realize who this is slowly, so there won't be a stunned, I-can't-believe-it moment at the door. I think I see a flash of movement in the barn, then I'm not sure. I walk to the front door and ring the bell. No answer. I check the metal garage, it's empty. When I come out, someone darts away from an upstairs window in the barn. Someone's up there. I walk across the long yard. I'm surprised how comfortable I feel here, not just because I grew up so close, but when Philips and I lived in Chicago almost a decade ago, we used the farm as a kind of weekend retreat, which Eddie and Irene encouraged.

"Hullo?" I yell into the barn. "Anyone around?"

Silence.

"I saw someone."

"Who wants to know?" A thin, reedy male voice that's familiar.

"Who's that?"

"Who's that?" It sounds like an echo.

"Aaron?"

"I asked who wants to know."

"It's me. Henry."

"Henry?"

"Your cousin Henry? Aaron, is that you?"

I hear furniture being moved and locks clicking open. Aaron is my first cousin, three years older, a gap that became troublesome when he hit junior high. We would've likely kept this distance through life except he was around for most of the Philips years and the two of them liked each other, so for a period of time, I saw him a lot. He's seen his share of trouble. After high school, he'd live at home and work for a few months to save money, then take off without a word to anyone. He drove his old rickety van to Alaska, to the Hudson Bay, up and down the California coast, throughout the Baja Peninsula, all the way down to Belize where he sold the van and took a boat back to Miami. He's worked on oil rigs in Colorado and on a fishing-boat based in Juneau. He spent two years in Hawaii helping a marijuana grower cultivate and harvest his crop, a period of time when he cut off all contact with family and friends. No one knew if he was alive or dead. When he came home, he told everyone he grew green tea on the sides of lush hills, only Philips got the whole truth.

I know he started a business at one point, a drive-through coffee place set up in the parking lot of a local supermarket, and that it had gone pretty well for a few months before an out-of-control bread truck drove right through it. His finances had been stretched to the breaking point and he'd never gotten insurance for all the espresso equipment, so he only received a small settlement from the trucking company, barely enough to re-start the business. Then he'd gotten ill with a rare inflammation of the veins in his legs, and he had to spend all of his savings getting better. Much of this drama was happening about the time Philips disappeared, so understandably, we lost touch.

It seems to be taking forever for him to come down. If he's been here since his business went under—I pause for a moment, figuring the math—that means he's been living at home for close to eight years. But maybe that isn't it, maybe he's here for another visit. I'd hoped he'd gotten away. When I used to think about him, I always assumed he would be fine, that he'd take a job here or there, meet a woman, the normal trip. But why is he living in the barn? It's old, leaning to one side, the wood slats deeply weathered, almost marbled, like driftwood, and inside on the first floor, the place is dirty with a thick earthen smell mixed faintly with a shit odor. There is a car parked inside but it's completely covered in dust and bird droppings, the kind of layering that might take months, even years.

There's a short stairway to the left and at the top, a trap door. I vaguely remember a loft up there. It had always been full of hay and mice. I start up and the door swings open, and filtered light comes through.

"Henry?" Aaron's voice is wobbly-sounding, like he hasn't used it in a long time.

"It's me, Aaron."

"I'll come down." The door slams shut, and I'm thrown back into darkness. I walk outside, the wind feels fresh and clean. The garden is close to the barn, the sweet corn stalks have a tint of brown and I can see green pumpkins spotting one section. Somewhere above me, an unseen crow squawks, an unpleasant noise that seems suitably gothic. I wonder if he's coming down at all, maybe this is how he deals with people now, by ignoring them until they go away.

When I turn around, he's standing right there, and I smile because of how familiar that face is. I smile in spite of myself because he looks awful, worse than awful, with a gaunt, hollow face and pasty skin, a belly that looks almost like a beer belly until you really look and realize it's set too high to be a beer belly—it's bulbous, like a growth, and under the belly, his legs are shockingly thin, the wind rippling loose pants over two pipe cleaners.

"Henry."

"Aaron, God," I say before I can stop myself.

"I've been sick. Didn't my mom tell you?"

I shake my head, half afraid of what I might say.

"Are you OK?" It comes out squeaky, fearful and he turns away from me. He's looking at the entrance to the barn.

"Where are Aunt Irene and Uncle Eddie?"

"Florida. They have a house in Sarasota. You didn't know?"

"No. I wouldn't know that. I haven't kept in touch that way."

"Yep. We got the place to ourselves."

There's a long, awkward moment while we both struggle to find something to say.

"I've been looking forward to the lane. Do you still go down the lane?"

"Yeah, I can still walk," Aaron says, aggravated. So we start for the road, cross it and begin down the lane, a bright green path running straight through the center of two fields, one of which is planted in soybeans, the other corn. It has an English hedgerow feeling and always has, as long as I've been alive. He moves slowly and within 100 yards, his breathing becomes labored and there's no chance of him keeping up his end of a conversation. The silence gives me an opportunity to recover from the shock of seeing someone I know so well, almost my own age, this frail and dissipated. What could have done this? How could my aunt and uncle have allowed this?

The ground finally levels off and his breathing eases. His snail's pace is maddening at first, but I get used to the idea there's nowhere to go and settle into the rhythm of his slow, lurching gait. He walks like a pregnant woman, leaning back, arms propped behind him, balancing out the weight of his belly. I'm not sure what to say.

"You've gotten older," he says. "Fatter."

And what I think is, he's not someone who should be calling attention to a person's body changes but at the same time—and maybe this is the source of his newfound brutal honesty—he's so fragile, his body so warped and asymmetrical, droopy around his face and neck, bloated drum-tight around his chest and belly, it would be cruel to respond in kind.

"Yes," I say in a tone meant to shut down further discussion.

"You're probably wondering," Aaron says.

"Yeah, I guess." I am, though I'm not sure what he means specifically.

The lane itself is lawn-type grass cut regularly, a soft, smooth path even Aaron can easily negotiate but lining both sides, they've allowed it to grow wild, an incredible tangle of jimson weed, milkweed, the pods hanging heavy and ready for a strong wind, small junk trees like poison oak and sumac, tiny slender green sassafras, a dozen other plants, yellow wildflowers, pitchfork and Velcro burrs; what all of Northern Indiana would look like if the land wasn't relentlessly groomed and cleared by people. I've spent a good portion of my life on this land, but that's not what I remember best. "Down the lane" was a favorite ritual for Philips and I, we'd sneak out after dinner, smoke a joint, toss our clothes aside and run around naked, which was always nerve-wracking at first, then liberating when we realized no one was coming down here after dark. We had a whole other life, naked in the dark in these fields, my wife and I, one of many whole other lives we shared. Or didn't . . .

As shocked as I am by his appearance, we settle quickly into the familiar, comfortable with silence. I bend down and rip up a two-foot sassafras tree, shake the dirt from the roots and then breathe in the rich, root-beer smell. I hand it to Aaron who puts it under his nose as we walk. The lane continues winding into a stand of woods heading towards a third crop field on the other side and a small, weedy lake and beyond that, more woods, all of it belonging to my aunt and uncle.

"Is that the elephant tree?" I say.

"That's further on," he says. "It's not much of an elephant anymore."

"What about the old beech? I'd like to see the names again."

"Gone. A few years ago, Dad sold a few of the oldest hardwoods."

"Shit, really? Why?"

"I don't know. Money. He sold them to a German company that makes fine furniture; maple, oak, cherry."

"But beech?"

"In the way."

"I wouldn't have known. It's not obvious."

"Not now. But at the time . . . "

"Time, I guess."

"Yeah."

We emerge out of the woods, ahead is a large apple tree covered top to bottom with starlings; it vibrates with the force of their wings and their voices. I made love to my wife under that tree, back when we were trying to conceive a child. It didn't work, but it was the best place we tried. We both wanted that time to be the one, to create a life in that wonderful, perfumed air with fruit blossoms floating all around.

"Do you hear from Philips?" he says in the calmest of voices but it's an explosive question, given all that's gone on and all that I'm thinking about at this moment. But Aaron's that way with me. We weren't always close, that three year difference weighed heavily through junior high and high school, but Aaron had the ability to tap into what I was thinking.

"That's a fucked-up question. No, no one does, as far as I know. Even if she does emerge, she sure as hell wouldn't contact me."

"But you're in touch with Cadence?"

"God Aaron. Fuck. Shit. No, I'm not. I'm not. Please," I say, unable to supply complete words to my outrage.

"You're not in touch?"

"No."

"How old is she now?"

"We're going to fucking drop this right now. I mean it. Right now!"

"I was just wondering."

"Quit your wondering, goddammit."

"You always curse too much when you don't know what to say."

"I think you should worry about yourself."

He remains calm, his demeanor so infused with weariness, I'm not sure he's capable of outrage anymore.

"What gave you the impression I don't?"

"What's up with you then? Why are you so messed up?"

"I'm sick. No one told you?"

"You asked me that. No. Who'd tell me? You tell me."

He flops down on the ground so suddenly I think he's collapsed. Then he leans back, stretches his legs out, his arms above his head. Even like this, his belly doesn't disappear, it's hard and fibrous-looking, sitting there like a basketball under his shirt.

"I don't get outside so much."

"I can see."

"Scurvy."

"What?"

"You asked. It was scurvy."

"Scurvy?"

"I was drinking, not eating, not going outside. No nutrition, just booze, equals scurvy. Did you know all the termites in the world outweigh all the humans ten to one?"

"What?"

"Kind of makes you think if a certain kind of life visited us, they might just conclude that termites are the dominant species on earth."

"I don't care about that. Are you getting better?"

"Better schmetter. I read a book about a boy who takes off one day, from family, house, school, job, and walks out of the city through the suburbs, through all the small towns surrounding the suburbs, into the country and he keeps going, drinking from people's outside faucets, eating apples from orchards, tomatoes and cucumbers from people's gardens, going until he can't see subdivisions, can't hear interstates, he walks until he doesn't see country stores, until the paved roads end and then the dirt roads."

Aaron stops, breathing hard with the effort of talking; he sucks in deep breaths to calm himself. Great puffy clouds have rolled in, a few more minutes and they'll be above us, and further on, I can see a dark line, a storm front like a mountain range rising in the distance.

"And pretty soon he's no longer seeing houses or any kind of structure, but he keeps on and fire breaks drop away, no use for breaks in a place that is uninhabited, and he keeps going until all he can see is trees and sky. That's all."

"Yeah? And he's happy? The book says he's happy?"

"The book doesn't know, he's off the radar screen. I am Legend, the last man on earth, that's what the book thinks. But it doesn't really know."

I sit, then lie down next to him. I desperately wish I had my opium mix but it's back in the truck and there's not much left, no more than two snorts. I feel like a fool, a pretender, floating far from home next to my cousin, "the last man on earth" slowly folding into himself. What does it matter if he is getting better or not?

"Aaron? You know where my mom's living?"

"I was wondering when we'd get to that."

Sonny & Sammy

They didn't think of it as a game, at least not at first, it was just that over time, they came to understand that people had notions about which twin was which. Sonny was the leader, Sammy the follower; Sonny wore pants and t-shirts, Sammy hated shirts and wore shorts even when there was snow on the ground. Sonny was the talker, Sammy liked to agree with his brother; Sonny usually had the ideas, Sammy was the one who carried them out. All of that was true. But sometimes, they simply switched roles without a second thought, they might run out into the neighborhood with Sonny shirtless and Sammy running ahead, talking and talking and deciding what they would do that day. It was why others had such a hard time telling them apart, not just because they looked alike or acted alike, but because they often seemed to be the other one. Except when they weren't.

But over time, it did turn into a kind of game. Third grade was special, and they kept it up the entire year, wearing the same color pants every day and switching t-shirts in the bathroom between classes. It helped that Sonny liked reading and writing and Sammy was better at science and at math, so they'd switch during the same school day, with Sonny taking all the English type exams and Sammy handling the hard sciences, getting A-minuses in both. The only trouble was their handwriting, which wasn't all that similar (to the annoyance of both), but they solved this by carefully printing.

The real fun was family gatherings, always with The Dude's sister's family, who lived on a farm outside of town. Christmas, New Years, Memorial Day, Fourth of July, Labor Day, Thanksgiving and all the birthdays. Irene and her son Aaron both were genuine challenges, they thought of it as a game too, and liked trying to figure out which twin was which. The twins spent days before a holiday thinking up ways to fool their aunt and their cousin. Sammy might run up to Aunt Irene wearing Sonny's favorite red t-shirt, but the shirt was only the first step in a process.

"Aunt Irene, Aunt Irene," he'd say and then proceed to give her a moment-to-moment detailing of the plot of the most recent movie he'd seen, which as everyone knew was one of Sonny's favorite rituals. Irene might listen respectfully, but such an obvious ploy wasn't going to fool her. "You're Sammy," she'd say, interrupting him. It was here the plan often broke down. The twins didn't usually think much past the initial deception and Sammy especially was never convincing once he was called out. He tended to stammer and get mad.

"I'm not, I'm Sonny, I am."

"Good try, Samuel," she'd say.

"I'm Sonny!" he'd say, then he'd stomp out.

"Hey Sonny," the real Sonny might say as he passed his brother in the hallway, making a last ditch attempt to salvage the switch. "Where's Sonny going?"

"Nice try, Sonny," she'd say to the real Sonny.

Fooling Aaron more often involved the physical. Everyone knew how much Sonny liked to throw, so Sammy would pester his cousin to play catch. Or when Aaron approached with ball and glove, Sonny would pretend he was Sammy and wasn't interested. Once Sonny dropped his baseball mitt and pulled off his T-shirt, yelling, "I can't take this anymore," like he was really Sammy pretending to be Sonny and had reached his limit on both shirt wearing and playing catch. That one worked.

The Dude was never much fun because he couldn't tell them apart even when they wanted him to, but Franny was the toughest of all. No bit of playacting was going to fool their mother. If either of them talked too much, she'd get it right away. "It isn't so much the words you say that gives you away," she told them once. "It's more when you choose to talk."

She would get body movement too. Apparently, they walked and ran and moved differently though the twins refused to believe there was any difference and it made both of them so mad at how easily she saw through them and at how proud she was of her "ability."

The Dude wasn't sure how to react; on one hand he thought he should be annoyed by all the switching, like he was being played for the fool. Except the twins never made him feel like that, it was Franny who often judged him poorly for his "inability". Despite his size, The Dude wasn't the confrontational sort; he'd never challenge her directly over an attitude he perceived as condescending. Instead, his anger tended to erupt at odd times, over seemingly minor incidents. He was more than capable of exploding over something he himself had caused; breaking a plate and angrily blaming it on who left it on the edge of the sink or leaving hardened chips of mud all over the kitchen floor then yelling about who had moved the outside mat. Still, anger never ruled the twins' household; The Dude was more often bewildered. The twins loved simple guessing games and he'd try to play along, but it was clearly impossible.

"I'm thinking of a number," Sonny'd say.

"Between one and one million," Sammy would finish the thought.

"You first, Dad."

"That's a lot of numbers, Kiddos."

"That's why it's a game."

"Um, seventeen?"

"Wrong!" Sonny would say. "Sammy's turn."

"Two thousand, six hundred and . . . seventeen," he'd say very slowly like he was figuring it out.

"That's it! Sammy-1, Daddy-nothing."

It might go on for hours like this if The Dude allowed it. Sometimes they'd guess colors or shapes or favorite movies or favorite trees in the yard or favorite mosquito bites, the only constant being that the twins always won, and The Dude always lost.

Franny found their "twinness" less perplexing than their wild streak. She was a naturally cautious woman from an early age, she never learned to ride a bicycle as a child because the speed and the open spinning spokes frightened her. And while The Dude had gone through a rowdy streak in high school, it mostly revolved around drinking and driving too fast.

From an early age, the twins were climbers and jumpers, and they were fallers. When Sonny was no more than three, he crawled to the top of the stairs and promptly rolled all the way to the bottom head over heels, bloodying his nose and terrifying his mother in the process. It was not an overstatement to say he could've easily broken his neck. She cleaned him up and warned the both of them in the most serious tone she could muster, but not five minutes later, Sammy did the same thing, and ended up with an identical bloody nose. Over the years, she got used to getting calls from the neighbors that one or both of her sons had climbed to the top of a telephone pole or was on the roof of their garage. She once caught them across the street on the roof of the Southern family's tool shed, their pockets full of raw eggs, about to jump to see who could land and roll without breaking the eggs. And one afternoon a few days before Halloween, Mrs. Kleinschmitt from three houses down called in a panicky huff and Franny had to stop in the middle of shaping her famous orange popcorn balls to take care of it.

When she arrived, Sonny was already on the ground rubbing his arm and sporting a golf ball-sized knot on his head, having snapped off the tip of his tree, and Sammy was at the very top of a twenty foot tall blue spruce, swaying back and forth like a metronome, determined to do the same to his. Mrs. Kleinschmitt was outraged and threatening legal action, but even so, it took ten minutes of yelling, using her most intimidating voice to convince him to give it up and come down. Sammy sulked the rest of the evening and part of the next day not because he was being punished—he was sent to his room without dinner or television and The Dude was making noise about canceling Trick-or-Treating in a couple of days—but because Sonny had done something he himself hadn't.

Franny

I'm surprised she's living in town. The last time we talked on the phone—years now, dating back to before I moved to the East Coast—she was going on about how much she wanted to move back to "the old neighborhood."

"The old neighborhood? What are you talking about?"

"You know what I mean, sweetheart," she said. "The real neighborhood, by the lake."

"Bullshit, pure and utter."

"Sweetie."

"I won't hear of it. Not a bit of it."

It was between 9th and 10th grades the two of us moved into town. Their divorce never did become official, him dying finally finished off a marriage that had been over for more than two thirds of my life, but that first move was the final physical split between them. My neighborhood friends, Tommy, both Dickies and Danny the girl, all swore they'd visit often, and I promised the same in return, but it didn't work out that way.

It was different living in town; no golf course nearby, no lake, not much open space, unless you count cemeteries and church parking lots, just block after block of two-story houses with postage-stamp front yards and a fenced-in back butting up against an alley. More than half of the houses were converted to multiple apartments and not everyone looked the same. There were Poles, Mexicans, Ukrainians, even a few black kids. The kids were like kids anywhere, but a lot of them had parents who couldn't speak any English, which was strange. Anything that happened kid-wise happened in the alleys, where we could throw a football, shoot baskets at a single rim bolted into the side of someone's garage, or drink a beer in peace. Maybe I would've talked about "the old neighborhood" the way she did if I'd never moved away, but all those years in Chicago living in Bucktown, Wicker Park and Ukrainian Village, neighborhoods with a similar feel to the one my mother and I moved to, made me realize this was who I was, what I think of when I think of home.

The address is a large Victorian split into multiple apartments off of Indiana Avenue in the "mansion" part of town, and without even checking the number, I know which apartment is hers. I know because from the outside, it's identical to the one we moved to all those years ago. Not the house—ours was considerably more dilapidated with a weedy yard and two rusty cars that didn't run clogging the driveway—and certainly not the neighborhood. Clayton Street was solidly working class while this is a once-wealthy neighborhood slowly going to seed, but the set-up is identical: a set of metal stairs bolted into the right side of the house at a steep angle, a wooden door at the top with a small overhang roof. I climb. There's a doorbell but instead I knock. Strangers ring the bell. Family knocks. Or maybe I have this backwards.

Someone's inside, I hear chairs scraping along the floor, a door bangs shut.

"Hello?"

"I've called someone," It's her, Franny, that husky voice, though it sounds hoarser than I remember. "You're in real trouble, mister."

"It's me," I say, and when this doesn't seem to be enough, I add, "Henry."

The door locks click, the door cracks.

"Henry?" she says, like it's not even a real word.

"For fuck's sake, yes."

"Henry," she says again, this time like she's trying it out to see what it means.

"Franny?" He says, with a mocking touch.

She opens the door, she puts her left arm across her body and grips her right, a gesture so familiar it's like I've never been anywhere or done anything. Just this, just now.

I can't say she looks good or the same; she looks older and fatter with craggy loose skin, and red veins popping around her nose, but her eyes and her mouth, they're the same. She's always had a friendly mouth and a great smile I spent a lot of years trying to provoke that smile. She looks at me without a trace of recognition except maybe somewhere deep because her next words are gentle, as if she understands there's someone known to her standing in the door to her apartment without knowing exactly who. I recognize a life that's taken a turn this way; towards becoming used to forgetting the familiar. There's no judgment to this recognition, my own life is heading in the same direction.

"Did you say Henry?" she says.

"Henry, yes. Henry. Catch up here, would you?" I've always been this way with her, caustic and bemused. Once when Philips and I were visiting her, my mother told me that was the exact tone my father used with her, and she hated it. "Really makes you think, that," Philips said later. "No it doesn't," I shot back, though of course it did.

"Henry," she says, finally getting the inflection just right. She takes my face between her hands. I smell alcohol mixed with cigarette smoke on her breath and something sour like old food on her fingertips. I've never known her to smoke. "Henry."

"Hey Ma," I say as casually as I can in an attempt to short-circuit the intensity of the moment. "What is this?" I raise her hand she's holding a can of Mace.

"Henry sweetheart." We hug and when I push away, she holds on tight.

"You feel the same. Isn't that strange?" she whispers in my ear. "All these years of grabbing you and hugging you, I haven't thought about it, not for so long, but right away, I remember, and I remember because it feels the same."

"Don't be dramatic, Franny, it's not been that long."

"It's been forever."

"Two years is not forever."

"You don't know. Nothing at all. You don't."

I've prepared a whole backstory to explain why I can't stick around Indiana. I have a new job at Portland State University teaching film, which I got through a friend and colleague. I make myself an adjunct film professor because Franny knows the nuances and her exuberance over a tenure-track position would be too much to bear. I briefly considered making the colleague female and mentioning a casual affair, just so she'll know her son is still capable of getting some, but that just seems too pathetic. Best to keep lies simple.

"Let me make you some food," she says, her voice just enthusiastic enough that I cringe.

"Ma, I got . . . Aaron's expecting me to make dinner tonight."

"Then make dinner. Doesn't mean you can't have a cup of Joe and some sugar toast." I settle at the kitchen table, she uses a French press for coffee, something she's always done even back when they weren't common. And I love her cinnamon toast, just a piece of white bread with butter and sugar and cinnamon, melted in a toaster oven.

We nibble at the toast and sip on our cups of coffee, hers with a generous dose of Sambuca judging by the smell.

"I can't believe this," she says.

"Right," I say.

"I can't."

"Well do."

"I want to hug you again. Not now, but again."

"Franny...?"

"I'm just saying..."

"OK."

"Now?" she says.

"How 'bout when I leave? I need to get back to Aaron. You know about him?"

"I don't know, I don't know about him. That's what I say now. Anyone asks me, I say 'I don't know, I don't know, I don't know.'"

"He's just really..."

"I can't sweetie," she says, softly crying. "I'm glad you're seeing your cousin, but I can't. Whatever's going on, I just can't. Do you understand?"

"Sure," I say. "'I can't' is one of my favorites. 'I don't know' too."

She laughs and pulls a small bottle of Sambuca out of her apron pocket and refreshes her coffee, her hand trembling as she pours. Years ago, she would hide her drinking from me. I'm not sure if this is progress or regression, but I suppose it hardly matters.

"The toast is good," I say. "Like always."

"Small mercies," she says. She brightens. "Hold on." She leaves the room and returns with a small package roughly the shape of a book wrapped in bright, flowered paper. No way she just wrapped this, which means either she's giving me someone else's present, or she's had this for a long time, waiting for the day I appeared.

"I got nothing for you."

"Just you is plenty."

"When did you start smoking, Mother?" I say, trying to deflect her attention.

A look of surprise, she hadn't realized I knew. "Well . . ." she says.

So it's true, after 40 years of not, she's actually smoking.

"It's a hard smell to get rid of," I say as way of explanation.

"I just did, that's all. I couldn't see why not, and it gives me something to do with my hands when I'm out." By out, she must mean bars. She goes out. To bars. This seems a major life shift, the entire time we were living together, she was an at-home drinker. Bars were seedy, she'd say, fine for the likes of low-life jerks like your father, but not for anyone with even the barest sense of decorum.

"It's just a bit odd is all," I say. "I don't even know if you ever smoked."

"Well I do now."

"I guess so."

"Since you know . . ." She fishes into her apron pocket and emerges with a pack of light blue American Spirits and a lighter and deftly lights one and takes a long pull, actually drawing the lingering smoke in through her nose. The effect is startling, being presented with the tough prison moll version of my mother, like that moment in a suspense film where a formerly trusted associate shows their true face. Smoking transforms her, gives her purpose, certainty, a sense that she knows who she is and what she's doing and isn't the lost, broken creature she's always seemed. I don't know how I'm supposed to feel about it. Not the smoking itself, the smoking's fine—whatever she needs to do to get by—but that she's not the person she's always been, she's transformed herself. Maybe taking up cigarette smoking and bar hopping in your middle sixties isn't most people's idea of personal growth, but from where I stand, it seems a quantum leap forward. Has that been her role in my life, as a reassurance that no matter how stagnant my own life is, it pales in comparison to the Queen of Inertia, my sad little drunk of a mother who can't manage to ever get out of her own way? The thought shows me in such an ugly, petty light, I have to leave. Sort this out somewhere else. I stand up and move towards the door.

"You're leaving?" she says, picking a piece of tobacco out of her mouth and flicking it. "I thought we'd do one more round of Joe and toast."

"Aaron," I say. "He needs me."

"Oh, well, if your cousin who you haven't seen in a decade needs you," she says.

"I'm sorry."

"Don't be," she says. "Sorry."

At the door, she hands me the gift, which I'd left on the chair.

"You know," she says, lighting a new cigarette off the old one. "You should invite me to Santa Fe sometime."

"What?" I ask. This is too much, completely beyond the pale. "What are you talking about?"

"I'd like to see some places . . . I'd like to see New Mexico. I hear there's a Spanish influence." She holds up her cigarette. "And these come from there."

"I don't live there. You know that you fucking know that."

"I went to a past lives therapist once," she says. "I guess you know that."

"Mother, just shut up about it. Please."

"You're the one who brought that into the house, all those books you bought, and the videotapes. And talking about it all the time. Past lives this, past lives that."

"I didn't talk about it all the time. I don't ever remember talking to you about it."

"Oh sweetie, you used to read passages from those books."

I did do that. Reincarnation, past lives, every book I could find, I read. It all seems so painfully obvious now what I was doing, I don't like to be reminded of it.

"And you know I have to have a book to read. Once you brought them into our home, it was only a matter of time."

"Apartment."

"Suit yourself. It was a home to me."

"It was a phase, Franny, like...I don't know...a phase you grow out of and besides, it was so long ago now, I don't even remember it."

"She told me I'd been a monk in Spain in the late sixteenth century and that I probably came over on a boat and ended up out in Northern Mexico, converting the heathens."

"She who?"

"The therapist. She said it was likely I knew Santa Fe. Maybe I lived there."

"So we've both lived there. You go, you don't need me."

"Don't think I haven't thought about it, buster." Delivered in her classic clenched-teeth style, meant to show she was serious when I was growing up, but now said with a shading of self-mockery, and I can't help but smile.

"Kiss your mother," she says, and with a cigarette dangling, she takes my head in her hands and rubs my buzzed scalp, I have to bend way over for her to reach.

"This worked better when I was smaller."

"You said a mouthful there, boy. I like your hair longer, your head's too small for your body."

"I didn't see that coming."

"My little pear-shaped boy."

"Thanks."

"We'll have breakfast," she says.

"Sure Franny."

"Before you go."

"Sure Franny."

"Maybe a few times."

"We could do a few times."

I would've agreed to come live with her later as long as I could get out now. I'm in my truck with the engine running and the transmission in reverse before I even hazard a glance, she's sitting on the top step of the porch. She gives me a wave. This is our dynamic since I went away to college. It used to take days, not minutes, for me to get to the point of panicking and fleeing, though until today, I'd never thought of it like that. I have the urge to do something nice for her, say something—I'll call you, Good to see you (not I love you, not shouted out loud)—or maybe just a couple toots on the horn, a wave and a smile, that'd be okay but even as I know I should, it seems as craven in its way as the original act, to expect to smooth over decades of behavior in one gesture.

I leave and head for the city park, backing into a spot overlooking Stone Lake. The trees on the far side are just turning, giving the lake a stunning checkerboard collar, greens and yellows and reds in dozens of shadings, their surface seeming to boil and roll in the wind. Stone Lake's always been the quiet lake, the swimmers' lake, because it's too small for water skiers. A few people stroll along the water's edge, two muscle cars are parked driver's window to driver's window—cabbie-style—their owners talking and laughing and taking quick tugs on a brown-bag bottle. A man and his little boy feed the large Canadian geese hanging along the shoreline. The boy keeps charging after birds as tall as he is, arms out, they both seem a bit unsteady, the goose waddling and flapping its wings, the boy lurching forward, like a stumbling dance. People doing normal, everyday things calms me. It's never easy seeing her. Why did she keep talking about Santa Fe? Our lives went off the rails there, she knows that. Our child Cadence lives there with my ex-wife's parents. A town that represents real pain and suffering, not the pseudo-versions I've grown comfortable with.

I remember the gift and open it without enthusiasm, suspecting an emotional time bomb. Still, I'm not prepared for what it is. A photograph, framed. I should've known it wasn't a book.

It's not the family I expected, though it has bite still. Philips and I together, with the baby between us, rock monoliths in the background. This was taken on a car trip through Monument Valley and southern Utah. Besides the drive when we moved from Chicago to Santa Fe, it was the only trip the three of us took together. But what a picture! I don't remember doing this, we've stretched my fleece jacket and zipped it in front with her left arm in one sleeve, my right in the other, Cadence positioned so we look like the three-headed monster. The light is low, and we are deeply tanned and healthy—happy even—with me caught awkwardly but good-naturedly in mid-word and Philips genuinely laughing (you could always tell when her reaction was authentic, she wasn't good at hiding how she felt) at whatever I'm saying. A spasm crosses the baby's face, a moment's bit of gas maybe, but her tiny hand extends through the neck opening and is reaching for my face. I marvel that my mother can keep this photo without being overwhelmed by all it entails. I've always admired that in my parent's generation, their ability not to over-react. Born around the time of the Depression, they were raised through hard times, taught to listen and do what they're told and not to talk or think about it too much, not to discuss it or analyze it. We're all miserable, we're all in pain, but only my generation and beyond is so aware of exactly what is fucking us up. And what does all that awareness bring? I'm not sure, but it's not peace and it's not understanding and it's not redemption.

I'm beginning to suspect I've stepped into a far more powerful and complicated psychic current than I could ever have imagined when I left New Hampshire four days ago. In a moment of denial bravado, I flip the photo out the window and put the truck in gear, inching onto the pavement, before I jam it back in PARK, retrieve the photo, and find a spot in the back, behind a box, under a soft gym bag full of socks. On the way to the farm, I even have a chuckle over it. This is my version of maturity. Ten years ago, I would've tossed it, driven all the way to Aaron's, sat around for a while obsessed over the photo, before dashing back to where I threw it and recovering it. Now I reduce the drama to three minutes total. Growth is growth, I guess.

Aaron

Uncle Eddie and Aunt Irene return in a week. I've promised myself I'll be gone by then, enough is enough. In the meantime, I have the farmhouse to myself. Aaron apparently sleeps in the barn, even when his parents are away. I tell myself it's important to spend time with him. Given his condition, it seems more than possible I'll never see him again. But Aaron shows little interest in coming out of the barn; we take a single daily walk together down the lane. Sometimes he appears at dinner and picks at whatever I've prepared. Other times, I hear him sneak into the house late at night and eat leftovers from the fridge. Though I'm initially annoyed—how often do I actually pass through town—his appearance is so wraith-like and fragile that within a couple of days, I'm happily ensconced in front of the television after dinner just like I live there. It's easier not to see Aaron, not to constantly face his condition.

He looks like a walking corpse, like he's dead already and just waiting for his brain to get the message. What happened to him? Aaron has never liked being around people all that much. When we were kids, he had a standing invitation to come to our neighborhood for Trick or Treat because theirs was the only house on the entire road and he never came. He'd carve his own pumpkin and even dress-up, but he hated going door to door with a large crowd of rowdy kids.

As an adult, he'd moved away from Denver because of the density of people and then away from home because of the proximity of family. He'd known a few girls but never had a girlfriend as far as I know, though it was unlikely he'd tell me if he did. He seemed happiest walking on the farm by himself; I'm sure it's why he came back home, the beauty of his family's woods and lakes and the serenity of walking in them. He and I have the same disease, different degrees. Philips used to say Aaron was me without all the crippling introspection which she meant as a compliment to me, though she and he had a genuine fondness for each other. It was important to Aaron that Philips was his friend and not just the wife of his cousin and she respected that. They shared confidences.

On our daily walks down the lane, Aaron refuses to stop talking, asking about Philips and the child.

"Fucking Christ," I say one afternoon as we lumber our way towards the distant woods, Aaron already huffing and puffing. "Do you really think I want to talk about this?"

"I think about her sometimes. Wonder where she might be. Imagine adventures, maybe a pet," Aaron says. He shows no interest in displaying the slightest bit of sensitivity about the subject. "You must think about her."

"No."

"You must."

"I choose not to."

"You can't choose not to."

I look at him, thinking he'd get the point of how ridiculous it is to say that to me; him so frail and dissipated he can barely walk, all of this in a body not even fifty years old. But if he does, he gives no indication. We walk in silence until the mood tempers.

"You didn't tell me about your mom," he says.

"She smokes now."

"Smokes? Like cigarettes?"

"No, a big Sherlock Holmes pipe."

"What?"

"Yes, yes, cigarettes. Camel no-filters."

"That's it? She smokes?"

"She can't shut up about Santa Fe either."

"And you think I'm screwed up?" he says.

*****

When we found out Philips was pregnant, things changed, at least for a while. We quit arguing; the intensity that always surrounded us was muted. We developed rituals and took pleasure in them; making love all the time when we first found out, not so much out of a grand passion—we were far past that point—but because of the opportunity to have skin-on-skin sex without fear or doubt; we became like two professionals happily doing our jobs each day. I started cooking for her again, the way we'd been when we first lived together. This time it wasn't me creating elaborate dinners but finding ways to satiate her odd assortment of cravings.

And she took great satisfaction in my attempts and showed a patience she never had before when I failed. Being pregnant blunted her edges, she didn't get angry as often and when she did, she got over it more quickly. And free from her relentlessness, I found the force of all I felt turned down a few notches. The baby was a drug, and we were patients being dispensed a full dose daily and mostly we were happy to be in the moment.

By the time she went into labor, it was all we could do to tolerate each other. Her irritability at being so large knew no bounds and seemed justified to me, so I found myself fawning, giving in, trying to calm her, playing the buffoon.

On the walk from the parking lot to the hospital for her final pre-delivery checkup, I noticed something new. Maybe it was how I was thinking that day but the way she walked pregnant with an uneven lilt, the bulk causing her gait to shift back and forth—she reminded me of those nature films of an elephant contentedly loping, shot in barely perceptible slow motion, trunk swinging back and forth— there was such a graceful cadence to her walk and I thought "I love this woman. It must be true. I do." I wanted to say this to her in a way she'd believe so I worked and re-worked the words in my head, considering every likely reaction, every possible offense (understanding, of course, that the elephant analogy was best left unsaid). Cadence. I knew what to say.

"I was thinking—don't say it—about what we should name her. Maybe we should consider a name now." We knew we were having a girl.

She didn't respond so I continued. "Cadence. Like in music, you know, I thought that'd be a good name. Cadence." And she walked a few steps and then stopped and looked at me and I remember being scared because she could look at me in a way that made me feel there wasn't a single comfort in the entire world. But she smiled and kissed me and took my hand and without ever saying so, that became our child's name. Cadence. The one thing I've given her no one can take away.

Philips and I moved to Santa Fe three months after bringing the baby home. I quit my job at the downtown college; they offered me benefits and an extra class to stay on but I had to say no. Whatever was working for us in Chicago—and looking back, the months of her pregnancy were among the most peaceful and fulfilling of our marriage—stopped when we brought her home. Those weeks were the hardest of my life.

Faced with the all-consuming task of caring for the child, we drifted into different responsibilities. We'd read very little about taking care of babies. Philips said people had gone 10,000 generations without books on child rearing, and I accepted that without question. But it wasn't always self-explanatory. Since Philips had given birth to her and was nursing her, she expected me to handle nearly all the diaper changing. First, she got a vaginal infection because I was wiping her baby shit the wrong direction. Dealing with her genitals made me more uncomfortable than I would have ever imagined, though I got used to it. I had no choice.

Philips breast-fed but was adamantly against using a breast pump— "I'm not a fucking cow in a stall" were her words—so we had to supplement her breast feeding with formula. Except she kept throwing up the formula. After a hellish month of crying (the child) and screaming (us), we discovered soymilk formula which she was able to (mostly) keep down. Getting up with her in the middle of the night was supposed to be decided on a case-by-case basis, but it was almost always me who warmed the formula. Who was I to argue? Philips spent all day with the kid and when she finally fell asleep, she'd be out until morning—unlike the baby who was up and crying every couple of hours.

Neither of us was particularly good in a crisis; those times when she had diarrhea, couldn't keep any food down, or had a blazing temperature. The proper course of action was never self-evident. Do we deal with it ourselves or take her to our doctor in the morning? Or do we go to the emergency room right now? I hated that feeling, that sense of rising panic as the baby cried and cried, pushing us to lash out at each other. I was lousy at it, Philips was worse, often flying into a panicked rage which infuriated me, and I'd scream back; neighbors top and bottom banged on the floor and ceiling and we had visits from the super more than once warning us to keep it down.

And when I'd look at the tiny baby, I wanted to see her chubby tummy and her soft, rubbery skin, I wanted to wonder at her downy hair and the way she suckled the bottle. But what I mostly saw was work and anger. She didn't smile, she had no personality at that age, all she did was cry and sleep. And the life I imagined, the three of us spending long hours naked together on our bed, sleeping and playing and laughing, wasn't possible. Philips didn't like me in the room when she breast-fed; she took to locking the door. At first, I was beyond resentful but over time, I convinced myself Philips and our child were creating a singular, unbreakable bond together, and what husband in his right mind would deny a wife that?

We picked Santa Fe because her parents had retired there and because they lived in what sounded like an interesting place; a town of some size where hopefully we could both get work, a western city with a literate population and beautiful scenery, a climate that was hot but not too hot in summer (her mother's words), cold but not too cold in winter (her father said, completing his wife's thought in a way that always angered Philips for no reason I could understand). And most importantly, it had her parents, babysitters ready and willing to take care of the baby so both of us could get some space.

"Maybe once we both have time, we can find the energy to get a divorce," I said, loading up our truck in Chicago.

"That'd be nice."

"Wouldn't it."

*****

One day when we're all the way down the lane, Aaron points to a spot in the woods back towards the old cabin. The cabin sits on the edge of a stand of white pine trees planted in rows decades before. It's misty and dreary, the kind of day that carries its own mood, not unpleasant if you give yourself up to it. Aaron hobbles his way past the fallen-down cabin and finds a thin path into the white pines. Covered in a carpet of brown needles and with the pines all board-straight and reaching seventy-five feet above, it has a muted, Oz-like quality to it; like the path is heading some place that doesn't actually exist. Breaks in the gloom roll in and clouds take form and the sky opens up in patches. He angles for a slant of sunshine hitting the ground. When we get there, I see a dozen foot-high, leafy marijuana plants in excellent condition. Nowhere near ready for harvest, but the richness of the green and the leafy elegance of the plants reflecting the bright sunlight is simply . . . beautiful. I'd never known Aaron to smoke pot, though since he was a child, he's been interested in growing plants and vegetables, and he had his Hawaii experience. He used to say when he inherited the farm, we could plant marigolds and tulips and poppies in both fields.

"I'll never get to these before they flower. I don't have the energy," he says with such a sense of resignation, he seems ready to lay down and never get back up.

"They're lovely still."

"They are, aren't they." He sits on a fallen log with a well-worn spot; this feels like a ritual, walking back here and basking in the splendor of his secret garden.

On the return walk to the house, he tells me he has an entire crop harvested and drying in the barn and he makes me a proposition. I would have done it for free, for just a small bag for the trip west, but he insists there be a quid pro quo between us. He allows me into where he lives in the barn and makes me sit at the table like we are completing a business deal and I finally understand how he is living. It's dusty but comfortable and homey despite the faint smell of illness mixed with oily disinfectant clinging to everything. He's set up an apartment inside the hay loft with tables, chairs, a sofa, a television, a telephone, even a toilet which is really just a bowl with a long tube leading outside to the ground one story below.

"You trim it up for me, put it in bags where I can get to it, separate it out and you can have half for yourself."

I agree and when we've shaken hands over it, I ask him about it, curious as to whether a part of his growing up was completely hidden from me, his secret life as a dopehead. All he'll say is the medication he takes makes him ill and that pot helps. He refuses to say more in a gesture I believe I recognize. Better to allow people to believe there's something remaining unsaid.

Aaron sets up a scale and offers me surgical gloves, which I first refuse but the weed is sticky and strong smelling and within an hour, my head is swimming from the pot-on-skin contact, and I take him up on his glove offer. He has me divide half of his cut into six one-pound bags, seemingly set up to sell, though I can't imagine who he might sell it to.

The other six pounds I put in two five-gallon paint cans near his bed which he covers with a bright Navajo rug. He uses the covered cans like a bedside table, with books, a lamp, an ornate wooden box, and a sleek-looking water pipe all carefully arranged on top. While he watches TV, he packs the pipe with pot from the wooden box, smoking dope constantly while I work cleaning and weighing.

My cut comes to eleven pounds, four ounces. It takes a while for the full meaning of this to settle in and once it does, I have to see this as one more sign. Twelve pounds! A major felony. I can't just sell this on the street. There's only one person in the world I know who might have the money and inclination to buy this much pot, an ex-cabbie named Clifford. And of course, Cliff lives in Santa Fe.

On the day I leave, I think Aaron isn't going to even bother to come out of the barn. I'm ready to go. Franny and I had breakfast five days running, she smoked as we ate and I found it difficult to see past this new tough version, but we were easy enough with each other. She cried a little this morning and I did too. We exchanged phone numbers (she has a cell phone!) and I promised to keep in touch and report back. Though I never did tell her I'm heading for Santa Fe—my Portland film adjunct professor lie is still in place—it seemed to me she knew; if not the particulars, at least that I was lying to her. I've written my aunt and uncle a long note and taken two home-canned bottles of spiced watermelon rinds, Aunt Irene's specialty. Nine years ago when Philips and I moved to Santa Fe, we stopped here to say goodbye. Aaron was wandering around Central America then. Philips had stuck her head out the car window and waved with both hands and Aunt Irene had waved back. She said only my aunt could do that in a way that wasn't corny, that didn't feel fake and she said it never failed to make her feel better about wherever she was going. Now, all I get is Aaron stoned and leaning against the side of the barn, smiling and holding his hand up in a version of a wave goodbye.

"Take care of yourself," I say.

"Funny," he says. "A jokester."

"Well . . . " I hadn't meant it as a joke. It isn't always clear how aware Aaron is willing to be about his condition.

"Tell Cady about her Uncle Aaron, will you do that?"

"I'm leaving now."

"Then leave."

"I'm going." I get in my truck, start it, and roll down the window. "I'm sorry," I say.

"You'll have to see her," he says.

"What?"

"Cady, you'll have to."

"I don't have to." But I no longer have it in me to believe that. Of course, I think. Of course.

Halloween

"I'm not scared," Sammy said out loud to no one, though he hoped his brother might be near.

They'd started fighting without a single word said. It happened sometimes. Sammy might look at Sonny or hear the way he said something, and he'd know and he'd be so angry and a fight would start because Sonny would know too and he'd be just as mad. It never mattered what it was about, and it'd be over just as quickly as it started. But this time, he'd run and run, laughing by the end, sure Sonny was right behind him, reaching for him, but when he finally stopped, he was alone. In the middle of the golf course. Dressed like a cowboy. Nine years old.

It wasn't that Sammy was lost, he knew about where he was and which way to go home but tonight, nothing was quite the same. Everywhere there were ghouls and goblins, ghosts, devils, astronauts, soldiers, rock stars, and the light of the neighborhood had never seemed so pale. The entire world was covered in a haze. He heard tiny voices squealing and laughing but they were so far away and sounded like death to him, the way someone might sound from six feet underground.

There was a hush in the air, like all the kids of the neighborhood were collectively holding their breath. You could hear feet shuffling through dried leaves in three directions, crackling like bones snapping and turning to dust. The night was warm for the end of October, even sweaty, and the sky was speeded up, clouds racing in crazy fractured patterns. In the light of the full moon, there'd be distinct shadows surrounding him one moment, flapping arms and shaking in the breeze, and the next, it'd be absolutely black where he stood, even as the cloud shadows streamed around him.

Then a shadow crossed the face of the moon and he said to himself, "A cloud, a cloud, a cloud," but it didn't look like a cloud. It looked like a demon or a witch. Yes, a witch on a broom, and he held his breath and crouched down in the darkness of a bush, hoping she wouldn't come back. A large, fast moving cloud separated into a thousand jagged pieces like a whole army of witches breaking formation and he wanted to scream when their shadows crossed over him, speckling the grass around him, but if he screamed they might see him so he began to cry and cry. He was so scared he was no longer sure which way his house was but it hardly mattered. He'd never try to cross the great stretches of open, moonlit golf course. He didn't dare.

The night had begun normally enough, for the twins anyway. Franny had caught them siphoning gas out of her car into a Diet Rite bottle. Sonny had seen it on TV and gotten the idea of making a Molotov cocktail; he said it'd burn, maybe even explode and both of them were excited, but their mom was not and demanded to know where they'd gotten such an idea. She'd taken the hose and poured the gas somewhere in the yard and she was not very sympathetic when Sonny got sick from sucking up gas.

Once it got dark, she went around and lit the pumpkins and then took pictures and shot some eight-millimeter movie film with its intense bright light that always made Sammy squint and turn his face. Sonny jumped up and down, clowning around and acting like an idiot. Watching home movies one time, The Dude had said at least in the movies, he always knew which twin was which. Sammy was the one squeezing his eyes shut, holding his hands up to block the light. Sonny was the star.

An hour after dark, they were both jittery, running around, wrestling, giggling, waiting for The Dude, whose job it was to take them trick-or-treating. They'd argued with her about this.

"Sammy will be with me," Sonny said.

"Sonny with me."

"All the best candy will be gone."

"Nothing but apples and gum."

"Yuck." Sammy sounded genuinely alarmed.

She was unmoved. They'd wait for their father. A few days before, they'd decided to be The Lone Ranger, both of them.

"What about Tonto?" The Dude said. "One of you could be Tonto."

"Maybe," Sammy said, unconvinced.

"Tonto? OK, we could be Tonto," Sonny said.

"We could," Sammy said.

"Tonto," Sonny said, thinking. "We'd need two Indian outfits."

"That's true," Sammy said.

"Wait a minute," The Dude said.

"Mom?" Sonny said, calling into the next room.

"Wait."

Franny appeared.

"We could use her wig," Sammy said.

"My wig?"

"Wait."

"We'd need two wigs," Sammy pointed out.

"When I said Tonto, I meant one Tonto, one Lone Ranger," The Dude said, confused.

The twins just stared at him.

"You have cowboy outfits already," Franny pointed out.

"That's true," Sonny said.

"Yeah," Sammy said.

"That'd be easiest," Sonny said.

"Two Lone Rangers?" The Dude said.

The twins just stared at him.

But The Dude did his duty, coming home early from work and taking his two sons out into the neighborhood, dressed in identical vests and cowboy hats, wearing black cloth with the eyeholes cut out across their faces, each with a tiny toy gun with matching leather holster. And he'd kept his mouth shut about it and walked the two Lone Rangers around, hanging back, letting them collect their candy house to house. He allowed them to disappear through a yard to have time to themselves, he knew they had soap and eggs and he remembered Halloween, so he let them go and picked them up one block over about a half hour later. He kept his mouth shut when they passed other groups of kids, children the twins' age who seemed to fill the neighborhood. He couldn't understand why they never made friends with other children. When the groups passed each other, he saw how the other kids were curious and how his weren't, not in the least. It didn't seem natural.

And towards the end of the evening, heading in the general direction of their house, he listened as always to their private language, the way one would say a fragment of a sentence and the other would immediately understand. Most of the time, he hadn't a clue as to what they talked about, it sounded like gibberish. When they reached the border of the golf course, the twins took off running without a word. They dropped their candy bags and disappeared into the darkness, and he knew he should yell for them to stop, but so little of what he thought and did around them had any effect. They lived in their own world, so he let them go. Five minutes later, he knew it was a mistake. They were gone.

He dutifully picked up their bags, one in each hand, thinking he needed to remember whose was whose until he realized with a bitter laugh that the bags were as identical as his sons.

He stood on the edge of the light cast by a streetlamp and stared out into the expanse of eighteen holes. He'd lived within a block of this course for over ten years, but he barely knew it, not being the golfer type. He had no idea where to begin looking.

"SONNY! SAMMY!"

He yelled again. A distant group of kids turned, looking for who was shouting, and The Dude didn't want to yell anymore. They were older than his sons, decked out in masks too bloody for his taste. He just wanted his sons to come back. At least they were together, he had that, the knowledge that they took care of each other, more than any two kids he'd ever seen or heard of. He had that. He called out one more time, then he waited.

And a while later, maybe as long as a half-hour, one of his sons emerged from the darkness, his outfit covered in smeared grass stains, missing his cowboy hat and his gun. The Dude squinted at him.

"Sonny," Sonny said. "I'm Sonny." And The Dude bent down and wiped the grime off his face, straightened out his clothing and Sonny allowed it, not squirming, and when it was done, he took his father's immense hand—gripping two fingers was as much as he could do—and The Dude felt a thrill. Such moments were rare.

"Where's Sammy? Where's your brother?"

Sonny looked away from him, so The Dude got down on one knee—he often felt more at ease on those rare occasions when he could deal with one of his sons alone—and he gently made Sonny look at him and he touched his cheek and could see his son appreciated it.

"Tell me, please. What about Sammy?"

"We had a fight," Sonny said. "I hit him and then I ran away." He began crying and The Dude kissed him and wiped his tears.

"We should find him."

"He's OK. I'm sorry I hit him. I'm really sorry."

"I bet he knows it, Kiddo, I bet he knows."

"He tried to hit me too. But I was the one who hit."

"I bet he's just as sorry."

"We got to find him." Sonny cried harder.

"We'll wait here."

"No, we should find him. Come with me, please Daddy, come." And what else could The Dude do but go along, being called Daddy and all. So he stepped off into the darkness holding two bags in one hand, his son's hand in the other.

Sammy waited, too scared to move. He closed his eyes and tried to summon up every bit of courage he had, which was a lot when he was with Sonny. But without? Alone? The fight was long forgotten, he couldn't remember what it was about. He couldn't even remember being mad. He just wanted to see his brother. And The Dude, he'd like to see The Dude with his huge strong hands.

He ran. After hiding awhile, the witches didn't seem as scary or real as they had. He could outrun them. He knew the lights on the other side of the course marked his neighborhood and once he got to his neighborhood, he knew the way home.

So he ran and ran, slowing as he went over a slight ridge, then the ground dropped away—suddenly it was simply missing—and when his feet re-impacted, he lost it all and started tumbling, head over feet, and when he stopped, he was at the bottom. His head throbbed and he was soaked by the dew.

He felt his face and then his outfit. His hat was gone, his gun missing, warm liquid flowed from his nose, and he understood it was blood, but he'd bled a lot in his life, and it didn't scare him. He knew it'd stop soon. But up was down, in was out and he was no longer sure which way the neighborhood was, he was too deep in the valley for any light to reach. Even the moon's light was at the wrong angle.

Strangely enough, he felt better. The tumble itself was fun, no bones were broken, just a bloody nose. And he could climb out in any direction, and he'd know where he was.

Then he saw light; pale, orange, quivering at the far end of the valley and he heard tiny voices and when he stared, he saw flashes of bloody flesh, skin gone green, mouths wracked by pain and evil, jagged teeth flashing in the light, heads shaking and laughing, a circle of monsters with kids' voices.

Sammy crawled for a while, then realized it was so dark in the valley, they'd never see him, so he stood and quietly worked his way closer. It was a circle of kids, still in masks, using a single flashlight held under their chins giving their demon faces an even more fiendish look and Sammy wanted to run away. His heart pounded, but their voices, so normal, so like his or Sonny's, calmed him and he moved close enough to hear.

They were swapping scary stories. He could tell by the way they talked, the words they used, that they were older than him, teenagers, and he didn't want to be caught. He was afraid of what a bunch of older boys might do to him. He wanted to run but he wanted to listen. And it was so dark. He moved within fifteen feet, and they still couldn't see him.

"Sssh sssh."

"Let him tell it."

"He's not telling it right."

"I haven't even said a word yet, how would you know?"

"I just know."

"Would you people shut up and let him talk."

"You shut up."

"Ssssssh."

"OK."

"Talk."

"I am."

"Tell it!"

"I am! It's about a boy and a girl and a car."

"It always is."

"Boring."

"Are there any tits in this?"

"Let me finish."

"How about starting?"

"I got a story."

"Fine, to hell with all of you."

"Your story was boring anyway."

They went on like this for a while, Sammy didn't like hearing the t-word; it was ugly to him, like they were talking about his mother. He backed away.

It was this movement that cost him.

"What was that?"

Sammy froze.

"Fuck you, what was that."

"I mean it, give me the flashlight, I saw something."

"We're not falling for that. Just tell your little story."

"Give me the goddamned light." Sammy had moved left so the light didn't hit him right away. When it did, smack in the face, he screamed. And the teenager screamed and dropped the flashlight.

"Oh shit!"

"FUCK!"

Sammy hated this word the most. The Dude used the f-word when he was really angry, and Sammy always thought it sounded wrong. It knocked him out of his daze, and he took off running.

"It's just some kid."

"Get him."

"Get him, get him."

Sammy was faster than Sonny, but both had been born with their mother's short legs and he was only nine years old, no match for a bunch of teenagers. They caught him in full moonlight on the saddle between two deep valleys, kicking out and tripping him, sending Sammy head-first into the grass, smearing green in a swath running from his hair to his chin. There were bits of grass and dirt between his teeth. One of the kids kicked his leg, then turned him over and when Sammy looked up, four boys, still in demon masks, stood high over him and the witch clouds raced above them. He was crying.

"He's a kid," one of them said coldly.

"A baby."

"I'm no baby," Sammy said, surprising himself with the strength of his voice. "I just got lost."

The four of them stood gigantic above him, immovable; green skin full of deep, craggy crevices; sharp, long teeth dripping with blood, a skeleton face with rotting skin drawn out long into a scream, and most disturbingly, a simple clear mask, blank, like a creature with no human traits or compassion, nothing human at all but the form. They stared at him, four wraiths dripping with evil. The sky over them was alive with winged creatures. Sammy couldn't imagine what horror awaited him.

"Help him up," one of them said finally.

They helped him up.

"You OK?"

Sammy nodded. He felt dizzy.

They all pulled off their masks, he could see two of them were younger, maybe even his age.

"You're one of those twins," said the tallest. "I've never seen you without the other one."

"Sonny," Sammy said, almost whispering.

"I know where you live. You know which way?"

Sammy pointed.

"That's right." They backed away from him.

"Shake it out, kid. Make sure it's all working." Sammy shook his arms, then his legs. No sharp pains, no weaknesses.

"I'm OK."

"Go home, twin."

"I'm going home."

"Quit sneaking up on people," another one said.

Sammy waved and the kids laughed. "Green teeth," the oldest one said and then the others shouted it out after him. It was a name that might have stuck, if there'd been that chance.

When he got home, Franny was beside herself with worry. The Dude and Sonny weren't back yet and here was her little Sammy with a black eye from one of his falls, smeared in green, most of his outfit gone, candy-less. She didn't know what to think when he refused to brush the green out of his teeth, flashing them at her at every opportunity.

"OK, Green Teeth," she said, laughing in spite of herself. Sammy grinned.

"Let me see again," Sonny said, hours later, under the covers with a flashlight, and Sammy beamed that green-teeth grin at him. "Eeeew," Sonny said.

"I'm going to school like this tomorrow."

"Mom won't let you."

"I just won't open my mouth all morning. I just won't."

The Dude had tried to be angry when they finally got home but Sammy kept flashing his teeth and showing off his black eye.

"You did that to your brother?" The Dude asked Sonny, too amazed to be mad.

"No way," Sammy said.

"No way," Sonny agreed.

"No way Sonny boy did this," Sammy said. "I did this."

"What happened?" Sammy told his story. He never tired of it, not the rest of his life. He was the first into the neighborhood, he'd tell Sonny. First contact with other kids, no matter that it was an accident, and they were older than he was. No matter that Sonny wasn't interested in the other kids or that Sammy had never seemed to be before. He was first and it meant a lot to him. It meant the world.

West

Small towns and two-lane highways have their own charms and in different circumstances, I'd be doing that route. Even stoned. It's pretty easy to negotiate the small town grocery store or mini-mart stoned as long as you do the responsible, middle-aged kind of pothead driving; cracking a window, putting the dope away in at least three levels of zipped pockets, rolling all the windows down and leaving them down for a few miles no matter the air temperature; lowering the radio volume in public areas, always making sure you have water for dry mouth and food to kill any smoke breath on the off chance you get pulled over. Driving like this, you can handle the semi-hostile stares by locals, simply the extra attention they give to a face they don't recognize. Nothing sinister about it, but if you're smoking cigar-sized joints and completely given in to the idea of trying to smoke every waking moment and to having the radio constantly at full blast, the Interstate is the only choice.

It is truly the last bastion of freedom in this country, at least for white people. Only a white guy like me can completely disappear into the great open spaces of this country. Really disappear. I also fall on the invisible side of the class divide; driving a beater no matter what color you are can attract police attention, but my truck is new enough to be read as a yuppie truck and people in yuppie vehicles get a whole different kind of attention. It still might be unfriendly, but it's not frightening in any way and a less frightened police person is a calm one.

I've pulled into a rest area 100 miles east of Amarillo, Texas and parked in a far corner near a scrubby field that smells faintly of manure. The only other people out this far are the most responsible dog walkers and a single van with large hippie flowers pasted on it whose owners seem to be in a situation similar to mine, a vehicle so saturated with marijuana smoke that the smallest cracked window results in a chimney-like rush of that stinky, all-too-obvious smell.

It's not clear there's any real need to worry, it feels like typical pothead paranoia. The families and old couples who populate these places don't scare me, though the large church buses I see everywhere are worrisome. Surely there's two or three reformed dopeheads amongst them, people who understand all the silly fears and rituals, who have the kind of strident self-righteousness about their need to steer wayward souls onto the correct path, and who instantly recognize the smell of that smoke; attuned as they have been for much of their lives to identifying it in large crowds of (hopefully friendly) strangers.

Not that I'm completely against the idea of someone taking the control of my life that has so far eluded me; it's just that twelve pounds of Aaron's marijuana is a tough sell to any cop as having a "personal use only" tag and going to prison is hardly what I had in mind. A day out of Indiana and it doesn't seem so destined that I have to go to Santa Fe. If I can smoke a reasonable chunk of this before I get there, there'll be no reason for me to stop and see Cliff. I can just pass Santa Fe by, continue heading west. I can settle in Flagstaff or go south to Sedona. I can keep going to Las Vegas. Cab driving in Las Vegas would be interesting for a month or two. Or I can stop in Albuquerque, get a job, and ease into my contact with Santa Fe. That's how I'm thinking.

I wander around inside the rest area, making ridiculously complicated vending machine purchases of combs and superballs and a tiny magnifying glass; getting lost in all the bright neon. I go through the obligatory blank-faced eye-lock on a particularly eye-popping part of a sign until I'm not sure how long I've been standing here and I'm afraid to look around because I don't want to aim my bloodshot eyes directly at anyone and then I realize I can't remember walking from my truck to the inside. I can't remember pulling into this rest area or the thought and resulting decision that led to this action, though I'm more than grateful it's working out. I find such questions quite common, particularly with extraordinary dope like this. It can make you paranoid and tense for about thirty seconds when you're going eighty and realize your head has been somewhere else completely and you have no idea how you steered the vehicle the last forty miles. But the paranoia usually gives way to a muted confidence in your own subconscious ability to drive a car, right before you forget all over again.

*****

Philips and I lasted four months at her parents' house in Eldorado, a large subdivision east of Santa Fe. In that time, we both basically gave the responsibility of raising the baby to Bonnie and Jim. We didn't even get up with the child anymore, Bonnie kept the baby monitor by her bed and if the baby cried, it was she or Jim who crawled out of bed to calm her or feed her. It was justified all around because her parents were retired and the both of us worked long hours in town. The first couple of months, it seemed like a great idea to have moved there, and not just because of the help they gave us. Living with her parents allowed Philips and I to bond against them. She needed someone to complain to and I was the only choice. If it wasn't exactly love, it was better than what we had in Chicago.

"Can you believe that shit?" Philips would say after another mother-daughter interaction.

"Yeah."

"Yeah," she'd say, mocking my answer.

"Why wouldn't I believe it? It's always been that way with you two."

But this bonding passed and soon it was Philips against everyone else as she set about making a new life for herself, separate from all of us. I can't remember a single night where the five of us were together in a common space after dinner; there must have been one, though it would have been uncomfortable with Bonnie and Jim sitting silently watching TV and Philips and I non-stop talking our way through commercials and programs alike. We could always connect over the television, right up until she disappeared, it was the closest thing we had to a fun time those last years.

What I do remember is a lot of nights alone with her parents; coming out of that tiny bedroom because I couldn't take the idea that she wasn't there—her actually not being there was a relief—and sitting without talking on the couch next to Bonnie; Jim in *his* chair, the sound on mute during commercials, nervous because I would try to listen for a car coming home and when I'd hear it, I'd have to quickly but diplomatically get out of there and back into the bedroom so Philips wouldn't catch me with her parents; she would judge me poorly for it. And there were nights when it was a false alarm and I'd find myself stuck back in that bedroom, and it was worse than watching TV with Bonnie and Jim, the being alone and the waiting.

Through a series of coincidences, Philips ended up with a job working nights as an apprentice sous-chef at the Hotel St. Francis downtown and she often stayed after, drinking at the bar with co-workers, not coming home until three or four a.m. On the nights when I worked, she'd be up and gone before noon, nursing a coffee at the Aztec, often with the same group of co-workers. I never knew this at the time; it came out later during the investigation.

I developed a grudging respect for Bonnie and Jim's silent, blank charms—mostly that they were so devoted to what was best for the child—but I had no loyalty. Yes, I'd agree with Philips, they're absolutely fucking batty, out of their heads, but they've changed their lives. That's what I'd tell her, they've changed their lives. This house feels nothing like the one you grew up in, I'd say, they've settled into a life here and if it isn't exactly happiness, it's not despair either. My theory, which Philips didn't dispute but had no enthusiasm for, centered around Santa Fe itself. Just waking up to another sunny day with snow on mountain ranges in three directions was enough. Maybe not enough to sustain a life but enough to get you through another day.

"Henry. Cady says hi," Bonnie would say with her grandchild on her lap, waving her tiny limp hand at me. The child might giggle and grab a handful of her grandmother's dress, or she might stare open-mouthed at the television.

"Hi, sweetie," I'd say.

"You want to hold her awhile," Bonnie said.

"Well . . ."

I held her. I'd already forgotten the months in Chicago where I changed every diaper, where I bathed her, and let her fall asleep naked on my bare stomach. I hadn't changed a diaper since moving to Santa Fe. She gripped my finger; I touched her round cheeks. Was she a pretty baby? I don't know, I'd never been around babies. Though Bonnie often said she looked like me, I could never see it.

She was a baby, with a monstrously large head and fat, short arms. And she'd begun to show a personality, which I never saw in Chicago, giggling at a private sensation; then her face and hands and feet would clench in a sour spasm, and a look of fear would take hold, but it would pass. She was good-natured and fair, meaning when she complained, she usually had something to complain about.

Philips was never interested in talking about the kid. Not that she didn't spend time with her alone, maybe more than I did, usually when I was working, but she wouldn't talk about her with me. She was still nursing, but instead of doing it behind a closed door as in Chicago, she'd nurse when I wasn't there. It was hard to see her indifference to me as anything but hatred.

"Maybe you ought to get the fuck out, get your own place," I yelled. More than once.

"You'd do well out here with my fucked-up parents, wouldn't you? You'd like that, you and Bonnie and fucking Jim, one big screwed-up family."

"You forgot your daughter."

"I forgot my daughter. That's rich, you saying that."

We stared at each other.

"I could hurt you, you know," she said.

I didn't know what to say. She was right. I had no defense.

"I want us to . . ."

"Stop," she said.

"OK."

"Just do."

"I said OK."

That's how it was between us, I wasn't allowed to hate back.

She agreed to move into an apartment in town together because that's what married people do. We were both tired of the fifteen-mile drive home after working all night. I knew it wouldn't change how Philips was living, it might make it easier, but still, I was hopeful. Neither of us had any way to solve the problem of what to do about the baby; we'd fallen comfortably out of the routine of taking care of her. Jim was more involved. When Bonnie said she'd take care of her until we settled in, we both agreed. We went to 100 percent formula, meaning anyone could feed her, and Philips no longer had to make the long drive out to Eldorado to breast feed.

And all the while, Philips continued creating a new life for herself.

"You should too," she'd say in her most reasonable tone. "Do it, take responsibility, get to know people. Don't just sit around."

"Where'd you get to know people? Your job."

"Yeah?"

"I drive a cab, I got no co-workers. I got a bunch of strangers I spend five minutes a night with."

"Who told you to get a job driving a cab? Quit, find a better job."

"I could work at the hotel. You could help me out."

She laughed.

"What would you say if I said I meant it?"

"Jesus, Henry."

*****

I've pulled off into the dirt near a famous kitschy sculpture with a line of old Cadillacs half buried in a field and I'm firing up the mandatory marijuana cigar. Philips and I did some of what normal couples do; we ate out, we went to a club in town and danced, we went to the Pink Adobe a few times to drink, we took hikes in the mountains, we had coffee countless times. We even discovered a new activity; she found out she liked to shoot pistols, so we bought a used 9mm Browning and we'd take it out into the country and fire it into the sides of hills.

I'm not sure what the cars are supposed to mean but it makes sense in a hillbilly spectacle kind of way. A symmetrical junkyard. I start to walk along a well-worn path through an alfalfa field, then stop. The land is so flat; it's a subtle wonder that takes a while to make an impression, as magnificent in its way as the Grand Canyon. I can see literally as far as the eye can; no tree lines, not a hint of a swell or a rolling ridge to block my view, just clusters of houses surrounded by trees.

I feel expansive, uneasy out of the truck, standing in that huge, open field; like my body is liquid and in all this vast flatness, I'll keep melting with no parameters to stem the flow. Stoned thinking.

Walking out to it is way too much work; plus a carload of teenagers has pulled up and already they're sniffing the air, trying to pick out the direction of that smell. They look like junior cops, which could be said about every Texan teenaged boy I've seen. So I get back in my truck, re-light the cigar and get on the interstate. Santa Fe is one day's travel away.

Vacation

Around Easter, The Dude began to talk about taking a big western vacation that summer.

The family took a week every year, but they always went north, usually stopping at Ludington or Manistee, 200 plus miles up the eastern coast of Lake Michigan. Last summer, they'd had two weeks and had continued past Traverse City and crossed the Mackinac Straits bridge into the Upper Peninsula. There'd been a big fight between Franny and The Dude over whether to cross into Canada at Sault Ste. Marie, with both refusing to budge. Franny said they were so close, the kids should be given the opportunity to visit a foreign country, even if it was just Canada. The Dude believed it was too much trouble to see "more of the same." Trees were trees, he said. The twins didn't care either way as long as they stayed in a motel with a pool. They'd been camping and while it was great fun running through the woods and rowing a canoe on the lakes, it didn't compare to the joys of a room and a pool. Then they found out firecrackers were legal in Canada and they abruptly and enthusiastically took their mother's side. In the end, the memory of what the twins had done the summer before with a single pack of bottle rockets finally convinced Franny to give it up. The twins sulked all the way home.

But now a year later, their father was talking about driving to the Rocky Mountains and taking three weeks to do it. Three weeks! There had to be lots of states with legal fireworks to the west, there had to be. Franny made a huge shopping list of camping supplies and spent two weeks getting ready, dragging the squirmy twins with her. The Dude traded in his Impala SS for a Dodge station wagon and bought an expensive set of driving and hiking maps of Colorado. Everything was set.

Then, a few days before they were to leave, the twins discovered an enormous mound of cut grass and weeds, deposited there by the golf course grounds crew, and had great fun rolling around and wrestling in the green softness. Within two days, Sammy had a full-blown case of poison ivy covering his arms, his neck and both legs. It didn't help at all that Sonny wasn't allergic, that they didn't share this.

Sammy was miserable for the entire drive to Colorado. Covered in pink Calamine lotion, which ended up on everything, even the food, he was forced to sit still in the back seat with the window rolled up. Moving just made it itch worse and wind on his neck drove him insane. Sonny wasn't happy either. Most of the time, when one of them was sick, the other was too. In those rare uneven circumstances, each felt a little lost and alone. For Franny and The Dude, this turned out to be the most peaceful part of the trip.

The only thing that made Sammy feel better was their own little book game they played together, even when one of them wasn't sick. It usually involved a reference text of some sort foisted upon them by their mother—the World Book Encyclopedia was a favorite—and some form of twenty questions, said in a scattershot style. For this trip, it was the *National Audubon Society Field Guide to the Rocky Mountain States*.

"Long-nosed leopard, Eastern Collared, Short-horned, Western Fence, Lesser Earless, Eastern Fence, Six-lined Racerunner, Great Plains Skink, Western Skink, Many-lined Skink."

"Snakes?"

"Nope."

"I bet it is," Sammy said, grabbing at the book. Sonny was known for occasionally lying when his brother got it right. "I bet it is snakes."

"Is it lizards?" Franny says, turning around so she can see into the back seat.

"Mom!" Sonny was outraged as he always was when she dared intrude on the game.

"Lizards!" Sammy said. "Lizards, lizards, lizards."

"She told you, it doesn't count, you told him, it doesn't count."

"Do another, do another, do another."

"Mom!" Sonny said because sometimes his idiot brother said the same words three times and wouldn't stop for hours or even days.

"What, what, what?" Franny said.

"Mom!"

"Do another, do another, do another."

"You're stupid, he's stupid, you're stupid."

"Just do another dear," Franny said.

"Dammit Kiddo, do another." The Dude weighing in.

"No cheating this time."

"No cheating, no cheating, no cheating."

"OK." Sonny picked through the book. "I got it. Pale Swallowtail, Pine White, Western White, Mustard White, Cabbage White, Large Marble, Sara Orangetip, Clouded Sulphur, Ruddy Copper, Blue Copper."

"Ooh, ooh, I know," Franny said.

"Mom!" Both twins said at the same time.

It might go on like this for hours, with Sonny reading about snakes, moths, wildflowers, song birds, moles, voles, shrews and all the different kinds of fungi.

By the time they arrived at the Grand Canyon, Sammy's poison ivy had scabbed up and wasn't itching anymore and the great twin chase was on. A leisurely stroll down the Bright Angel Trail turned into a pursuit when the twins disappeared around a bend ahead. The Dude understood they might walk all the way to the bottom without thinking about it, he finally caught them at the halfway point and forced them to turn around and face the hard climb out. The twins hadn't considered the walk out. It was a tough walk with no water, and both of them kept sitting down and complaining, and The Dude had to get fierce to keep them moving. When they got to the top, their mother was nowhere to be found and they wasted a lot of time looking for her before The Dude thought to check the car. The twins were sure there was going to be a huge blow-up, but after some frantic whispering, The Dude told them they were going to a motel for the night. Both of them cheered.

"None of that right now," he said. A catch in his voice made them obey. They could see their mother didn't feel well, she was sweating with her head against the window and her eyes closed and she didn't move or say a word the entire way, even when their father got out at the motel office to check in. He helped her into the room, then told them to put on their suits and go sit by the pool and wait for him. Their mother disappeared into the bathroom with The Dude and the shower went on. The twins put their ears to the door and heard The Dude say, "Are we sure?" and though they couldn't make out the words, they heard her crying and it scared the both of them into their suits and out the door. They were uncharacteristically subdued around the pool, though the twins weren't the sort to talk about their fears. Later Sammy cried when he found bloody towels bunched up in the corner of the bathroom. Sonny cried too when his brother showed him.

But by Mesa Verdi, she was up and around again and the chase was back on, through Chaco Canyon and the San Juan Wilderness, along the summit of Pikes Peak, and around the edge of Jenny Lake in the Tetons. It was in Yellowstone where a fully recovered Franny lost it publicly. Arthur had carried the brunt of the twin-handling since the Grand Canyon and with her now feeling better, he took it as his right to disappear and do some wandering on his own. From his point of view, he'd waited his entire life to come to Yellowstone and just once, he wanted to see what he wanted to see and at the pace he wanted to see it. As far as Franny was concerned, her husband had abandoned her along a boardwalk surrounded by patches of bubbling mud, geysers, and boiling bottomless pools with two hyperactive children who were a handful in open space. Her heart slowly dropped as she watched her sons giggling and laughing, building to what experience told her would be an explosion of running and wrestling and tackling. Their cousin Aaron said it was a little like watching Bugs Bunny chase Bugs Bunny. The Dude called it "Sonny and Sammy go crazy," and he wanted no part of it, forcing Franny to always be the one who had to bring them back to earth, usually by yelling and threatening. In the best of times and places, Franny disliked seeing them get this way, though she had trouble articulating why and suspected it showed her in a petty light. Maybe because in such moods, the twins were so locked into each other, everything else in the world, even Franny, didn't exist. She found it borderline creepy not to be allowed even bare access to her sons' most passionate moments and it hurt her feelings, even as she understood they didn't mean it that way.

But on the boardwalk of Yellowstone, the idea of the twins going Bugsy (her term) filled her with the deepest dread. They might simply run into Morning Glory pool and suddenly not be there and she wouldn't know where to look, what to do, who to tell. In her mind, she saw the crisis building to minutes, hours, days as people in uniforms searched with hooks in the mud pools and tried to shine lights down into the darkness of the holes. When she saw them both climbing the wooden fence, preparing to tight-rope walk (one of their favorites), she lost it and charged them screaming and when she got her hands on them, she swatted their butts and shook them until both of them went from giggling to incomprehension to tears. Arthur later admitted he heard the tirade from a distance, but never imagined it was his wife and children involved, an assertion Franny thought dubious at best.

The twins sulked as she marched them to the parking lot and stuffed them in the car and shut the door. Sonny said he was just going to go out the other side and Franny said in her most-focused, I-mean-it voice, "You try it, Buster." He didn't. She scanned the distance for her husband and wondered if she'd have to go find him. The idea that she might have to drag her kids out and make them follow her while she looked for their father, all the time keeping them quiet and in control, was completely unacceptable. She'd just wait. As long as it took.

Sonny had his nose touching the inside of the glass, glaring at her as hard as he could. Sammy was trying to duplicate his brother's face, but he really wasn't the glaring sort.

"You don't want to be looking at me like that, do you now?" Franny asked, honestly angry, something always scary to them.

Sammy looked away, he always backed down from his mother before Sonny, then was shamed to see Sonny hadn't. He was confused as to what to do because he was still frightened of his mother but hated feeling left out. Franny yanked open the door, rolled down the window, then shut it again. Sonny tried to keep it up, then seemed to understand the gesture and sat back on his seat and crossed his arms, showing more of a sulk. Ten minutes later, Sammy had his brother in a headlock, trying to jam him face first into the oval floor space, and ten minutes after that, they were asleep, on top of each other so haphazardly, they looked like rag dolls tossed on the back seat.

It was a relief but allowed her the space to think about how she and Arthur were handling what happened at the Grand Canyon. Mostly they weren't, with Arthur rebuffing her attempts to talk it out and even going so far as suggesting *she* was the one with the problem because she seemed to need help in understanding how she should feel about it. She'd used the word "miscarriage" once, and he'd gotten all sullen and pissy, like she was accusing him. She paced back and forth, circling their station wagon, trying to suppress a rising feeling that this was how her life was always going to be, standing around waiting for The Dude to figure it out. Or not. Not seemed a popular option for her husband lately. Maybe always. Maybe forever.

It took The Dude some ninety minutes to make his way to the car. In that time, Franny sat up on the hood of the station wagon, she leaned back on the windshield and stared straight up, she looked at the world of the parking lot all around her, and at the open, steaming space between the lot and the endless stands of pine trees beyond with its haze of steam and pillars of water. She stared at the grand hotel with logs as wide as their car was long,

and she studied the thousands of people scurrying to and fro:
fathers, mothers, children very much like her own. She saw clearly
there were no important differences between these families and
hers, and there never had been, a thought both comforting and so
oppressive, she had to raise her eyes past the human life all around
her. The dark intensity of the color of the Ponderosa pines was set
against a cloud-filled sky so fine-grained, it seemed to be boiling
and throbbing, revealing an extra level of three-dimensionality in
even the smallest visual details. Bugs gathered in great roiling
swarms above her, a flock of birds circled the immense hotel over
and over again, reacting like a school of fish, darting left as one,
dipping and diving and swerving. Far above the flock, a red-tailed
hawk was doing slow, lazy figure eights. Turkey vultures dotted
the sky, mixing in with the loose bits of retina floaters until the sky
was full of movement, chaotic in form, but not in purpose, the
birds seeming lack of urgency or objective validating her own
continued inaction. As she stared, a whole new world announced
itself. The difference between the old and the new was roughly
that of a tightly closed rose flower and one in full, glorious bloom.
She had stepped through a curtain and was seeing existence as it
actually was, it felt like her world, not anyone else's. Hers. It made
her want to cry out in joy. Tears welled up and she sobbed without
embarrassment. She didn't care. Nothing could touch her here.

When she finally spied Arthur trekking across the parking lot
in her direction, she knew what he'd say and in what tone he'd say
it. She knew he hadn't thought even once about the fetus she'd
miscarried a week before and that some part of her was never
going to forgive him for it. She knew she'd never have another
child. Yet she was strangely exhilarated. She was seeing the world
fresh, for the first time, and if she was smart enough to understand

her husband and her children were going to force her back into their worlds, she knew now there was a place that was only hers.

When they finally arrived home after a long and dreary drive back, there was a sense the vacation was somehow a failure. They did all the expected post-vacation rituals, including developing their slides and having Eddie, Irene, and Aaron over for a barbecue and slideshow, but it felt half-hearted. Gestures were left hanging and quickly forgotten.

Franny and The Dude never sat around recalling delightful moments or magical times. Franny found even the simplest, most necessary housework unreasonable and the physical equivalent of climbing a mountain, her life was being lived in a wilted funk. She'd be in bed when her husband left in the morning and some-times when he came home too, though often she'd switched to the twins' bedroom so she wouldn't have to face him right away. It wasn't that she ever spent an entire day without getting up, it was more as the time approached for her huge, rambling husband to return, she began to dread the moment when he'd walk through the door and she got that first fresh look at his face after a day's separation. So often, it was a complex look of trepidation and optimism she was sure she immediately squelched simply by meeting his eyes and allowing him to see her. And some days, she liked listening to him move through the house, the tinkling of the ice into the glass as he made his first drink, the growing heaviness of his steps as his patience wore thin, and finally his voice talking to the boys or yelling for her. It was a feeling that could be sweet or sad and was sometimes both, which carried the most satisfying bite of all.

Even the twins were affected and wasted almost a month watching cartoons and old TV shows. Franny knew she should encourage them to get out and not fritter away what was left of their summer vacation, but she was grateful for the peace of not having to worry about where they were or what they were doing. Sonny and Sammy emerged out of the funk first, taking baby trips around the neighborhood, and when their mother didn't complain, widening their wandering. By early August, they were spending the entire day outside, sometimes returning for lunch, sometimes not. Dreaded school was looming and there was no time to waste. They discovered places they didn't know about; a dilapidated shack in-between two fairways on the far side of the golf course where someone had pasted magazine cutouts of naked women all over the inside, a set of creaky stairs leading down the bluff to the lake that were so steep, Sonny said he was sure they could slide down them on a sled like it was a snow hill in winter, and Kabelin's Drain, a man-sized brick tube aiming back into the bluff and what seemed an infinite darkness.

They found it one day while they were kicking along the shore, looking for crayfish, or spending long, motionless minutes trying to catch frogs in the water.

"You moved," Sonny said, outraged.

"Barely moved."

"Moved is moved, idiot."

"You're the idiot. You are."

"We might as well go on," Sonny said.

They couldn't catch frogs or even crayfish, but they could scoop up tadpoles just both hands.

"Dare you to eat one," Sonny said.

"I will if you will."

"I will if you will."

"You first."

"I did the daring. You first."

Sammy looked at the tiny black tadpole flopping around in his hand; he shut his eyes, popped it in his mouth and chewed. "Eeeew." He spit then dropped down and drank up gulps of lake water. Sonny very smoothly cupped up a tadpole and swallowed it cleanly without chewing.

"You're not supposed to chew it."

"I know that now."

"I knew it then."

"You didn't tell me."

"I don't tell you everything."

"You do, you do."

"Well, usually," Sonny admitted. "I will next time we're going to eat a bug."

"Next time I'll know. You won't have to tell me."

"But in case you don't think of it."

"All right." They actually shook on it.

They knew the shoreline past the community beach from last summer when their mother took them fishing a few times, but they were curious about the other direction, towards the private piers with permanent boat stalls and the houses with grass yards leading right to the edge of the lake. A group of boys appeared standing in the water. One minute, the lake was deserted and the next there they were, laughing and kicking up water. The twins stared at the wonder of it, the mystery of life revealing itself, young boys living as lake creatures. Sammy walked into the water, trying to get an angle to see better and when Sonny couldn't reach his brother to pull him back, he reluctantly followed to a spot where they could both see.

It was a tunnel! It opened into the lake and headed back towards the bluff. The twins froze and stared the way they often did around other kids.

"I've heard about this," Sonny whispered.

"What have you heard?"

"A drain. There's a name, like a person's name. Like they own the drain."

"Drain? Drain?"

"They call it a drain. It's like miles long. One time The Dude showed me a place on the golf course where you can jump down into it."

"He showed you on the golf course? Where was I?"

"You were doing poo in the house. It was a round metal cover in the grass and he pulled it up and it was completely black down there.

"How come you never showed me?"

"I don't know. I forgot. The Dude said it was really deep and that it ended at the prison farm."

"Really, the prison farm?" Sammy said.

"Really the prison farm." They both liked saying it and they both loved driving past it. It was a trustee prison set on the highest point in the county and had exotic animals outside like buffalo, llamas and ostriches. They'd driven by it dozens of times on the way to the mall in the next town and still had never seen a single prisoner outside, which was a disappointment and made both of them slightly suspicious, as if the farm was really no more than cardboard cutout, designed as a cautionary tale for wild kids. Still, they wanted to believe.

When the kids in the water saw the twins, Sonny froze and appeared ready to run, but Sammy walked forward like he knew these kids. And the kids seemed to know him.

"Green teeth," the oldest one said. Sammy grinned.

"I had to brush them."

"I can see that."

"I tried not to."

"I bet your mom loved that."

"No," Sammy said seriously. "She didn't." The teenagers giggled. More of them emerged including smaller boys, kids closer to the twins' age. There were seven or eight of them now.

"Sammy!" Sonny whispered fiercely in his ear. He didn't like this, so many strange kids, he didn't like it at all. It seemed like the first protruding tip of a danger that threatened the entire world. He wanted no part of it.

"What is that?" Sammy said, meaning the drain.

"Take a look," said the tallest one.

"Sammy!" Sonny said again. But he followed his brother because it never occurred to him to do otherwise. They walked out into the water, giving the teenagers a lot of room. Only the tallest teenager paid any attention to them. Sonny recognized the younger kids from school, but he didn't know any of their names.

"You're those twins," one of the younger kids said. He was tall for his age, as tall as the biggest teenager, but stick-thin with wispy blond hair that appeared to already be thinning and a broad, friendly face. "Who's who?"

Sonny stared.

"I'm Sammy. That's Sonny."

"Tommy," the kid said. "Sammy with a shirt on his head. I can remember that." Sammy was, as usual, shirtless, and since Franny wouldn't allow him outside without a shirt, he'd taken to tying it tight around his head.

"Green Teeth wears a hat," Sammy said, like he was proud of it. Most of the group was already on shore, a few were headed up the bluff. Just the big teenager and Tommy lingered.

"Don't go too deep," the teenager said.

"Really," Tommy agreed.

Sonny moved past his brother and got in front of the tunnel. It was a five-foot high, perfectly round drainpipe made of brick, emptying out into the lake. Weed trees with vines hung low around it, making the brick structure invisible from anywhere but the lake. The flow of water was steady and about six inches deep.

"Our Dad says this goes all the way back to the prison farm," Sammy said.

"It goes pretty far."

"It branches off and stuff," Tommy said.

"You go back there?" Sonny said in a squeaky voice. He'd climb a tree high enough that it swayed under his weight, he'd leap off the steepest part of the bluff and roll head over heels to the bottom. But he didn't like dark, tight places.

"Sometimes. There's a little waterfall where the water is over your head. You have to swim. But that's really far back."

Now the teenager had joined his friends, leaving only Tommy. Sammy could see a gouge scar under Tommy's left eye that looked like a teardrop and made Sammy want to trust him.

"Come on, let me show you," Tommy said. The twins followed, Sammy in the lead. Tommy stood inside the edge of the drain, facing the lake. His head nearly touched the top, he bent down and plunged his hands into the flowing water, staring intently. Then he pulled a fish out and held it up. It was less than a foot long with loose, discolored scales.

"That's an ugly fish," Sammy said. Tommy laughed.

"Carp."

"What are they doing back in there?" Sonny asked.

"I don't know, maybe they get trapped when the lake is higher. You guys want to go back there?"

"No," Sonny said.

"Yes," Sammy said at the same time. Then "yes" again, to cancel out his brother's no.

Tommy led the way with the easy manner of a veteran tour guide.

"We'll go to the point where you got to make a turn. Past there you have to have a flashlight because you can't see the lake anymore."

"What do they call this?" Sammy said.

"Kabelin's Drain and don't ask me why because I don't know," Tommy said.

Sammy felt the top of the drain, it was moist, even slimy in spots. A couple of times, Sonny stubbed his foot against loose bricks hidden underwater though he was relieved to see there were none obviously missing in the ceiling of the tunnel.

"Sammy!" Sonny said though he had nothing else to say and his brother ignored him anyway.

"Do you think prisoners could escape through here? If it does go to the prison farm?" Sammy said.

"I guess they would have thought of that."

"Or maybe someone tried and that's how they found out," Sammy said.

"I never heard of that," Sonny said, though his brother had been talking to Tommy. He wanted to go back. Each step in, he wanted to turn around but he knew his brother when he was like this. Soon, they were far enough in that he couldn't make out the walls around them and had to turn to see the dwindling circle of light behind. Ahead, he could only hear the sound of Tommy and Sammy's feet pushing through gurgling water.

"How far do you think the golf course is?" Sonny said, forgetting for a moment about being nervous.

"Wow. I don't know. A long way, I think. There's a place up here where you can hear voices from up top. It's Judson Street," Tommy said.

"We live on Judson Street," Sammy said.

"I know."

Sonny wasn't sure where this kid lived. In the neighborhood, closer to the golf course. There were five houses that actually butted up against this side of the golf course; he might live in one of those. On the other side of the course was a sprawling neighborhood of newly built houses where corn and soybean fields used to be. But on this side, there were only five and all those families had fathers who worked in offices and wore suits. Many of them belonged to the country club. Judson Street was one street closer to the lake and Sonny couldn't think of any father there who worked in an office. The Dude drove large bulldozers and cranes. Mr. King next door was an iron worker; Walt Stone on the other side worked in the steel mills near Gary.

They kept going. The air in here felt different, much cooler but also wet and heavy and it seemed to Sonny he had to breathe deeper here, like there was less oxygen. He thought he felt dizzy but there wasn't enough light to know. Behind him, the entrance to the drain was now no more than a pinhole that wobbled so much, he wondered if he was imagining it. When he closed his eyes, he could see the same pinhole of light on the insides of his eyelids.

"Do you think we can hear the voices now?" Sonny deflated at the eagerness in Sammy's tone, it wasn't the voice of someone about to turn around and go back. But Sonny was ready. He knew how high the bluff was and he didn't like to think of how deep under the ground they were now—maybe a hundred feet, maybe more. If it all collapsed, they could never dig through that much. Not a hundred feet.

They kept walking.

"Oooooh," Tommy said.

"Hey," Sammy said.

"Whoa," said Sonny when a fish slimed past his bare leg. He reached out to touch his brother but swiped air instead. Just a few minutes in total blackness and you begin to lose your sense of space and sounds. He ran up against the backside of his brother.

"Don't!" Sammy sounded irritated.

"This is it," Tommy said. "Look."

Sonny looked, turning all the way around. There was no light, none. He held his hand two inches in front of his face and wiggled it and he couldn't see it. He started breathing harder, then Sammy touched him, and he calmed down.

"It's a real slow curve, you can't even tell."

"Can we hear the voices here?"

"Just a little further."

"Sammy!" Sonny pleaded. They couldn't go further, he thought. They couldn't. But they did. Sonny held on to his brother's belt loop. Pretty quickly, Tommy stopped again.

"If you stand here, there's a drain going all the way up to the street," Tommy said. The twins moved into place and listened. At first, all they could hear was water dripping but slowly they readjusted their ears and they heard male voices filtering through. It was strange, hearing it like that and knowing how high above you the people were and how they had no idea they were standing right on top of living human beings. Sonny started to get really frightened.

"I'm going back," Sonny said.

"Wait," Sammy said.

"We should. It gets deeper soon and there's lots of side tunnels, you need a flashlight to go deeper."

"OK." Sammy sounded disappointed but Sonny was energized by knowing they were going back.

"This is pretty cool here, huh?" He was speaking only to his twin, but it wasn't how Sonny normally talked, he was the one usually leading, pushing and pulling Sammy along. Now he was trying to deny how scared being here had made him.

"Yeah," Tommy answered. "I get kind of creeped out if I stay too long."

"I wanted to hear the waterfall," Sammy said.

"That's really far, just to hear it. You got to count tunnels left and right. I'm not sure of the number, I've never been there on my own. If you count wrong or take the wrong turn, there's side tunnels that drop off really deep. Supposedly you can start sliding and not stop until you're so deep, there's no way out."

"I'd like to see that," Sammy said. "Just to the edge."

They headed back. Sonny led, pushing towards the growing light. When he stepped out into the open lake, he felt like crying, it was so wonderful, the warmth of the sun on his face and the cleansing wind, the way the sunlight reflected into streams off the chrome of the cars across the lake and arced across the surface. A fish jumped a couple of feet away and Sonny laughed out loud, he couldn't help himself.

"You like?" Tommy said.

"Yes," Sammy said.

"Yes," Sonny said.

They climbed the bluff together. At the top on Judson Road, Tommy showed them the large round drain leading down into the tunnel now far below them.

"Hey there," Sammy yelled into it.

"Maybe you scared a fish," Tommy said. They laughed, the two of them. Sonny scowled, his sour mood had returned.

They separated like it was any day and they were regular friends, just a quick "take it easy" but back at the house, Sonny waited for an answer. He waited and waited until he realized his brother didn't know the question.

"I didn't like that," Sonny said.

"Oh come on."

"No, I mean it. I don't want to ever do that again."

"Oh come on."

"You come on."

"You come on," and just like that, they were over it, giggling and wrestling as they said "You come on" over and over, keeping it up through dinner and that night's television programs.

Cliff / Benny

On the edge of the Pecos Wilderness, a vast expanse of Piñon and Ponderosa pines stretching from west of Las Vegas, New Mexico to the very backside of Santa Fe Baldy, I perk up, hoping against hope that the turnoff to Cliff's place will be obvious. I need money and getting rid of an instant felony would likely make me less jittery.

First part of my idea? Stop smoking dope immediately. My attempt to smoke all of Aaron's pot in one 1,400-mile trip has ended in utter failure; even smoking cigar-sized joints constantly, before breakfast and again after and all day long, I've barely gone through two ounces. Not that it wasn't worth it; I've managed to push my state of consciousness off-center; my body has continued doing the normal things: driving, eating, shitting, watching motel cable television, but it's like my real mind has gone on ahead and I'm living in an after-image, my pot mind reacting too slowly to any introspective analysis my real mind might attempt. It can be a wonderful way to drive, but to live? Maybe, except I'm sick to death of it, my lungs ache and stoned is not how I want to be in Santa Fe. I need to be able to trust my wits. Now that I'm here, all that thinking about driving on past and not stopping seems foolish and infantile. Whatever it might mean, I'm here.

I pull off the road and wrap eleven pounds of it in a single grocery bag and make it tight with rubber bands, then stuff it under blankets in the back. I tie up the remaining two ounces and put them behind a pop-out plastic panel under the dash and cram it behind the glove compartment. No use being fanatical.

I remember the first turn off of I-25 with no problem, which I decide is a positive sign. Of course I'm ignoring the very real possibility that Cliff's moved on or killed someone or killed himself or been sent to prison or—the most likely—won't remember me or will pretend not to out of his own paranoia. I can't imagine the last eight years have been good for Cliff's sanity, given the way he was going. Cliff was a true piece of work; the original gun-nut-doped-out-conspiracy-theorist-cab-driver.

When I knew him, Cliff had his own radio show on a pirate station operating out of a secret (though no one was looking) house in the hills; it reached about half the town. The station was his passion; for money, he drove a cab and dealt pot, mostly in small quantities—ounces, halves, quarters—but a lot of volume. He lived in a rusty mobile home at the end of a long Apache Canyon dirt road that wound in and out, up and down, crossing the Pecos River at least three times, each a wet crossing. His trailer sat on the highest point of a wide, open area that Cliff took great pains to keep clear, presumably in case agents from the federal government decided to charge him from the woods.

Politically, he qualified as a demented Libertarian, a group that does tend towards the self-righteously insane though the basic idea makes a lot of sense. Stay out of my face and I'll stay out of yours was Cliff's philosophy. And he was capable of real insight, especially when you got him going about the evil influence of multi-nationals. His rap on the U.S. government was less convincing because he chose to embrace so many iffy sub-cultures: those who believe a space ship crashed near Roswell; weather watchers who believe the government controls the weather; fringe vulcanists who are convinced the government causes specific eruptions; geologists with long-winded, overly technical data showing someone is setting off earthquakes; fluoridians who continue to beat the tired anti-fluoridated water drum; paranoid gun enthusiasts who spend their lives cocking an ear and watching the horizon for the inevitable black helicopter invasion, on and on.

Cliff knew tons about Area 51, and he was hooked into a network of people who'd been used and abused by the federal government in shady and sinister ways; people who'd had nightmare run-ins with the FBI/IRS/DEA/ATF/state police/city police/county social workers/banks/car dealers/large corporations/city and state utilities. Fueled by crystal meth, Cliff could go on for hours. He could be sophisticated in his thinking about, say, the way the war on drugs was the greatest civil rights disaster of the late twentieth century and at the same time, he would pigheadedly take any official denial of the most luridly ridiculous alien abduction story as further proof of the far-reaching and diabolical nature of the cover-up. The cab owners were always having to talk to him about getting too political with the customers. That and his habit of carrying two pistols while he drove, one in his belt and one lying in the open on the seat next to him.

Philips and I had spent a night out there once; the only time we hung out with someone who might be considered a friend of mine. I wasn't sure; I was really more of a co-worker who got a kick out of his revved-up rap; I had no problem with him verbally venting his most explosive frustrations in my presence. When his energy played out, he could be meek and needy, so it was better to hang around when he was speeding, then make an exit before he collapsed into soppy sentimentalism.

The Pecos has no prominent landmarks; a few 10,000-foot rounded mountains but no obvious snowcapped peaks to mark exactly where you are. I know I had made the correct turnoff when I hit that first river crossing; the kind of place where the river is only raging about one month during the spring runoff; now it's no more than a few inches deep. The Pecos has whole areas that have a survivalist feel like Cliff's compound; pockets of mobile homes, ramshackle houses, tents set up in clearings; some have broken-down cars and trucks strewn about, others might collect every conceivable kind of metal junk. There are painters and photographers and sculptors living out here; the sculptors are the most obvious, their yards full of half-done steel pieces and lots of raw material in piles. The Pecos is also wild enough to have bear, mountain lion, plenty of coyote and even bighorn sheep in some of the more secluded, high altitude areas. It's crisscrossed with hundreds of miles of poorly marked trails, causing a couple dozen lost hiker incidents each year.

It's not really a community, since most people are living out here because they want separation from other people, but everyone tends to know the vehicles of everyone else so a strange truck like mine generates blank-eyed interest and a tinge of suspicion. It seems to me there are more houses now than eight years ago, but I'm not sure. It still feels isolated. Fifteen miles off the main highway, I find what I think is Cliff's road, but it's blocked by a chained gate. There's a crudely scratched sign that says to beep the horn three times and wait. I do it then turn the truck off so I can hear anyone approaching.

I figure out the numbers in my head, it comes to roughly 176 ounces. Aaron's pot is excellent, and in this day and age, Cliff would have no trouble getting $100 a quarter; that's $400 an ounce, times 176 is . . . a lot. Over $60,000 is my rough estimate. The number is scary, making me realize the size of the felony I'm carrying around. I'll ask for $15,000 and take $10,000 or any reasonable amount he might have on hand. That is if he still has that kind of money; if he's still in the business.

Ten minutes later, I hear the high whine of a two-cycle engine and one of those four-wheeled motorcycle carts comes up the road; the driver is way too small to be Cliff. They're coming so fast, I think they're going to crash through the gate, then at the last moment, they get sideways, kicking up dirt and rocks.

It's a child, a boy no more than twelve; he has a tan, weathered face and bright blond hair. He's also carrying a pistol in a holster strapped across his chest. He looks at me.

"I'm looking for Cliff," I say.

"I'm looking for Cliff," he says.

"What?"

"What?"

"My name's Henry. Henry Dolan. Cliff and I used to drive cabs together."

"My name's Henry. Henry Dolan. Cliff and I used to drive cabs together."

"You know, that's completely fucking annoying."

"You know, that's completely annoying."

"Got you," I say, because he omitted the curse word.

"Got you."

"I'm a big, fat idiot," I say, resorting to the classic ploy. The kid smiles at me.

"If you say so," he says, then kick starts the cart and tears back up the hill as fast as he came.

I wait a full hour before I hear, then see a horse coming this way. It's Cliff, I can see that right away. As he gets closer, I realize he's changed a lot. He used to be a mess, the raggedy, ripped-up baggy sweat-pants sort, usually with a dirty button-up shirt and a coat with the stuffing sticking out; but now, he is more Zen cowboy with immaculate pony tail and handsomely gray hair; a deep even tan which he obviously works on and a toothbrush Greg Allman beard on the underside of his bottom lip. He looks like a session musician or a rock roadie who's saved his money. He jumps down wearing snakeskin cowboy boots and studies me for a moment.

"I thought you were military at first with that hair," he says finally. "You've gotten fatter."

"Well thank fucking Jesus we're all so honest anymore. Yes, I'm fatter. What of it? Not you. You look great."

"Well yeah. Thanks." Flattered. Very un-Cliff like, being flattered. Then he turns and makes a sweeping move with his arm, like he's waving someone off, except it's sort of perfunctory, more for me than for any actual observer.

"Who you waving to there, Cliff?" I used to give him a hard time about his obsessive distrust, and I'm surprised how easily I slip back into it.

"Oh you know." He tries to mumble his way through it in exactly the way he used to, then he says, "The usual suspects." and I let it go. He waits for an explanation before he'll get near the fence. He's certainly armed, the way he's acting, wary-friendly, like a dog who's been beaten early in life.

So I go honest. As much of my story as I deem appropriate, heavy on the Aaron details to reassure him about the legitimacy of where I got the pot and the one-time-only nature of the deal, heavy on the state of Aaron's health to convince him I'm on the level, much lighter on alternative reasons as to why I'm back because I'm too confused there to offer a coherent explanation that doesn't come off as rationalization. Cliff would read rationalization as me hiding something.

I assure him of the quality. He says, "We'll get to that soon enough." He doesn't want to look at it in the open, afternoons being a particularly active time for spy satellites. He'll check it out inside. All in all, given his paranoia is fully engaged, I'm amazed at how calm and trusting he is with someone he hasn't seen or heard from in eight years. Later, after we've settled in and he's invited me to stay for the night, I kid him about going soft and being so trusting.

"I checked you out," he says.

"Checked me out? How so?"

"Two words, computer and database, as in I have one and there is one."

"A database where you can check people out?" I say, more snidely than I mean; Cliff can bring this out in me, a condescending sarcasm that's distasteful even to me.

"Plus, two more words. Motion and body, as in sensors; I got both all over this fucking mountain. Shit, I knew it was one person in one vehicle right away."

"Probably good I didn't jump the fence and cut through then," I say, kidding.

"Oh no," he says, in a concerned grandfather tone. "That wouldn't have been a good idea. Walking in my woods without knowing where to step? Not good at all."

In place of the rusty mobile home, he's built a two-story adobe house using straw bale walls. He has solar panels and two wood stoves for heat, a generator in case they lose power, one entire room enclosed in lead containing canned food and an impressive weapons collection. He's married with one stepson, the boy on the cart, and a blond, giggly four-year-old daughter who keeps crawling up and sitting on my lap.

He says he's not exactly in the business anymore, but he's "not exactly not" either, whatever that means. He'll only say he "knows someone who knows someone who knows someone" who might be willing to buy all of it and after I tell him I want no more than $15,000 and he can take whatever middle-man cut he deems appropriate, his enthusiasm for the enterprise takes a noticeably upbeat turn. He agrees to store it in a "DEA-proof" steel box of some sort, which is a huge load off my mind, and assures me my presence will not be necessary when the deal actually goes down. We settle the deal with a handshake, and he leads me into the dining room to meet his family.

"Benny," he whispers to me right before he introduces me. "They know I used to be Cliff, but I decided I wanted to be Benny with them. So Benny not Cliff."

His wife Doreen strikes me as a particular kind of new-age white trash; she has a blond, ethereal beauty with a broad, Slavic face and crooked teeth I can see were likely devastatingly sexy when she was twenty but now, the effect is mostly one of crooked teeth. She's familiar-looking in that generic way where half the population seems like someone I might have met once. She burns incense, has an ostentatious collection of wind chimes (which I soon realize drive Cliff/Benny insane, all that soft, wavy noise obscuring the possible sounds of approaching G-men), has tasteful Navajo rugs on the floor and on the walls. The house itself is a model of spare, simple grace with large open spaces and carefully placed tables, chairs, couches, floor lamps. She continues to cook as I suspect she always did. Tonight it is meatloaf with Ruffle's potato chips crumbled on top and baked apples covered in melted Red Hots—hillbilly food. But she's sweet and supportive, and Benny's most paranoid rants, considerably mellowed and toned down from when he was Cliff, bead up and roll off her without any apparent effect. We have a moment of bonding just after I've choked down a chunk of the meatloaf where she rolls her eyes in response to Benny going on about Art Bell, the radio personality, and how he's sold his soul to sinister forces.

Turns out Tommy, the blond boy, is going through a phase of repeating whatever anyone in the family says to him, which they mostly avoid by not talking to him. This actually may be the point, he seems content in silence and annoyed when first Cliff, then Doreen gently mocked him.

"Tommy the Magnificent, please pass the potatoes to your sister," Doreen says.

"Tommy the Magnificent, please pass the potatoes to your sister," the boy says, while passing the dish.

"Tommy the Dimwit, would you pour your sister more sun tea?" Cliff/Benny says.

Long silence, then reluctantly. "Tommy the Dimwit, would you pour your sister more sun tea?" He makes no move to help his sister.

"Mom?" the little girl says, then turns to her brother, giggling. "Tommy the Booger-Eater, could I have some tea please?"

There's an even longer silence this time while the entire table, me included, enjoys the boy's discomfort.

"Come on, boy, play it or don't," Cliff says. "You can't have it both ways. In for a penny and all."

"Come on, boy, play it or don't . . ." Tommy begins.

"Stop."

"Stop."

"You can't pick and choose what you repeat."

"You can't pick and choose what you repeat."

And so it goes through the rest of the dinner. It's a charming scene, beyond sweet in its way, knowing what I do about the man

Cliff used to be. One of his favorite taxicab raps was about the "tyrannical culture of children" and how "mommies and daddies the country over" intimidated the rest of us into kowtowing to the whims of their ugly little rug-rats.

"I'm so sick of the kiddie mafia," he'd say. "It's always the same, people with their kids. They're like, 'I got new pictures. You want to see my latest pictures? You want to touch the little mother-fucker? You want to hold him? You want to be the luckiest man in the world and hold my little baby?' Uh, no, I'll piss on myself and shit my own pants first, thank you very much." It was around this point that Cliff would suddenly remember Cadence and say to me, "Present company excluded, of course," which I thought was pretty funny at the time. It still is, though in a different, darker way.

There's an odd moment when Doreen stares at me an extra beat and it comes close to being hostile and I wonder if there's some contentiousness over Cliff's pot dealing, though a moment later she's seemingly over it and on to the kitchen to fill the dishwasher. Of course we have to try the pot, my vow of absti-nence not even six hours old, but he wouldn't appreciate it if I begged off, it might queer the whole deal. Cliff has a super-relaxed attitude towards his children, both of whom seem to adore him. He has guns all over including pistols in holsters loaded and sitting out; his explanation that the only way to have guns around kids is to show them how to use them and what damage they can do.

"If there's no dark mystery with all the hiding and the locked drawers, they become like any other tool in the house," he says. It makes sense to me. His attitude towards dope smoking is similar, the boy rolls the joint (he likes wearing the surgical rubber gloves) and comments on how sticky it is but shows no interest in smoking it himself ("Turning the forbidden un-, my man, Turning the forbidden un-, my man."), and soon disappears.

The little girl crawls up into the chair with me while we're smoking and squeezes herself into the small space at the exact moment Cliff hands me the joint, which I find unnerving until I see she's used to leaning her head away from any lingering smoke. She's a couple years older than Cadence was when I last saw her, but she's tiny and mute in a similar way, and she's so warm, like a little engine that never quits. I'd forgotten about that.

Later, Doreen appears with a pint of fancy ice cream and five spoons and we pass the container while she and Benny explain why home schooling is the only moral choice for parents in today's world. Tommy reappears for the ice cream.

"It's all about avoiding the well-established and built-in processes of indoctrination," Cliff says, and I can see his intensity heating up. "The ruling elites need a population they can control, and the corporations need workers who'll devote their lives to doing what they're told and consumers who'll follow the instructions as delivered through the corporate-owned mass media."

"I know Benny makes it sound like some huge, organized conspiracy," Doreen says.

"You're just too sweet-natured, sweetie, to see it clearly," he says.

"But it's more complicated than you make it out to be." Apparently, I've stumbled into an old argument. "It doesn't mean it doesn't end up in the same place, but not because the whole world's in cahoots. It's how our system's set up; because there's so many people and everybody is to some extent an individual, they figure the only choice is to teach everyone the same. And because politicians control it, it means the squeaky wheel gets the most attention. Yelling works in politics and deliberation doesn't. Problem is . . . education needs deliberation."

"That's why home schooling," Benny says, conceding the point to her.

Because it is in my nature, I look for qualifiers in Cliff's happy world and settle on Doreen, deciding she is, like he said, sweet-natured, but also a little too willing to stay back and let Cliff be Cliff, though also because it's my nature, I consider the complete opposite might be true, that she is firmly in control, using subtle powers to repress his exuberance. I see now the truth is in-between, that here are two adults meeting in some version of the middle and it's working for them. For the first time, I feel my astonishment over how Cliff's life turned out veering towards jealousy. I'm relieved when he suggests we retreat to his special lead-lined room "to talk business." I'm ready to hear the details of how he plans on selling my pot and being around the whole family is beginning to feel like work.

He keeps a large outside padlock on the door, and past that, there are three separate locks on the door itself. As he goes through the process of opening it, he proudly talks on about the door's make up, plate steel on either side with rebar-reinforced concrete in-between and a thin layer of lead embedded in the middle of the concrete.

The inside is incredible, every inch of wall is covered in layers of news clippings, photographs, posters of UFO gatherings, of conspiracy speakers, authors, scientists; the edges have curled, giving the room, even the ceiling, a fluttery, shaggy bark feel. There are four computer monitors, a half-dozen televisions of all sizes, set up at different angles; police scanners, a short wave radio set; two turntables, a reel-to-reel tape deck, a cassette player, a CD player and about two dozen speaker components—separated into woofers, tweeters, midranges—spreading out in an amazing spaghetti-confetti of multi-colored wires.

One wall is all canned food and bottled water, along another are three side-by-side gun cabinets, which he says are fire-proof. There is a lightbulb-shaped area in the middle that's the only place where you can safely walk, the stem leading from the door to the bulb where all the equipment sits along with a chair, a desk with a tiny oval of clear space, a tattered but comfortable couch. Benny bolts the door behind us and twists the two locks. He swallows a fat black pill that can only be pharmaceutical speed and offers me one.

"Well," I say, not wanting the speed now but thinking it might come in handy at a future date as a motivational tool. "My stomach's a bit dodgy, but I wouldn't mind one for later." As I hoped, he offered two and I found a safe shirt pocket for both of them. Then he drags a six-foot bong I'd originally mistaken for a floor lamp into the open and we once again fire up the merchandise. Though he agrees it's of fine quality, he keeps talking around the details of who it is he has in mind for buying my pot, and I'm having trouble making sense of it. The gist seems to be it might not be quite as simple as he first said, he's not the only person needed to make this work. I stress once again I want no more than $15,000 and will willingly drop it to $12,000 if circumstances demand it. I point out he could get four or five times that selling it piece-meal. I can see I'm getting through. He settles back and pulls out a calculator and enters numbers at a feverish pace. When he's done, he tosses the calculator aside and smiles at me. That's when the speed kicks in, signaling the end of the negotiations and heralding the arrival of the Cliff of old.

For the next two hours, he doesn't say another word about the pot. Instead, he goes on a Cliff-sized rant with hardly an aside to me, I might as well not be in the room. And while his mania sometimes threatens to turn into a hysteria, he lacks the despair and self-loathing that used to make being around the old Cliff so often painful. Now he's more of an entertainer and he's got his schtick down, wheeling out an amazing array of mysteries and arcane paranoias. There always was a lot of the verbal huckster in him, though after the first hour, I've come around to the same place I always reach with Cliff, needing to find some way to get him to shut up, even if only for a moment.

He holds me most of the way through a long-winded, overly technical discussion of remote viewing, something the military is supposedly involved in, a kind of collective mind-meld allowing a group of trained personnel to join together in seeing into the future. Of course, what they see is never good. Cliff/Benny is particularly nervous about a predicted series of solar flares in the next few years, which have the potential to wipe out all life on earth. He says he's seriously considering digging a shelter 30 feet down where he and his family could survive during the two years of deadly flare radiation bombardment, which quite naturally leads to an analysis of the various construction materials available and their relative merits.

I lose him completely on an interminable explanation of the evils of genetically-engineered seeds and the ways they favor corporate farming. I feel ready to nod off.

"I gave a cab ride to a guy who claimed he and his best friend were responsible for all the crop circles east of the Mississippi. He told me how he did it using this U-shaped tool to tap down the crops and a length of rope attached to the ground so he could make a perfect circle. It was all so simple."

He stares at me with a crinkled nose, like he's trying to figure out who I am and what I'm doing here, then launches into a new rant, as if he's been discussing this all along.

"What *I'm* talking about here is a whole switch in the national fucking zeitgeist, you dig? It's not that one hand doesn't know what the other hand is doing, you see? That's the beauty and the absolute fucking evil of it; it doesn't matter if one branch knows what another branch is doing. It's that there's a general all-pervasive feeling that we are children, that we need to be saved from our own worst instincts. Gun laws, seat belt laws, helmet laws, the fucking war on drugs and on terrorism, all variations of the same thing.

"You know, I believe those in charge think they're doing right by us, believe that we are children who need to be saved from ourselves. I even know the place and year it all began. Roswell, July 9, 1947, the day our government decided to cover up the single most important event in the history of the world, contact with beings from another planet. How dare they? How fucking dare they?

"I read all this shit day in and day out, lie after lie told by talking heads who no longer even know they're lying. Waco, Ruby Ridge, Oklahoma City, the WTC, believe what you want, let them say what they want, blame who they want. We know. That's why everyone likes to get on their snide fucking high horse about people like me, people who know the truth. Mock us, little ones, go ahead and mock, because history—whore that she is—comes around to the truth in time. May be ten years, a hundred, one thousand, see, but what these fucking insects don't understand is that living with the truth is a calling; it's not a way of life, it's a way of thinking and I can no more change how I think than I can my, my, my . . ."

"Name?" I suggest.

He stares hard right at me and for a horrible moment, I think I've blown it, that he'll get self-righteous and throw me and my eleven-pounds of pot out into the night. Then he very slowly looks up, as if he's watching an imaginary rocket take off, leaning his head until he's looking straight up at the ceiling, like a fully open Pez dispenser. I look where he's looking, there are dozens of newspaper clippings stapled there and I spend a full two minutes, squinting, trying to read what article he's reading before realizing he's out, mouth open, corpse-like; an appalling thought I dismiss with a quick ear to his chest. I give him a shake and am relieved when he makes a halfhearted attempt to rouse himself before re-collapsing. As sudden as it is, I have to admit the silence is blissful.

Getting out of Cliff/Benny's hovel of a room takes a dismal half hour of hands-and-knees type searching for the two keys fitting the two separate locks locking the door from the inside. Discreetly searching through his pockets, my thoughts are this: stoned a few hours after dramatically swearing off dope, stuck in a room fifteen miles by air, thirty-five by road from Santa Fe and I can't get out of one door, one room, one house; it is like being mired in quicksand, like treading water, diverted from my goal before I reach town. Worse than that, I realize I'm at this moment probably only four or five miles as the crow flies from Philips' parents, Bonnie and Jim, and the house where the child, Cadence, still lives.

But thirty seconds out into the cool, dry late-night air and my thoughts swivel 180 degrees; fate is not too strong a word for how effortlessly it has worked up to this point, better than I could have imagined. Free of a prison-threatening felony and hopefully up $15,000 besides, tomorrow I'll drive on into town and leave Cliff to it; all at the cost of a single day's delay and a little backpedaling on my abstinence vow. This registers as the kind of minor triumph I'd forgotten exists.

Philips

There is some mystery as to how someone like Philips could have come out of two people like Bonnie and Jim. Bonnie is a large blond woman, nearly six feet tall, from Minnesota, the daughter of a Protestant minister of Swedish stock. She'd aged well over the years until by the time I met her, she had a kind of handsomeness because of her size and because her extra weight not only smoothed out any lines in her face, it enhanced the shape. But as a young woman—I'd seen pictures and home movies—she was relentlessly plain and stolid looking, the kind of woman who attracted attention because of her height but then repelled this attention because of her looks which were vaguely square and doughy. She was neither thin nor fat, pretty or ugly.

So when she started dating Jim, a man she met at a bus stop in St. Paul—their first date had been for pizza across the street from the stop where they'd met—her family was pleased though their enthusiasm waned when they found out he had Indian blood in him. "Just enough to give his hair 'a little shadow'", she told them.

When they finally met him, they were crestfallen, then angry. "A little shadow" was an understatement, he was dark and looked Indian even though he claimed to be only one quarter Ho-Chunk out of Wisconsin. And he was good looking, better than Bonnie could have ever hoped for, they thought.

But his size! He said he was five-foot seven, but to call him five-foot three would be generous, he was a full eight inches shorter than her. And she came from a tall family; her father was six-foot six and all three of her brothers topped six-foot four. They had a cousin who was six-foot eight and at family gatherings, it was impossible to hide; little Jimmy—he started asking his in-laws to call him Jim after they got married because Jimmy sounded too childlike—a bush in a forest of trees. After he gained confidence, he insisted they see her family only on Christmas, Thanksgiving, Fourth of July, the major holidays. And after Philips was born, he took three trips in two months to Chicago without saying why and one day he came back with a job and there was nothing Bonnie could do but go with him to Chicago.

Philips had grown up in Munster, Indiana, no more than 40 miles from where I was raised; which over time became a symbol of how far she had failed to travel in her life, married to another loser from The Region; that scoop of Northern Indiana along the tip of Lake Michigan, an urban area held in disdain by the rest of the state. And until Santa Fe, Munster was the only place I'd ever seen her parents and even an hour spent in their Munster house made it easy to understand why Philips was so antagonistic about her childhood.

There was a stillness to the place, a pall. Their house had the hollow feeling of a diseased body; it invoked a vague sense of dread. At some point in their marriage, a doctor had prescribed lithium for Bonnie; followed by a series of anti-depressants. She may have been a "strapping six-footer" when she was young, but when I first met her, she was a gawky, uncertain woman who walked like she didn't trust her footing for even a single step. Sometimes I could have a conversation with her; at other times, she'd sit at the kitchen table with her hands folded in her lap, staring at some indeterminate point on the table in front of her.

"She'll sit forever like that." Philips would say as we'd flee to my car, so happy to be out of that house, if only for a few hours. This was before we were married—when we were still in love. When we'd return three hours later after a movie or taking a motel room so we could fuck and watch TV in peace, she'd still be there at the table and Jim would be in his chair in the living room in front of the television with the sound down. Footsteps on the tile kitchen floor were like rifle shots. I thought I grew up in a still house, but compared to theirs, mine was a cacophony of people yelling back and forth, my mother banging dishes, my father with the TV up full blast and sometimes, when he couldn't stand the television announcers of a sporting event, the radio too. So I was shocked by how every edge of life had been repressed in Philips' house.

"Two more people who should never have been married," she'd whisper to me when she'd slip into my room after they'd gone to sleep. We had to be quiet, holding each other tight, kissing but we didn't dare make love, not in that house. "It's creepy here," I'd say.

"Now you know," she'd say and sometimes she'd cry, and we'd hold on so tight, I could feel her heart beating against mine. She liked to sleep with candles burning, it gave the room a warmth and we'd make sure we woke up in time for her to sneak back into her bed. It's not like Bonnie and Jim would start in on her in front of me if they caught us. They'd wait until I was outside or at the store, then Bonnie would tell Philips her father needed to talk to her and Jim would explode, pacing back and forth, yelling, ranting, acting like he might hit her; every bit of emotion he'd repressed for weeks, months spewing out. I never saw this, but it happened a couple of times when we were visiting, always when I was out, and every time it did, Philips appeared ashen-faced with jelly legs, she'd melt into my chest and I'd hold her and kiss her forehead, smooth back her hair, reassure her.

If I called her Philips at the dinner table, Bonnie smiled blankly and Jim ignored it, taking the first chance possible to call her Jane. They never understood why she hated her given name so much. Maybe I didn't either, but I'd never known her as Jane.

One time, we snuck into their room and stole two of her lithium tablets and ate one each, then went to a movie. At first, it was wonderful; like a heavy curtain settling down all around you, traffic, people, loud noises all sounded the same; the impulse to brake at a red light was no different than the one to accelerate on through. But the movie was impossible to watch; it was as if all the rhythms and changes built into the film became invisible and we ended up leaving and running back to the house and rolling up a joint to cut into the thick fog. When we woke up the next day, we had to leave. It was too hard to think of any life being lived the way her mother's was.

One night in her house, I woke, feeling a strange, disturbing sensation in the air around me, like I was underground and the tiny lights I could see—the alarm clock, the thin strip under the door from the light in the hallway, and the orange patterns on the ceiling coming from the street—were really cracks to daylight far above. When I coughed awake, I spit up dirt. I sneaked down the hall and slipped into her bed.

"Oh baby," she said, kissing me all over and this was what I wanted.

"I never told you about the woman who lived here before my parents?"

No, no, no, I wanted to scream, no eerie stories. Just the smell of your skin and the feel of your body naked against mine. That was what I wanted, love and sweet silence. But she kept going.

"She killed herself in the garage."

"Your garage?" The house was a split-level with the garage directly underneath the spare room where I slept.

"The very one."

"Please." I meant it.

"She sealed off all the cracks and turned on her car and waited. She was unhappy."

"Please, please, baby."

"I grew up with this," she said fiercely, through clenched teeth. "You can live with it for one night."

"God."

"Turns out she tried a few times in the house itself. She tried to hang herself but herniated a disc in her neck instead. I did a report on it in high school. I researched back issues of the local paper and called a couple people she knew."

"You were a cheery little flower, weren't you?"

"My teacher thought it was weird."

"You think?"

"I used to be sure I could hear her breathing; it was like the whole house was her body and I was inside."

I squeezed her so tight, it took her breath away.

"It actually was the furnace going on and off and the way the house would settle. But still . . ."

That was life in the Leans household in Indiana. How Bonnie and Jim ever got the idea or the energy to move to New Mexico remains a mystery, but they were different people there, though it was tough to convince Philips of that. The Santa Fe house never felt like their other one. It was airy and full of light. During the day, they opened all their windows and let the dry high desert air flow through. At night, they burned fires in their fireplace, filling the house with the smell of piñon pine.

In New Mexico, Philips continued to insist there wasn't a single moment of love that had ever existed between her parents, and I took this as a compliment of sorts; there'd been plenty between us. But I also knew their marriage wasn't unusual, people get together for all kinds of reasons and for people like Bonnie and Jim, without a lot of choices, the reasons are usually as simple as one person asks the other to marry them.

"She probably couldn't think of a good reason to say no," I'd say to Philips in a quiet voice in our bed in their house in Santa Fe. It always seemed all the important things we had to say there we said in whispers.

"And that's a reason to get married and have a child?"

"They were different times. People didn't think so much."

"You're always defending them."

"That's not true. I wasn't raised with them, so I'm not pissed-off."

And then she'd laugh. "Different times, my ass."

I knew what she was saying, but I had no answers.

"Did you know your parents have sex every other day between four and five?" I said to Philips.

"They always did, as far back as I can remember. Next evidence," she said.

"Still . . ." I didn't believe her. She'd never mentioned her parents ever having sex, much less three times a week. It was pretty damned amazing to me, two people who'd been married as long as they had.

And Bonnie in Santa Fe was still on lithium but at a lower dose; she had a part-time job in town and a few casual friends. They both loved the child and treated her as if she was a second chance. Philips resented her "new" parents as much as her old ones and when I'd point out what an amazing change it was this late in their lives, her scorn for me was just as vitriolic.

"I don't understand it," Bonnie said to me one time, meaning Philips' attitude. This was as analytical a conversation as she was capable of.

"Like I do," I said, and she actually put her hand on my arm, an unusual (for her) gesture which I appreciated at the time.

Santa Fe

For someone born in a flat land, one of the great joys of driving a cab in Santa Fe was seeing nature play out against the mountain landscape; it never failed to move me. The way the light, gone nearly horizontal at the end of the day, bathed everything in a warm orange, stretching and outlining the rippled pools of shadow up and down the mountain. Earth and buildings alike soaked up the light, deepening the rich brown, as if the true color of adobe only existed in these few moments before sundown. Nature was one continuous drama, always a welcome relief to the more human, painful drama going on in my life at the time.

Santa Fe sits at the end of the southernmost spur of the Rocky Mountains; the peaks over Santa Fe aren't jagged; from anywhere in town, the impression is one of width, strength; of support; exactly what you might expect from the bottom end of a long mountain chain, as if these mountains had to bear the weight of the entire column above it, all the way into Canada.

There were times when it seemed the mountain carried the burden of the seasons; there were whole months down in the city where nothing much changed; one sunny day evolving into another. In fall, the aspens change color, forming a golden band across the face of the mountain. Snow comes as early as October up high while the town itself might go through an entire winter with only an occasional dusting. During the summer monsoon season, every day like clockwork, clouds build over the mountains. By early afternoon, they gather into a mushroom shape and expand; by 4 o'clock p.m., the main cloud will have spread over half the valley, threatening to join similar clouds building out of the Jemez to the west and the Sandias to the south. By 6 o'clock, narrow, column-shaped downpours of intense rain dot the valley and the sides of the mountain. I once saw the setting sun ignite a curtain of water into a lush, velvety red, the intense purity of it was something I could have spent a lifetime chasing. Cars were pulling over to watch in a town that sees a stunning sunset nearly every night. It lasted less than a minute, but for the time, it felt like a new kingdom was being announced.

The town itself starts in the hills and spreads out south and west into a shallow valley. When I lived here eight years ago, it was mostly a haves and have-nots town; the haves being principally white, extremely well off, and living in the hills north and east of the city. The have-nots occupied the areas away from the hills; the further you got from downtown, the flatter and cheaper real estate became. Down Agua Fria or out on Airport Road, there were dozens of huge mobile home parks with hundreds of trailers each; there were budget subdivisions with small, trailer-size houses and scrub yards. Many of the people living out there did so because it was what they can afford; a lot of them drove downtown to work in the upscale shops and restaurants. Even eight years ago, it was a miserable stop-and-go morning commute all the way in; the numbers of people living on the outskirts easily overwhelmed the capacity of the roads.

There was a lot of anger too, and I can't imagine a scenario where that's changed. The Hispanics don't trust the gringos and have scant respect for the Indians. The Indians distrust everyone for obvious reasons. Spanish-descent Hispanics often rebel angrily at being labeled Mexicans, usually ignoring the truth that the groups have been intermarrying for centuries now. The rich (mostly) white money allows many of the hill gringos to live completely oblivious to such anger, staying close to home, shopping downtown or venturing out to the health food supermarkets that rim the edges of the downtown, never bothering to drive down Agua Fria or Airport Road (unless they're going to the airport); living in their Manhattan to everyone else's outer boroughs.

There's almost no black presence in the city and the few here tend to be artists or art dealers; I knew a black cab driver who claimed he could name every African-American in the entire town.

City government is mostly Hispanic and tends towards Democratic; the town itself is politically left of the state which in turn is politically left of all the states surrounding it. People believe in government taking care of people. Land of Mañana is the semi-derisive term newcomers have for New Mexico, the idea being that shop-owners, mechanics, service personnel, etc. all have a "relaxed" attitude towards finishing a job on time. After I was here awhile, I quit thinking of it as a negative and more as a way to live life. Relax, chill, it will happen when it happens. Not a bad life philosophy.

My first sight of the mountain as I approach downtown via Old Pecos Trail has a calming effect, I'd forgotten the scale of it and the way it can change how you feel about your life.

Earlier at Cliff's, I'd had what could only be described as a panic attack. I'd woken before anyone and stumbled out to the redwood porch. The sun was hitting a small corner and I dragged a chair over to it and sat down, hugging my arms for warmth. There was still a chill and outside my little patch of sunlight, I could see my breath. The triumph of the night before—I'm $15,000 richer or will be—gave way to the realization I have to figure out what is next. I guess I knew I couldn't just keep driving west, that there was a reason circumstances brought me here, and when the two kids appeared and started tearing around the porch and the yard, it didn't help.

I thought I'd seen the back end of fear in those last months with Philips, but this punched through and beyond so fast and fierce, it sucked all the air out of my lungs. I was back in a place I'd never completely forgotten, no matter how much I pretended I had, and the force of that—all that has happened, all that will—sat so heavily on my chest, I couldn't draw a breath. My head felt like an expanding balloon on its way to a cartoon popping and my beating heart was heading off the rails.

Then I felt a hand on my forehead and one on my shoulder and someone helped me lean forward over the rail and I expelled what little I had left in my stomach and when I was done, I took in a full breath the way a drowning man finally breaking the surface might. It was Doreen. She pulled her chair next to mine and took my hand, I could feel her calm heart beating through her fingers, and slowly, slowly my own pounding heart matched hers. We just sat like that for a long time and by the time I felt better, the porch was fully in the sun. She then made breakfast for the four of us—Cliff never did come out before I left—and I even managed to eat. Whatever I'd gone through was still there, it was exactly like having an excruciatingly sharp pain out of the blue and even after it goes away, it leaves a residue that's not easily forgotten. I stumbled trying to find the words to thank her, she put her finger to her lips, telling me to hush, then she smiled. She has a beautiful smile, even with (or because of?) her crooked teeth and I wondered again how someone like her ever managed to hook up with Cliff. On the way to town, I decided she must be used to dealing with such terror moments, Cliff was a genuine and complete emotional mess when I knew him and if I'll buy that people can become saner as they get older, I also know insanity has a way of lingering. No doubt the two of them have spent some dark nights together.

I drive to the library. I have a few reasons, the most pressing is I have to use the bathroom. Driving a cab teaches you about a city's public bathrooms and I know them all; those you can use without being hassled, those that are large, clean, smell OK and have a lock on the door (a must for snorting drugs or enjoying a calming dump).

When I'm done, I walk into the main room of the library and look around and it's like I never left. I could be in the middle of a cab shift, stopping by for the bathroom. The interior looks the same, the views front and back haven't changed. I even think the woman behind the reference desk was working here eight years ago. Eight years? It's incredible. It would be so easy for me to believe that my wife is across the Plaza at the Hotel St. Francis getting ready for the dinner rush, that the child is fifteen miles east of here taking her first tentative steps. How can it be eight years? Almost a quarter of my life.

I've always been good at pushing thorny issues to the side, telling myself that since I'll have to deal with them eventually, there's no point in even thinking about them now. It's allowed me to drift along for years at a time. Though I've hardly forgotten the earlier attack, I already think of it as an aberration, inevitable given I've returned to this town.

I stand up and head to the city phone book section and look up Bonnie and Jim, just to make sure they're at the same address. They are, same phone number too, which only increases the sensation that the last eight years have been a kind of fever dream coma that I'm only now emerging from.

With no better ideas, I stroll to the Plaza, and it looks the same. Some of the shops are different and Woolworth's is gone, but the Indian jewelry merchants are still set up under the Inn of the Governor's awning and a seemingly interchangeable group of ragged youths are gathered near the center sharing a single cigarette, one of them playing an acoustic guitar.

Then I see Jim, right there in broadest daylight, driving by in the same car he had eight years before, in the same way, both hands tightly gripping the wheel, his head barely clearing the top, looking intensely ahead. Because he is so short, Jim never felt comfortable behind the wheel, the cars were all too big, the decisions too fast, it was a constant source of anxiety for him and anyone riding with him. He was heading towards Fort Marcy, a city-run sports complex where Jim went every day to work out, his one place of social interaction in Santa Fe ("But one place is one more than any of us would have expected," I argued to Philips, who admitted it got him out of the house). He's alone today. Bonnie used to go with; she took a low-impact aerobics class and had her own separate group of female friends.

I can't believe it. Jim right there driving past me big as fucking day, what am I to make of that? It's too much, like the cosmos has decided I'm a dullard who needs constant provocation.

I walk quickly back to my truck.

He's disappearing inside when I pull up to Fort Marcy. As with driving, Jim's self-consciousness about his height was all over how he walked; vigorously with his head down, never focusing eye contact on anyone, always projecting a sense of concentrated purpose as a way of shutting everyone else out. I pull next to his car. I'm nervous. I don't want to see him, not now. I believe Bonnie is who I should approach first about the child, if I approach either

of them. In my last days living at their house, Bonnie and I sometimes bonded as captives to the whims of her daughter, my wife.
She never showed the kind of anger towards me that Jim did—he
came to suspect I was the reason his daughter decided to disappear—though in the spirit of full disclosure, Medicated Bonnie (the
only Bonnie I've known) was incapable of any large emotions, and
more than once I mistook chemical befuddlement for unspoken
connection. Oddly, my initial reaction had been to wave at Jim. I'd
felt a huge relief seeing a friendly face until I remembered it
wasn't.

I consider staking out Jim for an hour or so, but I can't see the
point. I know where he's going. It occurs to me I may be hoping to
get caught as a way to avoid having to actually drive out to Eldorado and walk up cold to their door. This will not do; it is not the way
I want this to go. I'm beginning to believe that since I've half-assed
my way through whole years of my life, I need to do this exactly
right, without cutting corners. Or not do it at all. Those should be
my two options.

I drive out Cerrillos Road and take a second-floor room at the
Motel 6. Doreen offered their spare room for a couple of days, but
that's a long drive and besides, the bland anonymity of a motel
room can have a soothing effect on the nerves. When Cliff/Benny
does the deal, I'll move. Not too upscale, just a bit nicer. Maybe the
Residence Inn or the Santa Fe Motel.

After a shower and a change of clothes, I head back out. I have
a notion to sit down at a coffee shop somewhere and read the
paper so I can plan my next move. Downtown Subscription was my
favorite, though I could never get Philips to go there. She said it
was too full of "Upper East Side types," which I had to admit was
true (though she didn't respond well to my counter that her

favorite place The Aztec was populated mostly by the kids of "Upper East Side types"), but it still had a wonderful, spacious garden where you could usually find an out of the way corner, a perfect spot to read and nurse a cup of coffee for an hour. In keeping with a theme, Downtown Subscription appears unchanged. There's just enough chill in the air to drive all but the smokers inside, leaving most of the patio open. I drag a table and chair between two overgrown chamisa bushes.

I have the New York Times, southwestern edition, and I plan on wasting an hour over-concentrating on the paper, reading every story, every section. I'll just disappear into the world for a while, which (hopefully) has the added benefit of giving me some perspective on my own problems. By my third refill, I'm into the Arts and Leisure section, the sun has reached all corners of the garden, and people are trickling out onto the patio. At the table closest to me is an aging hipster, complete with thinning hair pulled back into a tight ponytail. It's easy to imagine him as a once-dynamic professor who'd had it going on a few years back, an energy, a group of adoring students maybe, a circle who believed he had answers, but the last few years haven't been kind to him. He's deflated. His skin hangs looser than it should for someone who must be approaching fifty, like all the connective tissue holding him together is slowly dissolving. I decide he's terrified of what's happening to him (He must be!), but he hides it well, settling into a loose-limbs akimbo pose, one long, thin leg draped over the other, a hand-rolled cigarette propped, picking bits of tobacco out of his mouth.

Past him, there's a boy with long hair wearing a Butthole Surfers t-shirt sitting with a girl with a shaved head and a t-shirt mini with a bright logo on the front of it. When she stands for a refill,

I'm able to read that it says, "Don't Suck Corporate Cock," which feels like a bold statement in this place. Not that all the dog-walking gay men or the baby-carriage pushing mothers would be against the sentiment, they just wouldn't approve of the brashness and I guess I don't either, though you'll never find me admitting that.

I watch two toddlers come together, brought by their respective parents, obviously strangers before this moment. They're walking their kids in the patio area exactly the way you'd let a dog into the back yard. This is the kind of observation I'd like to make out loud, but I am of course alone. The little girl is the boldest of the two, taking off after crabapples, kicking the wooden fence, nibbling on a green leaf, chasing the birds with her arms out in front of her, digging in the dirt. The boy follows her around, picking up what she's picked up and putting in his mouth. The "Corporate Cock" girl acts annoyed when one of them gets too close to her and I dislike her for it. Both kids are a little unsteady, like they're carrying an invisible weight on their heads and it's difficult to tell what is genuine interaction and what is random lurching. The boy's presence seems to agitate the little girl, but that isn't for certain. Their motivations seem clouded, like I'm watching two squirrels scurry around each other. I have an upsetting thought about absence and years missed and go for my fourth refill as an avoidance. When I come back, a middle-aged couple is clearing my paper to sit down and I have to stop them, though I let them take the table and one chair, leaving me sitting out in the open with no protection.

Now there are more kids running around the patio, the place has become quite busy and when I look up, a young girl is standing staring at me. For one awful moment, I think it's my own child somehow—she looks so familiar—and my mind spins out an absurd tale of an obsessed little girl checking all the coffee shops every day, month after month, year after year, waiting for that day when I reappear. Slowly common sense reasserts itself and I realize that not only is this child too young, my own wouldn't look familiar to me. It's Cliff and Doreen's little girl. I don't remember her name, I'm not sure I ever bothered to ask, which seems a monumental failing at this moment. Pretty soon Tommy shows too.

"I know you," he says.

"I know you," I say back.

"You're Benny's cab driving buddy, he told us about those days."

"You're Benny's cab driving buddy, he told us about those days."

This gets his attention.

"That's stupid, you're stupid," he says.

"That's stupid, you're stupid."

"This won't work, it never works." I can hear irritation creeping into his voice.

"This won't work, it never works."

"I'm a big fat idiot."

I have him and he knows it. "If you say so."

Tommy makes an exaggerated "mean" face. "That's so funny, I forgot to laugh."

"Is your mom here?"

"No I drove us."

"Right."

"I can drive," he says and he's serious.

"I saw. That little toy cart."

"It's not a toy!" I've made him mad, which of course is the point. "It's not! It can do sixty. Cowboys use them to herd cows. You're stupid to call it that."

"You're stupid to call it that."

He opens his mouth but doesn't speak.

"Is your mother inside?"

"I told you."

"You drove in yourself, because let's see, you and your sister needed a cup of coffee? Is that it?" I stand up and see Doreen through the glass doors. For some reason, I sit down quickly. I'm not sure I want to talk to her. She saw me in such a state this morning, I feel a bit like a teenaged boy who blurted out something inappropriate and too intimate to a girl he just met, embarrassing the both of us. I return to my paper.

When I look up and Doreen's standing there, I feel the smallest wobble in my legs. It's not just that she looks completely different from last night (this morning, I was too embarrassed to meet her eyes), though she does. She's dressed in black jeans and a pullover sleeveless flowered dress, worn like a long shirt, and her face has a baby-fat puffiness with delicate spiderweb lines fanning outward around her mouth. It's more that for years now, I've genuinely believed myself incapable of being spontaneously attracted to someone (more or less) my own age. I met Philips when I was twenty-two, she was nineteen, and in all the years since, I've never been drawn to anyone much over the age of twenty-five. I've always assumed it was a hardwired kind of imprinting, a slightly more complex version of the baby duckling fresh out of the egg that bonds forever with a coat rack. As I've gotten older and fatter and look more and more my own age, it's only added to an overall despair, a sense that human connection is comfortably in my increasingly distant past.

"Well look at you," she says in a tone a parent uses on a child, or so it seems.

"You too. You look different in the light."

"Different good?"

"Yeah, I think so, though I'm not sure I want to admit that you looked different bad when I first met you yesterday."

"First met," she says with a laugh that seems cryptic. What am I missing?

"Do you want to sit?" She shrugs her shoulders and I realize she does, but there are no chairs and no table.

"Why not walk me to my car?"

"Sounds good."

"Tommy, get your sister, we're going."

"Tommy," Tommy says. "Get . . ."

"Don't start with me kid," she says, and means it.

We lean against her truck, an oversized SUV of some kind.

"I'm sorry about this morning. I don't know what the hell..."

"No need. Benny told me what he knows, about...you know, and it's understandable."

"What'd he tell you?"

"Just that you had a daughter . . ."

"Have."

"That's what I meant, and that she lives here, and you don't."

"That's pretty much all of it. I'm glad you know."

Tommy approaches pulling the little girl along, Doreen opens up the door for him and the two of them pile into the back. "Why be glad I know?"

"I just . . . I don't know. You seem like someone I'd like to know."

"Careful there, son," she says, though I'm not sure if it's to me or to Tommy.

"You and Cliff . . ."

"Benny."

"Right, Benny."

"You going to ask me about my marriage? Is that what you're about to do?"

"I guess I was. Cliff . . ."

"Benny . . ." she says with infinite patience.

"Well Cliff, when I knew him, that's what I was saying. He wasn't someone I'd imagine with a wife and kids, and especially not—"

"Especially not?" she says. "Someone like me?"

"Even if I was going to say that—I didn't, so you can't hold it against me."

"Benny is at his core a decent man."

"I think that's true."

"It is true." A touch of irritation.

"But . . . ?"

"I don't think I know you well enough to complete that thought."

"He can be a lot of work," I suggest. "Maybe that appealed to you once, but . . ."

She holds my eyes in what seems to be a challenge. I may have gone too far, but the least I can do is hold her stare. She breaks first with a strange, off-kilter smile, showing her crooked teeth. "Like I said, be careful."

"OK."

"Men are work."

"I guess I proved that this morning."

"Hurray. He's capable of learning," she says, back to what might be considered a flirty tone. "Simple concepts anyway."

"We should have coffee."

"I got coffee."

"I mean some other time. A plan, a set time, like between friends."

"Are we friends?" she says, but I can tell she's enjoying this. And why not? Banter with an adult male not her own husband. It doesn't mean anything.

"I said 'like'."

"I usually try to keep my husband's drug dealing buddies off my social calendar."

"See, that hurts."

"I said 'usually'."

"You and me, coffee soon?"

"Only if you promise to use verbs next time," she says, climbing into her truck and shutting the door.

"Henry good coffee tomorrow," I yell after her car, then she's gone. That went well.

Sammy

By the time Sonny and Sammy went back to school, the pall was lifting on the household and Franny seemed to regain enough energy to keep up with the dirty clothes and dishes. Arthur took a couple of half-days off and came home at lunch and the two of them spent the afternoon in bed together like they used to do before they were married. With the twins gone seven hours a day, Franny could manage, and she didn't mind when they came home and started tearing around the house and yard.

The morning of the accident, the twins woke and decided they wanted to go sledding and the fact that it was a Sunday in the middle of September and 80 degrees out didn't matter, they grabbed their plastic saucer and headed to the bluff encircling the lake, making for the old staircase. Made of wood, condemned before either of them were born, and sitting over the steepest part of the bluff, the old staircase looked dangerous with off-kilter angles, wood splitting and splintering from age and rain, the middle buckling out a good twenty feet from the slope of the bluff. They ignored the replacement stairs dug into the bluff itself, a much more reasonable construction of dirt, rock, cement and railroad ties.

"This is really steep," Sammy said, giggling.

"Sammy and Sonny sitting in a tree," Sonny said. Sammy sat in front, Sonny wrapped his legs and arms around his brother; the saucer teetered back and forth on the edge.

Sonny squeezed the ridge of his brother's baby fat and shook.

"I wanna, wanna, wanna," Sammy said.

"I'm flying farther than you."

"Bet?"

"Bet."

"The Dude says Kiddo…" and they both broke out laughing. "The Dude says" always did that for them.

"The Dude says Sammy is a retard."

"The Dude says, we're going to fly today."

"The Dude says Sonny flies the farthest."

"The Dude says no pain no gain."

"Let's fly."

But they didn't, not right away. It was scary steep and Sonny was the one who'd have to make the final push-off.

"You ready, fat boy?" he said, his voice shaky. Sammy raised a determined thumbs up, the final okay, and he had no choice. He pressed palms on the ground, lifting them up and out and they were off, squeezing his legs tight around his brother and giving up to it; bang, bang, bang on each step and the gathering force put a chill in him. This is a mistake, he thought, it's too hard too high too steep, and he tried to grab one of the passing vertical supports, then they started spinning just like they would on snow and he could hear his brother whooping and hollering and then he was too, yelling to the sky and laughing with his brother, and it didn't matter at all that Sammy bloodied his nose on a rail or that Sonny banged his head so hard he saw stars, none of it did, just the speed and the air rushing and their path headed for open space at exactly the steepest part of the bluff; then they hit a support beam and maybe if the stairs hadn't been so old, it wouldn't have disintegrated on contact, but they were and it did, ripping Sonny free of his brother and launching him into space, spinning feet over head and with each turn, he saw his brother hanging above the stairs, flipping like he was flipping. On one pass, the red saucer floated free above him and Sammy the fat boy was yelling and laughing, and even though he was more scared than he'd ever been, Sonny couldn't help but laugh because he was flying, they were flying, and it was wonderful.

Then Sonny hit and rolled, impacting a tree which spun him, raised his body and sent his feet over his head and back over his feet. He couldn't see anymore but he could hear Sammy banging around like one of those cartoons where the villain falling down a high cliff hits every bush, tree and rock before finally, mercifully stopping.

Sammy was the first up, popping to his feet like a jack in the box. He paused to feel his cheeks and shake out his arms and legs, ignoring the heavy throbbing pain in his arm and his double vision. When Sonny came to, all he saw was his brother's face covered in smeared blood—Sammy's idea of a joke—with bits of dirt and grass stuck between his teeth. They found the saucer and climbed back up the bluff, Sonny helping his brother because clearly something was wrong with Sammy's arm. When they got home, the twins dribbled every ounce of blood they could squeeze out over Sammy and lay him out in the front yard, arms and legs hanging lifelessly-like over the edges of the saucer, the grass and dirt still outlining his front teeth, giving him a ghoulish appearance. Then Sonny rang the doorbell.

"Green Teeth!" he screamed when his mother opened the door, doubling over with laughter, causing his "dead" brother to shake from the giggles. Franny didn't think it was one bit funny. And after they went to the hospital because Sammy's arm was broken, The Dude showed, and he didn't laugh either. But for the rest of the night and all morning the next day, the twins broke into giggles at the mere thought of it.

The next morning, which was a school day, they had an idea. They'd switched places many times before, especially during test time, but they'd pretty much stopped because no one ever noticed and because Sonny's class was just as boring and pointless as Sammy's. On Mondays, Sammy had gym and he hated gym, especially with a broken arm, and Sonny loved it. They never gave a thought to what might happen on Tuesday when they'd switch back, never considered that surely the teacher would notice that Sonny Dolan had a broken arm yesterday and today he didn't. So when Sammy collapsed right in class that Monday, Mrs. Sanders had no reason to believe this wasn't Sonny. The attendants took 'Sonny' to the emergency room of the much larger, city hospital on the school side of town, this meant no one would know the twins. When The Dude showed and they peeled back the sheet to his child's neck, he took their word that this was Sonny and when his wife arrived, it was he who had the dreadful duty of telling her. It would be one more in a lifetime of things between them, The Dude not being able to tell his children apart even after death; Franny blaming him for something he was in no right mind to analyze.

Franny knew right away, leaning down to kiss her child's cheek, she'd smelled Sammy before she ever pulled back the sheet and saw the broken arm. Without a word to her husband, she sat next to her dead son and waited for people to bring his living twin to her, so he could see his brother and make whatever peace was possible in a time like this. When Sonny finally came, looking bewildered and frightened, still wearing Sammy's clothing, she couldn't bear it, couldn't allow him to look down upon a dead face in his own image. Instead, she asked him to find his father and tell him he was Sonny.

Sonny followed a thick yellow line on the floor in the hospital corridor leading to a waiting area. He marched up to The Dude, who stared ashen-faced out the window, and tapped his leg saying, "I'm Sonny, Dad." The Dude couldn't look at him, he couldn't. He put a stiff arm out on his son's shoulder, squeezing ridges of baby fat between his fingers but holding him away, unwilling or unable to pull him close, trapped together in a pose that would come to define their relationship for the rest of The Dude's life.

Cadence

Number each question, starting with number one. Don't worry about the order or about which question is most important. If you think of it, it's important. Keep the questions neat. Put an empty line between each. Don't worry about whether you'll ever actually ask any of these questions. Writing them down is what's important.

I wasn't sure how to start. Mrs. Garcia told us we could choose anyone in the history of the world to ask. It couldn't be anyone famous, like rock stars and actors. I wasn't sure whether I wanted to do what the other kids were doing, asking Abraham Lincoln or Geronimo or Billy the Kid. Mrs. Garcia would only say she thought I must have a lot of questions for real, living people. I knew she was talking about my mother and my father even though she didn't say that.

Ask what you want to know.

Mrs. Garcia said she'd start with a couple of questions. To get me started:

1. *My name's Cadence. No one has a name like mine. Why'd you name me Cadence? What other names did you consider?*
2. *Tell me about the day I was born. About the weather. About being in the hospital. Did any historical event happen on that date?*

I told Bonnie about it, I was having trouble getting going and thought she might help, but she told Jim and both of them were quiet around me for three whole days before they started talking to me normally again. But they never said don't do it, they never said anything. Then the questions came and once they did, I couldn't stop.

It is strange sometimes, the way I think. Like the other day, I was walking home from school, cutting through the green belt and I surprised a full-grown coyote. I wasn't scared—well maybe at first—but he acted like I wasn't even there, until I took a step towards him, then he took off like he was the scared one.

He was big and healthy-looking, almost fat, and I swear I could see gray hair around his mouth, meaning he was pretty old, and it made me wonder if he was alive when my mother and my father lived here. Maybe they even crossed paths, maybe the two of them were walking right where I did, and they startled each other in the same way.

I do that a lot with my questions. Did they walk here, did they sit in these chairs ("No!" Jim said once like he was mad at me. "We just bought these chairs."), did they help fill up this bird feeder? I know it's silly, but I can't help it.

Once after Bonnie told me my room had been theirs, I woke in the middle of the night after dreaming Janie had crawled under the bed and carved a note to me in the wooden bed frame. I got up and turned on all my lights and even went to the garage for a flashlight so I could see under the bed, but there was nothing there.

Another time, I found a really fat snake in the weeds near the train tracks and I thought maybe it was sick or dying because it didn't try to slither away when I got close, it had a lump in the middle and I realized it had just eaten, which was kind of gross but also kind of cool, and I bent over and picked up the snake and it seemed to know I wasn't going to hurt it because it didn't squirm or try to bite me. One time Mrs. Garcia played a game with the whole class, discover your Indian name. Mine was "Rhythm Girl" because of my name, Mrs. Garcia was "Long Enduring Water Buffalo," which made some of the kids laugh, but not me. I named the snake "Fatty Love Snake" because it was so round and didn't mind me picking it up. Then I sat it in the grass and watched it crawl away and I said, "Goodbye Fatty Love Snake, goodbye."

Vanishing

The one thing Philips and I discovered we enjoyed doing together in Santa Fe was shooting.

I'd grown up with guns, but I don't think Philips ever had any interest until she heard me recounting something Cliff had told me about shooting up junk refrigerators and sinks south and west of town. I bought an old Browning 9mm from Cliff and showed her how to load, point and shoot it.

We'd go out near the city dump, a wide, nearly treeless land extending all the way to the Jemez Mountains, full of dry riverbeds, rugged arroyos and, closer to the mountains, deep rock canyons. Almost no one lived there, a few stragglers set up tents and lived out the summer, walking into town to beg for food or pick up an odd job here and there; and there were scattered mobile homes, the kinds of places with a couple of non-running vehicles in front. The boundaries of the dump itself were loose and forever expanding.

After Philips and I had been a few times, blasting away at all manners of discarded home appliances, Cliff told me about this one arroyo where there were a lot of rats a person could shoot, rattlesnakes too, maybe even the occasional wild dog. You could shoot them too, if you had a mind, he said.

I didn't, not even the rats—I'd grown up hunting with my Uncle Eddie and had had my fill of killing—but one night, desperate for something new to say, I told Philips about it and she was excited. By then, it was as bad between us as it'd ever been, and I was eager to spend any time I could with her. On a typical late summer day, monsoons building over both mountain ranges, we went out, backtracking here and there until we found Cliff's rodent arroyo and sure enough, rats scurried when we drove up, disappearing under the small mountains of water heaters, refrigerators, burned-out cars, and endless piles of ripped open garbage bags.

"What's that?" she said.

"A water heater, I think."

"Cool."

We got out and I began setting up, laying a blanket over the hood of the truck, then carefully placing the pistol, two sets of ear plugs, three fully loaded clips, and two boxes of cartridges. Philips popped in a clip.

"I'm going to lay some hurt on that water heater," she said. "Just to get started." She looked good with a gun, like she was born to it, but even this bothered me.

When Uncle Eddie was teaching me, I wanted to shoot like in the movies—bang, bang, bang, bang—as fast as I could but he insisted on the proper stance, taking in a breath, letting out half, squeezing the trigger, then walking down and looking where you hit the target. And this is how I taught Philips, but she wanted to fire the entire clip at once, she wasn't interested in hitting the center of a target. And of course I understood—I wanted to join in and be like her—but I was to the point where I couldn't imagine not being in opposition to her; I no longer had the emotional tools to handle harmony.

So she shot up an entire clip right away, mostly missing but kicking up a lot of dust; birds flew, rats scurried for their holes, the wind gusted, scattering the sounds. I fired one at a time, hitting the water heater, splitting a sink, popping a can here, an old lamp there; all the time feeling her impatience, all the time wanting to break loose myself but holding back because I was unwilling to give in to her way. I watched while she fired fourteen shots as fast as she could pull the trigger.

"I like this!" she said. She was amazingly sexy; she'd lost all her pregnancy weight and with her hair cut close, wearing short skirts and combat boots, I couldn't bury the thought that in our prime, we'd have fucked at least once by now. Right there on the hood next to the guns. But we didn't really have sex anymore and seeing her out there, I couldn't imagine this creature wasn't fucking someone. She should have been; she was at some sort of peak, she should have been giving it and taking it, but it made me very sad because I knew it wasn't and never again would be with me. I hated her for making me feel that.

We circled around until we were on the ridge above the arroyo. She was committed to killing and wanted to wait it out until the rats came out of their hiding places. It wouldn't be so bad, would it? To blow up a rat? A fucking rodent carrying disease? Or a dog? She said she could kill a wild dog, what kind of life does such an animal have anyway?

"I don't know," I said. She had a way of making me feel simple, unable to say what needed to be said. "I've killed animals."

"I haven't . . ." she said, cutting me off.

"It's not one of the necessary experiences, believe me," I said.

"I don't," she said. "Believe you."

"What?"

"Oh come on now," she said, incredulous; like we'd long had an unspoken pact truth was better left out of our relationship.

"You come on now," I said angrily.

"Ooooh, Henry's pissed-off and he has a gun." I thrust the gun out to her, and she took it. She fingered it, expertly slid in the clip, checked it, then popped it back in the way a character in the movies might do in the middle of a gun battle.

"You know what I wonder?" she said.

"Like I give a flying fuck." I was still angry.

"We haven't seen anyone in an hour. Not a soul. If I shot you and say, dragged your body back behind that pile of sinks, how long would it be before someone missed you?"

"Bonnie and Jim, right away."

"I'd tell them you decided to go to Chicago, that it wasn't working for us. They have eyes, they can see. And they are my parents. They'll believe me."

"Now that's funny. They'll believe you. Rich even."

She was holding the gun out in front of us, not pointing it at me, but holding it in a way that made me think she could do it. Not really, but to think that, even if only for a micro-second, about your own wife, someone you've been with for years, is the kind of thought that can change how you think about everything.

"You condescending cunt, I wish I did have the guts to put you out of your misery," I said. She stopped smiling; she loathed that word. "See, I can say whatever the fuck I feel like saying too."

She turned away from me, and I thought I'd gone too far somehow, though at the time it didn't feel extraordinary. We'd had uglier arguments than this one.

"You'd have to explain it to our daughter when she gets older," I said, in an attempt to lower the hostility level. "About what happened to Daddy, what you did to Daddy."

When she turned back, she was smiling, but I could tell no good would come of it. "Oh poor Henry. Don't you know? Are you telling me you really don't know? I could leave your body to rot out here and still have her father explain it to her."

"What are you going on about?"

"Haven't you ever looked at Cady? Haven't you ever wondered how she doesn't look like you?"

I felt a chill. "She doesn't look like you either. She looks like a fucking baby. I don't know what you're trying to say."

"Don't you? Really now."

"Quit saying that! If you got some fucked up shit to say, just say it. Or shoot me. It'd be better than listening to you flap your fucking gums," I said.

"You're not Cady's father, how clear is that?"

"You're full of shit."

"Keep telling yourself that, big boy."

"You vicious bitch."

"I'll pay for the blood test tomorrow. I know who it is, I could tell you. You'd know too. You've met him."

"Why would you say that? Like that?"

"Because . . . it's true?"

At that moment, a dog appeared well below us, picking around the foodstuffs on the far side of the trash pile. She crouched down and moved to the edge of the arroyo.

"Philips, come on, you got to talk to me," I said.

"Shut up!" She was concentrating on stalking the dog and I was too stunned to know how to make her stop and talk to me.

She aimed, then fired. She missed by two feet, far enough that the dog jumped, looked around a moment, smelled the air, then tore off with its tail between its legs. She started running, paralleling it along the ridge top.

"Philips! Jesus Christ."

She ignored me. I wasn't sure what to do. I needed her here now, I needed her to tell me this was just another one of those arguments of ours where we say the worst possible thing we can think of to each other. I needed it, but she kept running.

Then she tripped, her feet kicked back, and she put out her hands to cushion her landing and when she hit, her finger must have squeezed against the trigger because the gun went off. It went off and there was silence.

I stopped and listened for any signs of what had happened. For a long moment she didn't move and in those seconds I made a plan. No one had seen us together. I'd have to leave our car, make my way back to our apartment, and wait for someone official to inform me of my wife's tragic accident. A terrible thrill ran through me, a dark exhilaration at the prospect of looming change, of being set free once and for all and I understood this was the best possible ending for everyone. It would be hard, sure, Bonnie and Jim would be upset, but little Cady was only a child. She'd never miss her mother and I could tell her about the good times. Only the good times.

Then she popped to her feet, grabbed the pistol, and took off running without looking back, disappearing over a ridge. She was gone and I didn't go after her. I walked, then ran to our car, and took off, leaving her there. I made it all the way to our apartment before turning around.

When I found her walking along the road leading out of the dump, appearing flattened and wavy in the heat rising off the hard baked ground, I was as far from knowing what I felt as I have ever been. When I got close, I could see she'd been crying, which made me cry. She got in our car and lay her head on my shoulder, squeezing my arm to her chest. By then, I'd had time to think about it. Cadence did look like me, especially around the eyes. Everyone said it, even strangers who didn't know we were related. We had the same eyes.

"Why did you say that? Why then?"

"Please," she said, and I knew she didn't want to talk.

"You got to say something."

"OK."

"You fucking got to."

"I said OK. I don't know why, I don't know, I just said it."

"Is that what you wish? That she wasn't mine? That I'm not her father?"

"No," she said quietly, after a long pause. "Not you, not that."

That's how we left it. I worked a full ten-hour shift that night and when I got home around three in the morning, she wasn't there. When I woke the next morning, my eyes were all crusted over, I couldn't open them without first delicately clearing the sharp crystals from my eyelashes. She still wasn't home.

For three days, I worked, came home and slept and told no one about Philips being gone. It was glorious in its own way, a step out of place and time. There was some mean delight in allowing her disappearance to linger, like I was rejecting her instead of vice versa. When I finally drove out there on the fourth day, I found out she'd left a note and Bonnie and Jim had been putting off telling me. They claimed they assumed she'd left me a note too, but it didn't track. Neither of them brought up my three days until much later, when Jim pushed for a police investigation.

Most of the note was about us, about how we'd become expert at hurting each other and how that was no way to live. Implicit was a deep anguish at the failure of our marriage, which surprised me. I didn't think I could wound her anymore, not in the same way she could damage me. She wrote very little to her parents, but she thanked them and kept her tone gentle. She used a "best interests of the child" argument about abandoning Cadence.

I stayed away from Eldorado for an entire month. The second week was the worst. At first, I expected her to call even though the letter explicitly said she wouldn't, but by week two I knew she was gone, and I couldn't get out of bed. Even now, I don't think on that time much, I was sick and filthy in a way I wouldn't have thought myself capable of. I worked my way through it literally, by laundering my sheets and all my clothing, by cleaning the floor, the dresser, by painting the walls.

By the time I went out to see my daughter and her grandparents, the bond between the two households was disintegrating. Jim was abrupt and huffy with me and made it clear he held me responsible for his daughter's disappearance. I didn't blame him and thought he and Bonnie deserved some effort, so I sat with them after dinner and held Cadence, I helped him with his nightly fireplace fires and feigned interest in his TV shows. We even drove up onto the top of Rowe Mesa with a firewood permit and filled my pickup to the top with cut piñon pine. But inevitably, my nightly visits turned to every other night and then two times a week.

Then for an entire week, they quit returning my calls. When I finally drove over there, everything was different. Jim had recovered his suspicious nature. He joined a victim's support group at Fort Marcy and was eventually encouraged to go to the Santa Fe police department (using contacts the group had developed over the years) and demand an investigation into the letter's veracity. After my very brief police interrogation was over, I confronted Jim. I may have been more forceful than was prudent, picking up a croquet mallet and brandishing it in his direction while telling him he knew fuck-all about his daughter. It turned frosty after that and

Jim made every visit to see Cadence uncomfortable, though Bonnie struggled to remain friendly in her own muddled way.

There was a page three story in *The New Mexican* about her disappearance, along with some details about her work life. None of her co-workers at the St. Francis expressed any surprise she was gone. I called the reporter and after some initial reluctance, she gave me an outline of the information that didn't make the story. Philips was part of a large restaurant crowd that often met for coffee before work and stayed after to drink. They were very proprietary towards her and seemed to think of me as a clinging acquaintance of hers, someone just short of a stalker. Many didn't know she was married, those who did held hostile opinions of her husband, even though I'd never met any of them. None of them knew she had a daughter. There was some talk of involvement with other men. Hearing about her other life went a long way towards changing my thinking about...well, everything; Santa Fe, Bonnie and Jim, my marriage, myself, the child. It was easier to stay away. Bonnie and Jim were increasingly hostile, they didn't want me there and Cadence was settled and seemingly happy. What were my choices? I couldn't bring her into town and take care of her, not by myself. And I wouldn't live out there, even if they were willing.

I came up with a plan. I'd return to Chicago for a while, get my teaching job back, save my money. I'd come get her when I could afford day care and eventually private school. Bonnie and Jim hardly reacted to the news, only the words "send for her" elicited the barest sneer from Jim. They knew I wasn't up to taking care of a kid. Philips disappearing came to seem like a license for me to disappear. As if we had, as parents, made the dual, but separately rendered decision our daughter was better off being raised by her grandparents. It was the last act of my marriage rather than the first of my new life.

"She'll be fine," I said to Bonnie. "Better than fine. And I'll visit whenever I can."

For my entire time in Chicago, I refused to consider I was anything but completely serious about coming back for her, it was only after I realized she was in school and (surely) had teachers and classmates she liked did my commitment to the plan waver, but I quit bothering to delude myself after I moved to New Hampshire. It didn't matter anyway, doing is the only thing that does.

And now I'm standing at their front door, having driven out here in a burst of energy and optimism after my chance meeting with Doreen. That burst is gone, and my knees are shaking when I ring the doorbell. Bonnie answers, looking exactly the same. Jim's TV is blaring in the background.

"Hullo, Bonnie," I say.

"Hullo Henry," she says, and turns her body to let me in like I've been living here all along.

Henry & Cadence

Bonnie is making coffee, being as vacantly pleasant with me as always, Jim keeps saying "Henry" in a non-committal tone, like a man trying to remember how to be angry. Finally, he returns to his TV and looks ready to sit back down.

"Go tell Cady he's here," she says, and Jim dutifully pads down the hall. She has our old room.

"We've got a pond now," Bonnie says, and I'm grateful for the distraction from my thoughts, which are drilling a serious hole in my guts.

"I like it. How long have you had it?"

"Two, no, three years now."

"Do you run it in the winter?" Twenty-questions is the best approach with Bonnie, she likes the back and forth.

"All year."

"What about the birds?"

"The quail come to the edge in groups, the piñon jays sit on the rock in the middle. We've seen the ravens washing their pieces of rabbit in it."

Cadence's bedroom door flies open, and she rushes out, then stops herself halfway and walks, eyes glued to the floor. She's tall for ten, though I haven't spent much time around ten-year-olds. But I'm tall and so is Bonnie's side of the family. Jim puts his hand on her head from behind, awkwardly laying claim, and I can see this isn't typical for the two of them, Jim's not someone naturally open to touching and being touched. Bonnie has her coffee and a stack of butter cookies. Cadence passes into the light and sits down across from me. She's so dark! That's the first thing I notice. Her skin is a deep olive color, darker than her mother, though a lot of that comes from living in the relentless sun of New Mexico. She has my green eyes and my long forehead too, which I don't remember.

"Hello," she says.

"Hello."

She looks down shyly. I'm staring, but I can't help myself. There's so much to see! It's amazing in a way I could never have guessed, the changes, the instantaneous animation of an infant into a whole, living creature, like someone sprinkled pixie dust over her and she grew up overnight. So familiar. Her eyes are still mine and look even brighter green set against her olive complexion, but that's not it. Does she have Philips' cheek bones, her mouth, her chin? Is that what I'm seeing? I'm not sure I can conjure an image of my ex-wife anymore.

"Do you want me to help you start dinner?" she says to Bonnie, who seems surprised by the offer.

"No sweetie, thank you. Dinner's in the oven. You just sit there and catch up. You want to have dinner with us, Henry?"

"OK, sure."

She won't look at me, focusing on a spot of the wall, and after a while, I quit staring. It only seems fair. Let her get used to my presence gently, with no pushing, no gawking.

No one says much at dinner. The Bonnie and Jim dinner table has always been a quiet one, Jim discourages talking (in happier times, Philips and I took some delight in annoying her father with our exuberant dinner table conversations), and Cadence continues the tradition, speaking only to ask for the salt or to say "Thank you" and, "You're welcome" in a soft voice. When Jim struggles to open a bottle of red wine, she giggles, and I can see she's a sweet child who loves her grandfather. I can't help but think if by some miracle, Philips and I had raised her, she'd be a beautiful adult child, talking on about herself, wearing make-up and hipster earrings. Following the New York fashions, her life revolving around what she doesn't have rather than what she does. This is the value of growing up with Bonnie and Jim, the lack of pretension, the way they treat her like any child and not someone preordained to someday change everyone's lives.

After dinner, we sit in front of the television with the sound down, her and I on the couch, Jim in his chair, Bonnie with her back to the set in a rocking chair.

"You're quiet, Henry," she says. "When did you get so quiet?"

"I guess this has left me speechless."

"And you, Cady. What about you? Talk to him, talk to your . . . father," she says, and Jim gives her a sharp look, meant only for her. She ignores it, though whether on purpose or because she simply missed it isn't clear. Jim still seems to be struggling to get his bearings, my appearance at his door has sent him reeling. Maybe this was his greatest fear come true, maybe he's confused about how he should be acting in this moment. I have sympathy.

"What about those questions you wrote down for your teacher?" Bonnie says.

"She said I should say them when we were alone," she says.

"We could take a walk," I suggest.

"Do you want to take a walk?" Jim asks.

"I don't know," she says and looks down. She wants to, but is smart enough to realize her grandfather is against it.

"They'll take a walk," Bonnie says, settling the tie in my favor. "Go get your jacket and get your pad; Henry will put his shoes on."

She jumps up and runs into the other room and her excitement frightens me, I feel a pressure that might have no outer limit. There's a genuine fear hovering around this girl, and the deepest one of all is that I'm not up to this. That I left the first time for a reason and I came back here in a rush of energy, the suddenness of New Hampshire to Santa Fe seems like a rocket ship, seen from where I am now. She's only a child, I tell myself, nothing's been settled, nothing's been decided.

"I'll use the restroom real fast."

"Some things never change," Jim says, the friendliest words he's said to me since I arrived, alluding to an often-discussed habit of mine of using the bathroom right before leaving, making people wait.

I wash my hands, wipe my face and run wet fingers over my hair. There's a set of fingernail clippers on the counter and I take the opportunity to trim both thumbnails and clean out the dirt underneath. I find their Q-tips and clean my ears, an old habit I find difficult to break. I stay as long as is reasonable for the situation and when I emerge, she's waiting by the door in a bright yellow jacket, and a black baseball cap that makes her look boyish. Holding a notebook.

"Well then," I say but my legs are unsteady, and I wish I could go back into the bathroom and sit on the toilet for a few minutes.

Outside is better, the cool high desert air dries my sweat.

"You kids take as long as you want," Bonnie says, and I have to wonder if she's on some other medication, a newly discovered pill that turns you into the perfect mother: friendly, accommodating, without possessiveness, envy or insecurity.

Our feet crunch on the gravel road, only the main roads of their huge subdivision are paved; we are heading downhill towards the railroad tracks. The silence builds until it feels palatable, suffocating. *She is a child*, I tell myself. *My child. Stand up to this.*

"Where do you want to walk?" I say. It comes out squeaky and frightened-sounding. I *am* frightened. I'm not sure why I'm here, what any of this means.

"I know where the coyotes sleep during the day," she says.

"I'd like to see that."

Then, "You know, I lived out here a few months with your mom when you were a baby."

"Bonnie told me."

"What'd she say about it?"

"Only that you lived here. And that my room was yours."

I nod as we walk down a short hill, then cut across open land, heading for a railroad trestle, a place where we can cross under the tracks and keep going. She has long legs and a short, hunched body—the opposite of me—there's a hint of gangly-ness to the way she looks, her feet are too large for her slender legs, but she seems far more coordinated than her mother. I have a flash of us walking along this very road holding hands and laughing. I think Philips had a skinned knee. Did that really happen here? Good times in Eldorado?

"Are you nervous?" I say.

"No."

I can feel her looking at me as we walk and decide not to look back. Let her stare for as long as she needs to.

"I saw a snake here last summer. It was bright red and blue and had just eaten a mouse," she says, breathlessly.

"Do you know what it was? Was it dangerous?"

"Snakes are big scaredy cats."

"Who told you that?"

"I picked her up." I can tell she is proud of this.

"You picked up the snake?"

She runs down to the trestle without answering, she seems impatient for me to catch up. We're standing underneath a short, wooden train bridge spanning two small hills; the path runs between. The tracks are twenty feet above our heads.

"There," she says, pointing to a corner where there's fresh dirt thrown around, the entrance area made smooth by constant coming and going. The hole itself remains hidden.

"Do you want to climb up there and look?" I say.

"Oh no," she says. I ignore her and scramble up the gravel and dirt hill until I'm able to grab hold of the underside of the trestle, then I work my way hand over hand towards the corner.

"I can see the hole," I say. "You should come up here."

"No." She doesn't like that I've climbed up here.

"It's OK, I'll help you. Come on."

"I don't want to. My teacher says you shouldn't get too close. The coyotes won't like it. They'll be scared."

I skin up the heel of my hand sliding down and have to press it against the inside of my shirt to stop the bleeding. She walks on ahead of me, I jog to catch up. We make our way to the train tracks, which are slightly elevated with grand views in three directions. It's clear enough out that we can see the craggy outline of the Manzanos south of Albuquerque and Mt. Taylor to the southwest, easily 100 miles, a mammoth single cone mountain sitting by itself, so distant it seems as much a trick of the light as a mountain. I point it out to her, but she just nods her head and keeps walking. She's grown silent and it feels like she's upset. Or maybe anxious. "Jim likes mountains," I say. "He taught me all the names."

She puts her hands in her pockets with her notebook tucked up under one arm. Five older teenagers pass us on mountain bikes pushing hard up a dirt path running alongside the tracks. They are decked out in stretch bicycle outfits. She doesn't bother to even look in their direction, she hasn't entered any semblance of a boy stage. Another reason to be thankful Bonnie and Jim raised her.

"Bonnie said you had some questions?"

She nods.

"For me?"

"Some of them."

"Why do you have questions?"

"Mrs. Garcia had everyone do it as an assignment." Her shyness borders on being sullen. Considering the circumstances, I shouldn't be surprised, but still am. I promise myself I'll keep trying and not get annoyed or defensive.

"What was the assignment?"

"Write out five questions you'd ask if you could ask anything you want to anyone."

"So you got five questions?"

"When it was over, Mrs. Garcia told me I should keep going so I did."

"So how many do you have now?" She holds the notebook up for me to see.

"The whole notebook? It's full of questions?"

"No, no. Not full. It's not full."

"Some of them are to me?"

She nods.

"Do you want to ask me one?"

She stops and cocks her head, as if listening. Again I'm struck by an overpowering sense of the familiar; in the way she looks, in her gestures, her pauses, in the way she gathers herself before speaking. It has to be Philips, it has to be her mother I'm seeing in her, but I don't remember Philips like this. Then again, I don't remember a lot of the ways of my ex-wife.

"OK." She sits down on one rail of the tracks I stand on the other with my arms out for balance. She leafs through the notebook, using her finger back and forth on the page. Wispy clouds have moved in, diffusing the light and turning our shadows fuzzy and the air cooler. I think about later in the evening and what it will feel like driving away from here.

"Here's one. Who's Philip?"

"What?"

"Philip. It's written in pen on the picture of my mother in Bonnie's room and I heard you say it. I know it means something, but I'm not sure."

"That's Philips, with an 'S'. That's your mother's name. Bonnie never told you?"

"Her name is Jane. Bonnie always says Janie."

"Philips was her middle name. Everyone but Bonnie and Jim called her Philips."

"Philips," she repeats to herself.

"It was Bonnie's father's name. Philip, but they couldn't give a girl that name, so they added the 'S'. I guess it's not a man's name with an 'S'. She never liked the name Jane."

"I like Jane better. I like Janie." She has a way of bending her knees towards each other and hunching her back so that she turns inward, like a turtle drawing into its shell. Pure Philips. She used to sit on our fire escape in Chicago that way watching the distant skyline. I'd make dinner and we'd sit outside together and eat off a single plate piled high.

"Ask me another."

She continues searching, then stops.

"I don't feel like it."

"You want to walk?"

I tightrope my rail and after a while, she does the same with hers. It becomes an unspoken contest, with each of us glancing over at the other while trying to keep balance. I fall first, and she walks an extra fifty feet just to rub it in. She's good, with natural physical grace, walking the rail as easily as walking on the ground. Bonnie told me she plays basketball and it's easy to imagine her handling the ball. This is my grace. She sure didn't get it from Philips, who always needed at least two people-lanes of space. She was all boots and arms whipping this way and that. And she fell. All the time. She'd trip over her own feet or career off of the corner of a parked car and she'd be down and back up before you'd even notice. People's first impression of her was always of an unfocused ditz. Until she opened her mouth.

"Your mother was a klutz."

"What's that mean, klutz?"

"She tripped. She'd knock stuff off of tables and bookcases. She fell a lot."

"Fell? You mean, fell?"

"All the time. Boom! On her face." Cadence giggles.

The mood lightens some as we head towards the house.

"You know, you can ask me more questions another time if you feel like it."

"Another time?"

"I might be around for a while."

"They didn't tell me."

"I didn't tell them. I thought they might not like it." I'm not sure how honest to be with her.

Back at the house, Bonnie sits on the edge of the fireplace, intent on stoking the fire; Jim is in his chair with the television on. Cadence disappears down the hall and the entire room freezes; Bonnie and Jim listen, seemingly thinking that our walk has been so upsetting that she's run to her room. But really, she's gone to the bathroom and when the toilet flushes, the whole room takes a collective breath and calms down. Cadence comes back out and sits on the couch next to Jim.

"You and your football," she says to her grandfather. Jim doesn't turn, but I can see it register in his eyes, this *is* regular between the two of them and they count on it being there, giving them both a small satisfaction.

"It's what I used to say," Bonnie explains. "She heard me say it."

We watch a nature show on elephants and when the host tells a story about elephants returning to a site and lovingly caressing the bones of long-dead relatives, Cadence's eyes glisten. She sniffles and coughs and turns away, not wanting anyone to see; it's so gentle and transparent a gesture, so perfect and timeless, it's like witnessing a small wonder and I have to look away myself.

Jim shakes my hand and Bonnie hugs me good night. Cadence disappears into her room. There's a long, awkward moment waiting, all of us unsure as to whether she's coming out again. Neither of them mentions further visits. Finally, I go to my truck and start it up. Cadence appears at the side door and puts her hand on the hood of my truck as if to stop me. I roll down my window. After a moment, I turn off the engine.

"I loved her, your mother," I say, an easy enough lie for me to tell. I'm not sure that what I felt for Philips really constituted love, ever. Or maybe it did then and doesn't now. Or it did sometimes and didn't others. But it was a long time ago, almost this girl's entire life. I think any child would want to know her parents loved each other, but she just stares at me, like she perfectly understands why I said that. Cadence has the same way of keeping you off-balance as her mother did, using the simplest of looks or certain silences to always make you wonder how much she actually understands and what she perceives.

"You like living out here?"

"It's the only place I've lived."

"I've lived all over."

"I know."

"You know?"

"I looked up Keene, New Hampshire and Chicago, Illinois on the map, I even found LaPorte, where my other grandmother lives."

"My mother?"

"Yes."

"You know about LaPorte?"

"I know that's where you grew up. Bonnie knew."

"I'm going to come back, OK?"

"OK."

"You could call me."

"I don't have a number." I don't either and since there are two Motel 6's on the same stretch of Cerrillos Road, I can't tell her which is which. "I'll find out and leave a message."

"OK."

I start my truck up and she steps back to where I can see all of her. Maybe it's seeing her whole like that—she's barefoot in baggy basketball shorts, her little feet turned inward in a way that's both cute and sweetly vulnerable—but I know right away what keeps nagging at me, what's so familiar. She looks like me. Not in some general parent-child sense, she looks like I did when I was her age. She stands like I did...like we did. She turns in her feet and hunches her back when she sits, hugging her knees. That wasn't a Philips' gesture, though an hour ago, I clearly remembered it as such. But Philips was a sprawler, she liked to lay back, arms and legs open, she liked her space. She's me. Us.

I take the back way home, behind Quail Run, and pull off to a dirt road I know that rises over a saddle between two hills. I sit up on the hood. Stars are out and the moon is behind me, blocked from view. There's just enough light left to make out dark boiling clouds hanging right on top of Santa Fe Baldy. There's a gun-metal cold wind out of the north that makes this little rise feel irredeemably sad and remote. I'm still alone. I've always been alone. Having a daughter isn't going to change that, especially not one I abandoned years before.

Later the wind shifts and there's noise everywhere; voices talking, laughing, doors banging shut, dogs barking, cars spinning their tires on gravel, and somewhere in the vast space between me and the Sangre de Cristo mountains, the high whine sound of a dirt bike rises and fades. I shiver and Cadence's face comes to me so quickly, it has the feeling of a haunting. I watch a pinpoint light move around the sky, at first I think it's an airplane, but then I realize it's too low, that it must be on the side of the mountain itself; maybe the ski basin; someone out grooming the slopes, except it's way too early in the season for that.

It feels intangible, elusive, full of meaning. I doubt what I saw was actually Cadence's face. Could it have been Philips'? Does Cadence look like her mother? She must, in some way, but I can no longer remember Philips' face. For the first time in a long time, I find myself wondering if she's alive. Through all the eight years she's been gone, I've had a spectral relationship with the memories of my ex-wife, a gnawing psychic connection, her presence looming just out of my perceptual reach but (often) as prominent as my life. I assumed when a marriage ends as disastrously as mine did, there's an endless amount of detritus left over and there's some comfort in that. She's gone, I'm gone, and in our absence, we're forever linked. I was always sure at the very least I'd know if she was no longer on this earth.

But what if that connection I've felt these eight years wasn't her, what if she drove a thousand miles, changed her name, and died in an anonymous traffic accident before I'd even managed to work myself up to leaving Santa Fe and our daughter? Or caught cancer, or stepped off the curb at exactly the wrong moment, or met a man who killed her? Maybe she's been long reborn and her new, improved presence is out there right now and that's what I feel. Or maybe it never was her. Maybe it was Cadence all along. She's the one I've been waiting for all these years.

Cadence

I have to wait through the entire day before I tell Mrs. Garcia, she's always got so many kids around her, and I don't want anyone else to hear. After school, I stay until everyone leaves and tell her. She doesn't act like I thought she would, she seems more mad than glad. She keeps asking me if I'm OK.

"Sure I am." I don't understand the question.

"It's a big event," she says. "I want to make sure you're approaching it in the right way."

"OK," I say, because I don't know what else to say. What's the right way? She's the one who started this, she's the one who got me going on my parents. She asked me lots of questions and I came up with lots more after I started. Bonnie and Jim never talked about them. They showed me pictures of Janie as a girl and they have one album with a single picture of him in the background, but I've never seen them together. I used to wonder if my father walked right past me on the street, would I even know who he was? Now I will.

"He isn't at all like I thought he'd be," I say. I want to talk about him. I want Mrs. Garcia to be happy. I thought she'd be as happy as I am.

"How so?" She doesn't sound happy.

"He's so big!" I say.

"You mean like fat?"

Suddenly I don't want to talk to her anymore. She isn't saying what I thought she'd say.

"Are you OK, Cady?"

"Yes, yes, I'm fine." I don't want to, but I feel like I could cry. I waited all day to tell her and now I just want to leave. "I should go home."

Mrs. Garcia comes over to me and I know now she can see I'm about to cry.

"Cady? Sweetie? Did your father say something? What did that man do to you?"

"What do you mean? We walked along the railroad tracks and I showed him where the coyotes lived. We talked about Jim and how he loves mountains. He used to live where I live."

"You just promise me to tell me if he does. You don't really know this man, not at all, and I think you should be careful around him."

"OK." I'll say anything now to leave.

"You promise?"

"I don't want to promise."

"All right, sweetie."

When I get outside, I do cry, but only a little. I don't know why Mrs. Garcia has to be that way. Even Bonnie and Jim aren't like that, they just don't talk for hours or turn up their television so there's no part of the house where you can't hear it. When Jim knocked on my door and said Henry was at the front door and that I should come out, I couldn't believe he was serious, even though Jim doesn't make jokes. Since Mrs. Garcia got me thinking about my parents, each time I had a wish like at birthdays or if Bonnie dried out a wishbone and we snapped it, I always wished for the same thing. Once Bonnie asked me what I wished for and I told her and she stared off in space like she does, but later she found me and put her arm around me and hugged me tight. And when I told Mrs. Garcia what I was wishing for, she said, "What a fine wish," but now that it's actually come true, everyone's acting strange, like I did wrong by bringing him here. Except for him. I can tell he's glad he's here.

Henry

When I wake, it's well past noon and the little red light on the motel phone is lit. I call the front desk, there's a message. "Cadence called." She must've found the number on her own and called me before she left for school, both of which seem hugely impressive for a ten-year old. I didn't expect this. Last night, when I returned to the motel room, I snorted all the speed-poppy mix I had left, but only after thinking hard on whether this wasn't a step back into my New Hampshire life. I decided to treat it like what it was, a unique and wonderful recreational narcotic, and I snorted it all, except this time, I felt lousy almost from the beginning. I ended up two hours sweating in the bathroom, always on the edge of puking, then most of the rest of the night watching one loud cable movie after another.

So now it's almost two in the afternoon and I've done nothing, but that's OK. I still have time. First order of business? Go downtown and buy Cadence a gift. I have an idea that came to me last night while lying on the bathroom floor. I even have a vague plan I'll buy the gift and then drive to Eldorado and surprise her when she comes home from school. That will make up for not answering the phone this morning.

Instead, I drive to Downtown Subscription and set up camp on the patio again. I tell myself I need coffee and food in my stomach, but I also know it'd be nice to see Doreen and her kids again. It could be worthwhile to talk to her about Cadence, she might see what I don't.

Except Doreen never shows and 3:30 p.m. comes and goes, meaning I missed picking Cadence up at school and I haven't returned her call. I'll have to go out there. It's the only solution;

appear bearing gifts. I head downtown. The store in question has exactly what I want, which I take as a positive sign. I pick up a couple other gifts for her on the spot, figuring I can give them to her as circumstance demands.

Their car isn't in the driveway. I ring the bell and knock on the door, but I know no one's home. Bonnie and Jim like to dine early, before the crowds arrive. They've probably gone out to eat. They used to have their favorite restaurants, but that was eight years ago. I wouldn't know where to start.

I decide to leave a simple note and my present. I can't give it to her unwrapped, so I tear out a page from my atlas (New Mexico) and use black electrical tape out of my glove compartment. I mark a star where Eldorado is on the map along with a large arrow and I leave it all behind the screen door. I consider waiting in the back yard but decide the possibility of a neighbor calling the cops is too high. I might have trouble explaining myself, at least until they got home.

Since I'm in the right general direction, I drive to Cliff and Doreen's without calling first, a calculated risk. They might not like it; Cliff was always a bit unpredictable. I'll ask him about my money and maybe he can tell me about his kids. I don't think they're both his, meaning he had to figure out how to be a father.

The gate is shut but not locked, which is the clearest sign of all how much Cliff's changed. Doreen is working in their garden alongside the house; it's a square patch of black mulch standing out against the hard-scrabble brown New Mexico dirt. She's busy pulling out dead tomato plants and turning under the soil with a spade. She waves and begins taking off her gloves to greet me.

"I'm glad you came," she says.

"Benny?"

"He's gone inside. He does this a couple of times a year. He locks himself in his survival room, usually when the kids are away. They're spending the week at their grandparents. There's no telling when he might come out. He stayed in there for fifteen days once."

"The lead room? There's not a bathroom in there."

She nods. "He comes out to use the downstairs bathroom. Just not when any of us are awake. It's not like I'm going to stake out my own bathroom just to see him." She leads me onto a wood deck, and we sit in padded redwood porch furniture and watch the sunset intensify. It feels exactly right, not to talk to Cliff, but Doreen. To just sit and talk to her.

"What's that about? The lead?"

"Benny had an e-mail friendship with Whitley Strieber, you know, the writer. Maybe this was his idea, I don't know, but Benny became convinced alien visitors can't abduct someone through lead. That's what he used to say, now he's too embarrassed to make that argument. Now, he claims the research on radiation bombardment is flawed and that every single person on earth is being slowly poisoned. He figures the longer he's inside, the longer it'll take to kill him with radiation. He likes to call it a cleansing." She seems to understand Cliff's idiosyncrasies and has no problem alternately revering and mocking them.

"What about you and the kids?"

"They go in with him sometimes, usually just for an hour or two. They like all the TVs and stereo stuff. He gets antsy with anyone else in there. I think that's OK. I don't want him kicking around my garden."

"And you?"

"Let's just say I'm more concerned with the interior than the exterior, if you know what I mean."

"Look inside yourself first?"

"That's the idea. Benny believes that too, most of the time anyway." She disappears into the house and comes back with two bottles of root beer, home-made bean dip, and warmed pita bread.

"You know, you gave me a ride in your cab once," she says after a long silence in which both of us are eating.

"You remember me?"

"Not physically. I mean, I don't recognize you. I was so drunk, I don't remember looking at your face, except you seemed familiar when I first met you."

"You did look at me sort of funny. I wasn't sure it was all that friendly."

"I'm sorry about that. I had some bad years, sometimes I meet people I don't remember who remember me from then. It's not pleasant."

"Except this time."

"Except this time."

"So how do you know it's me who gave you the ride?

"Benny put it together after you left the other night."

"So you knew Cliff back then?"

"Benny," she says, with no rancor. "We should call him what he wants us to."

"You're right."

"I didn't know him then, but I remembered that it was Cab Driver Number 50 because people kept talking to him over the radio. They called him Five-O."

"That's right. I'd forgotten. That was my number. Everyone said Five-O because they liked having a real reason to say that. But there must've been a few Five-O's over the years."

"Benny guided me back and we figured out the year. He says you were the Five-O then."

"Now you got me curious."

"I was a waitress at El Farol's and Wednesday's were my night to stay after. Tommy was at my sister's for the night and almost the entire shift had the next day off, so we'd drink at the bar until it was light out. Somewhere along the line, I went outside without my coat and because of some fucking drama I had going with the manager, I didn't want to go back in for it. By the time I got into a cab, I had the serious chills and couldn't stop shaking. The driver was really nice...you were, I mean, you were really nice to me. You blasted the heat, and when that wasn't enough, you let me crawl up front with you. I put my arms inside your coat, and you rubbed my back. I think you had to basically carry me inside, which I apologize for, by the way, even if you don't recall. I remember shedding clothing and trying to pull you onto the bed with me. I was more than ready to sleep with the big Five-O, but you made me get under the blankets and you found more and piled them on top and stayed until I quit shaking and fell asleep. It was just one night, but it was towards the end of a long slide in the wrong direction, and you helped me out when I needed it. And you didn't do what a lot of other guys would've."

I do remember, though my details are different. We kissed for one, she kissed me first and then I kissed her back. I also saw her mostly naked and even spooned with her under the covers for about thirty seconds, bolting at the moment where she turned her body, opened her legs, and began to unzip my pants. And after she fell asleep, I found her purse and took the fare plus a healthy tip. I'm not ashamed of the memory, but I wouldn't brag over it either.

"But you're giving me too much credit. We had a dispatcher and we had to account for our whereabouts. It'd have been pretty much impossible for any cab driver to ... you know, sleep with you in those circumstances."

"We both know that's not exactly true, but really, what I credit is that you took care of me, you got me to bed safely and in those days that didn't always happen. After Benny told me you were that Five-O, I thought I should thank you."

"It's weird," I say, feeling an urge to confess something in return. "Two weeks ago, I didn't know anybody. If someone forced me to make a list of the ten people closest to me in the town I lived in, I wouldn't even know the last names of half of them."

"Sometimes that sounds OK to me."

"Not knowing anyone?"

"When Benny does what he does, I've gotten to like it. I used to bitch at him about it, but after a while I stopped because I like being alone and I like sleeping alone. Like having the bed all to myself. Maybe not all the time, but once in a while."

"That's the rub. Your 'once in a while.' It's different if it's full-time."

We let it rest there until the clouds ignite and fade and it becomes more night than day. I'm not going to leave her side until she tells me to. I'll just sit here next to this woman who has a place not only in my present but in my past. The scant six inches of space between our knees feels charged, like my entire body is leaning towards her and all I need to do to fall is to not resist. It's been so long, a moment like this: to sit with a woman, knees touching. Nothing more than that, just knee to knee with a friendly stranger for a few minutes. As if she senses it, she suggests I go talk to Benny on the CB radio set-up they use to communicate when he's in his room. She says he might come out or he might not, leads me inside to the CB handset, and disappears.

I have to laugh because as odd as this is, it's very familiar, talking to Cliff over a radio. I try to recapture the tone of our old arguments, but it comes out nastier than I mean.

"Cliff, you insane dipshit. Get your ass out here and give me my fucking money."

Silence.

"One fart for yes, two for no." An old cab-joke.

"Who is it?" Cliff's reedy voice sounds shaky.

"Who is it, my ass, you fucking-well know who it is."

"My kids here?"

"No. Are you coming out?"

"That's not a good idea right now."

"Jesus Christ Cliff, get your fucking ass out here."

"Who is this?"

"Cliff. Seriously."

"What do you want?"

"I want my money, Cliff. I want to say 'hello'. I want to talk like normal human beings, you know, face to face."

"That's not a good idea right now."

"$15,000. How's that for a good idea right now?"

"Swim all you want in your little me-first capitalist pond, it ain't going to help."

"Pretty damn articulate when you need it, ain't you? Why would I take seriously some guy who locks himself in a lead-filled room for days at a time."

"You're supposed to take seriously the guy who has your $15,000."

There was a lot of speed around when we were both driving, mostly in the form of a white powder we snorted. It made everyone gabby, but Cliff's capacity for non-stop talk was unmatched. He'd alienated every driver who worked with him, which was why he was judiciously moved to late nights, where there were far fewer drivers to piss off. After a couple of months of delicate negotiations with him (the trick was to keep him from realizing we were negotiating), I managed to move all our conversations to the radio. No window to window, no meetings at Dunkin Donuts. After that, when he got worked up, I'd blare my stereo, turning it down at appropriate intervals and grunting "Yes", "Fucking A", and "I hear that", into the handset. We were both fine with it.

And soon, sitting on the other side of a locked door, talking to him over the radio, I'm again glad we're not face to face for the exact same reasons. His current obsession is the not-so-recent death of the expert who testified that flashes on the Waco video tape are FBI gunfire, which the Bureau continues to deny, meaning Benny not only has to explain a web of complicated and nebulous connections concerning the death, (he says murder), he first has to recap the entire Waco situation, including its links to Ruby Ridge and Oklahoma City. Listening to Cliff, it's like September eleventh never happened. He's only interested in home-grown terrors and feels the U.S. government is the most effective terrorist group in the world by such a wide gap, all others pale. I ask him why he's still obsessing on Waco when the world's exploding, and he says he's fighting for the soul of this country and doesn't give a rat's ass about "a few Bedouins and their bullshit."

"Nine-eleven was a grand dodge, a covering action so they could take out a little more of the slack, a little more of our freedom. It's like each time shit happens, we have to suck it in, give up more of this and more of that and each time, the mother-fuckers squeeze tighter until none of us can breathe."

There's a small break and I take it; I may not get another chance. I wanted to talk to Doreen about this, but right now, I'm ready to talk about something other than the nuances of his paranoia. "What's up with your kids?" I ask him.

"Say again?"

"Your kids?"

"Why are asking me about my kids?"

"Because I want to know what's up with them?"

"What's up with them? What does that mean?"

"What do you mean?"

"I mean, what do you mean? It didn't sound very friendly."

"I meant it friendly. I thought your kids seemed great."

A long silence. One lock clicked open, then the second, and Benny appears, squinting in the light of the hall. This is what he looked like when we drove cabs and his name was still Cliff, wearing sweatpants with long rips in them and t-shirts with cigarette holes and stains. He has a thick rope tied around his waist, the other end somewhere in the dark room behind him.

"Yeah," he says, smiling. "Yeah."

"The boy's yours? And the girl is someone else's? Is that right?"

"The other way around."

"Right, of course, she's the youngest, she's yours. Stupid of me."

"But I don't think of it that way."

"Really? I mean, seriously? But you didn't raise him from the beginning?"

"No."

"How did you go about it?"

"I don't know. I just treated him like a human being. You know? They're around and I'm around, little fucking people occupying the same space I am for a relatively brief period of their lives. I'm not buying into some ownership jag about the kids, Dory isn't either. We're four independent humans living under one roof. The big difference between us and them is we've learned a lot more because we've lived longer. That's all. And I can't see any reason not to let them in on it, that way they can know what I know and they're free to learn more. Each generation gets a little smarter."

"But did he resent you in the beginning? Did you have to deal with a lot of bullshit?"

"It wasn't an easy situation. His dad and Dory were high school sweethearts and when it started going bad, he lost it and went out and shot some dumb kid outside a bar. That was some bad shit for a while. But he's a good boy. Smart."

"But just being around kids all the time?"

"In for a penny, my man. Besides, I like my kids."

"Well, OK."

There's a long silence and I realize we're done.

Doreen walks me to my truck I feel the urge to linger. "We talked about your kids," I say. "I wanted to know about kids."

"I bet."

"We should have a drink, you and me," I say quickly, then regret it. "I mean, Cliff's inside, the kids are gone, I just thought…"

"Benny," she says mildly.

"Right, sorry."

"I don't drink anymore."

"I wasn't saying anything. It's just weird to find out you had an effect on someone you didn't even know that I did. Makes me think about . . . you know, shit undone I guess."

"Undone?"

"Not done."

"Not done," she says slowly and looks at me in a way I'd forgotten existed, a complicated look, but suspicion is at the heart of it, some tiny sense of betrayal. An anonymous taxi driver helps her at a particularly low point in her life and now here he is back telling her about things "not done." What could be "not done" but the fucking? She seems so vulnerable, brittle even, and isn't that the way of it? There's always at least one more mask behind the façade, I should've realized anyone who could put up with Cliff, even this dialed-down version, must have a lot of issues herself.

"I don't know what that means," I say. "I guess I just wish that everything I remember about Santa Fe isn't linked to failure somehow."

"I see," she says blankly. It's time for me to go.

By the time I return to Bonnie and Jim's, it's completely dark out and their car is in the driveway. From the road, their house shows only a wall and the garage, you have to turn a corner to get to the front. I ring the bell and wait. It takes a long time I can hear them fumbling with the locks. The screen is locked. Then the door opens on Jim, who looks down, bends over and picks up my gift and note.

"What's this?" he says.

"I came by earlier and left it. I thought she'd have it by now."

"We go through the garage, not the front door."

"I guess I didn't know."

"Maybe you didn't want to know."

"Why wouldn't I want to know? Do you think I could give her the gift? Hi Bonnie," I say past Jim.

"It's late," he says, using a hostile tone.

"It'll only take a second."

"Jim," Bonnie says.

"She's in her room for the night," Jim insists.

"No I'm not." Cadence's voice, but since Jim won't open the screen door, I can't see her.

"I got your call too late last night to call back," I say to her. "I thought I'd come out and bring you a small gift."

"Jim!"

Jim opens the screen door and steps aside. Cadence is wearing matching pajamas with pine trees all over.

"Cute pajamas," I say, and she blushes. "I got you this."

"What's the note say?"

"Just that I stopped by and left this. I assumed you went in the front door."

"Sometimes we do."

"Open it, sweetheart," Bonnie says.

She opens it, straining to read the package in the low light. She slowly figures it out and I'm delighted to see she's delighted.

"I read about these," she says. "I wanted to get some, but I always forget to look."

"What is it, sweetie?" Bonnie says.

"Stars. For my ceiling. They stick. They glow in the dark, so when I turn off my light, I can see hundreds of stars."

"Stars?" Jim says.

We have a quick cup of herbal tea at the kitchen table, Bonnie, Cadence and I. Jim watches TV with the sound down. Cadence tells me what happened at school—some older boys snuck into the school's science lab before class and dressed up the full-size plastic skeleton with hat, sunglasses and burning cigarette—and she does it in that breathless kid way, like she's desperate she somehow won't get it all told. Jim unmutes and the entire room fills with the sounds of squealing tires and TV gunfire. It deadens her excitement; she understands this is Jim's way of trying to wind the evening down and get rid of me.

"You should be going to bed," Bonnie says.

"You could put your stars up tonight," I say.

"Yes," she says.

"Say goodnight to Henry."

"Goodnight Henry."

"Goodnight Cadence."

She kisses both her grandmother and grandfather, but there's no question of her and I doing anything other than saying goodnight.

When I'm alone with Bonnie and Jim, I invite all three of them to go out and eat with me tomorrow night, my treat.

"Oh Henry," Bonnie says, like she understands the futility of the suggestion.

"We just ate out tonight. We don't eat out two nights in a row. We don't do that," Jim says.

"But you could."

"We don't."

"But you could."

"But we don't."

"Henry," Bonnie says.

"What if just Cadence and I go," I say. It seems important to me that I not be denied. "I'll come get her, we'll go eat, then I'll bring her home."

"Henry," Bonnie says, like she's trying to pre-empt her husband from saying something harsh.

"You know she'd like it, I'd like it, and you two could have an evening to yourselves."

"We don't need an evening to ourselves," Jim says.

"Bonnie?"

"Jim?" She asks.

"I just don't see the point," he says.

"If not tomorrow night, how about the night after? All four of us could go then."

"We're not going," Jim says.

"I think it's a good idea," Bonnie says, then looks embarrassed. "The night after tomorrow. You should be here by 5."

"I can do that."

"I just don't see the point."

"It's settled, Jim," she says.

"I'll see you tomorrow."

"The night after," Bonnie says.

"Right."

On the way to my truck, I glance into Cadence's bedroom and she's there on her knees with the window flung open. "Well, hello," I say.

"Hi."

"How are the stars."

"I always wanted some."

"Good. That's good."

"I don't know what to call you."

"Call me? Like a name?"

"Yeah."

"Henry, I guess. What were you thinking?"

"I don't know. Jim says it doesn't matter."

"Jim doesn't know everything either," I say, and right away it's a mistake. She's taking it like I'm badmouthing Jim. "It matters to me, that's what I mean. Jim wouldn't know that it matters to me."

"I don't think of you as a Henry."

I can't help but laugh at way she blurts it out, halfway to an accusation. "Well let's figure it out."

"Hank?" she says.

Hank? No one's ever called me Hank. No one's ever even brought it up before. "Do you like Hank?" I say in as gentle a tone as I can muster. I really don't want anyone calling me Hank.

"Maybe, I'm not sure."

"No one's ever called me Hank. People think of me as a Henry."

"I don't."

"Well OK. So what do you want to call me?"

"I don't know."

"You could call me Dolan. That's my last name." I've been called Dolan a lot in my life and never minded it. When she was born, we put Cadence Dolan Leans on her birth certificate only because we thought Leans Dolan sounded clumsy, but we agreed she could choose either if she wanted when she was older. The mutual disappearing took care of that and whether she knows her real middle name or not, I shouldn't be the one to tell her. Not now.

"I know. Maybe."

"Or HD for Henry Dolan."

"Can I call you Hank?"

I knew this was coming. "If you want."

"Nobody calls me Cadence but you."

"Nobody calls me Hank but you."

Hank

I hadn't planned on approaching Doreen so soon (I want to think of her as Dory, it sounds warmer, more intimate, but that's Cliff's name for her), but on the drive towards Bonnie and Jim's place, I was swept into such a sense of urgency because there's really no telling when Cliff might emerge from his lead room and her kids return in a few days. She said he spent fifteen days in there one time, but that was clearly unusual, he might already be out right now. I might very well pull up and the two of them will be standing there, arm-in-arm.

When I arrive, the gate is once again unlocked, hopefully signaling that Cliff is still inside his room, and amazingly enough, Doreen is sitting outside on the steps just like she's been waiting for me. I wave, she slowly takes a great pull on a cigarette and smiles like I'm an associate whose name she's forgotten.

"Hey," I say over the roof of my truck.

"Hey back," she said.

"Why you sitting out here?"

"Benny hates the smell of cigarette smoke in the house."

"Well he's not here."

"No he isn't."

"Why not sit on the back porch?"

"I was. Heard you coming."

"You knew it was me?"

"I didn't know, but it wasn't hard to guess."

"You figured I'd come back?"

"Didn't think about it." I can feel it slipping away, my rationale for coming out here has never seemed thinner.

"I wanted to . . . well, you know . . ." I say, then tighten up. And think about tightening up, which only makes it worse. Soon, I'm officially floundering. It's been so long since I've had a conversation that matters.

"You wanted to . . .?" she says in a mock helpful tone, but in the circumstances, I'll take amiable derision over darker alternatives.

"I wanted to ask you if you'd go with me to pick up my daughter from school." This is better, strong enough that it will confuse her, and it does. "You said you owed me for those years ago, I just need to do it and I need help."

"A smaller person would point out that I held your head while you vomited and washed your face with a cloth."

"Not you though."

She smiles and her laugh lines appear, revealing a lived-in beauty. It's thrilling in its way.

"So that equals me letting you sit in my lap to warm up in my cab, do this and we'll be even for carrying you inside and putting you to bed."

Now she's looking right at me, really looking, and there's a theatrical element to it, she's all but announcing to me that the next few seconds will decide our fate, that she's going to look into my soul and pull out the real me. I laugh out loud.

"You're laughing," she says. She doesn't like it.

"You're just so focused all of a sudden, it was like Joan Crawford. I mean, come on."

"You come on," she says like a petulant child and for the first time, I think this is a huge mistake in a direction I hadn't fully considered.

"I'm sorry."

She concentrates on smoking her cigarette, less self-consciously this time. I laugh again.

"What now?"

"We're complete strangers, right? Absolutely, except I've been in bed with you; seen you naked; you've held my head while puking then washed my face; you made me breakfast; and now we're having our first fight. It's funny, right?"

"It's funny," she says, mustering all her cool, and this she gets exactly right to the point where I'm not sure how to take it.

"You should come with. It'll be fun. Like I said, I don't know you, you don't know me, and she doesn't know either of us."

"So you want me to . . . what?"

"Just ride with me. It's not far. I'll tell my kid you're an old friend, we'll drive her home, I'll drive you back. That simple."

By the crow, the Eldorado sub-division is only a couple of hills away, but it's longer snaking our way around. I realize I have no idea how Cadence gets home from school. Does she have friends she walks with? Does she ride a bike? Take a bus? Pulling up to the school, cars line both sides of the road, parents there to pick up their children. But Cadence lives half a mile from here at the most, surely she's allowed to get home on her own.

I park behind the last car and check the crowd. A group of women gather in a circle, some holding bright blue bottles of spring water, others sipping on cups of coffee. A man with a shaved head stands a few feet away, his back to them, furiously pulling on a cigarette. When a puff of smoke wafts over, two separate women dramatically wave their hands in front of them like they're being overcome by smoke, then the entire group glares.

"Uh oh," I say.

"What?" Doreen says.

"It's them."

"Them?"

"Bonnie and Jim."

"The grandparents? Show me, show me."

I point my arm, scooting over so we're touching. She tenses but doesn't move.

"That's them?"

"That's them."

She squints to see better. It's an adorable look on her, clutzy and vulnerable and sleepy-sexy and what's better, she knows it. She's doing it for me.

Jim sits as straight as a board in the driver's seat, staring ahead and gripping the steering wheel like he's driving in fast-moving traffic. Bonnie sits just as vertical, her hands on her lap. They look like the dummy passengers people in large cities use so they can drive in the car-pool lanes. I say this out loud.

"Do they ever talk to each other?" she asks, ignoring what I think is a witty observation.

"Well, yeah, sure, like anyone else who's been married for decades, except maybe not as much. I think Bonnie's upped her medications recently, she seemed better just a couple days ago. That's how they used to be years ago; they could sit for hours like that. It made Philips furious."

She wants to ask about Philips, but she pulls back. I can feel it in the car, the way the vibe shifts, like the fluttery wings of insects around your ears, a changing pressure. The kids pour out of a double-doorway and Doreen, and I get out of the car. We cross the road and walk within ten feet of Bonnie and Jim and still, neither of them looks anywhere but ahead. Cadence is in a large group of fifty other kids, I'm happy to see she's friendly with several children and waves with both hands to three girls who wave the same way back. It seems as though Doreen and I and Bonnie and Jim are frozen in place and only Cadence is moving. She spots her grandparents first, then she looks past them and sees the two of us. She stops, confused. Bonnie senses something and looks at her granddaughter, then follows where she's looking and sees us. She appears ready to cry. Jim stares at me blankly, though I think it's meant to be surly, then he re-grips the steering wheel and waits, like he's decided the best approach is to ignore this unpleasantness outside his window. Cadence waves at us, but not enthusiastically, before continuing for her grandparents' car. Doreen and I approach from the other side, with Bonnie and Jim in the middle, looking like passengers in an out-of-control car right before impact.

Cadence

I tell Bonnie and Jim that maybe I should go with him. I don't want to, I say, but he drove all the way out here. And he brought a friend. See. Her name is Doreen. But I don't really want to go. That's how you have to be with them sometimes. Jim goes into his room, and I hear the television. Bonnie feels for the tea kettle like she is blind, her hands touching their way across the counter onto the stove.

"It's OK," she says so I stand close to her. Then I leave. Hank and Doreen are standing by his truck and when I see them, I remember my notebook and have to run inside.

I sit between the two of them. Hank plays the radio low. Sometimes they talk to each other and sometimes to me. He gives me a Power Bar, then gives me two more and says they're for Bonnie and Jim. Or I can keep all three for myself. They tell me we're going to drop Doreen somewhere, that it'll just be Hank and me. For some reason, this scares me, but I can't think of what to say so I just say, "Why?"

"Well . . ." Hank says.

"Uhhhh . . ." Doreen says.

We drive on the highway in the opposite direction from town for a couple of miles and then get off and head down a road I've never been on before. It curves around before it becomes dirt. It crosses a shallow river—Doreen holds onto me when I lean out and watch our tires drive through water—and then some railroad tracks. I guess Doreen's decided she wants to come after all. I'm happy. We start to climb.

I'm not sure how he knows where to stop. There aren't any signs or even a place to pull over. He parks on the edge of the road, and we walk. Hank says there's a cabin he wants us to see. He says it's owned by the same people who own Eldorado where I live and it's open to anyone living there. I'm not sure why Bonnie and Jim never showed me this place. Except maybe because Jim doesn't go out much and Bonnie doesn't like to drive. Even when Bonnie and I go for breakfast, she makes Jim drive us. He sits in the car.

There's one spot where we have to climb rocks, it's kind of like a small cliff. I like that. It's shaped like the Grand Canyon, or another famous cliff and you can see what those places would look like, except a lot smaller. And to ants and bugs and spiders, it is like the Grand Canyon. Bigger even. Except bugs in the Grand Canyon wouldn't think that. If you know what I mean.

We walk on a trail for ten minutes and then Hank says, "There it is," and I see it. A real-looking cabin. I run up to it and look inside without going in. It is empty and the sun shines through in places but there is also a big fireplace and a loft to sleep in and there are beer cans on the floor. Hank asks about snakes, but Doreen says, "Not very likely." I let her go in first anyway.

On the other side of the cabin, there is another cliff. I stand on the edge. One more step and I'd fall all the way to the bottom. The highway is there too, but too far away to hear. It looks like a straight line cut into the ground that goes on forever. We sit on the edge with our feet hanging over. Doreen puts her hand on my shoulder when she talks. I like that. Then we decide to eat my Power Bars, all three of them.

Hank shows me how the land has fewer trees off in the distance, how it gets flat and bare. He says it's because the mountains and the areas around mountains get more rain so more trees can grow but further south, it is a lot drier, and trees can't grow so easily.

"I spent New Year's Eve up here once with, well, with . . . Philips." Hank looks at Doreen, then at me, like he's embarrassed. He always calls my mother by that name, and it never sounds right to me. I don't think I'd want to know someone with a name like that. I like Janie better. "With your mother. We came up with firewood and candles and incense and a blanket. It was snowing lightly, and I liked that, our footprints being fresh. We made promises and sang and chanted and at midnight, we went out to where we are right now and sat about here. You could hear gunshots going off, but they were far-far away and behind us. In the morning, the snow had erased our footprints and there was a single set of fresh coyote tracks. They came, circled the cabin once, then headed down the path," he says.

"A coyote. That's good luck," Doreen says.

"Not likely," Hank says. "Given all that happened after."

"How would you know?" she says. "You couldn't know that."

"That's right. Maybe it's in my future somewhere, waiting for me to catch up." Doreen looks at him funny when he says that. I tell them both I like coyotes, that my teacher says it's amazing that they're everywhere. Doreen tells a story about wolves and coyotes and about some ranchers who wanted to get rid of both. They set traps with food and got all the wolves, but they rarely caught coyotes. She said the coyotes learned fast not to step in the traps and they would dig the traps up, turn them over, and pee and poop on them. I giggled at this part, but later when I thought about it, I was amazed an animal would do that. Doreen says it proves animals have a sense of humor and I like that. I like how she said that. I wish I had my own name for her. She's not a Doreen, not to me.

"What could I call you?" I ask.

"You mean like a name?" she says. "Doreen. You've already said it."

"I know, but . . ."

"She's into names," Hank says.

"And you don't like Doreen?" she asks.

"I don't know." She smooths my hair and clears it from my forehead.

"Some people call me Dory."

"Dory," I say, trying it out.

"My daddy used to call me Reenie, what do you think of that?"

"Reenie," Hank says, like he likes it. It makes me like it too.

"Reenie," I say. "I like Reenie."

"Good."

It is getting dark on the way home and Hank pulls over and says, "time for the surprise now" and he takes a paper bag from behind the seat. It has sparklers in it. Reenie says why don't I lean over her, so I do. We light the sparklers right there in the truck and start driving.

"Out the window, out the window," he says.

"Faster," Reenie says.

I've never seen anything like it. The sparklers stream along the side of the truck; I can see the tail through the back window. Hank shakes his and it turns the streams of fire into squiggly lines, it fills both windows on his side, sparks popping and dying in the air around us. Then Reenie shakes hers and I shake mine and Reenie is laughing and then Hank is laughing and I'm laughing too because it's like we are driving through a tunnel of fire. It feels like the kind of dream I've always wanted to have.

And after they burn out, I shut my eyes and the same pattern in bright yellow imprints on the insides of my eyelids.

Hank drives slowly the closer we get to home. We sit in the driveway, no one moves or says anything.

"I don't think I like Hank the name." I'm not sure why I say this. Maybe because of the sparklers. I don't believe a Hank would think up the sparklers.

"How so?"

"I don't know. I just don't like it."

"Maybe he'll work into it," Reenie says. "Maybe he'll be a Hank in a week or a month."

"Maybe."

"If not Hank, what?" he says.

"I don't know. I'm still not sure about it, but I like the way she says Henry. I like the way you say it. It makes me feel different about it."

"Henry then," he says, like he's relieved.

When I get inside, Bonnie is sitting in the dark staring at a candle on the kitchen counter. Jim is in their room. I can hear him snoring. I've never seen her do this before, sit and stare at a candle like that. But it isn't so strange really. Not really.

Franny & The Dude

For a week after Sammy's death, the house was no more than a still life. The Dude lay in his bed; Franny escaped to the spare room, a place she'd spend the next three years; and Sonny never left his room. Footfalls sounded like rifle shots; the noise of people outside—children playing, neighbors cutting grass, car tires on pavement—was obscene, echoey, distant; their entire house was buried deep and permanently. After a week, The Dude went back to work, his wasn't the kind of job that tolerated long, unplanned absences no matter what the circumstances, but their lives didn't change. He'd come home after work without a word to his wife or his remaining son and lie in bed.

Franny lay in bed and listened to the sounds of the neighborhood and wondered what it might be like to hear the world so innocently again. And she listened to her son. Heard his thick, wet, choked-back tears, heard him throwing up into the bucket by the side of his bed. Understood the silence those first few days just after, while he waited in vain for her or for his father to come in and clean the sweat off his forehead, empty his bucket, give him ginger ale to wash away the taste. Heard his feet creaking down the hallway, stepping lightly. It was heartbreaking to hear him trying to be quiet and knowing he knew no one was coming. Heard the sound of liquid hitting liquid, the flush of the toilet, the running of the bathtub when he cleaned out his bucket, then the return of his footfalls and the metal squeak when he lay back down. In that first week, that first month, that first season, she came to know his small rituals as well as if she herself were there with him, comforting him. As if.

And if Franny often couldn't bear to be around anyone, The Dude actively avoided his remaining son. It had been horrifying at the funeral to see one son in the coffin and his exact image standing outside, looking dazed, a ghost finally free of the corporeal standing looking at his former body. Too horrible. And now when he looked at his remaining son, he saw the ghost, only the ghost.

The Dude took to spending long hours in the basement, he had tools down there and about a month into his grief, he decided he should make something, a chest of drawers maybe or a foot stool. Turn the tragic into the positive. But he didn't know how to make a chest of drawers and the process of going out and buying the right wood in the right measurements for a footstool was too much for him. Being in the bright lights of department stores, hardware stores, grocery stores was like being tortured; his head throbbed, and he needed sunglasses against the light and even in sunglasses and a hat, he felt so visible, as if everyone knew and was judging him. Sometimes everything in this new life—music on the radio, TV commercials, the way neighbors looked at him after he'd turned away—felt like an accusation. Especially the presence and absence of his son.

So he sat on a stool in the dim light of a single bulb clipped over his worktable and he picked around with his tools, putting pieces of wood into the vise, then turning it until the wood creaked and split. Once he'd found a very dry chunk on the floor—he couldn't remember where it had come from—and when he'd put it in the vise, it had disintegrated, almost exploded, into wood dust. That was good, the closest thing to fun he'd had in over a month. But he couldn't find any more like it and when he tried to explain it to his wife, she looked at him like he had completely lost it.

Sonny ended up missing the entire school year. Franny stayed home with him, Arthur went to work, then came home. It was like that every day. Friends and family called in the beginning, her sister flew in for a week, his family was around. No one knew what to say, but it seemed to Franny they wanted to say, "You're lucky, you still have the other twin." It seemed perverse to Franny with people acting like Sammy was an extra, a bonus thrown in at the last moment, an identical child created to be knocked off should the situation arise. As if their grief should be less because they really had less than two; identical twins are somehow less, one person split into two, not quite a half person each but not a whole one either. Like people were thinking, OK, so now you have what everyone else has. A tragedy, yes, but Sammy's death was something to 'get past'.

Family and friends agreed it must be awful for Sonny who was barely ten years old. He had nothing but time and besides, kids are resilient.

"Mark my words," Irene said to Arthur; reported later to Franny because he found the idea comforting. "Five years from now, he'll be a regular teenager worrying about girls and getting his driver's license."

How can she say five years like it's five days? How can she? Franny thought. *Is she out of her fucking mind?* Then she said it out loud and The Dude actually winced leaning away from her like he'd been slapped and feared another.

"That's not the way to take it," Arthur said. "That's not right, taking it like that. It's not how it was meant."

Franny walked away from him. Just left him standing there, a tactic she'd discovered about a month ago and one which still seemed to surprise and wound Arthur every time she did it, though she was also convinced he was relieved by her absence. *Five years! The gall, the ignorance and from two people who spent a lot of time around the twins, one of them his god-damned father!* Sometimes it seemed to Franny she was the only person (other than Sonny) in the world who remembered the boys had been twins. With Sammy gone, there was no trace of "them" left. She understood now better than before that there'd been three little creatures living in their house—Sammy, Sonny and "the twins". Two of the three were now gone. Not half the tragedy but double. More than double.

It was never clear to Franny what The Dude thought about all of this. He'd always been the kind of man you had to pry feelings out of, the important ones anyway. She had no energy for that. And he wasn't around all that much, he was either at work, in the garage or in his basement. His silence, his absence, only reinforced Franny's growing sense nothing she might do mattered anyway. Maybe if they had turned to each other, they could have found a way to approach their sad lonely son. But they didn't, they couldn't; the pain of the first two months wasn't just the loss of a son, it was the loss of a time when every part of life was less burdensome, less exhausting. Now the only moments light and free were a few micro-seconds in the morning—before they pulled themselves to full consciousness and remembered.

Sometimes Franny walked through the house and heard her husband talking in the basement, not to himself but to his dead son, she supposed. It sounded crazy and she couldn't help but think he never talked to Sammy like that when he was alive. She knew such thoughts were not only unfair, they didn't help, but she had no energy to blunt them. Then she'd go upstairs, and Sonny would be crying quietly in his bed, and she knew what right would be; it would be to go to her husband and kiss him and hold him. Go to her son and wrap her arms and legs around him until he fell into a deep sleep.

Franny knew all right, but she didn't do it. She thought of it constantly, but never got past the thinking, going to her own bed or drawing a scalding bath and setting her turntable to play the same Elvis record over and over, the volume cranked all the way. She might spend a couple of hours, refreshing the water as often as she could, the entire room so steamy and dripping her tears were swallowed up in the scale of it. She could pretend she wasn't sobbing, but simply drenched. Most glorious of all were a few tiny moments each day when she'd close her eyes and conjure the saturated blues and whites and greens of the Yellowstone sky, brushing up against a time when a new universe was forming before her eyes, her universe. Maybe it all had been a cruel illusion, but she liked to think it was her world and she'd simply lost it and she'd find it again someday. It was what kept her going.

That first Thanksgiving as a family of three had gone better than expected, largely because The Dude took a new approach, treating the family get-together as a chance to step outside of the world that had been thrust upon them. When the three of them arrived, Sonny was as dutiful and silent as always. He'd always had so much personality when he and his brother were together, they lived large and loud. This version of Sonny shuffled sideways, as if trying to always show everyone a thin profile, and sank into sofas and chairs, folding into himself until he was barely there.

Franny felt wobbly and weak at the mere thought of interacting with a group of happy people and wasn't even sure she could walk from the car to the house. But The Dude took her arm—he'd been drinking—and greeted his sister warmly and he put his hands all over Sonny, like he was showing everyone how strong he was, how loving a father he could be. At the time, Franny hated him for it, for pretending nothing had changed. But for days after, she came to realize she'd felt lighter at Thanksgiving, less burdened. She started to look forward to Christmas. When Arthur began drinking in the morning while still opening presents, she didn't mind. It loosened him up and he was more The Dude when he was a little drunk. She didn't care about the driving, sometimes she imagined an accident; death would be wonderful but even a good maiming might help; give them all something else to concentrate on; an actual physical pain that could be treated logically, step by step. It couldn't be more unbearable than this life. It couldn't.

So they arrived and she watched while Arthur played The Dude which was how she thought about it now, as a part he had largely abandoned. He shook hands and hugged his sister, he swung Aaron around and threw the football in the snowy yard; he sat with the kids, his large, bony knees knocking up against the card table. He laughed at jokes and sculpted his mashed potatoes to look like an upturned butt, making the children (except Sonny) giggle.

After a while, he began spilling his drink. The Dude got sloppy when he drank, he'd become all elbows and trailing hands, knocking glasses over or turning too quickly and sweeping a hanging picture off the wall with his shoulder.

"I'm sorry," Franny said.

"Why be sorry?" his sister Irene said.

"Don't be," Eddie her husband said.

"I don't think it's bad," Franny said.

"Not at all," Irene said.

"You two have been through so much."

"It can't hurt. It might help."

It was Sonny Franny worried about. He barely existed at these family gatherings. He was so submissive, never speaking up, sitting with his hands on his lap, he wouldn't even take food if Franny didn't spoon it out for him, if Irene and Eddie didn't insist that he eat. And then he would but so slowly, each bite was an ordeal. Exhaustion ruled his life. And if his cousin Aaron, three years older, came looking for him, Sonny followed him the way a prisoner might trail a guard. Left on his own, he'd sit in front of the television for hours and hours.

After dinner, The Dude resumed drinking heavily. The large meal had cut into his buzz, and he worked to get it back. Every single thing he did seemed transparent to Franny. Sometimes that was a comfort and sometimes a provocation. Losing a child made parts of her life feel like she was forever surrounded by barren leaves and dead plants, but she was also aware in ways she'd never been before. Emotions hung in the air like smoke caught in the light. No doubt Arthur had his own reasons for staying away from her—and her reasons, too, were complicated—but a lot of why she avoided him was because he glowed with a confused hatred, a disgust at a way of life that had been forced upon him, even a resentment of Sonny. She couldn't stand to be around that. If she did, she'd end up hating him completely and absolutely. Looking at him closely was too much like looking at her own reflection.

So that Christmas, when Arthur started dancing to music in the living room, she knew it was just a matter of time before he found Sonny and tried to make him dance. And she knew this time he was much drunker, as drunk as she'd ever seen him, and she could feel his anger and she wanted to run, leave the room, go upstairs into the spare bedroom and lock the door. Or to the car where she could let the motor run with the car radio playing full blast, her own secret activity, which she did when driving alone.

The Dude grabbed hold of Sonny, but he slipped out of his grasp and flopped back on the couch.

"Arthur," Franny said as a warning, but she knew it wouldn't work. Couldn't he feel the whole room against him? How thick could a man be, with his sister and her husband watching, their arms folded, waiting for the worst? That was their family now, they always waited for the worst. Or maybe it was only her.

"Frances!" The Dude said, mustering every bit of drunken contempt he could.

"Artie," Irene said, using a name only she was allowed to use but this time, he flashed a look of such active malice she actually backed away. Eddie saw and stepped forward, but The Dude held his hands up smiling and went over to his son.

"I'm going to dance with my boy." Sonny sat there like he always did. He wouldn't look at his father. Franny loved him so much at that moment—people say you always love your kids and it's true enough, she thought, but mostly because no feeling human being could consider an alternative—but there were times when he'd look a certain way, he'd hold his shoulders in, his knees together, trying to make the smallest ripple in this world, that she wanted to stand up to The Dude, put her hand on his chest and scream "No!", drag her remaining son to his bed and put him under the covers and wrap her arms around him because that was what parents did for children in trouble. Dancing? Not that, not now.

"Come on, Kiddo," The Dude's voice boomed.

"He's just tired Artie," Irene said.

"Why don't you . . ." he said with such vehemence, Irene backed away. He pulled his son up as easily as a child might pick up a cloth doll, and with a similar lack of care. He smashed Sonny to his chest and never noticed the way the boy turned his head so he wouldn't have to smell his father's breath; the way he pushed against his father's chest as if he could get away from the embrace.

God, Franny thought, God. His arms aren't long enough. He's trying to push away but Arthur won't notice because his arms aren't fucking long enough.

The Dude spun him around, like a parody of a western hoe-down with The Dude the cowboy and Sonny the girl except his feet didn't come close to touching. The Dude laughed and whispered in Sonny's ear and laughed again and Franny couldn't tell if it was unimaginable cruelty or if it was a loving father saying what a loving father might say to his son.

It happened fast; there was no hope of stopping what was about to happen.

"Fine, Kiddo," The Dude said, loud enough for everyone to hear, and Franny looked, and she could feel Irene and Eddie look too and Aaron moved in from the corner of her eye—a considerate boy who cared about his cousin, who missed his other cousin, who'd get between Sonny and any oncoming harm if he could. The Dude let him go; just opened his arms and with Sonny pushing off, he sprang free and hung in space a long moment, parallel to the floor, as if purposely positioning himself for maximum impact. He landed solidly, squarely on his back; his head slapped hard against the oak floor. Franny heard a whoosh, the sound, she realized later, of all the air being pushed out of his lungs.

People froze. The Dude stood with a stupid, drunken grin on his face; a face Franny saw for years and years, a face that came, over time, to represent a lot more. Sonny lay motionless on the ground, his eyes—perversely, Franny thought—open; one arm cocked crookedly in the air, his mouth stretched wide as if in the throes of a silent scream. Later, Franny came to think of this as both a gift and a curse; circumstances perfectly aligning themselves to show her a moment she could never have visualized. When she replayed this in her mind, she saw Sonny, but her voice screamed "Sammy" right before he hit the floor.

Doreen

When I drop Doreen at her house, we sit in my truck for over an hour talking and if it's obvious that for whatever reason, we're two people who aren't ready to leave each other's presence, it's not easy. We're both in the peculiar position of knowing the worst there is to know about each other without knowing much else. She drank and fucked around, and it got to be more than she could handle. I lost my wife and my child, and I fully deserve the blame for that. But past that, I'm beginning to understand the ways she's still damaged and, though this may be a bit of the desperate romantic in me, I think she's seeing through to places in me no one's seen in years and years. There is no talk of "us" in any literal way and quite possibly not in an implicit one either, we talk around it or by it and while it's possible that "it" has parked itself on the end of the hood of my truck and is slowly working its way toward us, it's just as likely that such a concept as "us" has never occurred to her. After all, what has she done wrong? Sat in a truck and talked to a friend of her husband's? Planned a rare night out free from her children and her man (yes, she's raised the notion of going into town for a quick drink and I've agreed)?

Still, what is so extraordinary is how right and complex it feels from the start, we're not just telling each other what we want to hear. I rightly note that Cliff ("Benny," she says with a testiness I find glorious) is more than a little out of his mind and that surely she needs relief from his relentless paranoid energy ("You have no idea," she says, then refuses to elaborate, which I take as a further sign of the healthiness of our budding infatuation, we're not school children here, pushing each other on the playground as a way to hide that we like each other, we're fully functioning adults with adult problems all our own. No need to go into them.) and she points out that re-approaching an abandoned child is a lifetime's worth of work and that not only have I barely started, I have to be careful not to "derail" my forward momentum.

We even talk about Benny, which thrills me since it appears the old Cliff isn't nearly as gone as it first seemed. Like me and our fellow cab drivers before her, it isn't just his king-sized rants that exhaust her, his total spent collapse into soppy sentimentality afterwards has become just as distasteful. He'll drag her to bed and fold into the fetal position, forcing her to wrap her arms and legs around him, beg her to whisper to him the way his mother used to and rock him to sleep. I try to subtly suggest Cliff and I were never really friends, more like work acquaintances, that his presence as my "friend" has no bearing on whatever might and might not be happening here between the two of us. I touch her bare arm lightly, offhandedly, and she takes it like we do this all the time. As delighted as I am with this, I know my desire to scoot over and kiss her is best left not acted upon. She opens the truck door and gets out.

She walks all the way to her door, then stops and takes a couple steps towards me.

"We'll have a drink," she says, like she's answering a question.

"Let's."

She suggests a place I've never heard of and insists on meeting me there a bit later, rejecting my suggestion I simply follow her into town. She says she has to make some calls first.

From the moment I arrive at the bar, I'm off-balance. There are no signs or even a light to mark it, I eventually locate the building by the cluster of cars and chained bicycles out front. It's at the end of Industrial Road in an area with no other nighttime retail property around, just a stone's throw from the cab company offices. Doreen's way of reminding me of Cliff? And the building itself is a half-moon tube with corrugated metal sheeting all around, basic Quonset hut construction. Of course the door is locked, and I have to knock and answer some pointed questions, making for a miserable first few minutes as I fumble trying to remember Doreen's (Cliff's) last name. Turns out it's not really a bar, but more of a social club lacking a liquor license, which is why they screen at the door.

Inside is not like the exterior, it is well-lit with a bar cleverly and stylishly designed out of steel I-beams and a small Japanese white sand garden in the middle with tables set around it. The building is long, and the back end fades into blackness. Everyone sits up front, though it's easy to imagine they might light up the rear part for dancing. It's a younger crowd, I see a lot of tattoos, unnatural hair colors and faces full of metal. One boy with a mohawk wheels a unicycle from table to table, taking drink orders. The music is a bluegrass-ambient mix I'd never heard before, though against all odds, it works. I've been here almost twenty minutes now and Doreen has yet to show and my own natural paranoia kicks in. Surely, she knows what it's like to gain access to this place, is this why she sent me ahead? Some sort of test? Or worse, a way to get rid of me? If she no longer drinks, how does she even know about this place? I settle uncomfortably at a table and keep my eyes on the door. After maybe ten minutes, a man with wild hair and a ZZ Top beard waves me over.

"Ray Teal," he says, shaking my hand with a vice-like grip and holding my eyes in what could be considered a challenging fashion. "Dory's running late so she called me to hang with you a few."

"You know Doreen?"

He raises a single eyebrow as if to slyly mock the stupidity of my question. He's smaller than me but not by much and he has an oversized-elbows-and-knees kind of ranginess to him that, when coupled with his tight T-shirt and squeezed fists, suggests someone who doesn't need much provocation to get right into it. It doesn't help that with his wild facial hair, he's unreadable.

"Henry Dolan."

It takes me some time to get it. He keeps making cryptic remarks, the crux of which seems to be I'm missing something. My only clue is his name, which does sound familiar.

Ray Teal was an old western character actor, most famous for playing the bumbling sheriff on Bonanza. *Who else would know that? Who else would use that as a clue?* Then I get it.

There'd been a fellow cab driver years ago who knew every western ever made and liked to argue that the basketball played in the late sixties, early seventies NBA was far superior to any other decade. He had a special love for Jerry West and Pete Maravich.

We had many a spirited talk late night when we'd be the only two cab drivers working. Like Cliff, he had a bug up his ass about the government, seemingly with more reason (he'd spent a year or so in jail for dodging the draft), and there were rumors he was quick with his fists and even carried a gun on occasion, but I never saw any of that. He was a trained acupuncturist and was bitter about having to drive a cab to survive. He had insane stories about living for months on end deep in the Pecos Wilderness in the late sixties as a way of avoiding the draft.

"Eloy McIntire," I say, shaking his hand a second time. "Good to see you."

"So you finally get it and I'm suddenly Eloy and we're all friends?" he says, grinning widely. "I'm supposed to slobber all

over you because you figured it out? Well, Brav-fucking-O."
Strangers could be put off by the force of Eloy's delivery—I
remember that about him—but I can tell he's glad to see me. That's
the way he talks to his friends.

"Oh come on, I gave you my fucking name, plus if you know
Doreen, then you know Cliff . . ."

"Benny," he says. "He likes Benny."

"I've heard. So you know Benny?"

"Small town, son, there are no coincidences in Santa Fe, just a
lot of people who know a lot of other people."

"I didn't have all that fucking hair to hide behind either."

"I got it before you got it, end of story, you buzz cut, fuck-up-a-
wet-dream mother-fucker. I should've known nothing's changed."

"It's always that way with guys like you. You suck one dick, and
suddenly for the rest of your life you're a cock-sucker."

"You're a cocksucker whether you suck dick or not."

"Not you. You suck dick because you suck dick."

He waves over the roving bartender, signaling it is over.

"I was surprised when Dory called with your name, I remembered you as a total recluse. You didn't even like to sit window-to-
window on the late shift. Always over the radio was Henry's
motto," he says.

This is true. Listening to Cliff rage on in person had convinced
me the meeting of cabs in some dark parking lot was to be avoided
at all costs. It was much easier to ignore him when he was simply a
voice coming out of a speaker. When Eloy came on the scene, I kept
the same approach. "I figured you were wrapped up in existential
combat, valiantly battling the karmic forces unleashed by decades
of fucking up. Either that or you were a pill head who passed out
every night."

"Little bit of this, little bit of that. I was working on it. Still am. In theory, anyway. I've identified the problem and I'm stumbling on, though the correct route to take to get there isn't nearly as obvious as it seemed in the brochures. If you get my drift. And I came to have a drink with Doreen. Shit, if I'd known there was any chance of running into a low-life like you . . ." All conversation in the room dropped to a whisper and the music stopped just for a moment. "Place got quiet."

"I do get your drift. You ain't exactly Einstein, if you get mine. And it's only quiet for now. Later on, we'll get a second, third and maybe fourth wave and they'll fire up the dance floor and the vibe will elevate. By midnight, the back end will be bouncing, and it'll sound like someone's opened up your head and is jackhammering inside. By one, I'll have some pixie stick backed into the corner, explaining the facts of life to her."

"The facts of life according to a Texas shit-kicker? Thank fuck-ing Christ I'll be drunk by then." I feel elevated by the pixie stick comment and its accompanying implication that Eloy and Doreen's relationship might not extend beyond friendship. Why would it? He's a friend of Cliff's, she asked him to come along because she's not sure about me, like the equivalent of the fifteen-year-old who insists her best friend go with on a date with the boy she likes. It's possible, if not completely plausible.

"I know the way. Let me be your guide. What do we want to drink?"

I tell him, my only rule on drinking: never mix boozes. It's saved me considerable physical pain, though I've never had the same troubled, ambivalent relationship with alcohol that runs through much of the rest of my family. Opinions vary as to why. Philips loved getting drunk out, disliked drinking at home except with dinner and at parties and was often bitter about my unwillingness to go bar-hopping nightly. She claimed I was simple, that it was straight avoidance of a most boring sort, the kind of uncomplicated psychological explanation in which only a lesser intellect would engage. My parents drank so I avoid it. My argument back was she was making herself the dullard by assuming there was a pat psychological basis for it, maybe I just don't crave the taste and don't like to put up with the crowds. If someone asked me now, I'd say it's all self-medication and we're all doing it and that some people need to know why, and others don't. What's the difference? That truth is absolute? That it will set you free? Spare me. My mother drinks and who's she hurting? Me? Not anymore, not for decades now. Herself? It helps ease her way through the world, how's that a bad thing?

Besides, I'm all for it in the right circumstance and this strikes me as a prime moment, a chance to clear the pipes of all that pot I've been smoking and get out of my own head. We decide on straight Tequila with limes and salt.

"Cheers," Eloy says, and we touch glasses. He almost immediately launches into, basically, the story of his own life, which is fine with me. I'm not a talkative drunk, but I don't mind listening. He was born in San Antonio, the child of a Spanish mother from an upper class, Mexico City family and an Irish father, who ended up in Texas via Brooklyn, where he was involved in organizing dock workers. His father got knee-capped after some union dispute and limped his way out of New York, looking for a safe, sunny place to settle.

Eloy has a way with a story. He uses his Texas twang for dramatic effect and is able to switch the tenor of his voice to sound like a hopeless hayseed, a conniving southern con man, a stuffy

Tex-Mex oil baron, or a Mexican bandito, depending upon the demands of the moment. The details are all interesting, even fascinating—tales of intrigues, both political (his father couldn't stay out of local politics and was beaten up in Texas too) and familial (his mother came from a very wealthy, over-educated old money family specializing in screwing with each other as often as possible)—but I still lost the basic drift relatively quickly. I was beginning to worry over whether Doreen would even show. Eloy's commitment to literal truth is tenuous anyway—he told these same stories differently years ago—the real honesty is in the music of his storytelling.

I keep a steady eye on the door as he talks. The scene picks up as promised, mostly guys in groups and scruffy-looking couples, many with dogs in tow. A teenager in the corner appears to be acting out all parts of a violent movie gun battle to his friends, using his hands as pistols and conversely, flopping backwards, wrenching his body and clutching his chest in a fair approximation of a movie gunshot victim. And the inevitable hacky sack game is threatening to break out—a bald kid with one of those booger nose-rings, studs on either side, has the damn sack out and is ready to toss it—and two of the dogs tear up and down the length of the space. Their energy in turn invigorates the people around them. It's a mixed crowd, with about two parts skater-mountain-biker kids to one part scruffy thirty- and forty-somethings like Eloy and I (though Eloy is certainly a fifty-something by now). Young and old kind of all look the same; overwhelmingly, the two hair styles in the room run to long and tangled or buzzed close (women and men). Eloy and I could be the poster children for the two looks.

Now he is into his draft-dodging stories, and I feel the first blushes of the tequila. It's put me in a loose mood, alive to the moment in a way I rarely am anymore. Promise is in the air, and I only hope Doreen shows before my enthusiasm fades. He's already described in loving detail "the most beautiful mountain meadow you've ever seen" and how to get there and now he's gone lost in the minutiae of describing a day in the life while living in a tent in the wilderness. First the fine points of hanging food on a bear proof rope, and now he's going on about the amazing "shit ditch" he'd dug. When he becomes overly enthusiastic describing the superior qualities of using sand to wipe your ass ("Free yourself from the paper jungle, baby"), including how to avoid potential trouble ("Two words—sand burrs") I interrupt and ask after a bathroom, figuring the time has come for a quick walk-thru of the place. He points to the dark end.

"Our toilets are on the delicate side, so be gentle. If you're just pissing, we encourage you to step through the back door and take care of business the way man has for. . ."

"I got it, E. Back in a minute."

I wind my way around small clutches of people standing and drinking, dancing. Outside seems a grand idea, until I step out there and see three other guys pissing in random directions. I'm not good under pressure and have had more than one bladder-popping panic situation at large sporting or concert events where I was expected to share a piss trough with forty other men and couldn't perform to anyone's satisfaction. It is one of those (I say) rare situations when thinking too much only causes more trouble. I keep shuffling away from the growing crowd, and with the damned metal door banging every time someone goes in or out, my concentration is in tatters. I've unzipped and zipped three times and there still isn't enough space. I continue moving down the side of the building, away from the voices, looking for a quiet place to try again. Clouds have rolled in, blocking the moon, and it is very dark. Finally, I relax, and all those clenched tubes open up. The sound of piss hitting the ground spurs me on, until I reach that wonderful point where I'm free and nothing short of an alien invasion can stop what is now inevitable. It's going to be all right.

"Who's that there?" a woman's voice explodes out of the near darkness, forcing me into a panic spasm in mid-stream, sending me into a stumble forward where I simultaneously have to try to keep from falling (successfully) and not to piss on myself (not so, I splash a line of urine across my jeans). The saucer has landed.

"You yelled that!" I say, outraged.

"Just a little yell. I heard you but you didn't hear me."

"Doreen?"

"Loy sent me to look for you. I thought it'd be funny."

"If you could see my face, you'd know how hard I'm laughing," I say, trying for droll, but getting derailed by my annoyance at the interruption of services. There is no chance now, not with Doreen fifteen feet away. It doesn't matter how dark it is. While I contemplate my next move, I'm amazed to hear her unzip her pants and a moment later, she's peeing like there's no tomorrow. It sounds like a gate has been opened.

"I've heard quieter waterfalls."

"Me too," she says. "I guess I had to go."

"You think?"

"I'm sensing you have a complicated relationship to emptying your bladder in public."

"You're sensing? Based on . . .?"

"You're a dribbler for one."

"I refuse to provide an answer for that."

"And we're eighty feet from the back door where you started, you're actually in the unofficial women's area. I can only assume you kept moving away because you were spooked by other pissers. It's a common problem."

"See, I'd say you take the fact that you won't stop talking about pissing and combine it with the truth that you just dropped your pants and peed like a race-horse in front of someone you met two days ago, albeit one who can't actually see you, makes me think you have your own set of problems."

"You think?" Mocking me. "Or maybe I just pee because I have to pee and can't see any point in getting fucked up about it. Let's go this way."

"Back's closer." I stop and she walks into me in the dark. I touch her shoulder in a friendly way, the way a long-time boyfriend might, and I'm delighted she takes it in the same spirit. It would be so easy to lean forward and kiss her sweetly on her bare neck, here where I can't see her face to gauge her mood.

"We need to take care of something first."

"OK." I follow her to the front, crossing into the light and heading towards a grouping of cars and trucks parked up in the shadow of a row of cedar trees. Someone's standing there, the end of his cigarette glows bright, then dies. It's Eloy next to a mid-60s Ford Fairlane grinning and smoking.

"Big Five-O comes to town and the town takes notice," he says, and I'm beginning to understand. "The dopehead part anyway."

"None of that," Doreen says in a scold. "Let's do this and get it over with. Two minutes, we're done."

"Aye, aye, Cap'n," he says and pops his trunk, shooting bright light in all directions.

"Dammit! Don't be a fuck-up."

He drops the trunk, the light, then the dark scrambles every-thing and it takes a moment for their shapes to reappear.

"You got it, Cap'n," he says, doing a pretty good fawning pirate. "Light be gone, sis', no fuck-up be me." Eloy's drunker than I thought and an edge of playful menace has creeped into what he says. I'm not sure how seriously I should take it. Doreen seems unconcerned, she's all efficiency and cool, walking two cars over to her SUV and opening the back door, deftly reaching through and pinning the button so the overhead light doesn't go on, then digging into a laundry basket full of clothes and coming out with my package. Just like that, like she's done this a hundred times before. Of course she has, of course! She's been with Cliff eight years, surely this isn't her first drug deal. Maybe she was even central to their operation at some point. But not anymore, not in a long time. And this is what I've brought back into her life.

When she shuts the door, she has to let go of the button and the dome light flashes a moment and my heart with it. I hadn't realized how tense I've become. Anyone could pull in or come out and see us and even if it's unlikely they'd notice or even care, there is a chance. A cop turning around or doing rounds, a citizen with a bug up his ass and a cell phone, a chance.

She walks and now Eloy's with the program, smoothly opening the trunk just enough for her to toss it in, then slamming it shut.

"Outstanding," she says, clearly pleased. "The money?"

"In the trunk," Eloy says.

"Outstanding," I say dryly.

"No one's talking to you," Eloy says, somewhere between joke and threat.

"Let's get it open," Doreen says, once again grim and deter-mined.

They return inside, leaving me to take care of the money. It's in a manila envelope—thinner than I would've thought—folded tight with rubber bands. It looks exactly like what it is. I tell myself to play it cool, make a plan as to where I want to put the money, and then do it. I fumble about, try splitting it and putting it in three pants pockets before deciding I'll lock it in the glove compartment. Of course a car pulls in, its sweeping headlights catching me at the exact moment when I stuff the envelope into the compartment and try to bang it shut with my fist. Finally, I manage to clear enough space for the envelope, lock the glove compartment and the truck, and head back to the bar.

Inside, the mood takes some time to settle. Eloy is talkative, determined to recount some of our collective cab driving experi-ences and I'm willing enough, but Doreen seems wrapped in a funk, sipping her club soda through a straw and eyeing the door, and I'm not sure of the best way to play this. If she leaves now, I have to face the notion the only reason she came tonight, indeed her rationale for suggesting meeting in the first place, was to complete our business and get me out of her and her husband's lives. So I join with Eloy, and we regale her with some of our best cab stories.

There was the "screaming banshee from hell" handicapped girl off Calle Lorca who made the driver lift her into the back seat ("The bitch stank too," Eloy says. I'm pleased to see Doreen flinch at that word, and I try to catch her eye to show my shared out-rage), store her wheelchair in the trunk, and drive her three blocks to an all-night diner, where the ritual had to be performed in reverse. Or the guy on Camino Carlos Rey who'd always start out asking if you were wearing underwear and would end up offering a blow job ("For free, like that might be the final convincer."). We recount surly drunks and known pukers, women with incontinent pets, famous writers gone to booze, an aging actress who gave hundred dollar tips in the form of a check, then called the company the next morning to put a stop on them, the woman who was with Jackson Pollack when he died, the retired Sioux actor who had a way with a John Ford story.

For Doreen's amusement (she appears to be warming to the moment), we act out a couple of the more infamous incidents in our mutual cab company history, including the time Eloy and I joined forces to get a completely passed out drunken yuppie woman home. Evangelos had called and they were willing to pay up front, but they wanted nothing to do with moving her. I took her under the arms, Eloy grabbed her feet and we carried her to the back seat of my cab where we sat her up leaning against one door.

"She was decked out—I mean not flamboyantly but expensive shit."

"Like leather pants . . ."

"And a linen Armani blouse . . ."

"A couple grand's worth of clothes and shoes."

"The problem was, we didn't know where she lived, though the bouncer thought it was somewhere in the South Capital area."

"She was gone . . ."

"A fucking vegetable, ready for slicing and dicing. Since I'm driving, I figure it's only fair Eloy go into her pants and get her wallet. Except the dumb fuck refused."

"Fuck no. Fuck no. Sure as shit she would've woken up in the morning with a King Hell headache and no memory of the night before other than that the cab driver groped her. Screw that."

"You can see our dilemma," I say to Doreen, who smiles and pulls out a cigarette. "Every time I turned a corner, her body would kind of lean out into space, and then I'd straighten out and she'd whip back into the door, her head smacking the window."

"It thwacked," Eloy says, vigorously shaking his head in agreement. "She thwacked."

"Every time."

"That's a lovely story, boys," she says, setting her cigarette pack on the table with a lighter on top, like she's staying awhile, which energizes me.

"There's more."

"I bet."

"She managed to mumble out a street but no number, so we finally... uh, well, you know ..."

"No I guess I don't."

"We left her in a safe place," Eloy says.

"A safe place?"

"Face down on some cushy grass so she wouldn't do a John Bonham."

"What were our choices? We didn't tell the dumb fucking broad to drink herself silly." Doreen flashes Eloy a hard stare, then sees me watching her and turns away. Bad times, she said earlier, nights when she didn't get safely to her own bed. The end of a long slide in the wrong direction. She's been that woman more than a few times, that's what that look was about. And maybe Eloy was there to see some of it, maybe he really did understand the full implication of what he just said and if he did, I know there's some deeper psycho-drama going on between them. Maybe not current, but still touchy in the right situation.

"I'm gonna go drain the snake," Eloy says, standing. "You coming?"

"Me?" I ask.

"No, I'm talking to that other bald fuckhead. Yeah, fucking you."

"As fine an offer as that is, I think I'll pass."

"Suit yourself." We watch Eloy make his way to the back, weaving through the groups of people and looking unsteady. Right before he passes out of the light, a young guy wearing a Rasta hat bounces away from some friends laughing, showing a dance move, and runs into Eloy, who pushes him hard and then stands, fists clenched, daring the guy to respond.

"Some piece of work that one," I say.

"Some something."

"You and Eloy?"

"What do you mean?"

"I don't know. You two? I'm not stupid."

"I never said you were. And I don't see how any part of my life is your business."

"You're right. It's not."

"Well OK then."

"Well OK then."

"You're one of those men who gets through life by agreeing with everyone, that way you can pretend nothing gets under your skin."

I want to say, "You, you got under my skin," but it's too corny and probably not even true and definitely wrong for this moment.

"I don't agree with that," is what I say instead.

"Funny," but she likes the answer.

"Can I ask you something that is at least partly my business?"

She shrugs, which is a disappointment. I thought we were on the verge of banter.

"Would you have even come out tonight if there wasn't a drug deal to be made?"

"It's your dope. I didn't ask you to show up at my door and drop a felony right into the middle of my family."

"Which isn't an answer."

"It is. Just not the one you want to hear."

"I just want to hear the truth," I say.

"Oh come on," she says. "'Just the truth?' Talk about your Joan Crawford moments."

"That *was* my Joan Crawford moment, wasn't it?"

"Henry the Agreer."

"Sounds like an English king."

"One of the ones you never read about." She downs the rest of her seltzer like it's a whiskey, lights another cigarette, and waves the unicycle waiter over. She's finally having fun.

"So you remember that Joan Crawford comment?"

"It's not every day I get compared to a dead diva who also happens to be a famously monstrous bitch."

"Glad I could help."

"Is that what you call it?"

It happens off-handedly, seemingly always the way these things happen. I just put my hand on her leg, it feels natural and obvious, and when she puts her hand over mine, I'm not surprised.

I look at her, but she refuses to hold my eyes, knowing that would lead to the inevitable kiss, but we're holding hands, rubbing thumb against thumb, and now I'm tracing the lines on her palm by feel, writing out words there—*This is so nice*—until she pulls her hand away and I think I've gone over some line, and maybe I have, but at the same time, Eloy returns large and loud and in a fine mood, launching into the story about the infamous night the cab company's main dispatcher, Tommy-Niner, had a chemical melt-down over the air.

I join in because I'm confused as to what just happened – did she stop because it was too much or because she saw Eloy coming? Together, we act it out, Tommy's singing, then crying into the microphone, his refusal to acknowledge drivers trying to get him on the radio, how he'd send four drivers to the same address and ignore other calls for hours.

At one point, he started reading the sports page (Tommy was a nut about the Minnesota Vikings) over the radio like it was poetry, stopping in mid-word and beginning again on the next line. He told jokes (We remember one each, both bar jokes: "A horse walks into a bar and the bartender says, 'Hey pal, why the long face?'" and "A priest, a rabbi and a duck walk into a bar and the bartender looks at them and says, 'What is this? A joke?'"), he cranked *Exile on Main Street* right into the microphone and between songs, you could hear him banging into furniture and drumming (rather well) on top of the metal filing cabinets to "Turd on the Run."

All of this Eloy and I agree upon and we have good time telling it. Our mood seems infectious, and Doreen settles back, lights yet another cigarette, and orders another club soda when the waiter wheels by.

Trouble comes when we try to recount what happened when a handful of drivers returned to headquarters to see what was what. I don't remember Eloy being there at all, and he is just as adamant I wasn't. He claims it was the same night a helicopter searched the ground from above with a powerful spotlight all over the cab company neighborhood and they had to restrain Tommy from running outside and shooting at the cops with his Ruger 9 mm. But that's not right and I tell him so. Tommy had a gun that night, yes, but it was a .22 single action pistol with one of those Old West-type gun belts. He was practicing his fast draw, which alarmed everyone until he showed us it wasn't loaded. And the helicopter was "in the fucking winter"—I may have been a little more forceful here than necessary—Tommy's freak-out was at the height of the summer season.

"No, no, no!" Eloy yells this. "He had his Ruger and Tommy was out of his fucking mind paranoid about the copter. It took four guys to keep him from going outside and shooting at it. You weren't there, you wouldn't fucking know."

I know this isn't a good direction to go with this guy, but I'm worked up and not in the mood to back down.

"The .22 *was* a Ruger and I was the first guy to show up," I say. "You're the one who wasn't fucking there!" Eloy stands up fast, knocking over Doreen's club soda. He's had roughly twice the number of tequila shots I've had. He looks pissed enough to take a swing at me and with the alcohol and all, I have no problem standing up and getting in his face. Doreen simply swivels in her chair and leaves without a word, taking coat and purse, which has a calming effect on me. I smile at Eloy as a healing gesture and he smiles back, then pops me in the face, splitting my lip, bloodying my nose and sending me and the chair ass backwards, where, as luck would have it, the unicycle waiter is wheeling by. His momentum actually reverses mine and sends me into my own table which I paw at desperately, trying to break my fall. He flies across another table, sending beer and booze in all directions, and somehow, my leg kicks out, nailing Eloy right in the groin, because when I look up from the floor, he's also on the floor, holding himself and rocking and moaning.

It's here that I simply gather myself, stand on shaky legs, and walk out. I can feel the blood running down my chin and people are staring, but it all happened so fast, no one makes any move to stop me, even though the unicycle waiter took the hardest tumble of all.

Outside, the full moon has cleared the clouds and the ground is speckled a milky white. My lip throbs and I banged the underside of my elbow pretty hard, but I actually landed quite softly. I see right away that Doreen's SUV is gone and I'm beginning to wobble my way to my truck when the door flies open with a loud metal bang and Eloy appears, bent over, eyes wild, spittle flying.

"You fucking piece of shit," he yells. "You kicked me in the goddamned balls."

"You punched me first, shithead."

"I'll fuck you up."

"You punched me!"

"You lie."

He's calming down. I position myself in the light so he can see my face. He's dropped to one knee, still clenched from the kick, and has to twist his neck to see.

"I did that?"

"Shit yes, with no warning."

"That *is* the way to hit someone. Done it myself a few times."

"You just did it, not more than three minutes ago."

"Goddamn man, I'm sorry. I'm a little tore up."

"You think?"

"Don't start with me."

I help Eloy stand and drag him to his Fairlane. He's right on the verge of passing out—I recognize the signs—so I put him in the back seat, face down, and I find his keys in his pocket and hide them in the glove compartment. No way should this guy try to drive home, not with eleven pounds of my pot in his trunk. There's a gun in there, a Colt .357, which makes me want to get out of there as fast as I can, but I take the time to write him a quick note telling him where his keys are, and leave it taped to the inside of his car window.

On the way to Motel 6, I run smack into a police drunken driving roadblock near the corner of Siler and Cerrillos and have to talk my way through. It's not a problem, I'm polite and even thank them for the "fine job you're doing", but when I get to the motel, I'm all charged up from the night's events and for the third night in a row, manage to stay awake until dawn and sleep fitfully well into the afternoon. I wake to someone knocking and for one, awful thrashing moment, I think it's Cadence come to see where I've been. Light floods in when I open the door, causing pain to shoot behind my eyes. It's Doreen.

"Stinks in here," she says.

"I'll come out, give me a moment." I slam the door shut harder than I mean to and feel around for clothes.

Outside, I turn my face from the sunlight, and she doesn't see the bruising until I've settled against her vehicle, which seems even bigger than it did yesterday.

"Oh man, look at you. Bet it hurts."

"Don't go overboard with your expressions of concern."

"OK. Hope it hurts. How's that?"

"You drive a fucking tank," I say, because I'm not feeling up to more banter. I spent a lot of last night alternating between regret we hadn't found a way to that kiss and wondering over her motives. Maybe she was really there just to complete a drug deal. But she's here now.

"That'd make Benny so happy," she says, smiling. "The notion of me driving a tank."

She looks light and freshly scrubbed with her hair pulled back, wearing baggy yoga-type pants and a loose-fitting t-shirt.

"Eloy got a little frisky last night."

"Been there before. I know when to exit."

"It's OK, I was being an idiot too."

"Yes, you were. E called this morning; said he thinks he might've fucked up. I said, 'Fucked up covers a lot' and he said, 'Punched Henry. He kicked me in the balls, but I punched first.' and I said, 'You're both idiots.' He agreed."

"Sounds like a consensus. Least he remembers. That kick was a complete accident."

"Not to him. He's convinced you were punching and kicking like a pro on your way down, 'like fucking Gregory Peck stabbing that whale while he's drowning.' He's very impressed."

"You look nice this morning. Fresh." I remember her last night, the way she was smoking and drinking the seltzer water, like she was a seasoned bar fly settling into a familiar routine. On her way to another drunken evening. I like the morning version of Doreen better.

"It's almost two, but thanks."

The sun warms me and the two of us are content leaning against her truck. She has beautiful feet, I'm not sure I've seen them before, but today she's wearing sandals and her feet are thin and delicate with long toes and deeply tanned skin.

"What are your plans for the money?"

The money? I'd forgotten the money! It is still in my glove compartment; my truck keys are inside.

"I just remembered it. Shit, fifteen grand."

"Twelve. You said you'd take twelve."

"Twelve is OK," I say carefully, feeling a twinge of paranoia and then immediately feeling guilty over it. "Twelve is fine."

"I should thank you. We did manage to make a nice piece of change out of that, I don't want you to think we don't appreciate it."

"We could go out tonight. A simple dinner, the Zia or maybe Dave's."

"I believe you're eating dinner with your daughter tonight." Shit, Cadence. I'd completely forgotten Cadence. Would I have forgotten right on past the time to leave? This is a disturbing thought.

"I meant after . . ."

"Don't even try," she says, but her tone is light, playful. Our shoulders are only inches apart and we're feeling well-disposed towards each other again.

"Tell me about how you managed to leave this beautiful town and not come back for so long," she says, like she's trying to shift the mood, though whether it's to pull me out or dissuade me from amorous thoughts, I'm not sure. It seems a bold question, given what she knows of my history here, but once I realize I can fall back on my wittiest "doomed romanticism" tales of my marriage, I warm to it. I present my marriage as both a grand passion and a destined tragedy of suitably imposing proportions, using a practiced style bordering on schtick, which I figure I can get away with since we've only recently met. She laughs and grows somber at the appropriate moments, and I generally avoid getting too specific about what was involved in abandoning my child.

She counters with her own stories of how she met Cliff (in a bar) and the condition he was in (hyped up on speed, but talkative and sweet) and the state she was in (emotionally fragile having had an abortion a couple weeks before, drinking at noon, dating one pissed-off guy after another). She says she always fears meeting people from "the old days" who she remembers fondly (apparently, I qualify) because she thinks the resultant disappointment will reveal something small and mean in herself. I take this as a positive, since it implies that she feels less than disappointment in meeting the present-day version of me.

"About last night, you know . . ."

"Ssssh," she says and then leans over, and we kiss, deeply but only for a moment before she breaks it off. "That's what you were going to ask, isn't it? That's what you wanted."

"I don't know. I was hoping we both did."

She gets into her truck, shuts the door and starts it up. "There won't be any more nights like last night," she says.

"What about mornings like this one?" She smiles and I touch her bare shoulder and let my hand run the length of her arm as she slowly pulls out, twisting fingers together for one beautiful moment. I wish I had told her everything.

After she leaves, I find myself thinking about the words she'd used—small and mean—and wonder if what I'd done to my own daughter qualifies. I run upstairs to my room and dial Doreen's cell phone number. She only left a few minutes ago.

"It's me." I can hear the low rustling of a small crowd in the background, she's probably at Downtown Subscription.

"Who? I can't hear you."

"Henry."

"Henry."

"Henry."

"What's up Henry?"

"What I was going to say doesn't make sense now."

"OK."

"You know how that is." I can feel it slipping away, our connection, which felt special just a few minutes before, when I was ready to confess all to her. Now I'm simply another voice in the phone, a part of the overall white noise of a person's life and seen from here, not a very big part at that.

"We'll talk soon," I say.

"Okay," she says, clearly confused.

"I'm sorry."

"It's OK."

We leave it there. I still feel like I haven't presented a full, candid portrait of who I am and what I did eight years before and I fear that moment in the future when she finds out what small and mean really is.

Cadence

When I come home from school, Bonnie says she needs to talk to me, so I go to my room and change clothes and when I return, she's chopping vegetables and won't look at me. Like she's forgotten.

"Bonnie," I say and she says, "Just let me finish this." So I go back to my room and when I come back a second time, Jim's in their room with the door closed and she's on the couch, staring at the TV which is turned off. I can tell she's sad. I know she sometimes wishes I'd call her Grandma; Jim still likes me calling him Jim but I'm not sure with her. But it wasn't me who started that. I would have been happy to call her Grandma years ago, she was the one who insisted. Now I can't change.

"I meant to tell you," she says.

"Tell me what?"

"He's coming out."

"When?"

"Tonight. He asked if he could take you to dinner."

"Tonight?"

"Yes."

"And we're going to eat here or out?"

"Out."

"Just him and me?"

"Yes."

"When did he call?"

"He asked yesterday when he stopped by."

"You knew yesterday?"

"Yes."

"Why didn't you say something?"

She turns her head away like she does, and I know it's no use so I sit on the couch next to her and she puts her arm around me. She likes this, the two of us in front of the TV even if it's not on. I think it's strange she's only telling me now about the dinner. Later, she's in a better mood and we go to my room and she sits on my bed while I put on my jeans and pick a shirt. I wear the jeans with a wide cuff and one of Jim's old dress shirts hanging loose. She doesn't like it, but I like to wear my basketball shoes when I'm going to a restaurant.

"Do you have your list with you?" she asks.

"Got it." Jim's in his room, the door is cracked. It's almost five o'clock.

"I hope he shows up," Bonnie says. Why did she say that?

"I'm going to go outside and wait."

"Take a jacket." Bonnie disappears inside their room and closes the door, but she comes right back out. I'm happy she came back. "You have a good time, sweetheart."

"I will."

I wait in front, leaning against our car. He pulls up and gets out.

"Hi . . ."

"Hello." He's just the biggest man, it surprises me every time. "How are the stars?

"I always wanted some." I did.

In his truck on the way to town, I push in the music tape in his tape player.

"Is that OK?"

"Sure. You won't like it much."

He's right. It sounds like machines going all at once, and it's so loud and fast, I'm grateful when he turns it low. He sees my face and laughs.

"I told you."

"What is that?"

"It's called *The Jesus Lizard*."

"That's the band?"

"Yeah."

"I've never heard music like that."

"Sometimes I like it. Sometimes I'm in a mood."

"What does that mean? Do you know?"

"Jesus Lizard?" I nod. "It's a lizard somewhere in the world, I'm not sure where. It's pretty light and has wide flat feet and if it runs fast enough, it can actually run across the surface of water without sinking. That's why they call it that, because Jesus could walk on water."

It's not until we're in town stopped at a light that I really look at him and when I do, I start crying. I can't help myself his lip is all puffed up with a black scar. It looks ugly, like it hurt. Hurts.

"What's wrong?" he says.

"Your fa-face," I say, trying to stop.

"You're just noticing now? I just thought you were being considerate, not drawing attention to my clumsiness."

"Someone hit you." He turns his face out of the light so I can't see it.

"Yeah, someone did."

"Why?"

"You'd have to ask him."

"I don't know who he is." He looks at me now, glancing back and forth, then he smiles and even though I don't know why he's smiling, I smile too.

"We'll have a good dinner," he says.

He's a much better driver than Jim. I feel safe, like I don't have to always look forward to make sure we're not driving off the road. And he drives a lot faster and that's fun.

We drive through town towards Tesuque. I wish it wasn't so dark. I like it out here with the red canyons and the mountains, but Bonnie and Jim hardly ever come this way. We drive past the Indian casino and turn into the lot of a restaurant called Gabriel's. The parking lot isn't very crowded. We get out and he looks over the hood at me and I don't like it. How it makes him look, like he's not someone I want to know. Every time I see his face, I remember again and each time, I don't like it.

"So am I still Henry today?"

"I don't know." The face changes everything, though now that he brings it up, I'm not sure it was right even before I saw his face. He doesn't always seem like a Henry to me.

In the restaurant, I'm telling him about a dream I had where I was in a big city on top of a roof and there were white tornadoes in every direction, and I couldn't tell if they were coming my way but there were so many of them, one of them had to be. And then I looked at him with his puffy face and the ugly black scar on his lip and I don't want to talk to him. Maybe it's because earlier I'd been thinking about the way Mrs. Garcia had acted about him and what she said. And about why someone might punch him. I hold my notebook against my chest with both arms, right there in the restaurant. He's a stranger and I'm miles and miles from home. I think I could cry. I can feel him watching me, staring, but I keep my head down. I watch his hands; he traces an invisible pattern on the palm of one hand with the thumb of the other.

"You're a beautiful child," he says.

"Thank you," I say quietly. I don't believe him. I don't.

"Do people say they can see your mother in you?"

"No." Bonnie doesn't talk about that, not like that.

"Did she ever say anything about me? About seeing me in you?"

"No, I don't know. Maybe."

"Sometimes?"

I don't know why he keeps asking me. I'm right here, he can see me himself.

When the menus come, he reads every food listed and explains what each is. I start to forget about feeling bad.

"What's tripe? It sounds made up."

"It's the stomach lining of a cow."

"People eat that?"

"Some."

"Do you?"

"I have, but I don't really like it."

I have what I always have at Mexican restaurants – nachos and one chicken taco and one bean taco with red chile. Henry has vegetarian tamales, done "Christmas" which I've never heard before. It means both red and green chile. He lets me taste it; it's way too hot for me. Bonnie and Jim don't like hot food, so I'm not used to it. He doesn't eat any of my nachos but has a margarita with salt. Sometimes Bonnie will get a frozen one, but she always makes a big deal about them leaving off the salt. He tells me about all the work that goes into making a tamale. I don't like watching him eat with his puffy mouth, but it's easy to look away.

When we go out to the parking lot, he keeps walking past his truck, towards the dark.

"Let's take a quick walk," he says. "Philips and I used to take this little trail every time we ate here. Kind of worked off the food."

"Janie," I say. I don't like the name he uses, and I don't think it's right.

"What?"

"Janie."

He smiles. "OK."

We walk to the back end of the parking lot where there are some dry-looking hills. Close up, there's a path leading out between the two hills. It's really dark. He takes my hand. The path climbs and he lets me go first, often putting his hand on my back and pushing. It's pretty steep and the ground is loose. I slip three times and each time he takes my arm and helps me. He's very strong. When we get near the top, he reaches past me and grabs a tree and pulls the both of us to the top.

He's breathing hard. There's a place where the hilltop is washed away, it's like a cliff and we sit there, side by side with our legs hanging over. I'm not sure what to say to him. I have my notebook in my bag, but it is too dark to read and I don't want to ask any of those questions anyway. I'm not sure I ever do. Being out here with him, I could ask a lot of different questions. And I'm nervous. I'm not sure I like this. Bonnie and Jim would never do this, they've never even taken me to this restaurant. I wonder what they'll ask me when I get home. And what will I say?

"What grade are you in?' he says. I'm shocked he doesn't know.

"Fourth."

"Are you good in school? What are your best subjects?"

"English. I like reading and writing. I like gym class because I'm not stuck inside all the time."

"You like gym class?" he says, like he's surprised.

"I don't always like having to sit in one spot all day long."

"I hear that," he says. A car pulls into the lot and a big family gets out and goes in the restaurant. There are a lot of them.

"They just keep coming, don't they?" he says. It takes me awhile, but I get what he means, and I laugh. Bonnie and Jim never make me laugh on purpose. Henry seems funny.

"Your mother and I . . . Janie and I lived in this basement apartment next to a parking garage before we were married. If you climbed to the top, you got this great view of the whole campus and of the town across the river. Being up here reminds me. Sometimes we'd go up there when storms rolled in, you could see the entire sky full of lightning. We both liked the lightning."

"I like lightning."

"One night we saw a tornado. We couldn't actually see the funnel cloud, but we could see the trail of sparks as it cut through power lines."

I don't know what to say. I'm not upset, I like his stories, but I'm not used to talking so much. I like it, but sometimes I can't keep up.

"See Los Alamos? It looks so close."

"I know Los Alamos."

"Have you been there?"

I haven't, but I don't want to tell him that.

It's a lot scarier going down. I can tell he's scared too. He goes first and tries to help me, but twice, he slides out of my reach and I have to turn on my stomach and crawl backwards to him. It's scary enough I wish we hadn't climbed up there, no matter what I could see.

I'm better once we get in his truck and buckle up and I decide to ask him one of my questions. He kept saying at dinner I should ask him a question. I asked him to describe the best summer vacation Janie and him, ever took. He keeps glancing at me and looking away and I think he's not going to answer me. But then he does.

"I can tell you about a vacation the three of us took."

"The three of us?"

"You, your mother and I."

"The three of us? On a vacation?"

"You were really young. I was going to save telling it for the right time. Maybe this is it."

"You and me and my mother?" I've never heard of this.

"Yep."

"I've never heard of this."

"You wouldn't of. Bonnie and Jim didn't know much about it, just that we took off for a few days. When we came back, they didn't care enough to ask us about it."

"It's not that," I say.

"Maybe this isn't the right time."

"It is, it is the right time. You can't say it and then not tell me." He can't.

"I know, I know."

"You can't."

"Here goes, best I can remember. Like I said, you were young, maybe a year and a half, but you were walking like a champ and talking in a gurgly sort of way . . ."

"What does that mean? Gurgly?"

"You called me Clem."

"Clem? I called you Clem?"

"Sounded like."

"Clem," I say, trying it out. "Did I call her anything?"

"Yeah, but it was never that clear what. Sounded a little bit like Pips, except sometimes it was more like Plips. Cady, Clem and Plips," he says, like he thinks it's funny.

"I don't believe you."

"Sometimes we weren't sure you were talking at all, sometimes we thought you were burping."

"Henry!" He's making this up and I decide I'm not going to listen to him anymore, except he still hasn't told me anything.

"Go on," I say, making sure he knows I'm not happy about it.

"We drove west, cutting through Jemez Springs on our way towards Farmington. South to Chaco Canyon, then back north past Shiprock, on to Canyon de Chelly, Monument Valley and southern Utah. All but the Grand Canyon."

"I've been to the Grand Canyon."

"You told me. You've been to all the places I just mentioned too. That's what I'm telling you about."

"OK," is all I can think of to say. I don't remember any of this and if I don't remember it, how am I supposed to know what to say about it?

"We ended up in Southern Utah, this guy running the motel told us there were some Anasazi ruins along this cliff face. Basically untouched because to get to the cliff, you had to cross a swinging bridge over the San Juan river and then walk a couple of miles in. The bridge was kind of scary because it was high and bounced and swayed. I had you in one of those child backpacks, you were always sneezing and tickling the back of my neck. Sometimes you pulled my hair."

"You carried me?" I don't like the sound of that.

"You were two feet tall."

"Still . . ."

"We had to walk through these stands of thorny trees and once in a while, we might see a cow looking at us through the underbrush but if we stepped any closer, they'd stop chewing and stare and then run."

"Bonnie told me cows were like big, slow dogs, that you can just walk up to them and rub their heads and pat their backs, that they like it."

"Those are eastern cows that live in fenced pens. She's probably never seen cows like these living on the open range, a long way from anyone who could protect them. No wonder they're skittish."

"She would've told me if she knew." Sometimes I think Henry doesn't like Bonnie and Jim, the way he talks about them.

"I know that, I know she would've. Can I go on?"

I shake my head "yes".

"We found the ruins tucked up in the corner of a huge amphitheater cave where rock met dirt. The motel guy was right, there were two complete rooms, roofs and all, and a lot of vertical walls still standing. It was flat up top, and you could see how people lived, where they walked and how they built their houses."

"But where were the people? You just walked into their houses?"

"These were ruins, sweetie, the Anasazi Indians lived there, hundreds of years ago, but they're long gone."

"Like at Bandelier?"

"You've been to Bandelier?"

"Our school took us."

"Exactly like that. We crawled into one of the rooms, it was tiny, I took up half of it myself, but inside was just right. It was warm and the way the square doorway framed the land beyond was perfect with the thorny trees to the left, a bend of the river right and the tops of three skyscraper mesas poking above a distant hill. We didn't want to leave, we had food and plenty of water, so we didn't. We spent the night. We zipped our jackets together and put you in the front facing out so you could breathe, Janie's arms around you and my arms around both of you.

"On the way out in the morning, we found a tarantula on a sunny rock and you tried to pick it up and when it took off, you lurched after it, your little arms out. The spider wasn't as enthusiastic about being friends as you were, imagine that."

"What does 'lurched' mean?"

"Stumbled?"

"I lurched?"

"You weren't even two years old. You're kind of touchy, anyone ever told you that?"

"I'm not touchy!" He laughs.

"I like spiders, I like tarantulas," I say to prove I'm not touchy. "I made Jim pull off the road once when we saw one, except it turned out to be smashed."

"I'm sorry."

"It's OK. I cried at the time. See, I'm not touchy."

"I see that now."

"What else?"

"We crossed the bridge back, got into our car, and drove home."

"That's all?"

"It was the end of the trip."

After Mrs. Garcia read my question about the best summer vacation, she showed me a book in the library that had maps of every country in the world. It was huge and she had to pull it down for me and open it up. She showed me Paris, France and London,

England. We looked at Greece and Cairo, Egypt and Hawaii and Rio de Janeiro and Berlin, Germany. We found Niagara Falls in Canada and Miami, Florida and New Orleans, Louisiana and Yellowstone National Park. But I never ever looked at the maps for Utah or Arizona and I never in a hundred years thought their best vacation would be with me. How could I know that? No one told me. Bonnie and Jim should've told me, except Henry said he didn't tell them. But they knew I went with, they knew that, and they should've told me. They should've told me about Henry and that Philips was Janie, they should've told. It makes me wonder what else I don't know about.

April Snowstorm

Through fall and winter, the Dolan residence remained a ghost house—the grass uncut, the yard full of leaves, the snow unplowed. Going to work, Arthur learned to gun his engine and drive his car through the piled-up snow in his driveway, nearly ramming oncoming cars on several occasions. Some mornings, he'd get dressed, eat breakfast, drink his coffee, start his car, then sit there listening to the radio. After a while, he'd turn off the car and come back inside and go to bed, sleeping through noon.

Once Franny put the request in writing, no one in the school district bothered them again about Sonny's absences. Eddie and Irene and Aaron quit coming by; The Dude was never friendly when they were over; he either stayed in his basement pounding like he did on pieces of wood or sawing this and that—making . . . finishing, nothing—or he'd stomp around like an animal defending its turf, barely tolerating another's presence. And he was drinking every night and all weekend too. A part of Franny was appalled, but she was no longer capable of making others less uneasy.

It was on a bitter night in a cold house with the windows rattling in their frames that Franny finally went to Sonny's bed. She'd begun waking after midnight and going outside where she'd sit on the porch surrounded by cold and snow. The world at three in the morning was strange and gray and muted. The regular world had turned against her and being awake at this hour was a small relief. She liked listening to the steady whine of the interstate two miles away, trucks upshifting, then winding out their big engines, she thought of them as birds migrating south, heading to a place she'd never been, a better place, she assumed. One night, she was lost in a memory of her long-dead father, a man born before the Civil War who was almost seventy years old at her birth. He carried her high on his shoulders through a Tennessee tobacco field, singing as he walked, and she felt like a giant, the rows of tobacco plants far below her. This was her only memory of her father and she wasn't completely sure it was even real and she began to cry and when she looked up, Sonny was standing there. Her heart stopped. She squeezed her eyes shut and counted to ten and opened them. He was still there. Not a ghost or a vision or an accusation, just her son. Then he turned like it might be the last thing he did on earth.

"Baby?" she said so quietly she wasn't sure he even heard her. But he stopped.

"I'm sorry," he said.

"No."

He opened his mouth, but no words came out. Then he disappeared.

She found him in Sammy's bed where he slept most nights. He looked tiny and alone, shrunk by half with one pillow under and one over his head, face against the wall, his feet drawn in and tucked under the covers. She lay next to him and put her knees in behind his, her face into the back of his hair and smelled him. He never moved that night, but she came back the next and the next and after a time, she realized he was making room on his bed for her. This was how they spent their nights.

They were together all day too. He watched her soap operas with her and soon knew the characters and plot lines better than she did. Sometimes she'd get confused and Sonny always knew what was going on and he'd patiently explain it to her, and she felt a secret thrill listening to his voice after him being silent for so long. When they were twins, they were forever and always a mystery. But Sammy's death revealed Sonny to be exactly what he was, a frightened ten-year-old boy and what was worse, she understood he always had been. That was a special kind of guilt; not that she could have prevented Sammy's death but that she had a part in making a lot of his short life anxious. She'd allowed anger and perplexity to exist in their house, she'd never made the proper effort to make sure she and Arthur understood their sons, and her husband still wasn't making the effort and she was still allowing it. The kind of guilt that was not just about a failure in the past but about an ongoing moment-to-moment breakdown; a failure of will re-consummated every second of her waking life.

Sonny had never seen anything like the early April snowstorm they got that year. It started around noon, wet and heavy, right on the cusp of rain. It fell in straight streams of huge flakes and was still falling by night fall, more than an inch an hour.

Sonny ignored it at first the way he ignored anything that nudged his thoughts towards his brother, but it was too extraordinary an event and after watching it from the kitchen window, he gave in, bundled up, and ran outside to see.

It was deep and heavy and took serious effort to move through, but he found he liked pushing himself after sitting for so long. Fifty feet out into the yard, the lights from the house were no more than fuzzy blobs with yellow halos and he could clear a snowball's worth of snow off his hair every few minutes. All he could hear was the fat flakes humming in the air all around him. When a door banged shut somewhere, he recognized it as such, but had no idea in what direction.

Then a shadow crossed the blob of light and he saw the outline of his father. Sonny froze.

The Dude had come outside. Dim light flashed everywhere and nowhere, and he wondered if it was him, if he wasn't having some sort of attack. Is that what Sammy saw right before he collapsed, did the whole world start sparking along the edges? Then it happened again, and he knew it was lightning. Lightning in a snowstorm! The thunder rumbled like it was underground. His father high-stepped his way towards him.

"What are you doing out here, Kiddo?" The Dude said.

"Nothing."

"You ever see this? Lightning in a snowstorm?"

"No. Not that I remember," Sonny said, confused, because his father had experienced all the same snowstorms he had. It was always awkward between them anymore and Sonny had learned how to angle his body like he was stepping aside, making it easier for his father to keep walking. They'd become like acquaintances passing each other on the street, practical strangers. When his father spoke, Sonny was so surprised he was still there, he jumped.

"TV said this is lake effect snow. That if you go ten miles in any direction, it's dry," his father said.

"We're like an island."

"Exactly like. Hey Kiddo, you want to do something?" The Dude said.

"OK. I mean sure."

"Come on."

His father stepped confidently out into the heart of the snow-storm and Sonny followed, struggling to keep up with his long strides. They made their way first to the bluff, shaking heavily bent trees as they walked. The evergreens, their tips bent all the way over under at least a foot of heavy, wet snow, would spring up with what seemed like a palpable sigh of relief, becoming a ragged green scar in the puffy white landscape. The hardwoods were like pencil drawings of trees, with only a sliver of wood showing. Even the power lines had a thick frosting of snow precariously balanced on top.

"This is like a postcard," The Dude said. "Like something I remember from years ago." Sonny thought he knew what his father meant, it felt like a memory even as it was happening.

They crossed over yards and through woods and walked the deserted road, eventually making their way to the golf course, right to the edge of the deepest valley. By then, it felt like they'd trekked to the Arctic Circle together. Both of them were warm and sweaty, feeling loose and ready.

"I got an idea," The Dude said. Sonny couldn't remember his father being like this. Ever. Like he was really having fun. They made a basketball-sized snowball together and began rolling it. Within a few feet, it was huge, making every push an extreme effort and clearing a swath of green on the golf course as it picked up more snow with each rotation. They pushed it to the edge of the hill. By then, it came up to The Dude's waist, to Sonny's chin.

"One more good push." The Dude got to his knees for better leverage while Sonny slapped at the surface, packing and rounding it. Slowly, slowly, they pushed until the weight tilted out and the ball rolled on its own.

"Run with it!" The Dude said, then tore off down the hill after it. Sonny followed. He could feel his momentum going forward—he was falling—but he didn't care because the whole world was a soft, white cushion. He threw himself on top of the snowball and it rolled him under headfirst, leaving him sunken in a Sonny impression in the snow. The Dude tried to stop and lost his feet, sliding to the bottom. He crawled his way back up to his son.

"You OK?" The stricken look on his father's face should have made him cry; it would have any other time. But not tonight. He was in a soft hole being slowly buried from above and nothing could harm him here.

"Yep."

"Move your arms and legs. Make sure." Sonny did. He was fine.

When they got to the top of the hill, they made snow angels. Sonny threw a few snowballs, but the falling snow was so thick, the joy of the ball in flight was lost. Bouncing smudges of light floated along the horizon, seemingly free of their moorings. The thunder sounded like distant breaking waves, like news from the outside. They really were an island of the moment, contained and unreachable, a place unique in the entire world.

They walked slowly back home, cutting a fresh path through virgin snow. Both of them were soaking wet but reluctant to go inside, fearful of losing whatever they'd found. They cleared the patio furniture and sat down and recounted the adventure of the rolling snowball.

When they finally went inside, Sonny ran upstairs, pulled off his clothes as if someone was timing him, dried off, got dressed, and ran back down to a large bowl of buttered popcorn and a hot chocolate with tiny marshmallows. They were just in time for The Dude's favorite TV police drama. Sonny and Franny curled up under the same blanket on the couch and The Dude sat in his chair, drinking his beer and eating his popcorn until his chin glistened with butter. Franny opened a second bottle of red wine and spooned out some butter pecan ice cream for herself. Later she made an English muffin. By the time Sonny went to bed, leaving his dozing parents with the sound blaring, it was like every other evening.

But his life had changed. When Sonny woke early the next morning, it was still snowing, though in smaller flakes, and he dressed quickly, stepping lightly down the stairs. He found one of his father's blaze-orange hunting coats, and went outside looking, because he knew no one was going to school on a day like this.

Henry

We're on the highway heading up the long hill into Santa Fe. I think the dinner went pretty well, though the climb down from the hilltop was a bit hairier than I would've liked. And my split lip didn't help, especially in the beginning. She actually started crying, which was a real surprise since we were already in town, and I had assumed she'd already seen me and decided not to comment on it.

At the restaurant, there were a few awkward stretches and I know the way I kept staring made her restless, and not only because of my bruised face. But I couldn't help it, she does, she looks like me. Not me now, but when I was her age. I don't know what it means but it's got me thinking about a time in my life I haven't thought of in decades, a period I never wanted to think of again.

There was also a dynamic I would never have noticed if Cadence wasn't with me. It was like being admitted into a secret society I never knew existed.

We were a man and his child entering the restaurant and the hostess put a friendly hand on my shoulder as she led us to our table and touched the top of Cadence's head when we sat, the waitress talked to Cadence, then winked at me, other parents went out of their way to make eye contact and smile and on the way to the bathroom, a man in snakeskin cowboy boots said to me, "They're something at that age, aren't they?"

Even the negatives felt revelatory. Wondrous. At the table next to ours, there was a woman with her gray hair carefully sculpted into an approximation of a crew cut and her daughter, about the same age as Cadence, but dressed out in a leather mini skirt and leopard tights.

The woman paid no attention to us, but the two girls stared at each other, hostility seemed to radiate off the other girl, though Cadence's face remained blank, unreadable. Strange the way the two of them locked into each other that way, it was almost primal, like small animals of the same species living in a teeming jungle and sensing each other. Sometimes they'll be interested and sniff around, other times, they'll bristle.

"Katie!" the crew cut woman said sharply, and both girls looked her way. I smiled at the woman, who made a point of ignoring me. I had a strangely comforting thought; if Philips and I raised Cadence, she might be like this child, dressed in some version of the New York styles, acting snotty. Maybe there is some kind of cosmic plan to this whole sorry mess.

At dinner, I did keep gently pushing her to ask me one of her questions in her book because I thought she really wanted to ask one and was just being polite, but still I'm surprised when she comes out with it before we're out of the parking lot. Our "best" summer vacation, Philips' and mine. And I know right away what to tell her, even though it wasn't really the summer and was nowhere near our "best" and was in fact taken towards the end of our marriage, or at least the practical part since we're still techni-cally married. And though I was saving that story, now seems as good a time as any.

When I'm done, she seems stunned into a silence. No wonder. I've been around her enough to know she likes being in control and has a prickly sense of dignity. It must be tough to find out the parents you've never known knew you. Took you on a vacation. And your grandparents never bothered to mention it.

I formulated a plan. Why couldn't Cadence and I have our own little one day vacation? Something the both of us will remember.

She said herself Bonnie and Jim never take her anywhere. I'm thinking about Eloy's meadow, the most beautiful mountain meadow he's ever seen, he said. I know how to get to Jack's Campground in the Pecos where the trailhead starts. We could pack a lunch, find the meadow and spend the day together soaking in the sun and the stunning wildflowers. There's fresh snow on the mountaintops and Eloy promised panoramic views of Baldy and of Truchas Peak to the north. I try and compose the necessary words to convince Bonnie and Jim they ought to allow Cadence to accompany me for a day. I think it best not to mention the length of the hike—Eloy said it was six full miles round trip, some of it steep, rocky switchbacks—or the final altitude, close to 11,000 feet.

Still, trying to find the right words makes it seem impossible. Bonnie and Jim will never allow me to take her some place they've never been. They're skittish at best and since they don't do much themselves, any attempt to do anything will seem outrageous to them. Even a simple (if a bit long) day hike. What about town? Maybe we could do go to town, they couldn't object to shopping in town. I have money now I can buy her a gift. Nothing outrageous, but something Bonnie and Jim would never think to buy her. A new CD player or maybe simply five new CDs. Town is a good alternative. I feel elated, light, generous, which is not a usual feeling for me.

"Don't you want to ask me something else?" I ask. "We don't get that much time together. I'll be glad to answer any question. Come on, one more." I lean over and switch on the map light, illuminating the notebook on her lap.

"OK," she says, sounding hesitant. She leafs through her notebook, considering and passing by many pages. Finally she settles on what looks to be a thin column of words, it's difficult to say in the dark.

"Go ahead," I say as sweetly as I'm able.

"You told me what Philips was."

"That's right, you said you got that off the back of a photo."

"I also have other names and I don't know what they mean. Bonnie gave me a Christmas card once, she said Janie left it behind. I don't think Bonnie even looked inside, but there was a letter."

"A letter? Who from?"

"I'm not sure, but it was to Janie. I couldn't read it, the writing was bad plus the ink was smeared. I went through and wrote down every word I didn't know, every name I could find."

Maybe I should've suspected what is coming, but I'm in far too buoyant a mood to notice. I'm twelve thousand dollars richer and my child is talking to me! Asking questions! New worlds are bursting forth.

"Lay them on me, baby."

"What?"

"That means go ahead."

"Oh, OK. They're mostly names. Let me see . . . Franny?"

I take a deep breath. "Franny's my mother, your grandmother."

"She lives in Indiana?"

"That's right."

"That's what I thought, I thought I knew about that one. I'm not sure the rest of these are even names, but I wrote them down anyway. What's 'The Dude?' There was a part that said, 'The Dude' but I didn't know what that meant."

As buried memories go, Dad's isn't so bad.

By the time he died, there wasn't even much bitterness between us, there was . . . nothing. It goes back . . . well, it goes all the way back, I suppose, but it was the summer after my first year of college when he accused me of stealing an expensive set of tools from the job site where I was doing go-fer work. And not to my face, he called in the cops and had me questioned and then fired, all without ever talking to me.

Then he refused to pay my tuition for my second year, saying if I wasn't going to study mechanical engineering like he wanted, I could pay for it myself. I'd switched to film studies after my first semester and tried to get away without telling him, but he insisted on seeing my grades, which was how he found out.

But even that simple explanation overplays any bitterness between us, long years went by where I didn't see him or talk to him and didn't think of him much and I'm sure I didn't cross his mind either. Philips never even met him and on those rare occasions when our paths intersected, at Eddie and Irene's for example, we were friendly in the way you are with an old high school teacher you never much liked.

"That was my dad. He's dead."

"I'm sorry," she says.

"It's OK, it was a long time ago. He was . . . he . . . he liked storms. And he could build stuff when he wanted to."

"Storms?"

"Thunderstorms. Lightning and wind and rain, he'd sit outside and watch them."

"He'd sit outside in storms?"

"Yeah."

"And that was his name?"

"Nickname."

"What was . . ."

"Arthur." I'm trying to be curt here, but I can feel the urgency of her enthusiasm and it would break my heart to just reach out and squash it. That wouldn't be right. I always claim to admire people who buck up and handle whatever comes their way, I damn well can do that now, though it isn't questions about Dad that truly scare me.

"He'd be my grandfather then, right? As much as Jim."

"I guess so."

"What did he look like?"

"I'll show you a photo someday."

"But was he like you?" she persists. "So big and tall?"

Was he? I guess he was, physically anyway. Of course, he wasn't capable of over-thinking a situation, but maybe that doesn't matter, not when it comes to what counts, which is more in the doing. He did look like me, we're the same size, more or less, and I guess we're the same way too. I am The Dude, aren't I? In some way?

"We're almost there," I say, trying to shut down the conversation, but I'm surprised at how reedy my voice sounds.

"Can I ask one more?"

"I don't know, maybe not." We're finally off the highway and winding our way through the dark back roads leading to the house. Another five minutes . . .

"OK."

"I'm sorry, it's just . . ."

"It's OK." She's closed her notebook and is hugging it to her chest. It's the sweetest thing I've ever seen, this tiny child next to me, my daughter who cares about me. "Someone hit you," she'd said earlier, with genuine concern. "I don't know who it is," she'd said, like she might go after him if she did, like she cared enough. I begin to cry, but quietly. I'm not sad, I don't know what it is. I pull the truck over, two wheels onto grass, and turn off the lights. We're even with the Eldorado clubhouse, which has an open soccer field next to it.

"One more," I say, and I know she can tell I'm crying, but it doesn't matter.

"Just a short one," she says, and I'm amazed at how quickly she recovers her good humor. It means a lot to her, me answering these questions. And what's the big deal anyway? She hurriedly flips through her notebook.

"I got it." I have a curious moment of calm right after she says it when I understand I knew all along this was what she was going to say. I am already reaching for the door handle. "Sonny and Sammy," she says, in the sweetest child's voice, with no comprehension of how explosive two simple words can be. Once outside and in the cool night air, I feel surprisingly focused (though my stomach is roiling) and a little foolish for fleeing the car so dramatically. I see Cadence's face in the window, and I know she's scared, know it's been a long, confusing evening. I signal her to roll down her window.

"It's this New Mexican food," I say. "I used to love it, but it's a little spicy for me now." I get back in the car and put it in gear. I'm not going to answer her question, but she appears to understand this and folds her notebook closed and reaches up and turns off the map light.

By the time we pull into their driveway, I'm better and we sit in silence, neither of us making a move to get out of the truck. I've spent a lot of my life in anticipation of the appearance of ghosts, sometimes with hope, but more often with a suffocating dread. But in all those years, I've never sensed anything. Not a shadow crossing the light or a phantom lightly brushing past me, not a wind carrying more than just a metallic cold or a voice settling in the wall, not the sound of tiny footsteps outside my bedroom door. It's been the tragedy of my life, the complete absence of the metaphysical, and I've often wondered what I did to deserve it. And over time, I came to understand the mystical wasn't missing just in my life but in the larger world itself; that it is a man-made notion designed to comfort the inconsolable and explain the unexplainable, and that this brings its own kind of comfort.

But when I finally dare a look over at my child, I know why I stayed away so long and why I'm back.

Cadence

Bonnie and Jim send me to my room so they can talk to Henry. I turn on my television loud because I think there could be yelling. Bonnie never yells but Jim does sometimes. I'm not sure about Henry. The house has felt bad for days. Jim goes into his room all the time. Bonnie watches television with the sound down. They both run to the phone when it rings and if I make a call, they ask me lots of questions about who I was talking to. If I didn't have a television in my room, I'm not sure what I'd do.

I finally go out into the living room. Jim is sitting in Bonnie's spot, watching the television; Bonnie is chopping green peppers on the counter. I can't tell what has happened. I stand in one spot through a set of commercials, but no one speaks so I go back to my room. Henry is there kneeling next to my window. I shut the door and run over and open it.

"Hey kiddo," he says.

"Hello." I don't like "kiddo," I don't like names like that, but I don't want to say that.

"How goes?"

"OK." We're talking just like he is at the front door and not sitting with his head inside and his legs out.

"You're watching *Gunsmoke*? I watched *Gunsmoke* when I was your age, when it was on originally. That's pretty cool, right?"

He usually doesn't talk like that. Saying "when I was your age." Other people do, Jim and all of his Marcy Center friends. They love to say that. It makes me wonder.

"Another show was on when I went out to the living room. Then this show came on."

"Can I ask you a question?"

"OK."

"Bonnie and Jim said you were really upset about my split lip. That you couldn't stop talking about it."

"I guess," I say because it's true. I didn't like it and I did want to tell someone. I wanted to tell Mrs. Garcia, but I'm still mad at her so I told Bonnie and Jim. I'm over it now. Besides, it doesn't look like it hurts anymore. He's staring at me like he expects me to say more but I don't want to say more.

"I'm sorry," he says finally. "Sorry it upset you."

"It's OK."

"I'm coming out tomorrow to pick you up. We'll go and get breakfast in town. And maybe we'll do some shopping afterwards. Would that be OK?"

"Yes."

"Good. Maybe you should pack an extra warm shirt, maybe some socks. Wear a good pair of shoes."

"Why?"

"I was thinking of taking a drive out to the Pecos, maybe going on a hike."

"Where's that?"

"The Pecos? Not far, maybe 45 minutes east of here. They have a lot of hiking trails, I thought it might be fun."

"Why'd you come to the window?"

"Oh shit," he says.

"You shouldn't curse."

"I know."

"Even I know that."

He stares at the television. A man in a cowboy hat is shooting a rifle at an Indian who isn't wearing a shirt.

"Do you want me to ask Bonnie and Jim?"

"No. I think I'm asking you not to ask them. I already did. They don't want you to go on the hike."

"Oh."

"They said I could take you shopping in town, but they don't want you to go on the hike. I figured we'd just go if the mood strikes us."

"Really?"

"It wouldn't take any longer than the shopping. You'd get home the same time. And we can go shopping another day. What do you think?"

"I don't know."

"Tell you what. You pack a warm shirt, an extra pair of socks and wear good walking shoes and we'll decide tomorrow, after we eat."

" . . ."

"If you don't want to..."

"I can't if they said I can't."

"I am, you know...your father."

"I know."

"Well, I know you know. That's not why I said it." I'm cold so I say that to him.

"Just think about it. Promise me?"

"OK."

"Can you say I promise?"

"I don't want to."

"It's OK."

He disappears, then sticks his head back and looks at me for a long time, then leaves for good.

I'm not going to pack any clothes. I want to eat breakfast and I'd like to go walk around the Plaza with him, but I won't pack for a hike.

In the morning, I remember last night differently. I like that Henry came and knocked on my window. I like that he wants to take me to a place I've never been before. I wonder if Reenie is supposed to come and I decide I want her along. So I stuff a pair of socks and a warm shirt into my bag, and I do it in a way so Bonnie and Jim won't notice the extra bulge. And I wear my basketball shoes, which are my best shoes to walk in. I'm still not sure I'll say yes to going but what he said, what Henry said, makes sense. I can decide after we eat.

Henry

I feel Cadence looking at me when I drive past Bonnie and Jim's exit on Interstate 25 East, heading first towards Doreen's and the Pecos after that. She's not comfortable with this, going against her grandparents. She has her notebook open, pen in hand, but she's not writing in it. Breakfast had gone well. I took her to the Tecolate Cafe and introduced her to the joys of Tabasco sauce on hash browns and eggs over-easy and using toast to dip into the runny egg/hot sauce mixture. She only took two bites off my plate, the first one because I pestered her about it, but then she leaned over and dipped a second time without asking. It got me thinking about the hike again; it is a fine day (sunny and 65 degrees, which is what I tell Cadence—it's too nice a day to spend in town) and plenty of time too before I have to have her home. Close to six hours. Bonnie said she'd look for us "around two" and I'd countered with "it may be three or so if we decide to head out to Villa Linda and the Outlet stores" and she'd accepted that. An hour from here to the trailhead at Jack's Campground, three more to the meadow and back, plenty of time.

"Whatcha writing?"

"I'm not writing," she says, closing the notebook.

"I know. I guess sarcasm's like puberty, it comes when it comes."

She's staring at the landscape, and I can't blame her. Past the Eldorado exit, the highway drops steeply into a canyon surrounded by a ribbon-ridge mesa, the sides, the valley and the flat top all covered in piñon pine. I doubt Bonnie and Jim ever go this direction, this might be her first time seeing this and it's only a few miles from her house.

"The hike isn't for certain. We'll stop and see Doreen and see what she wants to do. Maybe she'll want to drive back to town and the three of us can go shopping."

She smiles at me, she likes this idea, and there's that face again—our face. It's unsettling and I'm already nervous about approaching Doreen. Still, when I pass through their gate (still unlocked, a good sign), I'm glad Cadence is with me.

We've parked and are both already out of the truck before I notice Doreen standing rock still on the porch, one arm across her chest holding the other elbow. She must've been there since we pulled in, but it's not until Cadence yells out, "Reenie!" that she walks down the short flight to ground level to greet us.

"Hello Cady," she says, then to me, "This is unexpected," using just enough of a deadpan to let me know she means the opposite.

"That's me. The Master of the Unexpected."

"Is that right?" Cadence says, genuinely asking, like it might be an award I won or a title I was granted. Deflating in context, but in an amusing way, and I'm relieved when Doreen smiles over it.

"It's just something people say," I say. "Like a joke."

"Just like," Doreen says.

She invites us onto the porch. She's made a pot of coffee and sets me up with a cup in the same redwood chair I sat in the other day, then she and Cadence disappear inside. She's getting the tour and I'm clearly not invited.

I hadn't noticed when I was first here, but the porch is built roughly where Philips and I spread out an overlarge, cushioned moving pad that Cliff had given us and curled up together a short distance from his ratty trailer. The night air was extraordinary, the Milky Way so present the stars seemed blurred, slicing the sky in half. She loved that about Santa Fe, the easy access to the heavens.

She never liked that she could pick out only the brightest stars from our apartment roof in Chicago and whenever we visited Aaron or Franny, we always ended up in some dark spot, staring upward. On really clear Indiana nights, she could pick out the tiny moving lights amongst all the stationary ones, satellites orbiting. Once long before Cadence was born, we drove to Starved Rock in the middle of the state and spent much of the night standing on a cliff over the Illinois River, watching a comet through binoculars, the earth spinning it towards the horizon. She couldn't get over it, "a celestial object flying by our planet, can you believe it?" she said.

Our evening here might have been a transcendent, even healing one, except for Cliff who kept coming out of his trailer and firing guns into the dark. When he'd realize we were there, he'd say, "Oh my God, sorry, sorry, sorry" and go inside and roll a huge joint and bring it to us for free. An hour later, he'd be back, having forgotten the earlier incident. And each time, he set us a bit more on edge, which was our natural state in those days anyway. The last time, he emerged with a Mac10 converted to full auto, the bullets kicking up firefly sparks off the rocks on the far hill. He was mortified when he realized he'd forgotten yet again and he worked out a solution. "I'll just rope the steps," he said and that's what he did, tying a clothesline blackened with shoe polish across the steps of the trailer. Sure enough, with the eastern sky beginning to lighten, he came out again, tumbling ass over head into the dirt. He hit hard, waking me, and though Philips snored all the way through, I heard him say, "Oh, right, right, Henry and his chickie. Sorry, Henry, sorry Chickie," before limping his way to the trailer. Maybe I'll tell Doreen that story, she might get a chuckle out of it.

Right on cue, the porch door slides open, and Doreen and Cadence emerge, talking a mile a minute.

"I don't know," Doreen says.

"'Cause Mrs. Garcia says animals feel pain."

"Of course they do."

"I'm glad you say that too."

"But that doesn't really answer the question."

"It doesn't, it doesn't."

"You should ask your father."

Doreen sits in the chair next to me and I don't notice at first that Cadence appears to have something draped over her, arms around her neck, legs wrapped around her waist. For a moment, I think Doreen's given her an overlarge stuffed animal of some sort, then I realize it's Robin. She's carrying Robin piggyback. Robin. The kids are back!

"The kids are here?"

Doreen simply raises an eyebrow, as if to mock the stupidity of the question.

"The kids," I repeat quietly to myself.

"Ask your father," Doreen says.

"You mean Henry," Cadence says.

"You got another father somewhere?" I say, with too much of an edge, though really, I'm recovering from the loss of possibility. No way I'll ever find time alone with Doreen with her kids home.

"No, just you," Cadence says, easing Robin to the ground, and though she means no offense, it strikes me she is her mother's daughter. That's how Philips would've answered, emphasizing the "just" part so I understood it was a cynical judgment.

"Hey, you," Doreen says and there's Tommy coming from the woods, carrying two dead floppy rabbits by their rear legs. "Rabbit stew."

"Hey, you rabbit stew," Tommy says back.

"Rabbit stew, rabbit stew," Robin says.

"Hey, you," Cadence says, though she's never met Tommy before.

"Rabbit stew?"

"Someone say rabbit stew?" A man's voice from behind, Cliff walks out onto the porch, fresh from the shower wearing only a towel. Cliff out of his room. Perfect.

"Tommy sets a few snare traps in the woods," Doreen says as way of explanation. "Once or twice a week, we eat rabbit."

Finding a sunny spot, Cliff whips the towel off and begins drying himself, one leg up on a chair so he can reach between his toes. Robin is sprawled on the porch playing rag doll and Cadence is bent over her, trying to lift her limp body at the waist, and hasn't seen the naked Cliff yet.

"You should probably look away," I say to Cadence.

"Benny, child in camp," Doreen says.

"You brought the bambino," Cliff says, delighted.

"Oh," Cadence says, finally noticing. "Oh."

"I thought there were a couple extra people on the porch, but I figured if Reenie was OK with it, it wasn't my business."

"Benny," she says.

"Righto. Back in a flash." He walks into the house, towel over his shoulder, his bouncing white ass dominating. Cadence watches until he disappears.

"Cadence?"

"When he said 'bambino,' he meant me?" She asked.

"I believe he did."

"What's that mean?"

"Kid. Someone's kid. You're my bambino."

"Is that an insult?"

"Don't think so."

"Sounds funny."

"I thought it was because he was. . . wasn't wearing, you know, clothes. I thought that might've upset you."

"It *was* strange."

Cliff re-emerges wearing what looks to be the top half of a karate gi, complete with a green belt, showing a lot of leg, but at least he's mostly covered. He walks right up to Cadence and sticks out his hand. "Benny. I used to drive a cab when your old man here did. We were pals." She gingerly reaches for his hand as if leaning over a chasm.

"Cady," she says.

"What a cute little chickie," he says, and Cadence gives me a sharp look, like she blames me for this verbal indignity.

"She is, isn't she? A cute little chickie."

"Henry!"

"Cady!" I say, matching her tone. She scrunches her face at me.

Doreen brings out two bowls of corn chips and salsa and we settle in a rough circle, with Cadence comfortable in a cushy chair and Robin between her legs, her head back so they're cheek to cheek, Cadence's arms around her. The tone of the conversation is much as it was a few days ago, when I first met Doreen and family, with no hint her and I have spent a good portion of the last couple of days together or that there was anything other than the most perfunctory friendship between us. And maybe that is the truth of the situation, but if it is, I don't want to know about it and I sure don't want to spend much time in its presence.

When she dutifully recounts to Cliff about the three of us walking to the shack near the overlook, I think, like a mantra, "not the streaming sparklers, not the streaming sparklers, not the streaming sparklers" because that's mine and has nothing to do with him, but she tells him anyway, using the word "spectacular" in such an impersonal way—she might be describing Mt. Rushmore or the Golden Gate Bridge—it makes me feel foolish for caring. The final straw comes when Doreen launches into a humorous re-telling of the night at the bar, presenting Eloy and I as a couple of drunken but goodhearted Neanderthals who can't help themselves—"men will be men" are her exact words—and I try to catch her eye, looking for a subtle wink or some hint this story is for her husband only and our version would be different, that we shared something beyond basic alcoholic squalor.

"We should start thinking about going," I say to Cadence in a slight break in the conversation. I see her instantly deflate, she likes it here and has a new best pal, Robin, who's somewhere between playmate and living doll.

"I thought you all'd stay for lunch," Cliff says, sounding disappointed.

"Stay for lunch Henry," Doreen says, finally looking at me and using a tone of voice she might've used when we're alone. It's too late and even if it wasn't, what's the point? Her kids are back, Cliff is out and in the world, what's the point?

"We'll get food on the way. Let's do this again," I say.

"Bring the little chickie-poo any time," Cliff says.

Cadence sticks her tongue out at Cliff, and he returns the gesture, then she makes a big show out of extricating herself from under Robin, who has her around the neck and won't let go. It seems designed to convince me I'm making a mistake, dragging her away from here. We could eat lunch and still have plenty of time to hit the downtown shops for an hour or two before making Bonnie and Jim's deadline. Doreen seems to understand how I'm thinking, she puts a hand on my shoulder and says, "Cady says you're taking her shopping today. You thought about where?"

"I haven't." I move out from under her hand. She should leave it alone.

"I shop for kids all the time; I might know some places you don't."

"You should listen to her, old pal. She'll get the little chickiepoo set up just right."

"We can shop anytime. I got other ideas."

"Fine Henry," she says, awkwardly petulant.

"I know it's fine, DorEEN," I say, exaggerating her name.

Cadence has been quiet through the twisty drive to a paved road and now I've reached the point of decision. Left is town, right the Pecos and both are about equal distance. Maybe the hike to the mountain meadow is unlikely at this point, but it doesn't mean we couldn't walk a mile or two, then turn around. I know she wants to go shopping, maybe I do too, but what I said to Doreen is true. We can go shopping anytime. I'll pick her up after school on Monday or Tuesday or Wednesday or all three days and we'll head straight for the Plaza or Villa Linda Mall. And it's getting colder, another month and any drive into the Pecos might mean snow.

"We can still shop when it's snowing," I say, taking the right towards the hike. She looks at me like she expects me to say more. By the time we reach the town of Pecos, I've told her about the Battle of Glorieta Pass, showed her the road Jim and I took years ago when we drove to Rowe Mesa to cut firewood, and pointed out the State Fish Hatchery, all to no avail. She appears committed to outlasting me, stubbornly keeping her eyes glued on the passing landscape, refusing to pay any attention to what I say. That's OK, I don't mind. It's been so long since anything I did had even the barest effect on anyone.

The Neighborhood

By the time Sonny saw the first cars, he'd been outside for an hour, tracking through yards, the ball diamond, the golf course, shaking loose every evergreen and bent tree he came across. His tracks snaked through the snow behind him and all those trees he shook were shocking smudges of green in an all-white landscape.

Then he saw the kids, three of them hanging behind a row of bushes, huddled up near the stop sign at the corner of Judson and Holton roads. The streets themselves were unplowed, only Holton had a single set of tire tracks running down the center. The kids were bundled up and he wasn't sure he recognized them, but maybe it didn't matter. A truck approached and they crouched, hiding, and Sonny was sure they were going to throw snowballs.

He stood in the open and with The Dude's bright orange hunting jacket hanging below his knees, he was impossible to miss and indeed, the driver of the truck slowed almost to a stop, staring.

This was all the kids needed. They dashed behind the truck and grabbed the underside of the rear bumper, squatting so they were resting on their heels and when the truck accelerated, they skidded behind, the three of them. They held on as long as they could, but their bodies were like shovels on the unplowed street, building up a wall of snow between them and the bumper, forcing them to drop off.

Sonny waited. What else could he do? And they came back, shaking the snow loose and laughing and pushing each other. Tommy was the one who'd been riding on his stomach, he was taller than last summer and appeared just as rail-thin, even under the heavy clothing. The second kid was the teenager, Sonny found out later he was the one who labeled Sammy "green-teeth." The third kid was smaller, Sonny didn't know him.

"What's with you and the stomach?" the teenager said.

"I like it better. I'm not a wimp like you pussies, having to ride on my boat-bottoms."

The teenager put Tommy in a head lock and swung him around, then picked him up and dumped him into the snow by the side of the road and everyone piled on top, rolling and wrestling and pinching each other, the big teenager smearing wet snow across Tommy's face.

When they were done, they walked over to Sonny like the four of them were friends. The teenager pushed Sonny, but it was friendly.

"You want to try?" he said.

"I'm Sonny," he said nervously. He'd spent a lot of time thinking about this, about what name he'd give, but chickened out at the last moment and said Sonny.

The teenager laughed and then the others too. Tommy smiled and Sonny remembered his smile from that time they walked into Kabelin's Drain together. Sonny liked his smile.

"Yeah, we know but thanks for telling us."

"You want to try this?"

"Sure." He did.

A car approached, actually plowing a layer of snow off the top. It was decided that the kid decoy was a good idea and Sonny got credit for coming up with it. The third kid did it this time, he pulled his ski mask down over his face and stood there spastically waving his arms.

"That's Dickie P., the one acting like a retard," Tommy said. "This is Dickie D.," meaning the teenager.

"But plain ole Dickie because I'm the original Dickie," he said.

"And I'm the full Dickie P.," the kid said from across the street, being helpful.

"Two Dickies?" Sonny said.

"Here we go."

He did fine, except when he let go, his hand slipped out of his glove and it went with the car with no hope of retrieving it.

"Holy shit," Sonny said. Sammy in particular hated cursing, but it seemed natural with these guys.

"Fun, huh?" the original Dickie said.

Sonny had a thought he'd sworn over and over he would never allow, that this was something *he* would've loved and that by stepping out into the neighborhood, Sonny was doing what his brother would've done, what he wanted. Sonny cried, though everyone was so wet and sweaty, no one noticed. Then it made Sonny strangely happy, like it was a brief visit from Sammy, then sad again, but not so sad, he couldn't go on. These kids were always on the move.

Next, they headed to a cul-de-sac of houses off Holton Road, a place the twins had always avoided because there were so many kids living on it. The kids helped a man Sonny didn't recognize get his car unstuck and another kid joined us—Dickie said his name was Danny—and it was almost an hour before Sonny got close enough to hear her talk and realized Danny was a girl.

"You throw snowballs?" she said, the first words she'd spoken to him, and Sonny knew who she was. He watched her in school once after catching Sammy staring at her.

"I'll throw whatever," Sonny said. Danny and Tommy argued about where to go. Tommy said they could walk the half mile to the highway, there'd be lots of cars there. They couldn't stay on

Holton Road everyone knew them and no one was going out besides.

"I know a spot," Tommy said.

"I know every spot you know," Danny said.

"Johnson Road."

"Not enough cars."

"How about between the two Griffith houses, we'd have the whole lake if they decide to chase."

"Shit man, it's been warm for a month. I ain't going out on no lake," Dickie D.. said.

They decided on the highway, cutting through back yards, jumping fences, crossing a wide road and then over a higher fence into a large horse pasture.

"You've done this?" Tommy said.

"No," Sonny admitted.

"Well, if they stop and chase, we split in five directions and head for places cars can't go. They won't get out and run. Not usually."

"Not usually?"

"No," Danny said cheerfully.

"Though it's happened," Tommy added.

"Yeah it has," Dickie said. Dickie P. nodded vigorously in agreement.

A few people were trying to go to work. Plows were finally out but the snow was heavy and deep enough, it took two passes to clear a single lane, so it was taking time. They took a position on a small tree-covered swell rising over the highway, a fence between them and the road. Each prepared a snowball; it had the feeling of a solemn ritual. Sonny's bare hand stung under the wet cold, but it helped mold the snow into a tight, hard ball. Two trucks passed.

"All we need is an angry shit head farmer," Dickie said.

"In a pickup truck."

"Carrying his deer rifle."

"All we need."

They waited for a car. And then threw, three complete misses, Tommy's glanced off the roof but Sonny's thudded solidly against the outside door panel. The car slowed a moment, the brake lights flashed, but it continued.

"All right!"

"Fergie Jenkins here."

"You said you could throw. He said he could throw."

Sonny made a second snowball. A truck approached.

"Let's do the truck."

"I don't know."

"Why not the truck?" Tommy said.

"The truck, the truck!" Dickie P. said.

Sonny was ready and when it was decided, he let fly again, this time connecting square on the passenger side window. It gave off that particular thump when glass goes right to the breaking point. Two other snowballs also hit, but it was Sonny's that really got the man in the truck going, it was that kind of sound – scary. He skidded on the brakes and without a word spoken, everyone knew to run.

Dickie cut straight across the horse pasture, hoping to make it over the road and onto the lake or the woods around it. Dickie P. seemed confused and ended up following Dickie; Tommy and Danny went together, heading for someone's back yard and beyond that, more woods. Sonny jumped the fence and dropped into some high weeds, which were now smooth mounds of snow and watched as the truck headed straight for the fence then burst through and over it, the front wheels spinning and chunking.

"Four wheel drive," Sonny said to himself in a way he never would have before. He felt focused, light. Free. The truck aimed towards Tommy but that was clearly hopeless, he and Danny had already reached the yard and were disappearing around a house. Sonny kept at a right angle to the truck, making sure to stay low enough not to be seen. It was a blast.

Now the truck went after the two Dickies. Dickie had gotten across, but he was hesitating on the shoreline, the lake was still ice-covered but there was a sliver of open water outlining the shore. Dickie P. was in trouble, exhausted by the time he reached the fence, his foot caught and sent him head over, his jacket catching on a barb, his body twisting in such a way that he was hopelessly entangled, and the truck went right at him, like it was going to run him over. But the snow in the field was heavy enough that the truck's forward momentum slowed, then finally stopped.

The driver got out, he was wearing a short-sleeved white t-shirt with black driving gloves and had muscular arms and huge hands. Sonny circled back, Tommy and Danny stood in the yard, watching, and across the street, Dickie D. crouched behind an overturned rowboat. Dickie P. was in a full panic now, flailing and kicking with his feet to get loose. Sonny rolled a snowball and used the warmth of his hand to crystallize it. The man removed his gloves and flexed his fists. He fired, the snowball whizzed past the man's ear and hit the corner of his cab, splattering him.

"Why you little mother-fucker. You think that's funny?" The man saw Sonny now and he had crazy eyes, one of them seemed to be rolling on its own and he had spittle on his chin. He was drunk, Sonny was sure of it. He'd seen Franny and The Dude that way plenty of times. The man threw wild snowballs at Sonny, but he didn't have much of an arm. Sonny formed another snowball and let it fly right past him into his truck, impacting the inside of the windshield. It was like standing on his back porch, hitting the trees in the yard. Easier even because he was closer.

"You fucking piece of shit," he screamed, his face beet red, spit and snot flying. Dickie threw from his side and Tommy from behind, while Sonny calmly packed another and threw again, hitting the man squarely in the chest.

"Fuuuuuck!" Snowballs were coming from three directions, but the man was only vulnerable to Sonny's. He bent down for more snow and the man understood the gesture the way a vicious dog understands. Dickie D. helped Dickie P. off the fence. The man slammed his door shut and for a moment, Sonny hesitated.

Then he kicked open the door and came out with a shotgun, firing wildly.

Sonny wasn't sure what to do—this man was firing a gun at him—so he stood in place and while he did, the man calmed down and aimed.

"Sonny goddammit move," Dickie yelled, and the man looked at him and by the time he turned to Sonny, he was making for the lake. The man fired and fired and on the second shot, Sonny felt a push and a sting at the back of his legs, but he kept running, leaping across the sliver of open water, heading towards Kabelin's Drain. The truck was hopelessly stuck in the field. The two Dickies followed, yelling for Sonny to slow down.

"You got to be careful. The water around the drain is always open," Dickie said.

"Some arm," Dickie P. said.

"Wow kid," Dickie said, agreeing.

"Sandy K."

"Sonny K.," Dickie said. He smiled.

They met up together on Holton Road. It was Tommy who first noticed the blood dotting Sonny's pants. They went to Dickie's house because his mom worked late and slept-in late, and his father was long gone.

"Look at that," Sonny said, reaching inside my pants feeling warm liquid, then showing everyone the blood on my fingers.

"Oh God," Dickie P. said.

"He's got to take his pants off," Danny said. "To see."

"Oh God," Dickie P. said.

"It's OK," Sonny said. "I'm not scared of blood."

He looked around the living room, he'd never been in the house of someone who wasn't a relative. It was strange. There were floor-to-ceiling bookshelves on two walls, but no books. His house was the opposite, the few shelves bursting with The Dude's father's books and more in tall piles on the floor and in boxes shoved under tables and behind sofas, not to mention all the books his mother accumulated and those four or five she was currently reading, usually left spine open in every room. Sonny always thought it was such a mess, even though he liked books, but seeing this—someone had tried to fill the empty shelves with plastic flowers and a couple of photographs in free-standing frames, which only drew attention to the emptiness—he understood Franny's was the better way. In this moment, it seemed special to have a mother who read so much.

There wasn't much else in the room, a coffee table and a television sitting on the floor. There was wall-to-wall thick orange shag carpeting that made footsteps when you walked, and everyone plopped on the floor like they'd done it a thousand times before.

They made Sonny lay down face-first and helped him pull down my pants.

"Ouch," he said when Danny touched him.

"I can see it, just below the skin. There's one other and lots of bug-bite welts where the shot didn't go through," she said.

"Is it bleeding?"

"Mostly it's stopped. Should we take them out?" He looked at Tommy who shrugged. Dickie P. was across the room on the floor squeezing a hairy, bored-looking cat. The house smelled funny, the carpet too, like food left out too long. Dickie came out of another room with a magnifying glass, mercurochrome, and a pair of tweezers and a matchbook.

"We'll take it out here. It's not bad, no more than a splinter but if we tell someone, then we have to tell them the whole story," he said.

"I'd rather not," Sonny said.

"To which?"

"To the telling. I'd rather just do it."

"Cool."

"It'll hurt," Danny said.

"It'll hurt if I go somewhere to get it done," he said.

Tommy did it because no one else wanted to. He sterilized the end of the tweezers with a match, then used their rounded tip to slide under and into the hole itself. It stung but it wasn't bad, and he was surprised when they were done.

"Yellow Leg," Dickie called, and Sonny realized he liked it, liked being around these kids. He promised to meet up later to check out the shotgun man's truck. If it was still stuck in the field and no one was around, they were going to make him pay for his wounds.

"Sugar in the gas tank for starters," Tommy said.

"I don't think a guy like that deserves a windshield," Danny said.

"And does he really need four inflated tires?" Dickie D. said. They all laughed, and Sonny laughed along with. Half an hour later, when they split to go home, Tommy and Sonny fired snowballs back and forth until they were too far from each other, then they waved with both hands. He entered the house feeling light, expectant.

Thus began his second life. His parents weren't sure what to make of it. It's what The Dude always wanted, his kid playing with other kids like he did when he was young. But by the time it finally happened, he was too deep inside whatever had hold of him— grief, alcoholism, a damaged stubbornness, probably all that and more—to react to it. Later, when Sonny played Little League and then Pony League, The Dude would often appear well down the right field line, his truck backed in close, sitting on the rear gate watching, but even then, he usually left after the last out, sometimes giving Sonny a little wave, sometimes not. His mother tried to put on a brave face, she smiled and rubbed the top of his head every time he went out, but she couldn't hide how sad it made her, losing her little silent companion.

Sonny didn't care, he couldn't. Summer was coming fast and school beyond that. Before that day in the snow, he hadn't thought about the summer or returning to school in the fall, but it now felt inevitable in a good way.

And it was, for a while anyway. They'd hang out before, during and after school. The core group was Sonny, Tommy, Danny and the two Dickies, but the neighborhood was full of children within three years of each other and any given day they might have two or even three times as many kids hanging out.

Usually, they started the morning with a swim at the community beach, then sandlot baseball. Afternoons were often spent at Tommy's place because he had a basketball rim with a paved driveway and his house butted up against the fifth fairway.

And he experienced the golf course in a way he never had with his brother. They used to hide in the woods and spy on passing golfers, they never even thought of approaching the old golf clubhouse, an immense three-story white building, somewhere between funeral parlor and barn, sitting on a hill in the center of the course.

These kids knew when it was best to approach golfers on the course with found balls to sell and where on the course you could run out and take a ball without being seen. And Dickie the teenager had worked at the golf clubhouse as a bus boy and knew what doors were unlocked and when they had food buffets, so they'd sneak in and eat and drink their fill.

And they might take the hand carts set in a row on the backside of the clubhouse and ride them down the hills like a sled, pulling up on the handle for balance. Or reach up and under the taut canvas covers over the electric carts and grab every golf ball they could get their hands on.

In fall, the group played tackle football, either on the baseball diamond or in an out-of-the-way corner of the golf course, and in deepest winter, on the frozen lake, they'd have contests to see who could hold on the longest dragging behind Dickie' P's snowmobile on their stomachs. Year-round, they threw at passing cars; snowballs in winter, tomatoes, eggs, and water balloons the rest of the time. Sonny kissed his first girl on a close summer night, huddled sweaty and breathing hard under a tree in the middle of the dark golf course, holding on tight to each other while they listened to a man enraged, his car having been splattered by a combination of eggs, dirt clods, and water balloons, his headlights two streams splitting the sky above us. It just happened, they kissed. She was Danny's cousin and Sonny was sure he'd never see again, and he never did.

His third summer in the neighborhood was his last; by late July, Sonny and his mother moved into town, leaving The Dude alone in the house, and when school came, Sonny had to go to the junior high on the south side of town where he didn't know anyone. They all promised to keep in touch, especially Tommy and Danny who were Sonny's two closest friends, and they tried a few times, but it was clearly hopeless because everyone was still too young to drive. The two Dickies fell in with an older, tougher crowd and began spending nights picking pounds of ditch weed along rural county roads and selling it to Chicago dealers who used it to cut the good stuff. Danny moved to Austin, Texas with her mother and Tommy drifted away, settling into golfer's crowd, becoming one of those high school kids who spends all his spare time hanging around the pro shop talking and playing golf. By Sonny's senior year in high school, he and Tommy didn't even bother to say hello in the hallways, not because of animosity, but out of simple indifference.

That first night after the first day in the snow, Sonny did something the two of them used to do, though he didn't think about it like that until later. They would kneel by the rattling window in winter, usually shirtless, candy cigarettes in hand, pretending to blow smoke instead of breath, a contest to see who could stand the cold air longest. They'd stay until their teeth chattered and bodies shivered, rubbing warmth into their arms and legs and giggling at the outrageous stories they'd invent around distant sounds and passing cars. One of them always caved, diving for the warm covers, and the other immediately followed and they'd thrash around the bed in a near panic, desperate to tuck all the blankets in around so no part of them was showing because monsters the size of mountains had been dropped on Earth by an evil alien race and were approaching the house, or vampires and demons had been let loose, floating into their room from the closet, sniffing around the edges of their bed, unable to get past the covers, which had magical shielding powers.

Sonny opened the window and the slight wind, chilled by the snow, raised the hairs along his arms and legs. He closed my eyes tight and started to cry, imagining he was beside him and all Sonny had to do was never open his eyes again and it'd be all right. Sonny spent countless nights falling asleep this way, sure his brother was right next to him. As long as he never looked. Except tonight, he looked, and he was alone, but it was okay. Sonny stopped crying. The snow had crusted over, and it glittered in the light from the street, distinct spider web shadows danced against a perfect white backdrop. The rear porch door opened, and he knew what was next; The Dude's huge feet crashing through the crust with each step and then the sound of water hitting the glassy surface. The Dude always peed outside when he watched TV, the back yard being closer than upstairs.

Sonny knew their routine by heart, for months and months it was all he had. The Dude would finally lumber up the stairs, closing the bedroom door behind him and Franny would take over the downstairs. It was like the changing of a job shift. He would click off the TV when he left and thirty seconds later, she turned it right back on, the result of a long-simmering mutual resentment that permeated every interaction they had, though over time, this act became an affectionate ritual for the two of them. They'd joke about it with Eddie and Irene (but only when they'd had a glass or two of wine), how pig-headed the other one was. "See what I have to put up with?" they'd say together and smile. "Can you imagine?"

She'd throw another log on the fire, make herself a coffee or pour another glass of wine and an English muffin swimming in butter, and watch the news and The Tonight Show and sometimes the Late Night movie. And after, in the pale stillness of early morning, she'd slip into her son's room and lie on his bed on the outside of the covers, her arms around him.

But not that night. Sonny locked the door and settled in front of the window. There was a blue light, revealed only in moments when the tree branches shifted. Sonny stared the longest time, trying to figure what it might be. It seemed supernatural, how it changed hues, shapes, and even colors, the way witnesses described UFOs, but this was barely above the ground, nestled in the heart of the neighborhood.

When it first happened, they all said a lot of stuff to Sonny, not just Aunt Irene and Uncle Eddie, but neighbors and family friends and people in stores he didn't even know. Mostly bullshit, though they meant well.

"He's gone to a better place."

"He's in heaven."

"He's with Grandma."

"He's at peace now."

"He's at rest."

None of it made much sense and they didn't seem to believe it themselves. Only Aaron helped. He patiently explained the concept of reincarnation, that when someone dies, their soul is reborn in another body, and Sonny decided he'd be reborn somewhere and in time they'd come back together.

He heard a truck downshifting on the interstate and wondered what it was like where that driver was going. Was there snow? Was it near an ocean, in the mountains, New York City? Was it sunny and warm? Do people wear shorts there? And in a moment as brief as a shiver, had the new Sammy been born in a place where they wear shorts in winter?

A television! That's what he was seeing through the trees, just someone's television. Instead of disappointment, Sonny felt buoyant. Another mystery solved. And there were people out there, living their lives, even if it was only watching TV. Then he started thinking he was seeing their own television, that he'd floated out of his body and settled in another house and was looking at Franny's TV flashing through the trees. Seen like this, it wasn't much, one small light lost in an infinite landscape. He might be Tommy or Dickie D. or even Henry. He could be a Henry. That his was just one in a sea of lives, no worse, no better, no bigger, no smaller, no meaner.

Cadence

I take out the map and look where I am. Only a single finger's width from Santa Fe. It's still the second farthest place I've ever gone without Bonnie and Jim. Our class went to Bandelier and Valle Grande once. That was really far. And I guess there was the time with Henry and Janie, though I don't think it counts if I can't remember it. Not that I've been much of anywhere with Bonnie and Jim either. They don't like to travel. Jim always says, "What if the car breaks down? What would happen?" Then Bonnie agrees. She always agrees. We drove to the Grand Canyon once and spent two nights in a motel. We went to a bunch of shops right on the rim of the canyon and had ice cream cones and listened to all the different languages being spoken. I wasn't even that excited when they told me we were going, I'd seen the Grand Canyon in books and movies, but I couldn't believe it when I first actually saw it. It was huge; wide and steep and scary to just look at, like if I got too close, I might get the urge to jump in and fall all the way to the bottom. But the next day and the day after that, we went to the exact same spot overlooking the canyon and then we'd go back to our motel while it was still day out and sit and read or watch TV.

On the way home, sometimes I'd shut my eyes in the moving car and pretend it was my real mother and father, not Bonnie and Jim, and we were on vacation together and lived in a house with a swimming pool and a big back yard where coyotes lived. And I'd have dogs and cats too, and maybe some friendly fish living in the pool, and even though the coyotes were wild, they were friends with my animals and came to visit.

Near the Arizona/New Mexico border, we stopped at a wildlife park on an Indian reservation. Mrs. Garcia told me about it and I told them. You drive through it in your car and it has all kinds of animals, even ones from Africa. The booklet said lions and leopards and bears and cougars and giraffes and elephants. But when we drove through the gate, Jim said we were really low on gas and he speeded up and wouldn't slow down. We almost ran over a herd of ostriches, and we hit a bump Bonnie said was a stick but looked like a snake. When I looked back; I think it was wiggling and rolling over.

And I saw the head of a giraffe in some trees, and I asked Jim to slow down, but he said he couldn't, we might run out of gas, he couldn't. So we didn't. Now whenever I ask about a vacation or read about an interesting place in a magazine, they bring up the wildlife park, like any vacation would be like that one.

When Henry asks me about cats and dogs, I decide I'll answer him. He's been talking a lot, trying with me and after a while, I'm not mad about the shopping anymore and remembering the Grand Canyon made me remember how I wanted to go down the trail into the canyon, a mile or even a couple of turns, but they wouldn't. They just wouldn't. A hike now might be fun. I don't want to just come out talking like I'm giving in so easily, but then he starts talking about cats and dogs.

"Bonnie and Jim don't like animals. Bonnie says they leave their hair on everything, and Jim says he doesn't want to be tied down." Henry laughs at this because when we had our dinner, I told him about our vacation and how we'd never had another.

"What do you think?" he says.

"I don't know. I think it'd be fun to have a dog. Or maybe a cat."

"Which?"

"Both, I guess. I'd get them small, and they'd grow up together so they're friends and are never lonely."

"That's smart," he says. "You should live with animals at some point in your life. I've had cats. Don't trust anyone who says they don't like cats."

"Jim hates cats. Bonnie told me her father used to shoot cats he found in the fields around her house. She said she'd cry about it. I think Bonnie would like a cat."

"Most people who say they don't like cats really don't like their independent natures. Dogs will follow whoever is willing to feed them, they want to eat, and they want to please you. You can't always figure out what a cat wants," he says. "I know a joke."

"OK."

"What's the difference between cats and dogs?"

"I don't know."

"A cat isn't afraid of losing its job." He laughs to himself, and I laugh too though I'm not sure why this is funny. I've never lived with animals.

"I've never lived with animals," I say.

"You said. You should sometime. You should try it."

"I'd like to. When I said I wanted a puppy and a kitten, I wasn't making it up on the spot. I wrote it down." I hold up my notebook.

"You'd like it. It's one of the steady pleasures in life. I can't believe all the time in my life I've gone without."

Then he looks at me strangely and I think he's going to touch me; put his hand on my shoulder or rub my head and I'm glad he doesn't. I like it when he does it without thinking about it. I want to ask him about the two names from last night, but I'm scared to because he jumped out of the car last time. I told Bonnie. She said, "Well, the food here *can* be really spicy" and maybe he cried because he had a tummy ache. I don't think that was it, but I couldn't say that. I wanted to ask her about Sonny and Sammy, but

Bonnie doesn't like talking about the past. She'll never say anything about Janie unless I ask.

"It's not far," he says.

"It's pretty here," I say because it is. There's a river running
alongside our road and sometimes we cross over it and back on
bridges. There are green mountains on either side of us and rock
cliffs like canyons and huge trees as wide as Henry is tall with red
trunks growing next to the road and there are places with cabins
in the woods and a lot of trucks pulled off with people standing in
the river fishing.

When Henry said we should get going, I didn't really want to
leave because Robin is such a sweetie pie and I like Reenie, but I
didn't like when that man came out without clothes. I've never
even seen Bonnie wear shorts and Jim always wears a long-sleeved
shirt. When I take a shower, I lock the door and bring all my
clothes with me, even though my bedroom is only three feet away.
And the dead rabbits too, I didn't want to see them anymore and I
sure didn't want to eat one of them. So I didn't really mind leaving,
but then Henry went the wrong way, and I knew we weren't going
shopping and I didn't want to talk to him.

But now we're close, according to Henry, and it hasn't been
more than forty-five minutes and I wonder again like I did when he
took Reenie and I to the shack why Bonnie and Jim don't know
about this place. There are mountains covered in trees and
streams and hardly any people other than the ones fishing and it's
so different from where we live, so different from Eldorado, it's
like we've gone to another state or another country. It makes me
feel funny that Henry has been here only a few days and he knows
places Bonnie and Jim don't know, even though they've lived here

most of their lives. I know he used to live here too, but I don't remember that even though I wish I could.

He pulls the truck over and stops, saying, "It's time to evacuate and eliminate."

I give him a look.

"Pee," he says. "If you have to pee, that's what it means."

"I know," I say, even though I didn't, but I didn't like how he said those words. It didn't sound like words he uses.

"I got some paper towels," he says, out of the truck and walking around the front. I get out too. "Just in case of...you know, just in case."

It takes me a second to figure out what he means. I'd never do that out here. I couldn't.

There are cows ahead along the road and on either side in the woods eating. I walk towards them thinking I might be able to touch one; cows aren't very scary. Bonnie says she was raised with milk cows and you could pet them or sit on them or squeeze their huge noses and they didn't care. But then I remember Henry's wild cows, and these are like that. They run away into the woods and hide behind trees and look back, they make a moo noise but meaner, like they're mad or scared.

When we're back in the truck, he starts talking about some tree. He leans over and points to it. At first, I don't see it, all I see is this dead tree trunk with no branches that's all black at the top. Turns out that's it. He calls it the buzzard tree.

"Each time we'd drive past here, there'd be like forty buzzards perched on it. We stopped and took pictures," he says.

"You and Janie?"

"Yes."

"What's a buzzard?"

"A vulture. Like an ugly hawk."

I know what a vulture is, but I'm still confused. How could forty vultures sit on that tree? There aren't any branches and I know vultures can't hang on sideways.

"There aren't any branches!" I exclaimed.

"There used to be. It was real craggy, four or five branches sticking out every which way and at several levels and all of them full of buzzards. Like out of a gothic horror movie."

"What's that?"

"An old time monster movie, with castles and burning torches and black cats and vultures waiting in trees."

"I've never seen a movie like that."

"I'll show you one some time."

I have an idea. "Maybe the buzzards aren't there now because there aren't any branches." I like saying that word. Buzzard.

"Makes sense."

I have another idea. "Did the buzzards quit coming because there were no branches? Or did the buzzards leave first, and the tree dropped its branches because no one was using them anymore?"

"Wow," he says. "Like the chicken or the egg, right?"

I don't know what that means, but I don't want to ask him because I'm not sure about what I said. Why would a tree branch fall off with no weight on it? "Maybe the weight of the buzzards broke the branches."

He laughs. "Better theory I think."

"But why would they just sit there all together on one branch?"

"I don't know."

"It's stupid of them to all sit on a branch until it breaks."

"I'm not sure they're thinking ahead that far."

"Do you think they did it because they were lonely, because they wanted to be with other buzzards?"

"I'm sure that's part of it."

"I think if I was a buzzard, I'd want to be with other buzzards."

"Sure you would."

"I wonder if any of the buzzards got hurt when the branches broke."

"They probably just flew away. We should go."

For a few miles, the road climbs slowly, then we pass a bridge and a sign pointing off left reading *Holy Ghost Ranch* and up ahead, there's a small store at the point where the road takes a sharp right and begins climbing up the mountain. A sign says: *Cowles Country Store*. I'm glad when Henry pulls in and parks because high roads make me nervous. When I went with my class to Valle Grande, the school bus slowed down so much for some of the curves, I thought we were going to roll backwards. If I kept my head raised, I could see the entire valley with roads running everywhere and the mountains over Santa Fe and the ones with snowcaps towards Taos, but when I looked down, we were right at the edge of a scary drop-off and it felt like the bus was leaning, maybe tipping over, and I grabbed the seat in front of me and I closed my eyes and didn't open them until I felt the bus on flatland again. My friend Peggy called me a scaredy-cat for closing my eyes, but Mrs. Garcia shushed her, and later Peggy said she was sorry and she'd closed her eyes too and I told her I'm glad we're still friends and she agreed.

It's not only food inside, they also sell fishing poles and nails and screws and disposable cameras and lots of batteries. Under a window, there's a barrel with dirt and worms next to a tin tub of tiny fish. When I touch my finger to the water, the fish swim away, then swarm right back. It looks like a circle getting bigger, then smaller very fast until it's all just fish again. They even have guns under a glass case at the counter. I don't like guns. We had a speaker at my school once and he said guns were necessary tools, like a hammer or a saw, but after he left, Mrs. Garcia said a hammer was made to build while a gun was made to kill. I don't think Mrs. Garcia liked that man being in our class.

Henry tells me he's buying water and food for both of us, but I should also go ahead and get whatever I want, and he'll pay for it.

"I'm serious and not just food. You need a watch or a pair of gloves or a hat, anything you want," he says.

"I don't need a watch or a pair of gloves or a hat."

"Don't be dense."

"I'm not dense."

"I know you're not. I'm sorry. Just look around, see what you want, and I'll get the food and water."

I walk through the aisles, but I don't want anything. I don't think he should call me names, even if I don't know what they mean, and I shouldn't have to buy something if I don't want to.

"Cadence," he yells from over by the worm barrel. "Cheap candy alert."

I walk over to see, it's an entire aisle of candy. I like candy OK but when Bonnie and Jim let me buy one item when they stop for gas, I buy potato chips or cheese popcorn. And they never eat candy themselves so it's never in the house.

"They got it all, all my favorites from growing up. Necco Wafers, Pixie Sticks, Circus Peanuts, Chik-O-Stiks, Boston Baked Beans. What do you want?"

"I don't like peanuts. I don't like beans. What's a Chik-O-Stik?" It sounds awful.

"Well . . ." he says. "I'll buy extra in case you take to it."

I end up with a cranberry juice and a small bag of white ched-dar popcorn. He has four bottles of water, a bag of potato chips, a bag of corn chips, a pile of his stupid candy and five or six Power Bars. There is a box of pens near the register, it says: *WRITES UPSIDE DOWN* and shows the picture of an astronaut floating in space and still writing. I've heard of these. I could lay in bed on my back and write with my pad above me, though my arms would probably get tired pretty quickly and I like writing on my side. I like to make a tent with my blanket and a flashlight and sometimes I read or write and sometimes I lay my favorite things in a circle around my notebook and sometimes I pretend I have a floating bed like a flying carpet, and I can fly anywhere I want.

"This too," I say, putting the pen next to the pile.

"Excellent," he says, smiling.

"I can write upside down now."

"I see that. You never know when that might come in handy." The way he says talks, I'm not sure if he's being friendly or making fun.

"What'd I do this time?" he says, looking at me until I look at him.

"Nothing."

"How'd I know you were going to say that?"

"I don't know."

He looks at me in that way he does, like he knows exactly what I'm thinking. "You can write in bed now," he says gently. "With your new pen."

"I do, I do write in bed," I say, because he's being nice again. "I make a space under the covers with my flashlight, and I put my notebook in the middle and then set out my rabbit's foot and my basketball cards and the silver boots I got from a boy in Guatemala and my fuzzy bear Bonnie bought me at the Grand Canyon."

"Like a fort?" he says.

"I guess like a fort."

"You have basketball cards?"

"Yep."

"Who's your favorite player?"

"Devin Booker."

"From Phoenix?"

"Yeah. I like Kyrie Irving too, but Devin's my favorite."

"I used to play ball some. A lot when I was younger."

"Bonnie told me."

Then we start up the steep hill and it keeps climbing and there are places where I can see all the way down to where the river is. I open my notebook because I don't want to look out. I think I'll write words but instead, I start drawing. I like to draw. Mrs. Garcia says the first maps of America followed the rivers inland and they knew what the rivers were like for a thousand miles, but they didn't know the land even a mile on either side. Only what they could see from their boats.

"You should use your new pen," he says.

I hold up one flap of my notebook so he can't see and keep drawing, but then I decide he's right, I do want to try my new pen. I struggle to get it out of the plastic wrapper. He reaches over and tries to help, and his truck swerves and I have to look up to see. The road's high here and very narrow. If another truck came right now, we'd hit them.

"Ooops," he says, like it's fun.

"Watch the road, please," I say, because he scared me.

"Aye aye Cap'n."

"I'll try my pen after we stop."

"Sounds like a plan." Again, I'm not sure how he means that. It's so different being with Henry. Bonnie and Jim never notice anything. They can't tell when I'm happy or mad unless I tell them myself. I've cried in front of the TV with them many times and even when they notice, they think it's the TV, even when it's just some stupid cop show no one would ever cry over. But Henry pays attention and so when I'm in a bad mood, he can tell, even when I'd rather he couldn't.

The Pecos

"Circus Peanut?"

She looks at the orange candy suspiciously, then takes a tiny bite off the end.

"It's not like a peanut."

"You like it?"

She shrugs. "I'll eat it."

"If you squeeze it flat—" I show her. "—it makes it more concentrated, less foamy. Like a cookie."

"I'm not going to squeeze it flat." She has a kid-like way of being outraged that's adorable.

"Your loss."

"I didn't lose anything," she says, now being sincere. "I still have it." She shows me.

"Squeeze it flat, squeeze it flat, squeeze it flat," I say, like a chanting crowd. She's got her notebook open again, ignoring me.

"I'll squeeze it for you."

"No thank you," she says, going quiet.

"Here." I reach over and make a fake grab for it, she twists away, hunching her shoulder so I can't reach it. My front bumper brushes the weeds on the side of the road, and I have to jerk it straight.

"Henry! Both hands on the wheel please."

"Both hands on the wheel please? Where'd you get that?"

She sets her face to a resolute scowl, then to my amazement, she smiles and laughs, and gets shy over it, turning her head away so I can't see.

"Cadence?"

She won't look at me. "Bonnie says that."

"Bonnie says that?"

"To Jim, she says it to Jim all the time. I never thought I'd say it."

"It just came out?"

"It did."

We've entered the near edge of Jack's Campground, the snaky road and accompanying campsites are cut into the side of a hill like a terrace farm. There are a handful of RVs at comfortable distances from each other, and a single bright orange nylon tent pitched well off the road, inside the edge of the trees. We're heading for the end of the campground at the top of the hill where there are three or four different trailheads leading into the Pecos. I pull into the informal dirt parking area and find a spot that'll still be in the sun when we come back. There are no other cars.

"Can I have another Circus Peanut?" she says.

"I told you. You'll be flattening it in no time at all."

She snarls her lip at me in a fair approximation of Elvis and takes a bite.

"What were you doing writing so much?" I ask.

Cadence hugs the notebook to her chest and looks up at me without moving her head, tilting her eyes upward. Philips used to do this. I feel like crying for a moment, not a sad cry really, more about making the connections in life; the way they appear and open up things inside of you.

"I made a map," she says.

"Can I see?"

She spreads it on the seat between us with a dramatic flourish, like this is what she's been wanting to do for a while. I'm taken aback. It's a detailed map of the route we just drove, starting with the buzzard tree and continuing along the road. There are stick figure men in cowboy hats standing in the Pecos River holding fishing rods, there's a detailed bridge and road branching off with the words "Holy Ghost Ranch" and tiny pine trees everywhere drawn to look like Christmas trees. My truck is at the highest point on the map, which she's drawn as an immense mountain, and she's written *Henry* at an angle coming out of the driver's side and *Cady* at the opposite angle coming out of her side. The map is incredible.

I grab her roughly and quickly, pulling her to me and kissing her on the top of her head, then messing up her hair. She pulls away, but she's smiling when she does.

"Do you think maybe I could get a copy of this? When we get back to Santa Fe, we'll go to Kinko's."

"I made it for you," she says, hiding behind her hair.

"You did?"

She nods her head.

"You made it for me?"

"Mm hmm."

"I w-want it." My voice falters and I raise my chin so she can't see my eyes, which are wet.

"Really?"

"Really... really. Would you sign it? On the bottom." She writes Cadence Leans in the corner.

"We'll leave it in the book for now. So it won't get messed up."

I pack my bag heavy, plenty of food and water. I have ibuprofen, two kinds of antacid, arnica cream and the health food store version of Ben-Gay in case my knees start aching, Calendula gel for cuts and scrapes, an entire roll of toilet paper, and a good wad of paper towels. I make sure Cadence takes along her extra shirt. We'll both be plenty warm on the way up but coming back it might get chilly. And lastly, I pack a brand-new copy of the *Nation-*

al Audubon Society's Field Guide to the Southwestern States, which is a close approximation of the one my family owned all those years ago. If the meadow really is as glorious as Eloy claims, we might want to be able to identify some of the flowers and bugs we see.

We find the trailhead just as Eloy said, with the wooden sign reading "Pecos Baldy" laying on the ground, riddled with bullet holes. I have a moment where I wonder if this is really a good idea. I'm unused to the altitude, out of shape, overweight and she's just a child.

"You good with this?" She adjusts the bag on her shoulder and gives me a determined thumbs up, raising goose bumps down my back.

"Let's do it," I say and step over the bullet-riddled sign. Then I stop and she walks past me, like that's the plan all along

"This is exciting, isn't it?" I ask. "Like an adventure."

"Yes," she says, over her shoulder, heading up the trail. "Like that."

Her calm is a help. I know I'm the adult here, but the fact that none of it seems to bother her makes me feel better. Adults can develop a lot of ideas and fears, our bodies and souls have been impacted in ways children might not understand. It's possible to be too careful.

Cadence

It's not very much fun at first. The trail is black dirt and kind of ugly and it's steep. When I'm playing basketball, I feel like I can run and run without having to stop, but the season hasn't started, we haven't even had one practice yet, and I don't play much in the summer and fall, so I'm huffing and puffing. I'm glad to see Henry is too. He's faster than I am and keeps hiking past me, but then he has to stop, and I catch up. Sometimes I stop with him and sometimes I walk on, just to show him I can do that too.

"Isn't this something?" He says to me at one of his stops. All I see is the top part of a large hill to my right and the bottom part dropping to my left. And trees, a lot of trees.

When we reach our first flat area, there's a gap in the trees going straight off in both directions and mountains in the distance with snow on them and they look completely different because I've never seen them from this side. And in the other direction, there's a green hill covered in trees and near the top, Aspens just beginning to turn golden. I've never been to a place like this.

"It is," I say, even though he'd said, "Isn't this something?" twenty minutes ago.

"What's that?"

"What you said earlier. Something."

He smiles and I like it when he smiles and doesn't speak. It makes me feel I've known him my whole life. Maybe I do remember that trip west with Henry and Janie. Maybe I remember his smile. When he talks, I don't know what he means about half the time and even though I like it because Bonnie and Jim never say anything I don't understand (they hardly talk at all), I trust the smile more. I know what that means.

I almost ask him about the gap in the trees, it seems awfully straight, and I don't know how the trees could just happen to grow like that, but then I'm really glad I didn't ask because I remember Mrs. Garcia showed us slides of this. It's a fire break! Men did this, cut the trees to control fires. I didn't understand it then, but seeing it now, I do. Fire would burn to the edge and then stop because there's no more trees to burn. Whew! I would've looked pretty stupid asking Henry that.

"How are we doing?" he says. "Should we keep going?"

"Sure."

"We'll keep going."

"Sure."

From the fire break it's easier walking, though still uphill. And prettier too, the trail runs next to a stream, no more than a foot wide, with tiny waterfalls and lots of green plants growing around. In places, it's so thick, it grows over the stream, and you can't even see it. You could step right in it and get wet if you weren't careful, except for the sound of running water. I like the sound of running water.

"I like the sound of running water," he says just before I do.

"Me too. I do," I say quickly so he'll believe me and not think I'm just agreeing to agree.

"I believe you," he says.

"Stop that," I say.

"Stop what?"

I'm not sure what. He's just talking, except he keeps saying what I'm about to say. I push past him and keep on up the trail. I can feel him watching my back, not moving, so I turn around and make a face, showing him my tongue like I'm gagging, and he laughs.

Soon the trail is steep and gets very narrow with a sharp drop left. If I fell now, I'd roll all the way to the bottom.

I've always been sure I was scared of heights. I tell people I am. I don't like climbing ladders and or walking across bridges. But I've been walking for almost an hour one stumble or slip away from falling down a long hill and I'm not scared. I know I'm not going to slip or stumble.

So when Henry says, "Will you look at that?"—it's the sun hitting a stand of yellow Aspens well above us—and he takes off past me like it's a race, I follow right on his heels, finally going around him where the path widens. Then he starts flicking my ears as we walk and pretending it's not him and I finally yell, "Stop it!" and keep going.

"Stop wha...what?"

"You know."

"It was bu—bugs."

"Bugs?"

"There's a lot of . . ." He's having trouble catching his breath between words. "Bu—bugs out here."

"That was no bug."

"A lot of b-bugs."

I beat him to the top, falling into some weeds and rolling around like I'm acting a part in a movie. He shows a moment later, huffing and puffing and sweating and spitting. He bends over coughing, he paces and holds his head back and twists his face like he's in terrible pain. He drinks water, pours more over his head, drinks again and spits. Finally, he puts the water away and comes over to me. The front of his shirt is stained wet, but he's smiling.

"Top of the world, kiddo," he says.

"Don't call me that. Kiddo. Why did you call me that?"

"I don't know."

"I don't like it."

"I get that. You want some food?"

I take a Power bar and a handful of his granola, which tastes like wet cardboard with sugar on it. He makes me drink a swallow of water, even though I don't need it.

"Is this it, the place we're going?" I ask because if it is, I have to wonder. It's an open area roughly the size of a basketball court and the Aspens we saw earlier are pretty, they're bright gold and shake in the wind, causing the sunlight to flash off them. But he said we were hiking to a place with wildflowers and it's all ugly green weeds here.

"I don't think so," he says. "We haven't gone far enough. My friend said it was three miles. We've gone maybe a mile and a half. Two tops."

"I wanted to see the flowers," I say, because I realize he's thinking we should stop here and turn around.

"Me too, but I'm not sure. It seems like it's getting kind of late."

We're standing in the sun, and it feels so warm, it doesn't seem late. And if we've gone two miles already, we only have one more to go.

"If we've gone two miles already, it means we only have one more to go," I say.

He looks at me and keeps staring, like he's trying to see right through me.

"I'm ready if you're ready," he says.

"I'm ready if you're ready," I say, laughing to myself because it sounds like a kid's game.

He pulls the bottom of his shirt up to wipe his face and I see his white belly in the sun, and it makes me want to reach out and pinch it.

"We'll go on," he says.

"Let's go on," I say.

"We'll climb and climb," he says.

"Let's climb," I say.

But how isn't as easy as I thought it'd be. The trail snakes through the open area but there are three different places where it branches off and no signs telling us which one to take.

"You choose," he says.

"What if it's wrong?"

"We'll just hike for a while and turn around. No biggie."

"Middle."

He smiles. "That's what I would've taken."

The middle path is easy and flat for a long time, winding through stands of pine and the occasional group of Aspens, all of them with pretty yellow leaves that seem to spin on their stems, then we reach the base of a high rock cliff. Henry finds the path up, it's rocky and more like climbing stairs than walking a path. There are spots where he has to squeeze through a tight place and another where he has to climb using his hands and then reach down and pull me up. There's no time to be nervous, but when we finally get to the top and catch our breath, we have the best view yet. We're on top of a cliff looking straight down and we can see the open area in the distance and the fire break and the snow-capped mountains. We're so high up, the three paths look like someone drew them in with a pencil. The sky is blue as far as the eye can see, except for near the top of Baldy, where a cloud like a white scarf blowing hangs off of it. The sun still feels warm and the tops of the Aspens below us seem to be glowing, but it's also close to the line of mountains to the west and soon will drop below it and out of sight. Already, most of the land is in shadow and I know we'll have to walk through that to get to his truck.

"Can't be far now," he says.

"Can't be."

"A half hour at the most."

"If that."

"Maybe fifteen minutes, maybe less."

"Maybe over that hill." I like talking like this with him. Fast. No one else talks to me fast like he does.

"We'll do one more hill or thirty minutes whichever comes first. Deal?"

"Deal." We shake on it.

He makes me drink more water, stuffs another Power Bar and a banana in my pack, then pulls out my extra sweater and puts it in his pack. I didn't ask him to do that, but it is lighter and feels less bulgy. I wait for him to go first because that's the way we always do it. The sun is creeping up the side of our mountain and we want to stay out front.

Henry

I sit up with a start, the sky is a deep blue setting off Ponderosa pine treetops, split and charred from lightning strikes. Embedded stars are emerging. We're surrounded by that deep-woods, western quiet, the wind through the trees, a lonely sound, metallic in its coldness, menacing in its distance. I didn't notice the burnt trees a few hours ago, when we first arrived in full sunlight. Cady wakes next to me, sits up, rubs her eyes, says "Is it dark out? It's dark out," and I know we're in trouble.

It didn't start like this. We found the meadow and Eloy was right, it was spectacular, though at first, I was in no shape to notice. The meadow is set at the end of a long uphill, and I was really sucking air by the time we arrived, feeling queasy and weak-legged, a loose ball forming in the pit of my stomach. I coughed spittle and thought about throwing up. My lungs ached like they did on the trip out when I was smoking cigar-sized joints one after the other, a dull throb pressing along my rib cage. The truck seemed so far away I couldn't imagine making the return walk. I staggered inside the rim of sunlight and sat heavily, hoping my stomach settled. That's when my heart tumbled and skipped, rolling more than beating, and I was still gasping for air, gagging and coughing, and it occurred to me I could die out here. A man in his forties, out of shape, unused to the altitude? No one would be that surprised. Would Cady cope? Wait for someone to come find us, sleeping next to my body? Or take my truck keys, hike out, spend a warm night with the engine running, find someone in the morning?

"Come see," she said, chasing yellow butterflies. "Oh my, look at that. Do you see that?" The meadow wasn't huge—the rough size and shape of a football field, set on a gentle slope—but bathed in the warmest sunlight with wildflowers from tree line to tree line. Cady grabbed my hand and made me stand and together, we stumbled about. To stare at the sheer variety of colors is to understand where the idea of fireworks comes from: petal explosions of yellows and oranges and reds and all the shades in-between, set off by large tufts of bright green grass and spotted by an intensely blue, delicate-looking flower in a daisy shape with a yellow center like a staring eye. The effect was heightened by the aspen encircling the meadow, their shimmering off-white trunks serving as the perfect backdrop to all that eye-popping color. We bent over and ran our fingers lightly across the fine down of the flower petals, we dropped to our knees to smell. We followed a black bug with a bright red 'X' on its back while it picked its way along the base of grass stems and over tiny clods of dirt. It approached a line of ants, circled a moment as if in a panic, then took off at a ninety degree angle, keeping its distance.

"Smart bug," I said, and she nodded her head in vigorous agreement. My strength was back, and I hadn't even noticed and only dimly remembered the despair of a few moments before. We were fine. We'd soak in some mountain beauty, hike out, drive home. No problems. We found a white rock with bright red-flame splotches velvety to the touch and shaped like miniature sea coral and we sat and ate a Power Bar each and drank water.

"Will you look at that," she said. The meadow had come alive.

"What?" I said, "What?"

The air above was thick with flying insects of a seemingly infinite number and variety. Honeybees and bumblebees moved intently from flower to flower, the air vibrating with the sound of their buzzing, and large flappy moths and butterflies filled the space with color and random, even chaotic movement while smaller flitty yellow moths with wings so paper thin the sunlight shone through, rose on the wind, above the tree tops, before dropping back to earth. Lady bugs settled a moment, showing that classic hard shell pattern, before alighting elsewhere, spiders re-appeared at the edge of their webs, and grasshoppers large and small jumped en masse, as if they were rhythmically coordinating their hops. It struck me a meadow is like the surface of a lake. Large creatures (like us) dive in and churn about, sending ripples to every corner. But if we hold still, the surface grows calm and all living things once again venture out. That was what we were seeing. A stick-body insect like a mutated dragonfly zipped in and held in the space so close to our ears, its tuning fork vibrations gave us simultaneous shivers. Cady stretched a finger and a butterfly with delicate brown mottling set for a moment. Swarms of speck bugs boiled in the air above, their wings reflecting a strobed sunlight, like smoke curling through light.

"Watch there," she said, pointing near the base of the rock and we did and sure enough, a small brown animal no bigger than a mouse, but with a pointed nose, darted across a small dirt patch, disappearing into a stand of grass.

"Shrew," I say.

"Shrew? Shrew? You're making that up."

"I'm not."

"That's a made up word. Shrew."

"It's really not. Here, here." I remembered my Audubon guide. "Let's look."

She leaned against me, her chin on my shoulder. I showed her the "shrew" page and we decided it was a vagrant shrew.

"Legs and feet short. Feeds on invertebrates and fungi in vole runways," I read.

"Very active day and night, year round," she read.

"OK, here's the game," I said. "I'll read some names out of the book and you tell me what animal, insect or plant." She raised her eyebrows and puffed out her cheeks like this was funny.

"Ready?" She nodded. I leafed through the book, holding it so she couldn't see. "Swallowtails, Hedgerow Hairstreaks, Boisduval's Blues, Dreamy Duskwings, Spangled Fritillaries." She squeezed my arm like a little hug, then subtly lifted her body and tried see the book.

"You can't look!" I said, outraged.

"I'm not looking."

"You tried."

"I didn't try, I didn't," she said. "I was just stretching." We both laughed. She had clearly been trying to cheat.

"What's your answer?"

"I don't understand."

"What's that?"

"The game, I don't understand the game."

"These are all animal names. You're supposed to tell me what kind of animal."

"Oh," she said, absently munching on granola. "Can you give them again?"

"OK, pay attention this time," I said.

"I am, I will. Go."

"Boisduval's Blues, Swallowtails, Hedgerow Hairstreaks, Spangled Fritillaries, Dreamy Duskwings."

She looked around. The sun-shadow line had moved closer but the meadow was still full of light and movement, and with the sun a few degrees more horizontal, it backlit the swirling insects, particularly the moths and butterflies, setting them aglow, leaving after-smears in the sky.

"Butterflies!" she shouted. Of course she was right.

"You looked."

"I didn't look. And even if I did, I didn't see anything."

"Bet you saw something."

"Bet I didn't. So I'm right? They're butterflies?"

"And moths," I said, annoyed she got it so easily.

We should've never laid back, using our packs as pillows, but we did. Shut our eyes too. Warm sun, the air above stirred to a gentle murmur, our bodies cooled off and dried out, our stomachs full, maybe it was inevitable.

"Shit, shit, shit," I say in the sick rush of how easily this has happened.

"You shouldn't curse," she says.

"I know."

"You just shouldn't."

"I said I know."

Her voice calms me. It isn't completely dark, not yet. The clouds above Baldy carry a deep blush from the dying sun, giving off general light, and the tiny ski basin buildings and metal A-frame lift supports on the ski mountain are outlined in perfect detail, making it seem like we still have a connection with people and places. But in five minutes, the clouds will be black silhouettes against the sky and below us, everything, including the trail entrance off the meadow, is already in the deepest shadow. We're surely at least a couple of hours late and likely an hour from the truck and another on the road to Eldorado. That puts us at least four hours behind our time.

"Bonnie and Jim," she says, like I'd spoken my thoughts out loud.

"Yeah, we screwed up, all right."

"Henry!"

"Screwed's not cussing. It means messed up."

"I know that."

"You say you do but you really don't."

"You shouldn't tell me what I know. Only I know that."

"Guess that made sense in Bizarro World."

She sticks her tongue out at me and folds her arms in what seems a parody of a petulant child.

"Why don't you have a cell phone like everyone else?" she says brightly, forgetting she's mad.

"Why don't you? All the kids have them."

"Bonnie and Jim don't even know what a cell phone is, I had to explain it to them."

"Bet that comes up a lot."

She almost says something back, but instead turns away to show her displeasure. She really is hyper-sensitive to criticism of her grandparents and seems to always understand when I'm doing it, even when I'm being cryptic.

"We can call from that country store," I say.

"That's a long way still," she says, but her voice betrays no upset, which gives me strength.

We find the trailhead easily enough but moving out of the murky meadow and into the trees is like stepping into a cave, immediate and total darkness. I can only see my hand if I raise it above me, the overhead sky retains a hint of blue. A simple flashlight would be worth all my food and water and toilet paper and pain killers. I stop and Cady runs into me.

"Hey," she says.

"Hay is for horses. Hold on here." I take off my button-up shirt—I still have a T-shirt and a jacket—twist it into long rope, tie one end around her wrist and wrap the other around mine.

"Just in case."

"Just in case," she says, like she approves. There's only one way the path can go and as long as I keep the up-slope close on my left, we should be fine. I look back at the meadow, it gives off a dirty radiance, more an absence of shadow than actual light, but still more than we have here. We're only an hour from my truck, I tell myself. Less than that if we move steadily.

A few hundred yards in though and the trail evens out and gently climbs. I don't remember this. I stop and again Cady runs into me.

"Hey," she says. "Don't say what you said about horses."

"Do you remember going downhill on the way up?"

"What do you mean?"

"We're going up now, which means we must've gone down on the way here."

"I don't remember. But there's no other way we could've gone."

"I guess." I'm not sure about this. Even if I didn't notice in the daylight, surely there is more than one trail leading to the meadow. What if we took the wrong one? We keep going and fifteen minutes later, we reach what I'm sure is the top of the small vertical cliff we climbed. I'd been dreading this since it was a bit hairy in full daylight and going down is always trickier, but in the circumstances, it at least confirms we're going in the right direction.

"I'll go first," I say. "And you have to do exactly what I say. I'll help you."

"OK," she says. "But shouldn't we take the path?"

"There is no path, remember?"

"There's a path right here."

She's right. It's a series of switchbacks set into the side of the cliff, the white dusty limestone seems to faintly glow before disappearing into total shadow half way down, but even what I can see seems a lot higher than the one we climbed on the way in. And how could we have missed this path? Even in this dim light, it's obvious. Again I find myself doubting my memory. Maybe the entrance to these switchbacks is less apparent at the bottom, maybe that's how we failed to see it. But I don't believe it, not really, it seems increasingly likely we took the wrong path out of the meadow. But this one is going the right general direction, isn't it? What would be the harm if we end up at Jack's campground a few hundred yards from my truck? No harm I can see and since the alternative is to make the long climb to the meadow and try to locate the proper trailhead in an absolute darkness, the only choice is to keep going.

"Is this the way we came?" she says, as if she just thought of it.

"That's what I've been saying to you for the last twenty minutes."

"This cliff is higher than the one we came up."

"I know."

"And there was no path."

"Do you want to go back to the meadow and find the right one?"

"Oh no, no, not that. We can't do that."

"Then I guess we'll keep going."

"It's in the right direction."

"That's my thinking too."

"Look at that," she says. A half circle of fuzzy white light has appeared above the peak of a distant mountain, the first blushes of a rising full moon.

"Let there be light," I say.

"Oooh, that's good, isn't it?"

"It is, like a little gift."

"Yes," she says. "Like that."

An hour later, I'm lying on my back in an open area I first imagined was another wondrous mountain meadow until the moon cleared the trees, revealing a denuded landscape of rock and sand with only the barest patches of scruff grass. The moon is outrageously bright, casting crisp shadows on the ground and turning an oval of the sky around it a faint blue. Cady stands over me making wiggling shadow fingers on my chest and face and above her, my retina floaters are in full bloom, flashing across the moon's face. We seem to have lost our momentum, though neither of us has come out and said so. About fifteen minutes ago, the trail started climbing steeply and finally there was no doubt we were on the wrong path and had no idea which way was which. We backtracked to this area a few feet off the trail to wait for the moon, hoping it might reveal the outline of a distant recognizable peak—Baldy or Truchas—but all we see are more trees and the murky shapes of the surrounding hills.

"This would be a lot easier in the daylight," Cady says and when I stare at her, she holds one hand palm up, oath-taking style, and says, "Well, it would."

"I know it would, but . . ." I don't finish.

But slowly it seeps in, and I wonder if she's right. Maybe the responsible thing is to find a spot, make a fire, curl up and sleep until dawn. We have clothes, matches, food, water. Bonnie and Jim will be out of their minds with worry, but we also could easily walk all night in the wrong direction, and then where would we be? In the morning, we can get our bearings simply by where the sun rises. The truck is south, the sun rises in the east. Easy enough.

"What is that?" she says.

"What is what?"

"Birds at night?" She points at the sky. Bats. Not retina floaters. Bats. At least three, darting in and out, diving close to the ground, then disappearing into the trees before reappearing.

"Bats."

"Bats?" she says, clearly excited. "Like real bats?"

"As opposed to...robot bats?"

"Henry! You know what I mean."

"I do know."

"You always say that."

"I do, I know."

"I do, I know," she says, mocking me.

"I'm sticking my tongue out at you. If you could see me."

"If I could see you, we'd be home by now."

"Bats," I say like it's a curse word.

"Bats," she says, like there's a hidden meaning in the word itself.

Bats and a warm summer night on the golf course, the two of us shirtless and in shorts and bare feet, running hard, the dew kicking up, both of us clutching baseball mitts. He figured this out on his own, Sammy did. He read it in a story in *Boy's Life* and then went to the World Book Encyclopedia and read more, all before we actually snuck out and tried it. We'd never done that before. Plan an action, research it, do it. And I haven't done much of it since. I've thought about that more than a few times: how maybe the differences were looming and just never got the chance to manifest, how I'm being wildly narcissistic, even disrespectful in my certainty that Adult Sammy would've turned out like me.

I threw the ball because I had the best arm and because Sammy wanted to watch. He was so excited, telling me over and over what I needed to do. "Throw as high as you can, but it's got to be straight up in the air. Straight up." With the first couple of throws, nothing happened, and as was typical of us, we bickered.

"This is stupid," I said. I didn't really like this—the planning, the reading, him not telling me what it was that was supposed to happen—it wasn't the way we did things.

"You're stupid," he said.

"You are, you are."

"Just throw it again. Please."

"Idiot."

"Please."

"Double idiot." But it would've never occurred to me not to do what he asked so I threw the ball again high in the air, catching it when it came down, then again and again. On the third throw, I saw a blur.

"Did you see that?" he said.

"All I saw was the stupid ball."

"Throw it!" He was trembling with excitement, which only further irritated me. I threw the ball as hard and as high as I could. This time it was more than a blur.

"Did you see?"

"I saw."

"Did you?"

"I did. I did see." Bats. The ball went high into the air and out of nowhere, a bat swooped in, dived at the ball, then darted away at the last second.

"Do it again, you've got to throw it again." I did gladly, caught up in the moment and in his enthusiasm. Each time I threw the ball, bats appeared on cue and Sammy hollered and ran in circles and howled at the moon and tackled me until we were soaked from rolling on the grass. I threw the ball until my arm was sore, until The Dude appeared, pissed-off because he'd fallen asleep in front of the TV and had to get up and go look for us, but Sammy wouldn't be denied. He was like that. When The Dude's baseball fantasy fell apart, Sammy bore the brunt of his anger—I was never blamed because The Dude knew I would've never quit on my own—but it rolled easily off Sammy. He even found ways to tweak the old man, though I was never sure if it was on purpose, pulling out his catcher's mitt and using it as a leather Frisbee, or tossing it high into a tree so we could throw rocks at it. We even played basic catch and sometimes The Dude watched from the porch, usually with a beer in hand, usually glaring in our direction, giving us both the giggles. "Well this is just about goddamned perfect," he'd say, waving his beer as if pointing us out to an imaginary friend before disappearing inside.

"Henry?"

This time, he grabbed our father's hand and pulled him onto the golf course, and we showed him with the ball and how to get bats to swoop at it.

"Henry!"

"That *is* cool," The Dude finally said, and little Sammy beamed. Sammy had this way of sliding past the bad and worshipping the good. Those few times when it seemed like Dad genuinely enjoyed being with us—usually he acted like he couldn't be bothered—Sammy was beside himself with joy and all past transgressions were forgotten. He loved to walk backwards while the old man and I went normally, carrying on a conversation the whole time, asking Dad breathless questions and becoming confused and vaguely dissatisfied by the answers. Why the sky was blue ("Because it's supposed to be.") or what a squirrel was thinking when it chased another squirrel ("Thinking might be a stretch, kiddo.") or do fish cry when they get a hook in the mouth ("I hope not."). Sometimes he'd trip or pretend to. I found it harder to forget the sting of our father's disinterest or the times he raged and bullied, and I didn't like how happy Dad in a good mood made Sammy. Our mother was like me, she carried a grudge, and she viewed Sammy's elevated mood around her husband with suspicion. I guess he was his father's son and I my mother's. Except he was more her and I'm him.

"Did you see that?"

The Dude stayed and tossed the ball himself and we even tried a brief game of night-time catch. On the way home, Backwards Sammy and I in mirror-image stride, The Dude told us about the time his father our grandfather, dead years before we were born, assembled this "contraption" he'd read about using a car battery, jumper cables, and two steak knives with the wood handles burned off as a way to stun night crawlers after a rain. Normally you had to be quick and move quietly because a worm keeps part of its body in the hole and they go on movement and ground vibration, disappearing fast. He walked to the softball fields near the high school, stuck the knives in the grass ten feet apart, and gave the ground a jolt, sending a "tingle" up his legs and stunning but not killing the worms.

"Did you see that?"

"Then it was all gravy, kiddos," he said. "Just took his can and his flashlight and went around picking up dazed night crawlers. Harvesting his crop, two dollars a pound at the bait shop and plenty more for his own use. Working smart, not hard, that was my old man."

"Henry, did you see that?" She says. Cady says.

"What?"

"That."

"What?"

"I'll do it again."

"OK."

"Are you watching?"

"I'm watching."

And she does it, she just does it, using a rock, tossing it underhand into the air, high enough to be visible against a moon-brightened sky, and three bats charge in and dart away.

"Hooray!" she yells.

She heard me tell the story, she must have.

"I just told you that," I say. "You heard me tell that story about throwing the baseballs."

"Heard you?" she says, clearly confused and more interested in what she's doing. "Help me find another rock."

"Wait a minute. Just wait."

"I want to do it again."

"Wait, goddammit!"

She stops as if I'd slapped her.

"Did I not just tell you a story about Sammy and throwing the baseballs in the air? Did I not just tell you that?" I ask.

"You shouldn't curse." Sullen.

"Please."

"Well you shouldn't."

"Please. Didn't I just tell you that?"

"When?"

"Five minutes ago."

"You didn't say a word. You were laying there on the ground. I called your name..."

"I didn't just tell you about the bats and throwing the baseball?"

"I don't know what you mean," she says calmly. "We studied this in school. Mrs. Garcia told us."

"She told you? What'd she tell you?"

"That bats have like radar and that's how they see flying insects even in the dark and that you can trick them by throwing a rock in the air. I raised my hand and said, 'What if they try to eat the rock? Couldn't they get hurt?' And she said bats are smart and can tell from their radar what they're able to eat and what they can't. That's why they go after a rock in the air, to see if they can eat it. I've always wanted to try this, I wrote it down, made a drawing with me and the rock and the bats and our house. Once I dragged Bonnie outside with me, but she couldn't understand what I was saying. She thought I was throwing rocks at the bats and said, 'Sweetie, I don't think you'll ever be able to knock a bat out of the sky with a rock.' Like I'd want to hurt a bat."

I ease down to my knees so we're eye level and take her shoulders gently, moving her so I can see her face in the moonlight. She squirms, then relaxes in my grip, as if she understands exactly what's going on. Looking at her, it's right there. She is me. Us. It's never seemed more obvious. A shiver takes hold, shaking me hard enough I cry out. Philips used to say the shiver was the body's way of "acknowledging the metaphysical"—she could talk like that in the right mood—an involuntary reaction to a passing phantom, a mischievous spirit, a ghost pack of coyotes, or the residue presence of a possibility considered and ultimately rejected.

"If your brother . . . if Sammy was alive today, where would you be?" she said one time, out of the blue, which was her style, especially when I first met her. She had a way of being so up front and direct with her questions, she made you search for an answer equal in emotional honesty. She knew about Sammy, of course, I told her more about him than anyone else in the world.

"We'd be right here, right now," I answered.

"We? You and me? Or you, me and Sammy?"

"Me and Sammy, of course," I said, without thinking. "But you too, you too. I don't know. That sounds crazy, doesn't it? You and me and Sammy?"

"It's wonderful, isn't it? All possibilities exist in their own universes, an endless number of them, which means somewhere out there, we're living that. Sounds OK to me."

"What?"

"The three of us."

"Does it?

"It does." I knew she was just going with the moment, but still it meant a lot to me.

"It does, doesn't it?"

"Sure."

Until I met Philips, I was convinced a major part of who I was supposed to be was simply missing, he was missing, and my position as a fractional human being was, if not unique, then uncommon, but she said almost everyone feels the same and those few who do feel whole tend to be young souls, on their first go around. I came around to her view and decided it all made a kind of organic sense. The body breaks down, the mind frays around the edges, memory and certainty suffer, and growing older becomes a subversive force, pushing you to doubt what you've always known as objective truth, obliging you to unlearn a life's worth of knowledge. It's all decay in one form or another and it seems as central to living as any of the primal life forces. But it's been such a long time, three lifetimes of this child or more, since I've believed rot can be reversed, that what is lost might return. Really believed.

"Sammy?" I whisper to her, the way a dotty man might gingerly approach someone who could be an old friend.

She simply dips out from under my hands and steps away. "I'm Cady," she says evenly.

"I know that."

"There you go again, saying 'I know', all the time 'I know.'"

She's playing this exactly right, going light, refusing to be drawn in, saving me from myself.

"I'll quit saying it."

"Sometimes you have to say it."

"I *know*," I say.

"Har-har, you're so funny I forgot to laugh."

I make a zipper gesture across my mouth, and she gives me an exaggerated thumbs up.

"I'm cold," she says.

"Let's make a fire, we'll get wood."

"Together?" The hint of panic in her voice brings tears to my eyes.

"Of course." I take her hand. In the lower end of the open area, we find a four foot high outcropping of rock with a flat face out of the wind. We'll build the fire here. I show her how we'll sleep with her zipped up inside of my jacket facing out.

"Just like when you were two feet tall and barely able to walk," I say, knowing she won't like it.

"Henry."

"Or to talk . . ."

"Henry!"

"Still in diapers . . ."

"Stop it. I mean it." But she doesn't really, she's smiling. Together, we search for wood, finding plenty of kindling and one Cady-sized log, all of it burnished dry and gleaming white like bones in the moonlight. I use paper towels as starter fuel and in no time, the fire is going and I'm able to ease one end of the large log on top. We settle together, me leaning against the rock face, her with my jacket around her sitting between my legs. I close my eyes and let my face rest in her hair, breathing her in.

We sat like this at the top of those stairs, those fucking stairs, my arms and legs around him, ready to push off. What if I'd been sitting up front? Would he have made that final decision to lift us up and out? Could he have held on tighter than me so we stayed together and if we did, would we have both survived? Or both died? And if it had been me in front that day and collapsing in school the next, would Sammy be sitting here now with a daughter who looks like he did? Like we did? I squeeze her so tight I hear a tiny gasp of air pass her lips.

"I can't breathe."

"Good," I say, easing up just enough for comfort. She buries her face inside my jacket, I lay my cheek on top of her head, eyes closed tight. Whatever happens tomorrow with Bonnie and Jim, it's worth it for this. Just this.

We used to pretend we were camping on top of Mt. Everest in our pup tent, set up right in our room near an open window because there was too much snow outside. We'd tie the flaps down and make whooshing noises and shake the wooden stake like the wind was howling and dive into our sleeping bag and pull the cord tight until there was only a round air hole no larger than a baseball.

Sometimes Franny crawled into the tent, and we'd act like a lifeless lump, and she'd say, "Where's Sammy? Where's Sonny? Where could they be?" until one of us giggled or kicked the end of the bag or thrashed it open, yelling "Surprise!" like she didn't know we were there.

Sometimes she sang to us, I think she sang to us. *Swing low, sweet chariot, coming for to carry you home . . .* or *Michael, row your boat ashore . . .*", which was my favorite because the words were easy.

When they finally let us put the tent outside, it was The Dude who came with a bright light and a deck of cards. Sammy was in paradise, his dad and his brother in a tiny pup tent, but I wanted it to be Mom. I always imagined she did too. Maybe I even looked out the tent flap and she was standing there in the kitchen picture window, her fingers lightly touching, her forehead resting on the glass, maybe that's why I remember that night.

My heart thumps strong and even against Cady's back, the rhythm sends me pleasantly drifting.

I wake out of a spinning dream with a start. It's still dark out and we're in the same basic position, Cady a dead weight in my arms. Incredibly, she's snoring. The fire is only coals, but putting out warmth, though my back is cold, and I have to pee. With the moon gone, the stars are so thick and seemingly close, they're like

3D projections, like rods of light near enough to reach out and touch. I gently lay her on the ground and arrange my jacket over her like a blanket. She stirs, brings her knees closer to her chest, and continues snoring.

Then I hear it, a lone coyote high on the mountain, and re- member it reaching into my dream, appearing as the siren of an approaching fire engine, it's howl almost supernaturally piercing, the sound slicing and spreading through the immense blackness all around us until it is everywhere, as palpable and present as the stars, the darkness, the hard ground underneath, the lacey light- ning-scorched trees above. It is such a singular howl unlike anything I've heard before. Coyotes normally run in packs and their calls sound as a series of warbly yips building to bloodlust, but this is beyond simple communication, this has real feeling and though I can't pretend to know how an animal might feel, it sounds plaintive and defiant at the same time, telling all creatures for miles around it's here. I can't imagine any waking creature within earshot ignoring it. Surely meadow voles and hoary marmots are quaking in their hiding places, mule deer grow restless while jackrabbits dart for their holes. I have a moment's urge to strip naked and run through the woods, to feel a part of something so much larger than myself, to find a place where I can go lost like that coyote's lost. I climb to the top of the rock and the animal calls like it knows I'm listening.

Below I see her, my daughter, curled up sleeping, no larger than my fist held out in front of me, a small forest creature at home and at peace. Was he that small when he died? Was I? I've always told everyone, even Philips, that I didn't look at Sammy in his coffin, but I did. It was more that it didn't mean much to me. Sammy wasn't there, and I couldn't bear to answer questions of how it made me feel. Her live face cuts me in a way his dead one never did, him in his coffin is not an image that's ever haunted me. This child should be the person in the world who knows the most about me, not the woman who drank her way through the years when I was still looking for a parent, and certainly not the one who left and has stayed gone, but somehow Cady's innate sagacity brings out the same in me and I know there's much I can't yet say to her, not to a ten year old girl.

But when it's time and over time, I'll tell her. I'll remember the kids of the neighborhood to her, Tommy and Danny and the Dickies, the ones I met after Sammy. I'll describe Aaron as a young man and Aaron today and I'll tell her Aaron says hello. She'll like that, someone she's never met or even heard of thinking of her. And I'll tell her about Sammy, and her other grandmother and maybe even The Dude. And she'll want to know about her mother, anything and everything, and it strikes me I have the perfect narrative, I can start with only the good now and as she grows into a teenager and beyond, I'll explain the more complicated aspects of our marriage. I'll tell her my theories of why she left, and she'll develop her own. I'll say, "I wasn't always like this," and we'll both laugh. Maybe all my stories will begin that way. I wish I could start right now, talking and talking until I've said all there is to say, but I can wait. I know how to wait.

Cadence

I don't mean to fall asleep inside his coat, even though it's really, really warm. I close my eyes so I can make better wishes. I wish I'm standing in our kitchen, watching Bonnie outside filling the pond, I wish I'm on the back porch with Jim and Henry and the summer storms are coming in from the mountains, I wish I have a dog or a cat like Henry said, and I could hold her to my chest and feel how warm and sweet she is. And just like that I'm asleep.

When I wake, he's gone and there's an animal howling like it's in terrible pain and for a moment, I think it's me that's screaming and I pull off his jacket like it's on fire and look everywhere, but it's so dark, I can't see more than a few feet. Then I see Henry standing on top of the rocks, looking as big as the trees, as large as the hills, like those men in one of Jim's western movies, alone but not frightened and I feel better right away. Henry is here.

"You hear that?" he says.

"Of course I do."

"Coyote."

"I know."

"There you go again, always saying, 'I know, I know,'" he says.

I can see my breath and scoot closer to the fire, wrapping his coat tight around me.

"Will you come down now?

He jumps off the rock and kicks at the fire, sending coals like fireflies into the air, and starting a fresh flame. He lays the few pieces of kindling left on top.

"You cold?"

"A little. You?"

"A little. Sometimes it's kind of nice to let yourself get really cold, as long as you have a warm place to go."

"Like in your coat with both of us?"

"Exactly."

"But I'm cold now."

He laughs and takes his coat and shakes it out and puts it on. I get in and he zips me up, but he stands back to the fire, forcing me to look out at the night.

"You OK?"

"I am. OK. I worry about Bonnie and Jim."

"Me too.

"I'm glad you do too."

He kisses the top of my head. We're clumsy getting to the ground, zipped up as we are, and he has to let go of me and I swing free, stretching his coat out even more.

"Your poor coat," I say.

"Yeah, I'm going to have to eat a lot to fill it out," he says. I close my eyes while he squirms, getting comfortable. When I wake up next, it'll be light out and we can go home. When he starts talking about Sammy, it takes me a second to realize what he's telling me and when I do, I'm wide awake. I'd wanted to ask but was scared to because he gets strange when that name comes up. But then he just starts talking like I had asked.

"I want you to know," he says. "There is no Sammy without Sonny." For a long moment, I think that's it, that's all he's going to say, then he tells me about two brothers, twins, and how they grew up doing everything together, how they never even thought of being apart. They took baths at the same time and peed together (yuck!) and slept in the same bed and went to school on the same bike, with one of them on the handlebars and one of them peddling—it didn't matter which—and how they looked so much alike, they were able to fool teachers and doctors and even their own father. He says when the two brothers were together, the world made sense in a way it didn't when they weren't, like they were one person split in two. He says it's like being in nature, like being out here and feeling you're a part of all of this, not a human being aside from the trees and the plants and the coyotes and the bats, but just one more living creature like any other living creature surviving in the wilderness. I don't know what he means, but I like the name Sonny. I'd like to know someone named Sonny.

"Then Sammy died," he says, and his voice cracks and I remember how he said "Sammy" to me a few hours ago and the look on his face when he did and I'm glad I can't see his face now.

"Oh no," I say, because I want him to know I think it's horrible.

"He was your age," he says.

There's a long silence and I'm still confused. "But who was Sammy? Why did you call me that name?"

He hugs me so tight I can hardly breathe but I don't mind, we're lost in the woods at night with coyotes nearby, I don't mind.

"I was…Sonny," he says very slowly.

"You were? Sonny?"

"That's right."

"Then Sammy was your brother?"

"That's right."

"And he was my uncle? Sammy was?"

"I guess so. He would've been."

This is so sad it makes me sniffle. I've wondered what it might be like to have a brother or sister, but I've never thought one of them could die. He kisses the back of my head again and leans down and puts his scratchy face next to mine.

"I like the name Sonny," I say. "You could be a Sonny."

"That was a long, long time ago. No one's called me that in thirty years or more."

"I could call you that. You seem like a Sonny to me."

"I seemed like a Hank too. And a Henry."

"But you never did, not really."

"I don't know."

"And that way, I'd be the only person who called you that. It'd be all mine."

"I don't know."

I'm still not sure why he called me Sammy. I'm a little scared to ask, he doesn't seem to want me to call him Sonny, but I'd like to know.

"But you called me that name, you called me Sammy."

He shifts his body, unfolding his arms from around me, and for a moment, I think he's mad. High in the night sky, the tiny light of a jet moves amongst all the stars, and I wonder if anyone is awake on that plane and if they can see our little fire in the darkness. But then he gets comfortable and hugs me tight.

"It's complicated," he says slowly. "You look like him for one. Like us, around the face, you look like I did when I was your age. When we were. When the worse that can happen happens, you think of ways to help you get through it."

I know what he means. Bonnie thinks something terrible happened to me, even though I don't remember. Sometimes when I wake in the night and can't go back to sleep, I imagine my mom and what she might do, like buying shoes or riding up escalators. About what kind of car she drives. I'm pretty sure she lives near water, so I'll bet she swims and goes on boats. One time, I pretended she and I were in a hurricane together and we had to hold on to keep from blowing away. We huddled in a small room, and she held my hand and whispered in my ear, keeping me calm. Another time we had a floating bed like a flying carpet, and we flew around New Mexico, skimming over the trees and landing on mountaintops.

"Ideas can accumulate a lot of power just because you've been thinking about them for so long and never bothered to ask yourself if it was a good way of thinking in the first place . . ."

I'm very sleepy now and his talking only makes me sleepier, I don't know what he's saying, but I'm glad he's saying it.

I have the strangest dream. I'm walking barefoot in a dark tunnel with leafy plants touching my legs and gurgling water like a mountain stream. Fish swim past my ankles. There are other people with me, I'm not sure who or how many. We come to a gigantic room, as big as a mountain valley with a rock ceiling and a high waterfall and green moss growing on the ground like carpet and light coming through in holes in the ceiling. At the top of the waterfall, a tiny figure yells and yells and I know it's her, I know it's Janie, though she's too far away to see clearly. I know she's calling to me, though I can't understand what she's saying, except suddenly I *can* see clearly like I'm looking through binoculars and for a second, I see her, a woman in gray with her hands cupped around her mouth, but it's so fast, I'm not sure and what I see now is a coyote, sitting down, nose in the air, howling and howling, so loud I have to stuff my fingers in my ears.

Awake, I wait for the coyote call, my heart beating fast, before I remember it was in a dream. There's no wind and it's quiet except for Henry's breathing.

I have to pee and would rather wait until it's light out, but I can't.

Unzipping isn't easy since my arms are on the inside, but I reach through the neck hole and pull down. I'm surprised how cold it is outside of his coat. I'll just find a tree for balance, do it, and get back where it's warm, but it's trickier than I thought. I'm not sure I've ever peed outside before.

When our class was at Bandelier, Peggy made me get off the trail with her and keep watch while she went behind some green cactus with hard yellow flowers and said she'd do the same for me and even though I had to go, I couldn't. Not squatting outside in broad daylight.

But it's night here. I see stars through the trees, but they're more faint than bright and that's when I notice light, low in a gap between two hills, and I think the moon's back, except that can't be it, the moon never returns the same night. Daylight! The sun is coming up, though it still looks like darkest night in every other direction.

Then I hear a coyote. I get scared for a moment, but it doesn't sound like my Janie coyote from the dream, and it's far, far away. I've heard coyotes all my life around the house, they bark and they're scariest in packs. It always sounds like they've surrounded a smaller animal and are laughing at it before they kill it and eat it. But this is like the one before—maybe it's the same one—long and drawn-out and seems even lonelier because it's so far away. Like the way a kid will sometimes yell as loud as he can just so someone knows he's there. Then I wonder how far that coyote really is. When you live in a neighborhood like I do, you sometimes think there are mean children or bad adults close by, but you also know their houses and their yards, and your yard and your house is in-between. But out here, there's nothing between me and that coyote. I don't know much about animals, but I know they smell a long way. Maybe he can smell me. How long would it take to get here if he were to run straight at me right now? I get goose bumps all over and hurry up and finish, but when I reach Henry curled up on the ground, I feel fine again. I'm bigger than a coyote and Henry makes four of me. He turns and looks at me like he's been wide awake the whole time.

"You snore," he says.

"I don't snore."

"Do too."

"I don't believe you."

"Believe me."

"I said I don't."

He pokes at the fire with a thin branch that keeps breaking at the tip, making it shorter and shorter.

"Snorer," he says, not even looking at me.

"I'm no snorer."

"Are too."

"You lie." I stand in my spot with my arms folded to show him I mean business.

"Aren't you coming back?" He says like he just noticed me standing here.

"I *am* cold," I say, because I am.

"Me too," he says and opens the wings of his jacket. I lay down and roll close, face out.

"It's getting light," he says.

"I saw."

"Another hour and we'll start home."

"Good."

"It is good. We'll call your grandparents first."

"I want to switch from Henry to Sonny," I say, surprising my-self. I hadn't even been thinking about it, but then it came to me and seemed a good idea.

"You said."

"It seems more, you know . . ."

"You said."

"If you don't want me to."

"Maybe we should think about it."

"OK." I wish I could see his face.

"I like to think about things."

"I know."

"I know you know." I'm not sure if he's making fun again.

"If I said, 'Hey Sonny,' what would you say?"

"I don't know."

"Hey, Sonny."

"Doesn't work because I know you're talking to me. It's got to be casual."

"OK Sonny," I say, trying to make it sound casual, which is harder that it might seem.

"Better," he says. "But still not there."

"But you're going to think about it?"

"As long as you don't fall asleep again. Hard to think with that foghorn snoring of yours."

"Henry!" I thought we were done with the snoring.

"Warm enough?" he says, like he's trying to stop me from being mad.

"Plenty warm." He kisses the back of my head, then scratches my face on purpose with his beard. The coyote howls again, closer but still not close, and it doesn't matter anyway. He's so big and warm, it's like sleeping next to a giant—like being in my own living fort where I can't be harmed, where I can close my eyes and dream us home or to a desert island with palm trees and the lights of passing ships in the distance or on that jet plane flying to a place we've never been or even to where Janie is so we could all see each other again—the safest place in the world.

Epilogue-Franny

The first time it happened was a complete fluke.

She'd taken to carrying the letter in her purse and pulling it out at odd times—waiting for the traffic signal to turn green, sitting at the High Hat—so maybe it was inevitable someone might ask.

Patricia, the counter woman at the Temple News Agency where she takes her late morning coffee (because they're the last place in town to allow indoor smoking) said, "What do you got there, Fran," and she'd proudly read aloud a couple of short passages—she began to invent elaborate reasons to publicly open the letter.

At the library where she is well known for reading two, sometimes three books a week, she'd gone to Miriam the librarian and asked her what a certain word meant. After Miriam told her ("specious" and of course Franny already knew it), she'd said, "This is from my son. He's a college professor. Would you like to see a photo of my grandchild?"

Miriam's interest was perfunctory at best—Franny wonders how people she's known for twenty years can maintain a complete lack of curiosity about those around them—but little Mele, bless her heart, all of sixteen and working as an assistant after school, said, "Let me see, let me see," and she'd said all the right things ("What a darlin'"), though Franny was disturbed by the news that Mele knew not one but two Cadences in her high school.

Franny had never heard of the name before and if she was skeptical years ago ("Cadence?" she'd said to him. "Is that even a real name?"), she'd come to cherish it as a true original.

Other times, she'll pretend to be opening it for the first time—she uses white masking tape to repeatedly repair it—splitting the seam with a fancy wooden opener, then pinching one corner of the letter and with a flourish, flicking it open with her wrist. Sometimes she'll laugh out loud. At the High Hat, she said, "Well I'll be!" and Ted the bartender asked. Now there isn't much to Ted beyond being a bartender, meaning Franny is pretty sure he talks to customers only because it's his job and left to himself, he isn't the sort to say much, but still, it was nice to be asked.

"My son," she'd said and then she gave him the most cursory bit of back story and showed him the photo.

"Cute kid," Ted said.

"Yes," she'd said, near tears. "Yes."

He'd sent a two-thousand-dollar money order too, though she didn't bother re-creating the discovery of that each time. Why would she? Money's nobody's business. He'd written: *For a first-class ticket*, but she's already sunk half of it into her '91 Accord, thinking she'll simply drive.

Driving as a concept has always appealed to her (flying never has), the notion that you can walk ten feet out your door and step into a machine that can take you to either ocean, to the jungles of Central America and snowy wastelands of Alaska, to New York City and New Mexico, Baja California and Hudson Bay.

But the reality is she rarely ventures outside of a block-radius around her apartment. Gas station, video store, post office, bank, supermarket. She walks to her job downtown and the High Hat is a mere two blocks west. She hasn't been to the mall in Michigan City in a couple of years and hasn't seen Lake Michigan, a scant twelve mile drive on easy roads, in at least five, and that was from the South Shore on a trip to Chicago at Christmastime to see the lights.

She had so loved swimming in that lake with The Dude when they were first married. They were a pair, the two of them, running around like kids ("We were, we were."), tearing up the sides of sand dunes and rolling to the bottom.

That first climb over the line of dunes rimming the south end was a revelation for a girl from Kentucky, that amazing expanse of blue, as endless as any ocean, except on truly clear days when the faint shadow of the skyscrapers of Chicago bled through.

Still, she believes she's an excellent driver and driving on the Interstate is one of the calmest, easiest kinds of driving. Just hundreds of miles of straight roads. She can do that.

Besides, she's heard of western states where it is legal to drink and drive (some research might be necessary), as long as you're not legally drunk. There was a Hemingway book she'd read many years ago, the one on bullfighting, where he described the hissing of a tight stream of wine out of a full wine skin as it hit the throat of some Spaniard. That's what she wants. Pack up a full wine skin and head west where there's wide open spaces and no worries.

Though there are nights late when she lay in bed and can't get her mind to shut down when she wonders if it isn't all insane. She can't drive there, it's too far, too hot, she'll never make even five hundred miles a day, she can't afford the motel rooms. What will she do all night long in a motel room? How will she pass all that time in the car? It'll cost too much, it's too far. And she knows she'll never get on an airplane.

But other nights, she feels fiercely resolute. All I have to do is pack up my stuff and get in the Accord, she tells herself, get on the Toll Road going west. Once she's started, she's sure she won't turn around and go home. She's sure of that. All she needs is to get started.

Of course, even in the clarity of daytime, she knows it's a long way and when she's tired, her hands shake and her knees knock together, but if that happens, she'll simply find the first motel, one where she can sit poolside, smoke cigarettes, and watch the kids splash.

It'll be like a vacation. It is a vacation, isn't it? The first one she's had in decades. Besides, she has her own money, what's left of his, and a single CD worth about fifteen thousand, though she'd just as soon avoid cashing it in.

That was a surprise, all right. When she got the call from a lawyer a month after his passing, she was sure Arthur had found some way to stick her with a bill from beyond the grave. It had taken her almost five years to pay off the credit card debt that he had (mostly) run up after they split for good. Instead, she inherited twelve thousand dollars and it's gone up since then.

It didn't begin to make up for what he put her through, what they did to each other, but in a way, it softened him to her. The memories often come in a rush, vivid and touching in a way she wouldn't have thought possible before the money. How about the time the boys set up their new pup tent (Christmas) in the back yard during a snowstorm? Arthur took his beloved Coleman lantern to them and ended up staying. She could see three distinct shadows against the inside of the canvas from the kitchen window. And when she finally put on her boots and trudged out to check, he was asleep. Snoring while the boys played Slap Jack on his chest!

Or how just after they discovered she was pregnant, they acted like two teenagers in rut, going away each weekend to places like the Wisconsin Dells and Brown County. Four short weekends, really just a day and a half each, but still the most (only?) intense and passionate period of physical activity in her life, her own little romance novel. She'd always suspected romance novelists hadn't done a tenth of what they wrote about; that they got a lot out of mileage out of one or two quick experiences, like, say, a month of weekends.

Once before the boys were born, she woke to find him over her, he'd lifted her shirt and tugged the waist of her panties down and he was lightly touching her line of pubic hair. "I love this part," he said, and traced his finger along the line and into the hollow running along the inside of her thigh. He loved that part. Imagine that!

It is Ted from the High Hat who first hears about it. Franny had mentioned the house she used to live in on more than one occasion, it even got to the point where a couple of regulars made mean-spirited "here we go again"-type remarks over it and she decided "to hell with the lot of you" and shut up, but by then, all the High Hat regulars knew she'd lived in Bluffside, on the north end of Pine Lake, third house west of the S curve on Judson Road.

Ted was riding his bike in the old neighborhood and saw the FOR SALE sign. Now Franny herself used to regularly drive past the house, slowing each time, making note of every change. Over the years, she's had to admit they've made improvements; they've blacktopped the driveway, erected a handsome wooden fence all around the property, cleared all the weedy bushes in back, opening up an actual sight line to the golf course.

They even had a small square-patch vegetable and herb garden, which was one of Franny's dreams.

She's surprised the house is for sale, the family had put enough money into the place it didn't make sense to sell. There's no market for houses in this town, at least not the kind where you make a profit by fixing up a house and selling it.

She considered calling the realtor and setting up an appointment to see the place but couldn't bring herself to invent a plausible story and (likely) a fake name. Who would believe the seventy year old previous owner with a fifteen hour a week job and no discernible savings could afford a house? But then she saw the Open House notice in the Weekly Trader (truthfully, she was looking) and decided it was kismet. She's roughly planned to be on the road to New Mexico by next Sunday, but his letter said, "any time" and followed that with "I mean it", so a few days won't matter. Besides, she's nervous about the trip beyond the long drive. He'd written that the child looks like he did at that age and if the photo doesn't show this (except maybe around the eyes), she understands photos capture moments and meeting her grandchild in the flesh might be a whole different experience. What if she really does look exactly like they did, like Sammy did? For years, she detested how little of the boys she could see in the adult Henry, but over time, she understood the genius of that. Better to not always be reminded. How will she handle it if what he says is true about Cadence? Could she?

On the day of the Open House, she dresses and re-dresses three times. She starts with the best dress she owns, a sleeveless green linen piece that hangs over her knees, but her upper arms look particularly flabby and jiggly today, plus she doesn't want to appear to be trying too hard. Who dresses up for an Open House?

She pulls it off over her head and in doing so, catches a glimpse of her sagging body. She's been heavy most of her adult life and is an expert in averting her gaze at appropriate moments; in front of mirrors, while entering stores with reflecting glass doors, so on that rare occasion when she really takes a look, it's always a shock.

This one (quick) look drives her to her everyday outfit, which shows her in the best light. Black Levi's and a T-shirt of some kind—she picks a well-worn orange shirt that reads "Columbia

College" on it, a present from her son when he was teaching in Chicago years ago—and Nike running shoes.

At the last moment, she jams a hat over her hair, a "Gilligan" hat Sonny'd called it at one of their breakfasts, using that mocking tone of his which sometimes seems the way he says everything. But later he said she looked like someone with style because she doesn't give a shit, she has no style, which was typical of him, a backhanded compliment.

He can say more and make less sense that anyone she's ever met. She'd bought it on a whim, because in the store, she thought it made her look like someone else, the kind of person who'd wear a hat like this, she supposed, but still... And she is going in disguise, isn't she? In a way?

On the drive over, she has two things on her mind. One, will she give her real name? The woman might recognize it. Though Arthur had been living in it on his own for nearly 15 years when he died, the house had always been in her name and all the papers she'd signed had Franny Dolan in bold letters. And second, would she prefer a crowded house or one in which she was but one of a handful of guests? She decided one depends upon two, if there's a crowd, she'll introduce herself as Franny and trust that even if the woman makes the connection, she won't care because she has a house full of potential customers. And if she's one of a few, she'll invent an alternative. Maybe one as simple as Francis, which isn't really even a lie, or Fanny. Henry used to call her Fanny, and though he meant it as a swipe, she didn't mind. She even has a laugh about a block away when she pulls out a silver flask full of vodka from the glove compartment and sees herself in the mirror taking a quick sip; a grandmother in a "Gilligan" hat sipping from an expensive silver flask, going to see the house she'd once owned. It just seems funny.

The driveway is full and there are cars on either side of the road, but even so, she guesses there can't be more than a dozen people inside tops. Not super crowded but enough. A good number. She parks well down the road, pops a mint, and makes her way.

As it turns out, there's no decision to be made. Catherine was her realtor and she's handling this one too, greeting people at the door. Of course the woman would use the same realtor, why wouldn't she? How could Franny be so thick?

"Franny? Thinking of buying it back?" Catherine says loudly, but her voice is gentle, welcoming. She amazingly looks no different; same scooped, aggressively blond hair, same painted-on eyebrows and baby-smooth face, though the skin around her neck seems gathered, like a too-long pants leg bunching up. Years ago, Franny was definitely the younger of the two. Now she appears to be older.

"I'm sorry, Catherine, I hope this is . . ." Franny sputters with the worry Catherine will know she has a little buzz on. "Just wanted . . ."

"Not at all."

"Get a look at the—I know that's strange—at the old place."

"Happens all the time." Catherine takes her arm, as if she understands Franny is fragile and isn't put off by it. "You and Elena never met, did you? Come on, we'll give you the full tour."

Elena the owner turns out to be much older than Franny expected, maybe a decade younger than her, but Franny had it in her head Elena and her husband were twenty somethings when they bought the house. Early forties then and late fifties now, would be her guess. And there's no talk of a husband, though Franny doesn't have the gumption to ask, "Dead or divorced?"

Elena is tall and wafer thin, though broad, meaning straight on, she appears a most substantial woman, a hefty Midwestern housewife, but from the side, she nearly disappears altogether. She has a regal bearing, which Franny initially reads as snobbishness, but then she detects the overwhelming frailty in the woman, moments when she seems ten or even twenty years older than she is. A good wind would blow her right over, a storm might sweep her up and away. She's not overly friendly in the beginning and with Elena's fine linen pants and lovely, gauzy blouse, both of them falling perfectly on her skeletal frame, Franny feels awkward and out of place, an ancient, unwanted hayseed in her jeans with their bulges and her ridiculous running shoes that have spider-web patterns. She takes her hat off for a while, then puts it back on because it's too strange carrying it.

But Catherine and Elena leave her to wander at will and eventually, she makes her way through the entire house. Nothing goes like she thought it would. The house itself has little power over her, the kitchen is completely different to the point where she can't recognize it, even the main window has been moved and there's a bathroom now where her laundry room once stood. Walls separating out the library and TV alcove have been removed, opening up the entire living room (which seems distressingly dinky, even with the extra space). The black support beams are now hidden under dry wall and the windows all have treatments that aren't to Franny's taste, too much lacey billowing, too girly.

Upstairs is even more foreign, starting with the steps, which are now a straight run. Gone is the "Caligari Stairwell" (so christened by her son years after they'd moved out; she had gone to the library and rented the video and after, she thought she understood what he meant) with its angles and rickety black railings. Their bedroom is still the master suite, but it's been expanded to include the bathroom.

Only the basement throws her and makes her reach out her hand for the nearest wall. It is the same; same low ceiling and crawl space entrance in the far corner, same metal pole supports, same dark corner where the coal bin had been. She flashes on herself, and the boys huddled here in a storm, fighting her own growing panic (as a child and young woman, storms terrified her), Sammy—or Sonny—holding the candle high, his little hand shaking, throwing watery shadows all over the basement and giving their faces a transparent look, as if they were superimposed on the dark, but the moment fades quickly. The basement was Arthur's, he spent whole years by himself down here and she never could figure out how he stood it. "At least fix it up, put up some dry wall, warm the place up a bit," she'd yelled at him once. "You're not the boss of me!" he'd screamed back. Good old Arthur, the man made a life out of missing the point.

Still, she has a moment locked in the bathroom when she cries. She cries because Elena is much closer to her own age than she thought and still elegant, because she's sure when Elena sees her image reflected in the corner of her eye, she sees the seventeen year old Elena, tall and thin, with beautiful delicate fingers. She cries because Arthur surely spent some dark, dark nights in this room after they split and because she's pretty sure none of them involved agonizing over her, she cries because one boy is gone and one has been missing for so long, he might as well be. She cries because, because, because.

She washes her face and blows her nose, but still has to tightly grip the rail on the way downstairs, her legs are shaking so. Catherine sees her and does a subtle double-take, like she's surprised Franny is still here. Time to go, she thinks, and Catherine confirms it by gently taking her arm and heading her to the door. But Elena intercepts them and hooks her arm inside of Franny's like they're friends and says, "Would you mind, dear, talking to this lovely woman now sitting on the back porch, she's interested in the history of the house and Catherine tells me you have knowledge in that regard."

"Sure," she says. "Sure I will."

The woman's name is Nancy and like Franny, she has no interest in purchasing the house (likely the reason Elena pushed Franny on the woman, but Franny doesn't mind. More the opposite). She calls herself a reporter and says she's researching a freelance article about the history of Bluffside as a resort area near the turn of the century, but she takes no notes and seems more like a middle-aged woman filling up an afternoon. Franny relates. She tells her what she knows of this house, that it was built around 1895 at roughly the same time as the golf course. Old Mrs. Collins across the street once told her the house had originally been a barn and that parts of the house were probably twenty-five or thirty years older, maybe more. Maybe all the way back to the Civil War.

"Of course there were no battles in Northern Indiana," Nancy says.

"No," Franny says. "But I bet some men who fought in the war stepped through the doors of this house."

"That's a fine way of thinking of it," Nancy says.

"When we remodeled the kitchen and tore up the linoleum, we found newspapers spread out. Used as padding, I guess. All from 1919. Arthur was stuffing them in a garbage bag, and I didn't notice right what we had. Newspapers fifty years old! I put a stop to it and sat there right on the floor. He grumbled, probably cursed too, but I didn't care. I pulled out the papers sheet by sheet, they were so yellow and brittle, they'd tear everywhere if you weren't careful. I made a pile. Then the boys came running and Arthur gave up. He knew he wasn't tearing up any more linoleum that day."

Franny hesitates a moment to give Nancy a chance to step in or signal her patience was waning, but she doesn't. She's not the most effusive listener, Franny decides, but she had her chance to put a stop to it.

"I got some scotch tape, made it into a game; put it back together, like a puzzle. Sonny worked the tape and Sammy held the rips together. They had this way, this look, like there was nothing else in the entire world but completing this task. And they did, sitting there with their pudgy little legs crossed. Later, we took turns reading some of the stories. Sammy read about the construction of the new lighthouse in Michigan City and Sonny found a gruesome article about some local boys who'd been gassed in the war, I'm sure it appealed to his morbid side, though he didn't really show that until later."

"Surely they've grown by now, your boys," Nancy says, shocking Franny, who is pretty sure the woman is plastered and assumed she was only semi-conscious and incapable of such a question.

"Yes..." Franny chokes on the answer. "A college professor out west."

"That's fascinating. Both of them college professors?"

"Yes." Then she adds, "At different colleges, of course."

"Of course."

Fortunately, Nancy doesn't pursue it further, which is good because Franny isn't up to even one more fabrication in the direction of Sammy. Or Sonny for that matter since, quite apart from the wonder that he wrote her at all, it's obvious from his letter he doesn't have a teaching job waiting for him in Portland.

Even after Nancy stumbles off, Franny stays and Elena rewards her by asking her if she wouldn't mind replenishing the food trays on the porch and Franny does that and more, uncorking the wine and pouring for guests, standing for long periods talking to strangers, making it clear she's only helping out, but also often letting it slip she once lived here. Astonishingly, a couple from Chicago assumes she and Elena are former lovers and "thinks it grand" they've stayed close. And if she never finds as willing (or as drunk) a listener as Nancy, she still has a fine afternoon offering her insights into the house and the neighborhood, the kind of day she used to dream of having with The Dude and the boys. A full house of casual friends, plenty of drink and food and talk, it's what this house could've been. It could've been that for her. And for them, all four of them.

By late afternoon, only Elena, Catherine and Franny are left, sitting on the porch, sharing the knowledge of a job completed and well-done, sipping wine and absently watching distant golfers make their way to the green.

"I love that you can see the golf course," Franny says, hesitating a moment before allowing Elena to pour her another glass of wine. "I could've spent hours sitting out here, watching the people stroll by."

"They're a boorish lot in general," Elena says. "And I don't care for the sport myself, if you can even call it that."

"Still . . ." Franny says.

"One time, I watched a horrible man in plaid shorts remove every club in his bag and methodically bend each of them around a tree, like twist ties. Then he just walked away, leaving them there."

"Oh boy." Franny giggles.

"Priceless," Catherine says. "I may just use that in my sales pitch. Like live TV in your own back yard."

"Why not?" Franny says.

"Why not indeed," Elena says. "Drama on the half-shell."

That pleasant bottom-heavy anchored feeling that comes with being a little drunk descends over Franny and she can't imagine a better place to be than this. The Bluffside house, her house, her porch. In her wildest dreams, she couldn't have imagined this; to be sitting on her porch with a glass of wine in her hand, talking to newfound friends, even as she knows she'll likely never see either of them again. That's not what matters. A letter from her son inviting her out and now this. She shivers a moment, flashing on winter nights sitting in this very spot, ugly nights when she had no idea what she was thinking, when she couldn't stop her thoughts from spinning out of control. Sometimes even now she wonders if it isn't spinning still, that she's simply gotten used to it. The way Sonny came to her for the first time on one of those winter nights, on this porch—she might well have been sitting in this very spot— and how she thought he was a phantom come to haunt her with a lifetime's worth of accusations. How can you make sense of that? Who would want to?

She pretend-coughs as a way to hide her sniffles, then forgets herself and downs the entire glass of wine in one gulp. Both appear not to notice, but Catherine stands to leave only a minute or so later. Franny stands with her, except she doesn't want to leave, not this moment. She doesn't want her final memory of her beautiful porch to be of those endless winter nights when it didn't matter how cold it was, she couldn't bring herself to go back inside. Or that one night when he was the one who finally came to her. She asks Elena if she wants a quick hand with the dishes.

"There's not much."

"I don't mind."

"Well, then, that'd be lovely." Since she used mostly plastic cups and plates, they make quick work of it and return to the porch. Elena pours Franny another glass of wine.

"Thank you. It's so nice back here."

"Appreciate the help."

"If you don't mind, can I ask after your husband?"

"Gone." Franny waits for more in vain. There's a vacancy about Elena, like someone stuck an empty box smack in the middle of her soul. Or maybe it's more like she's off wandering somewhere on the edges of her mind and there's a hint of weariness each time she's forced back to deal with the present.

"Can I read you this?" It hadn't occurred to her until this very second, but it seems perfect for an awkward moment.

"Sure can."

She pulls out the letter. It's only been two weeks, but the letter has already been folded and re-folded so many times, the seams are delicate, discolored. She's embarrassed for a moment for making such a big deal over it, it's only a letter, a single page at that, maybe half of it filled with writing.

"There was this also, my granddaughter." She hands Elena the photo, who studies it with what seems to be genuine interest.

"A cutie-pie."

"Isn't she? She is, right? I'm not always sure."

"She is. She looks determined."

"I'm going to visit them soon."

"That's fine."

"It is. It is fine."

"Let's hear the letter." Franny smiles at her, grateful for her gentle interest.

She silently peruses the opening greeting and nearly chokes up as she always does here. So simple, these two little words, but each time she reads them, she remembers the lengths he'd go to as an adult to avoid calling her any name at all. Or if he did, it'd be with the smell of derision all over it—Mother, Mommy, Ma, Franny, Fanny, Fraulein, Fran—so these two words are wonderful. Wondrous even.

"Dear Mom," she reads out loud, and continues to the end.

About the Author

Michael Backus' writing, fiction and non-fiction, has appeared in *Digging Through the Fat, Exquisite Corpse, Oyster River Pages, Prime Numbe* magazine, *The Writer, The Sycamore Review*, and many more.

He teaches creative writing for Gotham Writer's Workshop and *Zoetrope Magazine.* He resides in Albuquerque, NM.

www.cactusmoonpublishing.com

Made in the USA
Las Vegas, NV
06 October 2021